# 1954

## or, Just Press the I Believe Button

# Byron Grush

Published in the United States by Broadhorn Publishing, Delavan, WI

ISBN-10: 0-9985454-1-4
ISBN-13: 978-0-9985454-1-7

In Memory of Bill Mego (1944-2017)
We might have written the sequel together, old friend.

# Duck and Cover
## A Forward

On July 14, 1954, twelve million Americans died in a nuclear attack—well, no...it was just a test. A drill. A simulation. A what-if. There had been public awareness of the dangers of nuclear war since the US had dropped the first atomic bombs on Japan. In 1951, school children were indoctrinated by a safety film called "Duck and Cover." When you see the flash, they were told, you should stop what you're doing and get under some cover. Drop to the ground, lie face down and cover your head with your hands. Get under a desk. Stay away from windows.

The nation-wide Civil Defense drill was called Operation Alert. It began in many cities with a blast from an air raid siren. Times Square in New York City was cleared in under two minutes. It was estimated that only two million New Yorkers would have been killed had the attack been real. It was considered a successful drill. In Washington, DC, the president was whisked from the White House by helicopter to a secret mountain retreat. The key to survival was advanced warning.

In Philadelphia, in a later, city-wide drill, results were also deemed successful. The major, Joseph Clark, led over 25,000 workers and residents from the area around City Hall to a designated evacuation site some quarter of a mile distant. It was orderly. The city's population, however, was just over two million people.

There would be more drills all over America. School children would be led to the subbasements of their school buildings to wait in darkness until the "all clear" was announced. Suburban residents would clear out a section of their basements as a shelter or even go to the extent of building fallout shelters in their backyards which they would stock with water and canned food. And guns.

There was a fool-hardy notion that survival, if you had adequate warning, was possible through duck and cover, and that orderly evacuation would take the population (those who hadn't been standing near windows) out of harm's way into the woods or the mountains where deadly radiation would not reach them. The President was calling for the construction of an interstate highway system to aid in the evacuations. The drills would teach people to be aware of the exits—now if only they could learn the difference between the "alert" siren and the "all clear." Up to the advent of the first thermonuclear bomb test at Bikini, this might have made sense.

One year later, a second Operation Alert took place in which not only the President, but members of congress were to be evacuated from Washington. 55 cities on the continent and 6 in US territories were theoretically wiped out by nuclear bombs. A five megaton thermonuclear bomb struck New York City. The Federal Civil Defense Administration estimated 5,000,000 were (theoretically) killed and another 5,000,000 injured. 10,000,000 persons had been made homeless. Well, that was better than the twelve million dead of the previous year.

Was it a successful drill? There was some confusion. In New York City the "alert" siren sent people indoors while the "all clear" brought them back into the streets—streets which should have been evacuated. The baseball game at Yankee Stadium stopped, but the spectators, numbering around 17,000, remained seated.

Philadelphia was one of thirteen cities who were not warned of the drill. A hydrogen bomb fell on it dead center. The evacuation was described as "spotty," with slow moving vehicles clogging the avenues. In Houston and Denver the participation was even smaller. In Peoria, Illinois, Civil Defense officials refused to participate. The President sped down Pennsylvania Avenue in the Presidential Cadillac. School children waved at him as he passed along a supposedly secret route. Some cabinet members had left well before the drill began, having known long before when it would occur. Secretary of State John Foster Dulles declined to evacuate and stayed in his office.

In a Federal Civil Defense Administration document issued just before the third Operation Alert in 1956, an evaluation of the previous year's drill admitted that the test had clearly exposed the nation's unreadiness to cope with a thermonuclear attack. The administration had been coming under attack in hearings held by a House Government Operations subcommittee who were afraid that the nation really had no adequate national civil defense program. It was "ineffective and fragmentary…worse than no program at all." Adding to the uneasiness about the civil defense program had been the President's (mock) declaration of national martial law—who, in effect, was in control?

But the FCDA carried on. In the new test, 63 cities, 9 Air Force bases, and 4 Atomic Energy Commission installations would be hit by 139 nuclear devices dropped from airplanes or launched from submarines. The yields would vary from 20 kilotons to 5 megatons.

In a secret document issued by the Executive Office of the President's Office of Defense Mobilization for "Briefing for Operation Alert 1956" (declassified in 2009) the assumed damage and fatalities as well as the proposed actions to be taken by the president "without waiting for any delegation of authority to act" were outlined. On the day of the attack there would be ten million fatalities with another ten million injured. By the end of the week this would rise to twelve million fatalities. After 72 hours radiation would kill another three million people and injure 1.2 million.

Actions proposed to be taken included: declaring the existence of war with the aggressor, phasing into wartime operation, federalizing the National Guard, authorizing the use of nuclear weapons, convening Congress at a relocation site, controlling entry and departure into and from the United States, apprehending and detaining all persons considered dangerous to the national defense, controlling domestic enemy aliens, establishing an Office of Censorship, implementing the plans for economic and psychological warfare, implementing gasoline and food rationing, and requisitioning privately-owned small craft and automobiles for military use.

In addition, the document goes on to stress the importance of economic stabilization. The "unprecedented economic consequences" of the attack would place "the highest kind of priority on the resurrection of our kind of economic and credit structure, *through any means available including military support*." (Read between the lines.) There would be indemnification for war damage, or "affirmative steps short of announcing full indemnification" in order to attempt to "create an atmosphere which would at least temporarily have to substitute for the usual facets of our credit system." The government would also determine the need for "orthodox direct controls" on prices, wages, and rents. On page 28 there appears this chilling proposed action: "Recommend utilization of evacuees from target cities in carrying on essential farm activities."

Heck, war is hell...even mock war. Reading these government documents gives one a sense of the thoroughness with which the problems were anticipated and solutions were offered. Just the many pages detailing the intricate bureaucracy necessary to assign the various responsibilities gives one an insight into the military mindset. A well-oiled machine never complains. What is frightening at this outset is the notion that the powers that were, those in the know, believed not only in the possibility of nuclear war, but in its *likelihood*.

In 1954 there were ill-defined, sometimes nebulous, sometimes fictional enemies with which to grapple. The Communists, certainly. Spies in the military and among highly placed government officials—just ask Senator McCarthy. Juvenile delinquency was a common concern with rising crime rates, drug use, promiscuity and deviate sexual practices rampant among our younger generation. Just ask German-American psychiatrist Fredric Wertham.

Wertham had, in April of 1954, published his book, *Seduction of the Innocent*, a pseudo-scientific study that sought to link juvenile delinquency with comic books. Wertham, in spring of 1954, was testifying before The United States Senate Subcommittee on Juvenile Delinquency, telling its committee chair, Senator Estes Kefauver, that graphic depictions of violence, sex, and drug use found in crime and horror comics led children to act out in similar ways. He sited interviews with troubled adolescents who had committed crimes they saw in the comics. Batman and Robin were homosexuals, he said. Wonder Woman was a lesbian and into bondage. There were hidden pornographic images in the drawings of super heroes' muscular bodies. Yep.

His "scientific" research was discredited, but his effect was to alter the comic book industry forever, putting one of the better publishers, EC Comics, out of business, and to instill in the conservative public the notion of censorship as a panacea for society's ills. But Wertham was junior league compared to the Senator from Wisconsin, the (Dis)honorable Joseph McCarthy. McCarthy, in 1950, had waved around a paper claiming he had the names of Communists working in the State Department. When he was discredited by the Tydings Senate Committee who investigated his charges, he declared that Senator Tydings was himself a Communist sympathizer. Tydings lost his bid for reelection as a consequence.

McCarthy's influence grew. He became chair of the Senate Committee on Government Operations in 1953 and sought out Reds in the Executive branch. Black lists and loyalty oaths appeared in the Hollywood movie industry and in publishing concerns. By the end of the Korean War, McCarthy had turned his venom on the United States Military, in particular, the army base at Fort Monmouth, New Jersey, where Julius Rosenberg had worked in the early 1940s. Rosenberg and his wife had been convicted of espionage and were summarily executed. McCarthy maintained that their spy ring still existed at the fort.

McCarthy's accusations proved ineffectual, but the Army counter-attacked, accusing the witch-hunter of seeking special favors for a whistle-blower named David Schine. The Senate Permanent Subcommittee on Investigations took up the conflicting charges, turning the tables on McCarthy and televising the hearings. These, the Army-McCarthy hearings, were the beginning of the downfall for the duplicitous senator. In December, the Senate voted 67 to 22 to censure McCarthy. His influence was gone. Gone, but not forgotten.

It is no wonder then that in the atmosphere of paranoia that was the 1950s, people would begin seeing things…unidentified things…flying things…alien entities…circular things. Flying saucers.

There is something about circular shapes that harkens back to primitive humankind's attempts to understand and explain existence. The circle is constantly with us as the sun and the moon, in the shape of our pupils, in natural forms and in our dreams. As a symbol it indicates the Self, God, Eternity, the cyclic movement of the seasons, the cycles of birth and death and the idea of resurrection or reincarnation. It is found in all cultures and all religions in some symbolic form whose meaning is essential to the evolution of the individual within the context of its belief system.

Thus we look to the sky, we see something we cannot fathom…perhaps an airplane, a bird, a weather balloon that seems out of place or moves strangely…it may be the smashed body of a bug on the windshield or the reflection of a passing automobile along the edge of our eye glasses. For a moment we cannot place the object within some previous, normal experience. We reach into our subconscious for a symbol with which to associate the phenomenon. We find the Universal Circle. We connect this with the unpleasant rumblings of our fearful consciousness: the threat of annihilation by bombs, invasions, disease; or something as simple as a bad day at work, a loved-one's recrimination, the loss of money or opportunity, the death of a pet.

We need some explanation of the event to center it in reality. There is power in the suggestion that we are not alone in the universe. Thus we adapt an anomaly to complete the fantasy which we want to believe. We see a flying saucer.

Or maybe it is real.

According to the National Investigations Committee on Aerial Phenomena there were 3,015 reported UFO sightings in 1954 worldwide. 58% of these were in Europe and 21% in the United States. The month of October had the most sightings with 1,150 being reported, most of them in France. Donald Johnson, writing about "The Worldwide UFO Wave of 1954," a statistically rich essay, describes four of the reported encounters with aliens during that time period:

...all involved small spheres, cones or disc-shaped craft and dwarfish UFOnauts who were between 0.9 to 1.0 meter tall, wearing diver suits. The first occurred at 12:15 a.m. in Nivelles, Nord, France. A 20-year-old metallurgist, Marcel Senechal, witnessed a spherical object three meters in diameter land in a meadow near a canal. Two one meter tall beings were seen talking to each other. Their heads were very large, and they wore luminous suits. The second occurred at dawn when Angelo Girardo, a 55-year old stockyard worker, was going to work in Bressuire, Deux-Sevres, France. He saw a three meter diameter circular craft with a small figure wearing a diving suit standing close by. The object took off at a fantastic speed.

The third humanoid report occurred at 6:45 p.m. Rene Coudette and B. Devoisin were riding bicycles with a third witness between Rue and Quend, Somme, France on Route D27, near the village of Vron, when they saw a glowing orange object, shaped like a beehive, on the road ahead of them. A small strange "man" wearing a diving suit, about 0.9 meters (3 foot) tall, was standing close to it. When they got within 70 meters of it, the object took off very fast. Less than three hours later the same or a similar orange object chased a car down a road in Quend for eight kilometers, then flew away toward the sea. The witness was a butcher named Georges Galant. The fourth humanoid report occurred later that night and did not involve a UFO sighting. A young baker's apprentice, S. Pouchet, was approached by two small shadowy beings, about three feet tall, in Marcoing, Nord, France.

—http://www.nicap.org/reports/waveof1954.htm

In the story which follows, people and events are presented within a historical setting that is well documented. Most of it is real. Most of it happened. A bit of it is fiction—the author suggests in order to integrate these elements into a cohesive whole, that the reader press the "I Believe" button.

# 1

## Bellingham, Washington, April 11, 1954

It would be touted as the most boring day in history by journalists who struggled to find anything worthy of note to report. Up to today the year had been ripe with exciting events: in January, movie actress Marilyn Monroe had married ball player Joe DiMaggio and the world's first nuclear-powered submarine, the USS Nautilus had been launched by First Lady Mamie Eisenhower (who swung a bottle of champagne against its bow); in February the first mass vaccinations of school children with the new polio vaccine had begun in Pittsburg; in March, a very large thermonuclear bomb had been exploded over the tiny atoll of Bikini (more on this later), Puerto Rican nationalists opened fire in the US House of Representatives wounding five people, and Edward R. Murrow and Fred Friendly aired their televised report on Senator Joseph McCarthy and his communist witch hunts.

But today there was absolutely nothing newsworthy. Sales of the new color television were slow (at $1,000 each), and there was some parental concern about this new music called "Rock and Roll" (instigated by the release of a record called "Rock Around the Clock" by Bill Haley and His Comets), and the French were still battling the Viet Minh in Indochina—but these stories were dull, dull, dull. If only something would happen!

Nathaniel Mirko (Nate to his friends) drooped; He got through his prosaic work day like a wilting thistle which had unfortunately attempted to grow up through a crack in a blisteringly hot macadam back road. Not that it was hot (it was a warm 65 degrees); it was the bending over to scrutinize the pavement that made him feel like a weed in a hot place. But this job, dull though it might be, had its compensations. He was outside. He proceeded at his own pace. He was supervised only by the random bird or squirrel, harassed only by feral cats or curious dogs, and he was getting some excellent exercise. Nate was a sidewalk inspector for the Greater Bellingham Public Works Department.

Armed with a spray can of orange paint, Nate walked the cement paths through neighborhoods rich and poor, looking for uneven fractures that might trip the unwary pedestrian. He would spray various sections of walk with hieroglyphs of dubious meaning, leaving directions for the maintenance crews that would follow (eventually). Grind this piece down, fill this hole up, tear this completely off. Dig, pour, smooth. His word was law; that was a good feeling. He was an environmental architect, marking his concrete drafting board for an improved design. A delusion, perhaps, but Nate was pronoid (the opposite of paranoid): he suspected the world was a conspiracy for his own benefit; his importance bloomed no matter how menial his compelled activity.

Plus, what the heck…Nate liked sidewalks. The sidewalks of his childhood informed his adult sensibilities. Sidewalks covered with spring's first maple seeds or the crisp dried leaves of fall. Sidewalks crunching underfoot with the shells of 17 year locusts. Sidewalks icy in winter so you could slide in slippery street shoes (but not in buckled rubber boots). Sidewalks fresh with rain puddles and writhing earthworms, confused by their new cement world.

Sidewalks with cracks you couldn't step on for fear of breaking your mother's back. Sidewalks incised with the trademarks of "Goodwin Cement Contractors, 1946." Sidewalks of brick, of octagonal tile. Sidewalks that bent around trees grown too close and too large like the "Alligator Tree," an ancient maple he remembered with roots exposed like a great reptile waiting patiently for an unsuspecting child to pause there on the way home from school.

School neighborhood sidewalks littered with candy wrappers or melted ice cream dropped from cones carelessly held. Tiny ants swarming over the ice cream or erupting from cracks in angry waves of some ant-centric ritual dance. The fragile blue shell of a fallen robin's egg or the occasional dead bird or squirrel carcass blocking your passage.

The memory of tricycles, bikes with training wheels, then the first two wheeler you triumphantly maneuvered down the sidewalk in front of your home. Metal skates clipped to your shoes catching edges where settling had raised or lowered sections of sidewalk. Chalked squares and numerals of hop scotch. Names and dates, hand prints and dog paw prints pressed into wet cement to forever immortalize a moment, a place once lived, a passage. Sidewalks that ended inexplicably. Sidewalks that led home.

Sidewalks that provided you with a summer job so you could afford to go back to U-dub in Seattle to finish your undergraduate work. Nate had spent much of his college years working at odd jobs. It was going to take him six or eight years to get a degree, but he had an elderly mother to support. Mother Mirko had frightening episodes of memory loss. Sometimes she couldn't remember who her only son was or whether she had eaten anything. The doctors had suggested she had Alzheimer's disease. There wasn't much known about it; there was no cure. Nate couldn't take on a full-time job that would keep him away from her for long periods of time—once or twice she had walked aimlessly out into the street.

Now he came upon a place where the roots of an ancient elm tree had pushed the sidewalk blocks up, cracking them and exposing jagged ridges of concrete that could trip a mountain goat (should one be ambling along the walk here). He studied this and decided that in order to save the tree he would reroute the sidewalk around it in a gentle curve. He spray-painted arrows to indicate where he wanted the new sidewalk to be placed.

At the curve nearby, a female motorist was waving her hands to flag down a passing police car. Nate wasn't prone toward eavesdropping, but he couldn't help overhearing the exchange between the citizen and the cop:

"My windshield! It's full of tiny pits! Must be vandals, officer. Vandals with a BB gun or something. Same thing happened to my neighbor down the block."

The woman was pointing to the windshield of a '52 Ford station wagon (green with pale yellow trim). The officer was squinting to inspect the damage. Nate couldn't see anything from his vantage point on the sidewalk, but it was clear that the policeman was concerned.

"Yours isn't the first report we've had of this kind of vandalism, Ma'am. We are keeping a sharp lookout for the perpetrators. You should file a police report so your insurance company will pay for a new windshield."

"That's all you have to say? You're keeping a sharp lookout? What's with kids today? Are they all crazy? It's comic books, isn't it? Comic books and that boogie-woogie music."

Nate chuckled to himself. It was so typical of people to blame juvenile delinquency on external influences. It couldn't be their home life, their lack of economic opportunities, the conservative social environment they were thrust into, or fear of polio or of the bomb. No, it must be a communist plot of some sort.

What it was, Nate believed, was that *the war was over*—the big one that had devastated a generation of young people, killed millions, provided evil enemies to hate and fear. Remove that enemy from the equation and you only have yourself to blame for your shortcomings, your failures, your misdirected journey through life's consequences. The only thing we have to fear, Roosevelt said, is fear itself—make that the fear of *one's self*.

Mrs. McCredie, a kindly lady from next door, was sitting with Nate's mother when he arrived home after work. Laura McCredie was a couple of decades younger than Mrs. Mirko, but she was a Christian woman who always volunteered to help out and actually enjoyed sitting and talking with Beverly Mirko, even though the conversations were mostly one way.

"She's fairly lucid today," McCredie told Nate as she rose from the rocker, collecting her knitting and magazines. "She remembered who I was. We had a nice chat about everything. She did keep asking when Herman was coming home, however."

Herman Mirko had been Beverly's husband, deceased now for the last twenty-some years. It wasn't unusual for her to ask after him, as if no time at all had passed, but it was troublesome. Nate imagined that the "chat about everything" Mrs. McCreddie just described had entailed everything about Mrs. McCredie's life, relatives, neighbors, and possibly the price of potatoes, and nothing from his mother. His mother was gazing at him with blank eyes, probably trying to place him in the pantheon of unfamiliar people that filled her days.

"Land O' Goshen," McCredie continued, "what a world…what a world! Did you know what my William discovered this morning? The windshield of his car was full of little holes…well, pits I guess you would say…they didn't go all the way through, but…"

"That's strange," said Nate. "There was a car near where I was working that had the same thing happen to it. Do you think it was vandals? The police seem to think so."

"Well, I don't know. It looked like somebody threw a hand-full of gravel at the car. Who would do such a thing?"

"Well, you take care now, Mrs. McCredie. Call the police if you see anything suspicious."

After Mrs. McCredie had left, Nate busied himself preparing dinner. He flipped the television on; it was good to have the noise and to provide a distraction for his mother. The evening news was on, although there was little news that day. The commentator was discussing a recent speech by President Eisenhower during which he had warned about the spread of communism by using an analogy that would come to characterize public attitude about the cold war and give rise to a colorful catch phrase: the "Domino Theory."

This suggested that if French Indochina was taken over by the communists, it would create a domino effect in Southeast Asia causing neighboring countries to also fall. "You have a row of dominoes set up," Ike had said, "you knock over the first one, and what will happen to the last one is a certainty that it will go over very quickly." The loss of Indochina would result in "many human beings passing under a dictatorship that is inimical to the free world," Ike had said. Burma, Thailand, the Peninsula of Vietnam and Indonesia would follow and even Japan would be endangered.

The new Evil Empire: The Union of Soviet Socialist Republics, the U.S.S.R., the Red Menace—a fine 1954 substitute for the Yellow Peril of World War II.

"Mother," Nate called, "I'm putting your food on the table. Can you make it in here on your own?" There was no answer.

Nate went to the living room where he had left his mother sitting on the davenport. She was not there. He called. He searched the house frantically. Oh no! Not again! The front door was ajar. And there she was, toddling up the street, her bathrobe trailing, neighborhood dogs barking, motorists honking. This has got to stop, thought Nate. I must do something. But what?

The city sat on the edge of Bellingham Bay which, cradled by the Lummi Peninsula and the Lummi and Portage Islands. The bay opened onto the Strait of Georgia. To the east lay the foothills of the North Cascade Range and off in the distance beyond these one could gaze at the snow-capped peak of Mount Baker. To the southeast was situated Lake Whatcom, the source of the city's drinking water. Across from the bay, centered between the Strait of Georgia and the Strait of Juan de Fuca, was the archipelago of the San Juan Islands. A mere 17 miles to the north lay the US-Canada Border.

An important link to the Alaskan fishing and canning industry because of its proximity to the Inside Passage (which was the water route to the Alaskan Territory), Bellingham boomed as a coal mining center in the late 19th and early 20th centuries. Its shipyards were robust and crucial to US Navy during World War II. All in all, it was a pleasant town, perched near the end of the world and often shrouded in fog, but rich in adventure and natural wonders, especially for a boy growing up in its environs.

As a youngster Nate played with his buddies along the waterfront of the old Fairhaven section of town. There they marveled at the Navy ships fitting out as submarine fighters; watched depth charges being loaded. He experienced the blackouts, the ration cards, the rubber drives, the Victory gardens. He remembered being told to watch out for floating airborne bombs: the Japanese had launched thousands of large balloons made of paper and filled with hydrogen and packed with incendiary devices and fragmentation bombs with long fuses to drift over the forests of the American west and to set fire to those forests to demoralize the enemy. The bombs killed six people.

Seattle and Renton to the south were the hometowns of Boeing Aircraft, a major supplier to the government's war effort: notably the B-17 Flying Fortress and the B-29 Superfortress. Seattle had seen the removal of its 7,000 Japanese immigrants and ethnic Japanese citizens during President Roosevelt's internment camp program. Mayor Harry Cain of Tacoma refused to support the program—but later he would be an ardent supporter of Senator Joseph McCarthy. Yes, the Pacific

Northwest was in the thick of things during the war.

Nate's formative years, 11 through 15, spanned the US involvement in that second war-to-end-all-wars. Fatherless…Herman Mirko had died when Nate was 4 years of age from a series of strokes, then a fatal heart attack…the boy had an affinity for the patriotism and bravado of home-front America. He watched soldiers and sailors come and go, gazed at a sky filled with airplanes, a harbor cluttered with floating armada, parades with flags—the crowds cheering the troops. He watched older cousins marching off to war; coffins draped with wrinkled flags coming home one final time.

## Bellingham, Washington, April 17, 1954

Nate stopped into the Fairhaven Pharmacy on Harris Avenue on his way home from work. He was a little perturbed today. His supervisor, Harold Petersen, had called him on the carpet for routing the sidewalk around a tree last week. "You think I don't check up on you?" Petersen had said. "We don't make sidewalks go *around* trees," Petersen had said. "This is Washington. We cut *down* trees," Petersen had said. "You wanna keep workin' here? You follow the procedures as put down by your boss…me!" Petersen had said. Nate wasn't so sure he did wanna keep workin' here.

He reached for the local newspaper, the Bellingham Herald, but the headline of the Tacoma News Tribune caught his eye. He read:

# Windshield Plague Hits City
## Hundreds Of autos Damaged
### Phenomenon Bewilders Everyone;
### Speculation Runs From H-Bomb to Vandals

There had been a little blurb in the Herald about people finding pits on their windshields and the police had chalked it up to vandalism. But now, apparently, the pitting had spread south to Seattle and Tacoma. Hundreds of autos damaged? He bought several newspapers to study when he got home. He was also looking for ads placed by nurses and caregivers who made house calls…even lived in. He had to have someone watching his mother as soon as possible.

When he got home, Mrs. McCredie met him at the door. "She's

had one of her bad days. Had to force her to eat something. Isn't there some medicine or something? The poor old soul is going to forget to breathe one of these days!"

"Mrs. McCredie," Nate began, "it's been wonderful of you to sit with Mother, but I can't keep asking you to sacrifice your time like this. I've decided to hire a full-time nurse."

McCrdeie harumphed. "And how exactly will you pay for that?"

"I'll get a full-time job. A good paying one. It'll be enough...I hope."

"And college? What about college?"

"It will still be there when I can get back to it."

Nate showed Mrs. McCredie the newspapers he had bought with the headlines about windshield pitting. Anything to change the subject.

"I knew it!" she exclaimed. "It's them A-bombs. Dropping radio-stuff from the atmosphere."

"H-bombs. And yes, that seems to be one of the theories."

"Now my William, he says it's sand fleas. You know those little buggers can lay their eggs in the glass windshields and when they hatch...pop goes the windshield!"

"How do they...oh never mind. Anyway, it can't be vandals. It's spread all the way from Vancouver to Tacoma."

After Mrs. McCredie had left, Nate helped his mother out into the backyard where they could sit under the shade of a redbud tree. The garden had turned into a jungle of weeds and tall grass that choked the perennials Mrs. Mirko had once considered her pride and joy. She had lost the ability, the interest, and the knowledge to preserve the garden with her once green thumb. Nate hadn't the time or the inclination to pick up where she had left off, and so the phlox, the coneflowers, the daylilies, the foxglove, and the hollyhocks were being strangled by bristly hawksbeard, redroot pigweed, bull thistle, and bittersweet nightshade.

"Mother," Nate said, "I am going to get you some help...a companion to come and live with you. Do you understand?"

His mother had been smiling, and humming an old children's song that Nate didn't recognize. Suddenly she sat up straight, looked at Nate fearfully. "Who are you?" she asked, her voice trembling. "Oh, you're Herman, aren't you? You need a haircut, Herman."

Later Nate searched the newspapers for live-in caregivers and nurses. He selected three advertisements and jotted down the phone numbers. He would begin calling in the morning. And he would place his own ad in the paper. Next he scanned the help-wanted ads. Nothing particularly interested him: warehouse work, truck driver, taxi cab driver—that one had potential but he was dubious about the pay scale. He'd return to the job search tomorrow. Now he was tired. He turned to the various articles about the windshield pitting epidemic. He learned several intriguing facts and/or suppositions:

In Anacortes, law enforcement officers had set up roadblocks south of town in order to apprehend the suspected vandals. They arrested no one. More than 2,000 cars had been reported as damaged in Bellingham and Oak Harbor. The number of calls to police had necessitated the hiring of extra help to answer the phones. On Whidbey Island, Geiger counters had been used to test the pitted glass and the owners of the automobiles for radioactivity, but nothing had been found of that nature. The Navy's million-watt radio transmitter at Jim Creek was accused of causing oscillations in the glass windshields. Cosmic rays were blamed, and unknown atmospheric anomalies were suspected—although no one could say exactly what these might be. Pitted windshields were reported in at least nine states and Canada, including Oregon, California, Wisconsin, Illinois, Indiana, Kentucky, Michigan, and Ohio.

Dr. D. M. Ritter, a chemist at the University of Washington, worked with authorities on the case. His conclusions? Tommyrot! People must be dreaming! Seattle Mayor Allan Pomeroy wired Governor Arthur Langlie at the state capitol in Olympia, and President Dwight D. Eisenhower at Washington D.C., asking for help. None was forthcoming. Odd shaped granules or small pellets of gravel were found near some of the damaged cars. These reportedly reacted when a lead pencil was placed next to them. Another report stated that over 3,000 cars had been affected including entire parking lots. Some people said they had witnessed pin prick sized holes expand to pits the size of a dime as they watched, thus giving rise to the "sand flea egg" theory.

The most logical suspect was Castle Bravo, a 15 megaton nuclear blast which had taken place over a coral reef in the South Pacific earlier in May. Fallout from the explosion was known to have rained down hundreds of miles from the blast site. Minute particles of coral reef may have been sucked up into the stratosphere to drift over the

Pacific Northwest and other parts of the North American continent. Skeptics called the phenomenon a classic case of mass hysteria, or at least, mass delusion. The pits had always been there in the windshields, they said. People just began to notice them and so the reports snowballed. Fear and anxiety about the recent H-bomb tests caused people to seize upon the pitting as the least lethal result that could have happened—the act of phoning the police was cathartic and reassuring.

Or it might have been gremlins.

# 2

## Bikini Atoll, South Pacific, May 1, 1954

Bikini Atoll, part of the US Pacific Proving Grounds, had seen nuclear testing as early as 1946 when the fourth and fifth atom bombs exploded by the United States were detonated in Bikini Lagoon. But now the bombs were bigger. The Proving Ground was to be host to a series of tests of very high-yield thermonuclear devices. This was called Operation Castle. The objective of the operation was to test the feasibility for an aircraft-deliverable thermonuclear weapon.

Two years before, in 1952, on the nearby atoll of Enewetak, the world's first Hydrogen bomb, Ivy Mike, exploded with the equivalent of 10.4 megatons of TNT, leaving a crater one mile in diameter and obliterating the island of Elugelab. Ivy Mike, because of the complicated mechanism needed to store its liquid deuterium, was three stories tall and weighed around 82 tons—clearly not a deliverable weapon. New research began on the use of a dry fuel. The Atomic Energy Commission and the Department of Defense had now joined together to test several approaches to deployable weapons with maximum yields.

The schedule called for seven detonations during March and April: a test designated as Bravo using a TX-21 prototype device nicknamed "Shrimp," (which was anything but, with a predicted yield of 4 to 8 megatons—it would reach 15 megatons), a test called Union, aka "Alarm Clock," (3 to 4 megatons), a test Yankee, called "Jughead," (this with a predicted yield of 8 to 10 megatons), Echo, called "Ramrod," (a pipsqueak of a mere 125 kilotons), Nectar, called

"Zombie," (1.8 megatons), Romeo, called "Runt," (4 megatons), and Koon, nicknamed "Morgenstern," (1 megaton). All were scheduled to detonate at Bikini Atoll, on the reef or on barges in the lagoon, except Echo, which was to be placed on Eberiru Island. The best laid plans of mice and men, of course, would alter the schedule; weather, failures and the unpredicted Armageddon-like spectacle of Bravo would shuffle around troop ships, unmanned vessels, and recording devices like pieces on a chess board.

The fleet of joint Task Group 7.3 gathered in the Marshall Islands: the USS Philip, the USS Bairoko, the USS Estes, the USS Patapsco, the USS Reclaimer, the USS Granville S. Hall (YAG-40), the USS George Eastman (YAG-39), the USS Molala, the USS Nicholas, the USS Curtiss, the USS Epperson, the US Renshaw, the USS Grosse Point, the USS Gypsy, the USS Mender, the USS Apache, the USS Cocopa, the USS Sioux, the USS Tawakoni, the USS Belle Grove, the USS Shea, the USNS Fred C. Ainsworth, and the USS Terrell County.

Each of the Navy vessels had specific tasks to perform: providing security for the area, operating a boat pool to transport personnel and equipment, providing shipboard assembly facilities for the experimental devices as well as a mobile radio-chemical laboratory, housing, weather monitoring, communications, positioning and mooring device barges, recovery operations, conducting surveys and analysis of the site, decontamination of drone vessels, providing an aircraft carrier (USS Bairoko) and support for fighter and patrol planes and helicopters, operation of the radio-controlled drone vessels (YAR-39 and YAR-40), and, most importantly, evacuations.

One workhorse of that fleet was the ocean tug, the USS Cocopa. She was launched in October of 1943 and joined the US Navy in 1944, seeing action during World War II. She had participated in Operation Removal in 1951 when her commander, Lt. Commander James B. Johnson, went ashore to the island of Anatahan to accept the surrender of Japanese holdouts—by some accounts, the last surrender of World War II. During the Korean War she sailed to tow a grounded Canadian destroyer, the HMCS Huron out of harm's way. She received a battle star for her services in that war.

The USS Cocopa was an Abnaki class Fleet Ocean Tug with 1,240 long tons of standard displacement, a length of 205 feet, a beam of 38.5 feet, and a draft of 15.33 feet. She could achieve 16.5

knots. She had a complement of 85 men and officers. She was equipped with one 3 inch/50 dual-purpose gun, two twin 40mm antiaircraft guns, and two 20mm single antiaircraft guns. She wouldn't be using these at Bikini. Here she would be taking underwater pressure measurements, installing and retrieving moorings and buoys, and towing instrument barges from the fallout area.

It was at the end of the Korean War, after the USS Cocopa had evacuated a Marine garrison at Wonsan Harbor, just north of the DMZ, that Seaman Recruit Christian Resnik, temporarily stationed in Tokyo, Japan, became Seaman *Apprentice* Christian Resnik and boarded the USS Cocopa. Now he had two stripes on his sleeve and had been bumped from E-1 to E-2—not a big deal of a pay raise, but enough to swell his pride.

Christian (his buddies called him Chris…or sometimes "Shitbag") adapted well to the small ship. At first he hadn't thought he would. Everything was grey that day: the overcast sky, the dirty brine swirling against the rotting wharf, the ship itself—a dull "Navy haze grey" swabbed spotless and boring. Life on this tin can? But he hefted his seabag (name and number stenciled roughly across the green canvas) and saluted as he stepped onto the deck. He squeezed into quarters where the racks were neat and the happy socks were tucked inconspicuously under the thin blankets. He found an empty rack and dumped his seabag. He reported to the Chief Petty Officer.

But after they had sailed out onto the blue water his mood changed. A bright Pacific sun had cut through the clouds as they sailed past Yokohama and out into the North Pacific. Sea birds followed the ship as it bobbed like a toy boat on the rolling ocean. First stop was Pearl on the island of O'ahu where they took on passengers—passengers? Eggheads and specialists in all manner of secret things; things not discussed within earshot. Something was up; a clusterfuck was imminent.

The crew was a varied bunch from lifers to fuzznut kids just out of sailor school. There was one sailor, a Petty Officer First Class (two strips and an eagle), name of Charles (Chuck) O'Bannon, who in another era would have been called an "old salt." Chris noted that he walked with ever-so-slight of a limp and tended to squint when on deck in the bright sun. Chris almost expected to see a florescent colored parrot perched on his shoulder. O'Bannon took a liking to Seaman Apprentice Christian Resnik and occasionally (rarely, due to the rigorous routine of a ship at sea) they could gab while on deck and watch dolphins breaking the surface of the deep blue in acrobatic leaps.

On one such occasion Chris braced O'Bannon: "Where we headed, Cap'n?"

"Don't call me Cap'n, boy. It seems the compass is stuck at west-south-west. The scuttlebutt is the Marshalls."

"What's there? It's the middle of nowhere."

"Ever heard of Bikini Atoll? Where they set off the big ones? I think we're headed for another fine Navy day."

"Oh great. We get to visit paradise…and blow it up!"

Indeed it was paradise…or had been before a series of nuclear tests had left it uninhabitable and one in particular had left a crater large enough to be seen from space. Bikini Island was one of 23 small islands set along a ring-shaped reef, the upcropping of a submerged, truncated volcanic mountain. The Marshall Islanders who lived there had sustained themselves by fishing and planting, had raised chickens, ducks and pigs; they had lived simply, weaving pandanus and hibiscus leaves into clothing; they had built ocean-worthy boats and visited other atolls within the Marshall Islands. There was no poverty. Some islanders worked in the copra plantations run by the Japanese. Some built western-style houses and even had servants. Then along came their Uncle Sam.

In keeping with a long tradition of relocating indigenous peoples, the US Government instructed the islanders to "temporarily" leave Bikini "for the good of mankind and to end all world wars." Officials of the Atomic Energy Commission explained that the nuclear tests were in the "interests of general peace and security." The Marshall Islanders, they said, "had no medical reason to expect any permanent after-effects on the general health of the inhabitants." Of course not.

In 1946, Operation Crossroads forced the inhabitants to relocate on Rongerik Atoll. Six times smaller than their homeland. They starved. They believed that the island was haunted by the Demon Girls of Ujae, sisters who would jump from the branches of the Kio tree and kill them—this was not a good place. When they were told their homeland was too radioactive to be resettled, they were moved to tiny Kili Island. They would be unable to return to Bikini for over thirty years. They had become Nuclear Refugees.

In a report (DNA 6035F) issued in 1982 by the Defense Nuclear Agency (an executive agency of the Department of Defense) detailing the procedures and results of Operation Castle in 1954, consideration was given to issues of personnel contamination as had been expected, and as had occurred (two different things). *Initial* exposure to radiation was neither expected, nor did it accidentally happen: the first few minutes of radiation emitted by a nuclear device, if experienced, would be accompanied by a heat wave and a lethal blast, rendering radiation inconsequential (basically, you're dead). However, neutrons emitted by the explosion could alter other materials in the environment, rendering them radioactive. This *residual* radiation could affect personnel over a longer period of time; it had varying rates of decay.

Thus it was paramount to maintain "personal radiation exposures at the lowest possible level consistent with medical knowledge of radiation effects and the importance of the test series." This included avoidance of the contamination of populated islands and local shipping, and significant monitoring of weather conditions. Protecting the 17,000 persons involved at the testing sites required two major approaches: barriers, to restrict access to radiation exclusion areas, and training, to acquaint personnel with the problems of radiation. In addition, radsafe clothing and radiation badges were issued and decontamination centers were set up on the Bairoko, the Curtiss and on a barge alongside the Ainsworth.

There were not, however, enough radiation badges to go around, nor enough staff to analyze them. Badges were issued to "representative crew members" and the results averaged. These and other calculations, such as intensities topside due to "shine" from contaminated water, radiation from the ship's hull and saltwater systems, and fallout that landed on the deck and on personnel were used to determine the dose. But. One wonders at the logic when reading through another DNA report (DNA-TR-89-256) from 1991 where one encounters:

*It is emphasized that the calculated dose is only applicable to a "typical" crew member aboard each ship. Only those contributions to dose that impact the entire crew are used in the dose equation.*

And this:

*Individual exposures accrued while performing decontamination work onboard these craft are not considered, as they do not impact the dose for the entire crew. It is assumed that personnel who had a potential for exposure while performing "non-typical" crew duties were badged, and that dose is in addition to the calculated doses presented herein.*

The DOD and the AEC underestimated, misrepresented or just plain deleted accurate data from public reports. Experts estimate the radiation doses may have been considerably higher than reported. But we are getting a little ahead of our story.

Petty Officer First Class Chuck O'Bannon and Seaman Apprentice Christian Resnik leaned over the side of the USS Cocopa and watched a family of pelicans swim past the salvage tug's anchor chain. The day had arrived for the first detonation in the tests. It was March 1st here, and February 28th on the other side of the International Date Line. Everyone had been evacuated from the atoll, measuring devices had been set, and the device (code name "Shrimp") was waiting patiently on an artificial island which had been built just off Charlie Island (code name "Nan") on Bikini Atoll for this, test Castle Bravo.

The Shrimp was roughly 180 inches long and 54 inches wide with a fuel of 40 percent lithium-6 deuteride encased in uranium. It was light, with an aluminum case instead of the more common steel. There was a lithium-7 isotope in the lithium, originally expected to be inert, but which would fragment into tritium and helium when high energy neutrons collided with its atoms, increasing the energy yield of the weapon. The head of the Los Alamos Theoretical Design Division, J. Carson Mark, had stated that he thought the Shrimp could produce an explosive yield as much as 20 percent more than estimated. It would yield 150 percent more.

"Ever seen one of these, Cap'n?" Resnik asked.

"Naw...and don't call me Cap'n! It'll be bright, I guess. That's why they issued us these dark glasses."

"Think we'll get radioactive?"

"Naw. They said we is upwind of the blast. Navy knows what it's doin', don't they?"

In fact, the Task Group 7.3 fleet was 30 miles south of Nan—upwind. Or so they thought. The test control bunker was on Eneu Island about 20 miles from the test site, also thought to be upwind. The Navy had established a safety zone of approximately 57 square miles around Bikini Atoll, primarily for security against enemy intelligence gathering. Airplanes patrolled the area as best they could. A Japanese fishing boat, the Daigo Fukuryū Maru (Lucky Dragon), was working 13 miles outside of the safety area. No one spotted it. There were Marshallese Islanders still on the atolls of Rongelap, Utirik and Ailinginae and US soldiers stationed on Rongerik Atoll, 110 miles away. These locations were assumed to be out of harm's way. They weren't.

0645 hours. Chris Resnik has donned his dark glasses—this is a good thing. Although it is daylight, it is if someone has set off a flashbulb in a darkened room. The light sustains, grows impossibly brighter, as if the entire sky has ignited. Chris can see the bones silhouetted in his hand as he holds it up to shield his eyes. Now the light becomes focused in an ever-expanding point of light surrounded by the blackest of blacks—now the universe is all red and orange and black and Chris can feel its heat. A gigantic fireball is rising. Fireball? Call the very sun a flickering candle! It is the birth of a star; in fact this fireball is many times hotter than the surface of our sun. It is a bulging, boiling, mass of hell fire that grows in slow motion. Rings of smoke encircle it. It rises upon a pedestal of heated particles of what used to be the earth, the water, the coral reef—becoming the classic "mushroom" shape now familiar to the inhabitants of this, the atomic age.

Now there is a crater in the reef 6,510 feet in diameter and 250 feet deep. In the first minute the mushroom has reached 50,000 feet above sea level. By the second minute it has climbed to 100,000 feet. By the sixth minute, the top of the cloud is at 130,000 feet. Two more minutes and it has a diameter of over 25 miles. The "stem" of the mushroom is 7 miles thick and the bottom of the fireball cloud is 55,000 feet above the now nonexistent reef. These numbers stagger the imagination.

Chris involuntarily grabs Chuck's arm. The two men are stupefied. Part of their awareness has been dislocated from them, leaving them in shock. On the deck on which they stand are other men, paralyzed, unable to shout, scream, cry out. The silence is eerie; they are thirty miles from a blast whose terrible rolling thunder has yet to reach them. Soon it will. Two sailors on the forecastle drop to their knees and begin to pray; they are seasoned veterans, witnesses to the horrors of war—but nothing, nothing like this.

There are people in the control room bunker on Eneu Island. The radiation level there is rising. They retreat to a heavily shielded room in the bunker. Rad levels[1] will reach 40 R/hr within an hour. (3.9 was the maximum allowable exposure for AEC personnel.) Measurement devices in the area have been destroyed by the blast. The Navy ships, including the Cocopa will receive their first fallout by the end of that first hour. Rad levels will be at 5 R/hr, causing crews to leave the decks and retreat to the lower areas of the ships.

On the Daigo Fukuryū Maru, fisherman Ōishi Matashichi has also witnessed the initial blast, an unbelievable "flaming sunset" that envelops sky, boat and sea. There are 23 crewmen on the boat. They are contaminated with fallout. They receive a dose of 290 roentgens. All will become sick with radiation poisoning. One, Aikichi Kuboyama, will die. The Japanese Government, understandably skittish of nuclear warfare, will protest and relations between them and the US Government will become strained. Eventually, the US Government will give Kuboyama's widow a check for 1 million yen (only $2,800!) and pay the Japanese Government two million dollars for losses in contaminated fishing grounds and other damages.

It is five hours after denotation. Fallout, wafting its way in a plume that stretches for 160 miles, has dusted Ailinginae, Uterik, Rongelap, and Rongerik. Rongelap is covered with a fine, white powder; children play in it, thinking it is snow. They lick it off their hands. Islanders on Rongelap, Ailinge, and Utrik receive doses of 175, 69, and 14 roentgens respectively. The islanders living here will be evacuated, but not for another two days. The so-called safety zone will be expanded from 57 square miles to 570,000 square miles. Better late than never.

Cocopa and other Task Force ships had been ordered to sail south, out of the apparent fallout area. Now, five hours later, Cocopa returns to Bikini to commence operations. Radiation intensities on deck measure 110 R/hr. The ship's wash down system is deployed to decontaminate its surface. She sails into the lagoon where she will be engaged in decontaminating a project barge left there during Bravo, and lay instrument cans for the upcoming Romeo detonation.

Resnik and O'Bannon are issued radiation badges for their top-side activities during the next several days. O'Bannon's comment on the Bravo shot is "That, my boy, was one butt-puckering experience!" Resnik's response is "Getting through this is like a monkey trying to fuck a football. I just hope we don't step in any shit."

---

[1]The **rad** is a deprecated unit of absorbed radiation dose, defined as 1 rad = 0.01 Gy = 0.01 J/kg. It was originally defined in CGS units in 1953 as the dose causing 100 ergs of energy to be absorbed by one gram of matter. A related unit, the roentgen, is used to quantify the radiation exposure. The **roentgen** (symbol R) is a legacy unit of measurement for the exposure of X-rays and gamma rays up to several megaelectronvolts. It is a measure of the ionization produced in air by X-rays or gamma radiation and it is used because air ionization can be measured directly. The roentgen equivalent in man (abbreviated **rem**; symbol rem, or often but incorrectly R̲) is an older, CGS unit of equivalent dose, effective dose, and committed dose. Quantities measured in rem are designed to represent the stochastic biological effects of ionizing radiation, primarily radiation-induced cancer. These quantities are a complex weighted average of absorbed dose, which is a clear physical quantity measured in rads. There is no universally applicable conversion constant from rad to rem. According to the National Council on Radiation Protection and Measurements (NCRP, Report No. 160, Table 1.1), the general U.S. population receives about 0.62 rem per year from natural background radiation sources (radon, cosmic rays, and rocks) and man-made radiation sources (medical diagnostic x-rays and consumer products). As a basis of comparison, a standard diagnostic chest x-ray delivers a radiation dose of about 0.02 rem. In Operation Castle, 3.9 was the maximum allowable exposure for AEC personnel.

# 3

## A Country Girl

## Bellingham, WA, April 19, 1954

Noreen stood on the porch staring at the screen door, perhaps willing that it was stuck, swollen from the rain or painted shut; that it wouldn't open, wouldn't be opened so that she wouldn't be obliged to smile nicely and say, "How do you do, I'm Noreen Ashley. I'm here to apply for the care-giving job." Why was she reluctant to pursue a great opportunity like this one? It had sounded ideal when she had talked to the man over the phone. The woman was elderly but not infirm. Just a little absent minded, apparently. And Noreen? She wasn't shy or lacking in confidence. No, it was something else. A fear of success perhaps. A reluctance to be tied down, to be responsible for another person's welfare. And then there was that one condition—living in. Living in another person's house, at their beck and call, on call constantly. A big responsibility. And after all, she was just a country girl.

Noreen had grown up on an apple farm outside of Granger in Yakama County. Father had been a sort of sharecropper on a big company-owned orchard; He had brought his family to Granger in '41 when the Farm Security Administration had opened the Crewport Farm Labor Camp, a government sponsored project to counteract the effects of the Dust Bowl. Later he had found work with Thackeray's Fine Fruits. Mr. Thackeray appreciated Ashley's hard work, his ability to organize the other workers (never into labor unions) and his interest in developing new types of apples. Thackeray offered him a hectare of trees with which to experiment.

Their single-wide was set on the edge of the valley where orderly rows of young trees swayed in gentle winds and basked under a smiling Washington sun. Noreen could remember running barefoot through the orchard, picking up a freshly dropped red delicious or a winesap. There was nothing like an apple right off the tree! Its unique sweetness, its juicy, crunchy, spurt of favor wouldn't last until market, but it would still rival any pommes from Michigan. Noreen knew a lot about apples. She knew that trees were a member of the rose family, that apple seeds were poisonous—someone had once died from ingesting a cup of apple seeds.

Father had helped develop a strain of golden delicious that was highly resistant to disease. Unfortunately, before he could reap any rewards from his achievement, he fell from a ladder and broke his neck. Noreen's mother had subsequently run off with a man who had worked at the tile factory: a swarthy type of man's man she had met at Murphy's Bar in Granger, who had bought her drinks and danced with her to the scratchy 78s that filled the gaudy, flashing juke box, who enticed her with promises of city life (they would travel south, to LA and get into the record business—wasn't she a looker? Couldn't she sing like a bird?), and so she left with him, leaving Noreen on her own.

Mother and father gone, Noreen thought it would be advantageous to pursue a career in medicine. Nursing, for instance. She managed to get through the first year of nursing at the University of Washington before her money ran out. After a series of odd jobs that went nowhere, she applied to a company in Bellingham that ran a nursing home. She worked hard to become certified as a caregiver, a category just a bit below that of nurse's aid. Working at the home was depressing, but it paid the bills and gave her experience that would be valuable once she had saved enough to return to nursing school. Then she had seen the job advertisement which Nate had placed in the paper.

So now she stood on the porch, staring at the screen door, hoping it wouldn't open. It did open. A sandy-haired young man peered out at her. He wasn't handsome, she thought, but he had the kind of rugged good looks that attracted her—why was she even thinking about this? She still hadn't shaken the uneasiness she had initially felt. She sensed a kind of foreboding that seemed to permeate the very atmosphere—nothing baleful, nothing dispiriting or fretful—just a touch of disquietude that lingered, crept around the edges of things like a cold fog that blurred and disoriented. Then, suddenly, it dissipated. He had smiled.

"How do you do," she said, "I'm Noreen Ashley. I'm here to apply for the caregiver job."

It hadn't taken long for Nate to make his decision regarding the caregiver job. No, it wasn't because Noreen was a rare beauty, a dignified young woman who imbued confidence, intelligence and trust, or a gentle being capable of bestowing positive regard and careful attention. She wasn't what Nate would have called beautiful—not cute, not extraordinarily pretty, but pleasing. Very pleasing. Nice to look at, and that, of course helped. However, she seemed a little nervous, indecisive, perhaps searching for the proper word or gesture. But when Nate introduced her to his mother he sensed a connection between the two. Beverly Mirko seemed to gain color in a spontaneous glow of delight. Noreen's nervousness evaporated. Nate instantly knew Noreen Ashley was exactly the proper panacea for his mother's malady, and the key which would unlock his own custodial prison doors.

She stayed and sat a while with her new charge even though Nate had suggested that the end of the week would be soon enough for her to commence her live-in status (the details of this hadn't been formalized) and her familiarization with Beverly's needs. Mrs. Mirko was having one of her good days. She babbled exuberantly to her new friend about imaginary events of the day, people who had called upon her, the great success Herman was having. Noreen took this all in her stride, aware that the repartee was mostly delusional. Noreen was supportive, which appeared to be a successful tactic, and this small success greatly encouraged her in her own attitude toward the job.

They were seated in the living room across from a bay window which looked out over the lawn. Because the house was situated on a slight rise in the landscape, the view included an unobstructed skyline against which rose the foothills of the Cascades and in the distance, the peak of Mount Baker. Beverly's eyes became fixed on this vista as she talked. Her dialogue suddenly ceased, then she said, "Oh…how pretty! The evening star in the morning. Isn't that strange and wonderful?"

Noreen looked out the window. There, silhouetted against the shadowed foothills was a shining oblong object like a fat cigar—only silver and gleaming as if it reflected and intensified the noonday sun. It hovered, then moved slowly to the north, then rose rapidly upward, turned sharply toward the distant mountain, and in a flash, was gone. Oh my God, she thought, I just saw a flying saucer!

The eye is a fragile organ, but oh so intricate! It has sensors dedicated to intensity (what we call black and white), and others reacting to the wave lengths of spectrum we call red, green and blue. Put it all together and we see colors. Not only is the effect of light sensed by this wonderful device, it also tracks movement: horizontal or vertical—this by a marriage of nerve-endings with the cerebral cortex. This eye-mind stabilizes our vision, keeping the world upright even as we tip our heads. It is truly a miraculous system. It can sometimes allow us to see things that aren't really there.

There is a short story written by Edgar Allan Poe entitled "The Sphinx." In it, a man is seated by a window with a view of the Hudson River. His mind has been occupied by the current cholera epidemic that is devastating the area. As he gazes out his window he suddenly sees a fearsome creature advancing across the landscape. The story has all the drama of a horror film and Poe's description of the creature sends chills up your spine. However, it turns out that a small insect "of the genus *Sphinx*, of the family *Crepuscularia*, of the order *Lepidoptera*, of the class of *Insecta*" had been dangling spider-like from a thread just in front of the man's eye. His eye-mind interpreted the insect, superimposed against the landscape, as being as large as an ocean liner. Fear, paranoia, and optical illusions can create quite a bit of mischief with our psyches.

So a drop of water running down a windshield and catching the rays of the setting sun can become an alien spaceship slowly landing on the road before you. The "floaters" in your vitreous humor, those annoying little fragments of retina that appear in your vision can seem to be gigantic one-celled animals or translucent reptiles. Their movements are not unlike those reported by observers of unidentified flying objects: hovering, slowly moving and then darting off quickly. This can be perturbed by anxiety and given meaning that does not exist. It explains some of the sightings of flying saucers like the one Noreen has just experienced. But not all of them.

In 1952 the United States Air Force began a study of unidentified flying objects, recording and analyzing the reports of sightings by the Air Force and civilians. It was an extension of a project begun in 1947, after the notorious Roswell, New Mexico incident. The first study, named Sign, and a second named Grudge, had been characterized as "the most poorly written piece of unscientific tripe I've ever read," by the Pentagon's Air Force Headquarters Intelligence director, Major General Cabell. But then, in 1951, Air Force pilots started seeing things that would lead to a new, more comprehensive study.

On September 10, 1951, at 11:10 AM, an Army Signal Corps radar operator stationed at Fort Monmouth, New Jersey, recorded an unknown object moving faster than his equipment could accurately plot. He tracked it as following the coast line at an estimated 700 miles per hour. At 11:35 that same morning, Major Edward Ballard was on board a T-33 jet piloted by Lieutenant Wilber S. Rogers. As they flew over Point Pleasant, New Jersey, Rogers spotted a dull silver, flat disc-shaped object, possibly the same object tracked by the radar operator. He and Ballard witnessed the object below their aircraft and estimated it to be about 30 to 50 feet in diameter. The UFO began to descend toward Sandy Hook. Rogers turned his plane to investigate more closely when the object suddenly veered off at a 90-degreee turn. They lost it over the ocean.

A prime concern of the study was whether or not UFOs were a national security threat (if operated either by Russians or outer space aliens or crazy beatnik radicals). Project Blue Book, as it was called, recorded 12,618 UFO reports by its end in 1969; over 500 of them could not be explained. According to a FBI report on Project Blue Book, the year 1954 had a total of 487 sightings with 46 classified as "unidentified," that is, sightings which could not be explained as clouds, weather balloons, experimental aircraft or swamp gas.

Already by the end of April, 1954, there had been several unexplained UFO sightings in the United States. On January 28, in Rangeley, Maine, Wilhelm Reich saw two bright lights moving into a valley against a background of mountains. The event lasted fifteen minutes. On February 26, R. M. Pierce, an architect, and George Avery, a marine engineer, witnessed a silver disc with a white trail at Newburyport, Massachusetts. It made a loud roar. There was a sighting in Pennsylvania on March 2, and one in the Nevada desert on April 4. In Chicago, Illinois, on April 8 at 4:30 PM, Lelah Stoker watched as a white round-topped disc with a humanoid suspended beneath it skimmed over water and landed. The occupant, wearing a green suit, walked around and then took off very fast. The incident lasted 30 minutes.

There were more in April. On April 23, in Pittsfield, Maine, Mr. and Mrs. F. E. Robinson reported seeing a silver dollar-shaped object with a dome and a flashing light, which made a sound "like a swarm of bees." It hovered, tilted, flew horizontally, and rose vertically. Stones under it moved. The next day in Athens, Georgia, at 7:35 PM, C. Cartley and Mr. and Mrs. H. Hopkins and their daughter saw fifteen to twenty yellow objects in a V-formation flying south for 10 seconds. Also on April 26, in Danville, Virginia, around 6:15 AM, Rev. W. L. Shelton saw two domed ellipses, 20 feet long, 8 feet thick, 10 feet at the ends, glowing silver or orange, which hovered, then climbed side-by-side while brightening. This was a 2 minute long observation.

# Bellingham, WA, April 29, 1954

It was nearly one week since Noreen had moved her sparse belongings into the spare room at the Mirko home. Things had been going well—Mrs. Mirko had her ups and downs, but all in all there was nothing Noreen couldn't handle. No escapes out the front door. No calls to the police about nonexistent burglars. No refusing to eat, save for one time when a plate of spaghetti landed on the floor after Beverly Mirko swatted at a very large, nonexistent bug. Nate was often absent during the day but showed up for the evening meal. He cooked at least half of the time, a circumstance that delighted Noreen and gave her some small insight into the character of the young man. He was serious, held up his share of the responsibilities (he hadn't found a job yet and the search was tedious, but he was dedicated), and he was personable when they sat down to dinner. Nothing to complain about.

The knock at the door came shortly after Noreen had successfully convinced Beverly to take an afternoon nap. She looked through the decorative glass of the front door to see a man, distorted by the diamond-shaped prisms of the glass, standing with his hand held out holding something she couldn't quite distinguish. One of those religious types with a pamphlet she would chuck into the trash as soon as he left? Some lanky high schooler selling candies or football tickets? A city worker with an eviction notice? She decided to open the door, at least a crack.

"Noreen Ashley?" the man asked. "My name is Second Lieutenant Leon Blackman. I am with the 4602nd Air Intelligence Service Squadron. We function within the Air Defense Command of the United States Air Force. I am here to ask you a few questions, if you would be so kind as to accommodate me."

He was still holding his ID card with his picture, name and rank on it. Noreen looked closely at this, noted the briefcase the man carried, considered that this Second Lieutenant, who wasn't in uniform, looked more like a high school senior than an airman, and began to wish that he had in fact been a high school senior selling candy bars.

"You better come in," she said.

They sat in the living room, Noreen on the davenport and Blackman in the rocking chair that their neighbor, Laura McCredie preferred during her visits. McCredie's visits! Noreen thought she now knew why this official from the government was here to ask her questions. She hadn't told anyone about seeing a flying saucer. No one, that is, except Mrs. McCredie. Mrs. McCredie had paid one of her visits to Beverly...most likely to size up Noreen...and during that visit, which had been one of Beverly's better days, the subject of the curious evening star that had shown so brightly during day came up. McCredie attempted to dissuade Beverly from her fantasy, a tactic to which Noreen's program of positive regard was opposed. Noreen admitted she had seen the "star" as well. She might have hinted that it looked for all the world like a flying saucer. She never imagined Mrs. McCredie would tell anyone about that.

"Why aren't you in uniform?" Noreen asked, trying to forestall the inevitable inquisition.

"When we interface with the civilian public we don't wish to appear formal. It usually puts people at ease. But I can see that you have some concerns?"

"What are you investigating?"

"Investigating? Oh…no, no. Just a sort of questionnaire. Our peacetime mission is to follow up on any reports of unusual activity in the skies. Unscheduled aircraft…that sort of thing."

"But I didn't report anything."

"Ah…but your neighbor, a Mrs. (here he pulled a clipboard from his briefcase and flipped through a page or two) Laura McCredie, said you told her you had seen a flying saucer."

"Why would you take someone's word for that? I never said…"

"Yours wasn't the only sighting that day, Miss Ashley. Of course, we don't believe in flying saucers…we prefer the term, Unidentified Flying Objects…the other presupposes outer-space aliens. Which of course is absurd. But we follow up on such reports on the outside chance that there has been an invasion of our air space by a foreign power. There is a cold war on, you know."

Noreen had been clenching her fists. Her knuckles were turning white. "I see," she said. "Of course, anything I can add…"

What Second Lieutenant Leon Blackman wasn't telling Noreen Ashley could have filled volumes. UFOs fell under the auspices of Project Blue Book but the current head of the project, Captain Charles Hardin, only had a staff of two. Field operations were impossible. The AISS (Air Intelligence Service Squadron) had been given the task to instigate when needed. Their official duties were to secure domestic crash sites of US and enemy aircraft, but this was extended to include UFOs. Their training was extensive: it included skiing and Arctic survival skills, horse and pack animal operations, and parachuting. They studied and became fluent in the Russian language; they were cross trained in technical intelligence and interrogation procedures. And they were excellent public speakers.

But the CIA and the FBI were also interested in Project Blue Book and the data gathering carried on by the 4602nd AISS. This raised internal tensions considerably. In addition, the chief of the Air Technical Intelligence Center, Harold Watson, at the request of Major General Cabell, had looked into the matter, and had told Hardin that his investigators were logging in too many unexplained observations. He insisted on more *Identified* Flying Objects. Was the AISS now intimidating witnesses to get fewer unexplained results?

Were they covering something up? It sounded like a good plot for a television show—but that wouldn't happen for many more years.

Second Lieutenant Leon Blackman opened his field guide, the UFOB Guide, which was designed to help agents organize data according to common sense, make it easier to rule out contradictory evidence, and which tended to skew things toward explainable conclusions. There were no categories for the most extraordinary details of the sightings and as a result of the use of this guide, unexplained phenomena dropped sharply as a percentage of reported incidents.

"Would you say that what you saw could have been an aircraft? Either a commercial jet or an Air Force trainer?"

"It was shaped like a skinny egg or a fat cigar…I don't know, an oval."

"And it was flying high or low?"

"Both. It stopped and hovered, then it took off straight up and then it shot off to the north. I've never seen an airplane fly that fast."

"So it could have been an airplane. An experimental one, maybe. From one of the Air Force bases."

"I guess so."

"Well, thank you, Miss Ashley. I've got everything I need. I'll be leaving now. Please don't be too verbal with your story, and caution Mrs. McCredie that…you know…loose lips sink ships, and all that."

Second Lieutenant Leon Blackman was satisfied that there was nothing significant in this particular sighting that needed to be noted in the record. A hysterical woman who couldn't tell the difference between an airplane and a cigar! What was that old saying about a woman and a cigar? No matter. He drove down the Pacific Highway toward Seattle where he would catch a shuttle flight back to the Air Force base in Colorado Springs.

He had passed Lake Samish and was in rugged country about 5 miles north of the little town of Belfast when his engine died. He turned the key and pumped the gas pedal but all he could get was a dull click. There was no electrical power. He started to exit the vehicle in order to lift the hood and check all the wires for a break or a short but the door wouldn't open. It wasn't an electric lock, just an ordinary mechanical one. But it was stuck. He tried the window. The crank wouldn't turn.

A dark shadow surrounded the car: an almost impenetrable curtain of darkness that blocked the view in every direction. It was as if night had fallen early. Then came the light: a fierce, blinding cascade of radiation from above that slammed against the car as if it, like the darkness before it, were a solid mass or some viscous liquid. Blackman felt a vibration that mounted until it took on the proportions of an electric shock. He was paralyzed, as if he were melting into the vinyl seat. Yet everything was cold, silent, suffocating in the absence of anything but that veil of light. He sensed rather than felt that the car was moving, rising, being drawn upward. Then he lost consciousness.

# 4

## Shore Leave

## San Francisco, June, 1954

By the end of June, the calculated dose of rems for the USS Cocopa was set at 2.2—remember, the AEC had recommended no more than an average dose of 3.9. Good news, yes? Need we repeat the rationale for the calculation? "It is concluded that the reconstructed doses well serve to complete the exposure records for crewmen whose 1954-totalled doses do not fully or accurately reflect their individual exposures." Huh? And what individual exposures might not be reflected in this calculation? "...for a one-day badging period (30 April) for USS COCOPA, there is a cohort of one Boatswain's Mate Chief (badged) and nine seamen; the reading is 785 mrem (a mrem is one one-thousandth of a rem). There is an individual badge for the Chief Warrant Boatswain with a reading of 240 mrem. The remainder of valid cohort and individual badges for this ship for the same period are all less than or equal to 40 mrem." Okay, so what happens to the 785 and 240? "Two badges for the period 1-7 May with readings from 1,300 to 1,500 mrem for cohorts of 2 and 3 personnel are deleted as atypical. A third badge with an obviously anomalous reading of 3,150 mrem is also deleted." Hmm.

The men of the USS Cocopa deserved a break, nuked or not. The ship and its crew had been the principal unit in recovery and buoy servicing operations for the first three Castle shots. They had towed and decontaminated project barges, laid mooring for instrument cans, shuffled between Bikini Atoll and Enewetak Atoll, and received fallout from all six of the detonations (seven were planned but one was a fizzle). The ship routinely ran its washing system and streamed through clean ocean water to reduce its own hull contamination. The crew recovering the instrument buoys wore protective clothing. No one complained of adverse symptoms. Yet there was an overriding strain from the months of caution, doubt, and the fear of "stepping in the shit."

Resnik and O'Bannon found a little bar on Broadway, just a few blocks from the Embarcadero. The Brown Betsy hadn't as yet become a gay bar, like Mona's or the Black Cat or the Why Not. The two swabbies might have been interested in some of the drag queen performances at these establishments, but shore leave time was fleeting, and a few beers were all they could fit into their schedule. It was funny, thought Chris, here we sit, our recent experiences so otherworldly, so bizarre, that we are set far apart from the ordinary people in this dark, smelly room…they haven't any inkling of the apocalypse that could be coming, should someone press the wrong button!

"So, Cap'n…oh, sorry…Chuck, which of the big bangs was your favorite?" asked Resnik once the bartender had placed a shot and a beer in front of each of them.

"Don't spec' we're to talk about it…not public like. But that first one, Bravo, that was abso-fucking-lutely awesome. We were one cunt hair short of being fish bait."

"Ya, man…fuck the Navy." Resnik dropped his shot glass of whiskey into his beer; foam cascaded over the top and onto the bar.

"Hey guys," said the bartender, "keep the deck clean, huh?"

"Roger that," said O'Bannon. Then to Chris: "Let's go over to that booth by the back door. A little privacy wouldn't be bad."

They moved to the booth, its high-backed wooden benches afforded some shelter from the boisterous bar crowd that milled and back-slapped and chatted up each other. The wood was painted dark green and varnished to a near shine; the table top was black Formica with silver flecks and a chrome border. Easier to wipe spilled beer…or other fluids. As they talked, a tall, heavy-set man with a soldier's posture and gate walked briskly over to their booth and motioned "could he sit down?" O'Bannon gave him the once-over. He recognized him as a jarhead: a Marine.

"Well if it isn't one of Uncle Sam's Misguided Children," O'Bannon said, lampooning the acronym (for US Marine Corps).

"Thought you POGs might be Gator Navy," answered the man, responding with an acronym of his own which meant "Person Other than a Grunt."

"The gator-freighter's in the garage, Chief. Can't give you no lift to nowhere. But sit down and take a load off. We's always friends with squids."

Chris looked at O'Bannon quizzically. "What's a squid?" he blurted without thinking.

"It's a higher form of Marine life, son," answered the Marine. This your sea daddy here? He looks real Joe Navy to me. Fartin' dust yet old man?"

The niceties over with, the three began to trade introductions and stories—stories necessarily incomplete on the sailors' side of the conversation. The Marine's shore leave was up and he needed to get down to San Diego by tomorrow morning. O'Bannon regretted that he couldn't offer him a lift on the Cocopa. She was at the Navy's dry dock getting scrubbed down so that she didn't start to glow in the dark. The Marine, whose name and rank were First Sergeant Andrew H. Millender, cocked his head at the "glow in the dark" comment.

"We were across the pond recently…Japan," O'Bannon offered, hoping to defuse his potentially ship-sinking slip.

"Giving condolences to the families of Japanese fishermen?" asked Millender. "Don't worry. It was all over the New York Times front page the other day. A FOOBAR of the highest order…dustin' a fishing boat! At least it wasn't the Marines or the Navy that fucked up. Those eggheads were sure limp dicks if they couldn't add the numbers right. And those flyboys should have seen the boat."

"Oh, that's not quite fair. They were outside the safe zone. Trouble was, the safe zone was too far inside the danger zone." (This from Chris Resnik.) "So, you know anywhere around here we might find some pootang?"

"You boys'll be visiting the pecker-checker if you're not careful. Just walk down Broadway tonight. And watch out…under that heavy lipstick some of the chickies may be twinks."

"Don't mind Seaman Schmuckatelli, here," O'Bannon commented. "I'm going to the head. Be right back."

"I'm leaving, myself," said Millender. "It was a good time we had here. Much appreciated. One thing…do you register those two guys at the table across from us? They seem a bit strange to me. Been scopin' us out the whole time. Something funny about them."

At a round table, the only seating arrangement with a good view of the booth, sat two men. Strange men. Strange men in the sense that they were unusually tall—definitely over six feet and maybe more. They had thin, pinched faces and what O'Bannon would have called "squinty eyes" in a less than complimentary assessment. The most unusual aspect of the men was their complexion: pale, almost colorless, with a subtle tint of grey that deepened their angular features. They stared with unblinking eyes at the three companions. They were as motionless as if they had been mannequins in some bizarre department store which catered to horror film actors.

O'Bannon would later admit that a shiver ran up his spine when he looked into those "squinty" eyes. He slid out of the booth and headed toward the back of the bar where the bathrooms, marked "Heifers" and "Bulls" were situated. The Bulls hadn't been cleaned recently and the stench was stifling. O'Bannon hurried about his business, but had to pause to gaze at a calendar which graced the otherwise graffiti-covered walls. It was from December of 1953—no one, apparently, had had the desire to change it. For it showed a bright red cloth background against which was posed a most beautiful, sexy, blond and nude woman, her legs curled up seductively, one hand almost touching a knee, the other hooked behind her neck, her breasts thrust forward (the most sensual nipples O'Bannon had ever seen on a photograph—or in person). It was titled, "Golden Dreams" and O'Bannon knew, although it was not credited on the picture, that this was a photograph of Marilyn Monroe, taken in 1949 at a time when she had needed $50 to make a car payment and slightly before she became a matinee sex idol.

Man! Is that Joe DiMaggio a lucky stiff! Well, it was just an image, wasn't it? O'Bannon had never, and would never know the pleasure of touching the flesh of such a gorgeous woman. Yes, it was aptly titled, "Golden Dreams." He returned to the booth but it was empty. Millender was gone. Resnik was gone. He looked around the room: the two fugitives from a circus side show were also gone. He went to question the bartender.

"Seen where my buddy went?" he asked.

The bartender swirled a stained cloth over the surface of the bar, wiping away peanut shells and cigarette ash. "He left a few minutes ago with those two weirdos. They Chinese or sumpin'?"

"You didn't see which way they went, I suppose."

"Can't say I didn't…can't say I did." The bartender paused here in his wiping, perhaps readying his hand to receive a bill or two from O'Bannon to aid his memory. O'Bannon considered doing this but logic voted against it. The law of diminishing returns—he'd heard that expression somewhere, and now he understood its meaning. Resnik was long gone.

"Damn!" he said. "Well, thanks a pant load." Now he would return to the base and wait for Resnik to show up. Some great odd story the kid would have to tell, wouldn't he? Those men…Chinese? O'Bannon didn't think so. FBI maybe, arresting him for blabbing about the nuclear tests. Or Russian spies! A little obvious for spies though, wasn't they? Coincidence that they left together…yes, that must be it…coincidence.

O'Bannon walked up Broadway toward the waterfront with its piers clustered with boats, old men with fishing rods, and gangs of jabbering sea birds. Trash littered the sidewalk: paper wrappers, a broken whisky bottle, a discarded sock perhaps dropped from a laundry bundle—no cigarette butts however—these were picked as prizes by the indigent who huddled in alleyways and slept on old cardboard pallets. One such unfortunate sat propped against the side of a building next to a row of battered, overflowing, metal garbage cans. The man's eyes followed O'Bannon but his head remained motionless as if he were a gargoyle on some French parapet, forever frozen with a grim gaze across the ruined landscape.

O'Bannon noticed a tattoo on the man's bared forearm: an anchor. A seafaring man? A down-on-his-luck sailor tossed back onto shore by an unfeeling ocean that took his ship, his livelihood, his pride? A sailor-soldier home from a barbarous war that had shattered his mind, eaten his soul? Or just a drunk, no longer with a spouse to badger him, children to embarrass him, a boss to berate him? Ah, matey, better you than me, thought O'Bannon. He searched his pockets for a few coins and laid these at the man's feet.

Along the waterfront were rows of piers; along the piers were rows of boats. At the first pier were sail boats with their sails furled, masts rocking in a rhythmic array like slender saplings in a wind-swept landscape. Here the water rippled and coiled, distorting the reflections of the swaying masts into a mass of undulating serpentine shapes. It was visual music to the old salt. He strolled farther along the waterfront past wharfs where fishing boats were docked and gulls swooped up tidbits from their decks; past landings where mid-sized shipping vessels were tied, their crews ashore in the bars and bawdy houses; where rotting piles provided perches for sea birds; where fishermen had stuck poles between planks, spending their lazy vigils dozing or talking or playing cards or checkers...waiting, waiting, waiting for the zinging sound of line unreeling, for the tug of war between fish and man.

O'Bannon caught a bus which ran down the Embarcadero and over to 3rd street. He exited at Quesada Avenue and walked the remaining six or so blocks to the Treasure Island Naval Shipyard at Hunter's Point where he was stationed during the decontamination of the USS Cocopa. From the south gate at Crisp Avenue he proceeded to the seamen's barracks and reported in.

The shipyard dated back to 1870. By 1916 the drydocks there were the largest in the world, attracting the attention of the US Navy who rented the shipyard from World War I to the beginning of World War II. Treasure Island and the surrounding property were then acquired by the government for shipbuilding and maintenance. It became the site of the Naval Radiological Defense Laboratory. In 1945 the USS Indianapolis, docked at Hunter's Point, was loaded with components of the first atomic bomb, the one that fell on Hiroshima. After Operation Crossroads in 1946 the yard was used to decontaminate ships used in nuclear testing. The site became so radioactive that (in another reality) in 2017, parts of it are still being decontaminated even though private industry has taken over the former shipyard and built and sold hundreds of condominiums.

Waiting to be assigned back to active duty, O'Bannon had some time to kill. He walked down Spear Avenue past the fire department building, the electric shop and the paint shop, and stopped briefly at the cafeteria to look for other crew members of the Cocopa. No one he talked to had seen Resnik return to the base yet. He continued walking and found himself at drydock number 3 where the USS Granville S. Hall was being scrubbed down to remove any remaining traces of radioactive contamination. She had been the YAG-40 that had entered the lagoon under remote control and had received some of the highest doses in the fleet.

The USS Cocopa was at the next dock he came to, drydock number 2. She had apparently received the highest dose of any of the fleet, a circumstance not explained to the crew through the official channels; the usual ad hock scuttlebutt had supplied this information. O'Bannon entered the machine shop next to the drydock and again inquired about Resnik. Again no one had seen him. He strolled up to the large drydock number 4 to gaze at the carrier, USS Bairoko. Having been launched too late she had missed seeing action during World War II, but she was a seasoned veteran of several atomic bomb tests. Sixteen of her crew had received beta radiation burns from the Castle Bravo test.

The big ship was an awe-inspiring sight, O'Bannon thought...a big fish out of water and formidable as hell. She towered over the surrounding buildings. The only thing taller than her bridge was the huge crane that was visual behind her. Her flight deck was eerily empty, a flat wedge of grey steel against a blue sky void of clouds. Her naked hull glistened where water rolled down from hoses welded by radsuited men. Pelicans and gulls avoided the scene. Wouldn't O'Bannon like to ship on her instead that miserable tug he was stuck with! You couldn't pick and choose in the Navy, however. You went where you were told. And this cold war...at least it afforded opportunities to get out on the open ocean, even though your duty brought you close to eternity in the person of the hellish Mr. Atom Bomb. Oh for a normal war with a normal enemy!

Two days later O'Bannon was ordered to report to Chief Petty Officer First Class Daniel Otameyer at the Hunter's Point Naval Base Administration Building. This wasn't the manner in which new orders were issued—a tour on the Bairoko or some other decent ship was clearly not in the offing. Something else was afoot. Something ominous. He located the office on the second floor, down a drab, isolated hallway that needed cleaning. The door to room 238 had a hastily-lettered sign on yellowed paper taped to its milk glass window.

It read, "Chief Petty Officer First Class Daniel Otameyer."

Having knocked, entered, reported, been confronted by Petty Officer Otameyer, our own Petty Officer First Class Charles (Chuck) O'Bannon sat on a folding chair (metal) facing a vintage wooden desk (oak) as he was directed, and waited patiently to learn just what the something else was going to be. Otameyer had not taken the seat behind the desk but stood facing O'Bannon. Suddenly he snapped to attention and uttered, "Ten-hunt!" O'Bannon immediately stood, turned, and saluted.

"Sit," said the officer who had just entered. "I am Lieutenant Commander Nicholas Hamilton Mitchell with the Judge Advocate General's Corps, US Navy, Washington, D.C. You are Petty Officer First Class Charles O'Bannon, assigned to the USS Cocopa?"

"Aye, aye, Sir," answered O'Bannon.

"You may leave us, Petty Officer Otameyer," said Mitchell. He walked around behind the desk, extracted a handkerchief from a pocket and brushed off the wooden chair. Sat. O'Bannon had remained standing at attention.

"Please sit down, Officer O'Bannon. This will be very informal. Just a few questions." O'Bannon sat.

"Excuse me, Sir, but is this about Seaman Apprentice Resnik? I've been quite concerned…"

"You were seen leaving the base at 1800 hours on June 24 in the company of Seaman Apprentice Christian Resnik. Seaman Resnik subsequently failed to report back to the base and was assumed to be AWOL. Can you offer any explanation for his whereabouts or his behavior?"

"No, Sir. As I said, I was concerned because Seaman Resnik sort of…disappeared. We were in a bar…"

"Called the Brown Betsy. Yes, we know all this. Seaman Resnik informed us of at least that much. You were still in the bar when he left it. Resnik can't, or won't elaborate on his activities between that time and 0800 hours this morning when he stumbled through the front gate here at the shipyard. He claims to have no memory of where he was or what he may have done during the time he was AWOL."

"I went to the head. He was gone when I got back."

"There were reportedly two suspicious men in the bar who left with Resnik. Do you have any knowledge of these men?"

"No. Were they spies or something?"

"That is yet to be determined. We need your help with this matter...unless, of course, you are complicit in something un-American."

O'Bannon shook his head. "No! Where is he now? Can I see him?"

"He is in the brig. And yes, I would like you to visit him. See if you can get him to talk to you. Find out who those men were. Get him to tell you if he met anyone else, talked to anyone. This is a matter of national security...do you understand?"

"Aye, aye, Sir. I understand."

"At this point we have no reason to believe that you and Seaman Resnik conspired together for anything other than a couple rounds of beer. However..."

"Aye, aye, Sir. Anything I can do. I will certainly try."

# 5

## Majestic 12

Dr. Albert Forstinger sat at his desk in the corner room he used as an office in his vacation home on Longboat Key. He stared at the plain brown envelope before him and considered the large red letters across it which read, "Top Secret." Damn! He had just gotten away for a week of relaxation and sun—and now this! Dr. Forstinger was a member of a clandestine government group called Majestic 12 (or MJ-12 for short). He could be summoned at any time.

In 1947, when news of the crashed alien spacecraft at Roswell, New Mexico, was leaked to the press, President Harry S. Truman authorized Project Sign, later called Grudge, and then Blue Book to investigate. This group would later become known to the American public. Its main purpose would be to debunk UFO sightings and run interference with the press. Another crash of an alien spacecraft occurred on February 13, 1948, near Aztec, New Mexico. Then another in March of that same year at the White Sands Proving Grounds. It became clear that a more robust investigative entity was needed—a secret one: Majestic 12 was born.

Twelve men were chosen from the ranks of the military and

civilian elite: men like Dr. Vannevar Bush who had been head of the Office of Scientific Research and Development and had worked on the first atomic bomb; Admiral Roscoe Hillenkoetter, the first director of the CIA; Dr. Donald Menzel, an expert in cryptanalysis; General Nathan Twining, Chairman of the Joint Chiefs of Staff, Chief of Staff of the U.S. Air Force, and commander of the Air Materiel Command at Wright-Patterson Air base, where the alien bodies from the Roswell crash were taken; and others of equal renown.

By the end of 1952 there had been 16 downed alien spacecraft, 13 in the United States and 11 of those in New Mexico. 65 bodies had been recovered including one live alien who was nicknamed EBE, short for Extraterrestrial Biological Entity. He had been found wandering in the desert after the Roswell crash. The alien became ill and died on June 2, 1952. Majestic 12 was tasked in the recoveries and study of these extraterrestrial encounters and was charged to keep knowledge of the true existence of alien visitors from the public at any cost.

Dr. Forstinger had joined the MJ-12 group in 1949 after the death of one of its original members, James Forrestal. Forrestal had been Secretary of the Navy and later Secretary of Defense under Harry Truman. He was exhausted from the intense level of his work and had become severely depressed. He received psychiatric treatment and was housed on the 16th floor of the National Naval Medical Center at Bethesda, Maryland. On the morning of May 22, 1949, his body was found on the third-floor roof beneath a window across from his room. It was concluded that his death was a suicide, although various assassination theories surfaced.

The brown envelope beckoned. Forstinger reached for the letter opener his wife had given him on their fifteenth wedding anniversary: a miniature katana, a samurai sword. He drew the opener carefully from its sheath (he had once sliced off a piece from his thumb with the sharp instrument). He ran the blade across the top of the envelope and withdrew its contents. He read:

# TOP SECRET

June 28, 1954

FROM: General Hoyt Vandenburg, Director, MJ-12 Security and Intelligence

TO: Admiral Roscoe Hillenkoetter, Admiral Sidney Souers, General Robert Montegue, General Nathan Twining, Dr. Lloyd Berkener, Dr. Detlev Bronk, Dr. Vannevar Bush, Dr. Jerome Hunsaker, Gordon Gray, Dr. Donald Menzel, Dr. Albert Forstinger

SUBJECT: Transcript of the interrogation of Navy Personnel allegedly having had contact with the extraterrestrials.

PURPOSE: To determine 1) the veracity of the reported incident, 2) the likelihood of an information leak, and 3) a course of action to contain potential leak.

PROVENANCE: The attached transcript came to MJ-12 in the following manner. Seaman Apprentice Christian Resnik was aboard the USS Cocopa at the Bikini Atoll nuclear tests called Operation Castle earlier this year. On June 24, while on shore leave, Seaman Resnik went missing for 24 hours. He was arrested for being AWOL. Lieutenant Commander Nicholas Hamilton Mitchell with the Judge Advocate General's Corps intervened in the case when it was learned Resnik had had contact with unknown persons of a suspicious nature. Resnik pleaded amnesia. Mitchell allowed a shipmate of Resnik's, Petty Officer First Class Charles O'Bannon, to interview Resnik; O'Bannon had no intelligence training, nor did he or the subject know they were being taped. After listening to the extraordinary narrative documented below, Mitchell forwarded the tape to Captain Charles Hardin of Project Blue Book. Pursuant to the directive forbidding government personnel to divulge information relating to alien interactions with humans, Captain Hardin forwarded the tape to me. This is the only transcribed version of the tape. As always, it is for YOUR EYES ONLY.

Tape recorded on June 26, 1954. Participants are Petty Officer First Class Charles O'Bannon and Seaman Apprentice Christian Resnik. Location, brig, Naval Base at Hunter's Point, San Francisco, California.

O'BANNON: Hey, kiddo, how they hangin'?

RESNIK: Hi, Cap'n. Can't complain. Food's decent.

O'BANNON: So, they tell me you got amnesia. Why'd you go off like that? Find some chippies? Somebody you don't want to tell about, like the Admiral's daughter, or something?

RESNIK: I'm beginning to remember some things. But…I can't tell them about it. I just can't. They'll put me in the loony bin.

O'BANNON: Well, you can tell me, old buddy. I won't tell anyone.

RESNIK: I remember we were at that bar. Drinking with that ground-pounder. You went to the head. The jarhead left. The next thing I remember, those two guys, the real tall ones with the pale faces, came up to the table. I remember looking into their eyes. That's all I remember about that part.

    I must have blacked out or something because I woke up in an alley behind the bar. I was lying up against the wall of some building and this feral cat was licking my face. I figured they had rolled me, but I still had my money and my ID in my pocket. It didn't make any sense. Then the MPs found me. They told me I'd been missing for 24 hours! How could I have slept for 24 hours? They locked me up and questioned me. I told them about the two weirdoes and about passing out. I couldn't remember anything else. They didn't believe me.

O'BANNON: I know. They asked me to talk to you. See if you could remember what happened. They think those two guys were spies. They think they may have pumped you for information about the nuclear tests.

RESNIK: What the hell would I know about it? I was just an enlisted punk that had to press the "I believe button" to get through the day. You know what they say about those three balls—put a sailor in a room with three balls, come back an hour later and one will be missing, one will be broken, and one will be pregnant. Anyway, those guys weren't spies…at least not the Russian kind.

O'BANNON: How do you know that?

[Here there is a pause of about 30 seconds]

RESNIK: You're going think I'm crazy. Well, here goes. This is what I remember…little pieces of it come back to me. I did wake up before the alley. I was in a room that was kind of like a hospital room, with all kinds of equipment…stuff I'd never seen before. I figured maybe I was in the emergency room. I was lying on a table, a cold table made out of some stone or metal or plastic or something. I was naked. There were these…people, if you can call them that. Standing around me. People just like those two in the bar only even taller. Those eyes!

O'BANNON: Take it easy. You're safe now. Just concentrate. What else do you remember?

RESNIK: The eyes…there was this fellow bending over me, compelling me somehow to look into his eyes. You know, they were like slits, but then they opened wide…so wide!

[There is another pause of a few seconds]

RESNIK: They didn't…they didn't actually talk. I just sort of knew what they wanted. I couldn't avoid it. He never blinked. I felt…it was like he was scanning my mind through my eyes. There was a tingling sensation. In my head. I blacked out again.
    Later when I awoke there were several of the creatures surrounding me. One ran his fingers all over my naked body. Another had these needles with long wires coming from them. He would stick them into me in places…well, you know…like my balls. It was funny, though, it didn't hurt at all. Then they all left the room and it seemed to fill up with a fog.

Some kind of gas, I think. I blacked out again.

When I woke up they had turned me over on my stomach. I could feel that they were sticking something up my ass. A probe of some kind. This time it did hurt. I tried to call out but I couldn't make a noise or move. I think the gas must have worn off too soon. I knew by then that these weren't human people. I think they were from outer space. That's crazy, isn't it? But that's the only explanation I could come up with. I was scared shitless.

When they were done they turned me over on my back again and gave me something to drink through a straw. It was like nothing I've ever tasted. Sweet, refreshing, like the clearest, coolest spring water you could imagine. It made me feel...I had this, what do you call it? Euphoria. I felt important, chosen. And kind of horny.

They left me alone for a while. Slowly my paralysis eased and I could move my arms and legs. I sat up. As I did that, two of the creatures entered the room. They helped me down off the table and steadied me as they walked me around. I got a better look at the place. The walls weren't flat, they were curved. The floor was curved too. My sense of up and down was disjointed, like I could have walked on the walls if I had wanted to. Then they took me on a kind of tour.

In another room there were a bunch of big glass jars filled with some yellow liquid and...and...it looked like fetuses. I thought they were human, but they had those eyes with the dark round pupils just like the creatures...spacemen...whatever they were. I got the idea...and this is really crazy...that they were *growing* them like vegetables and that they were hybrids...hybrids of humans and aliens! Yeah, I was scared.

It was a ship. It must have been. At one side there were a series of small portholes with very thick glass. I looked out and saw...no, you're going to think me totally wacko...I saw what looked like the earth below us! And stars. And then I think I fainted again.

When I woke up the next time I was in the alley. I couldn't remember anything that had happened. Not until later. When it came back to me I realized I couldn't tell anyone in authority about it. No one would believe me. You don't believe me, do you?

O'BANNON: Well, sure I do, buddy. Sure I do. And you're right. I don't think you should tell anybody about this. I'll tell them I talked to you and I really believe you can't remember anything. You have amnesia…right?

RESNIK: Yeah. Amnesia.

End of transcript.

---

Subject Resnik remains in custody. Subject O'Bannon has returned to active duty and is under surveillance. He has apparently not repeated this conversation to anyone. Recommendation needed as to containment of incident. A formal meeting of MJ-12 is not at this time warranted. Please advise using the usual secure channels.

Dr. Albert Forstinger was troubled. This description of what was clearly an alien abduction of the sailor was too similar to others he had had to review over the last four years. It was probably real. None of the other abductions had been leaked to the press or the public— not yet. That wasn't going to happen on his watch! The leak at Roswell had been a blunder that had precipitated scores of UFO sightings. Some of them real, most of them just mass hallucinations. Either way was bad. It was an untenable situation.

It seemed to him that at this juncture the sailor was unlikely to repeat his story. The problem was that Resnik didn't have a cover story for the missing 24 hours. The authorities could wear him down to the point where he would blab. Forstinger would suggest to the group that Resnik be given some kind of story to tell. He would be admonished never to reveal the truth…or what he thought was the truth. It would be a shame to have to terminate the boy, or lock him up indefinitely. He would also recommend that the Greys be advised that their memory loss techniques weren't being successful.

Then there was O'Bannon. Could he be trusted not to talk? There would be no incentive for him to remain quiet if he was at sea and the crew started to spin tall tales for their amusement. Forstinger sighed. It seemed likely he would be boarding a plane for California soon. He would need to interview both men to determine a course of action. He swiveled his chair around to the credenza behind him upon which sat a vintage Underwood typewriter. He slipped a sheet of paper through the roller. No carbons for this communiqué. Top secret stuff had to be carefully handled.

# 6

Bellingham, June 22, 1954

They hadn't laughed together before, not like this—almost uncontrollably with tears in their eyes—and with a huge hug like two old friends or lovers separated and now reunited. They remained in the embrace longer than two people who were not old friends or lovers should, perhaps unsure of what had just happened, unsure whether to be embarrassed, surprised, or elated. They pulled apart and stood uncomfortably, each watching the other for some clue, some response. Then they laughed again.

The occasion of the laugh was the result of Nate having brought home something for dinner that he had spotted at the A & P in the frozen foods aisle. Something new. He had three boxes in the paper sack which he proudly drew out and displayed for Noreen's approval. The colorful packages were labeled, "TV Brand Frozen Dinner" by Swanson and Company. Each box contained an aluminum tray covered with foil and divided into compartments in which were a thick slice of turkey, mashed sweet potatoes, early June peas, and cornbread dressing. Pop it into the oven at 425 degrees for 25 minutes said the directions.

Just why these items produced such a bout of hilarity was not clear. It must have been because the release of tension from the past several days was an absolutely necessity and inevitable. Nate's mother was considerably worse and it looked as if she might need to be hospitalized. This abrupt change meant that Noreen's presence in the Mirko household was no longer needed. Not only did this mean a new job search for Noreen, it presented Nate with the prospect of living in an empty house; a house devoid of the stability of matriarchal authority (albeit a matriarch with Alzheimer's); a house devoid of the charm of a young woman whose presence had become important in so many ways.

Noreen had baked an apple pie. She knew everything there was to know about apples and her baking skills were more than adequate. So there they were, eating TV dinners and home-made apple pie. Nate had to chuckle.

"So what? You think my pie is funny?" Noreen said.

"I think your pie is delicious. I think the combination of synthetic food and real food is funny. This TV dinner stuff is awful!"

"It will probably be a big hit with consumers. Quick, easy, cheap and futuristic."

"Someday mankind will go into space and eat TV dinners."

"Speaking of space…" Noreen had eventually told Nate about seeing something in the sky and being visited by a government agent. Nate had dismissed the entire episode as a lark, although the fact that an agent had questioned Noreen bothered him.

"Did they ever come back? The FBI man, I mean."

"He wasn't FBI. Some other handful of capital letters. They investigate flying objects that they don't believe in."

"Not to change the subject, but you know, Noreen, that you are welcome to stay here as long as you need to. Until you find a position. Even…" He was going to say "after," and he might have been thinking "indefinitely," but he caught himself and continued: "…though my mother will be in the hospital."

"Not to change the subject back, but I wanted you to know…I saw it again. The flying saucer or whatever it is. You had to work late last Monday, you remember? I went for a walk in the early evening hours. As I sat in the park, looking up toward the mountains, I saw that strange shape again. It zigged and zagged like some sort of insect…a firefly maybe. No airplane flies like that, Nate. It must have been something otherworldly."

"It must have been a mirage. You know, atmospheric conditions can magnify things on the ground and make them seem like they are in the sky. I'll bet there is even a name for it.[2] Like when people see castles in the sky."

"Castles in the sky! You see, Nate, you *are* a romantic."

"Just a cockeyed optimist, Noreen. One that believes that the world is a good place. And in the logic that says creatures from outer space just don't exist." Nate began to hum the song from the musical, *South Pacific*, "They Called Me a Cockeyed Optimist."

"Do you have to work tomorrow?"

"It's Saturday. That's our big day, especially since we're not allowed to be open on Sundays. Blue laws! How is a person supposed to make a living when they won't let you be open?"

"Well, maybe on Sunday then. Will you take me for a drive in the mountains? Perhaps it will cure me of my delusions."

Nate Mirko now worked at Honest Harry's First-rate Used Cars and had become its star salesman. The job wasn't going to make him rich, but it put food on the table, paid Noreen's salary, and allowed Nate to make payments on the automobile he was buying (at cost, or so Harry had said).

Harry Bertram was honest as the day is long, or so Harry said. He would never turn back the odometer to make it look like a vehicle had traveled fewer miles than it had. He would never give a high-ball offer over the phone on a trade-in then retract that offer maintaining the car had numerous defects. He would never sell a stolen car or a salvaged car with a washed title. He would never, ever, pressure a customer. No, Harry Bertram was honest, even on short days.

This Saturday wasn't going to be a short day. There was a young couple looking at a 1952 Chevrolet Deluxe (a coupe with a two-tone paint job and only few dents) at one end of the lot, and a middle-aged man wearing a tweed jacket examining a 1952 Hudson Hornet (whose rough-running engine had been quieted by Harry's application of some oatmeal) at the other. Harry Bertram was stuck in the middle of the lot trying to close the deal on a Studebaker Commander Starliner Hardtop (which had arrived one evening under questionable circumstances). Thus Nate had to shuffle back and forth between the Chevy couple and the Hornet man.

Later, the two salesmen retired to the prefab building that served as an office, tired but happy, as each had made a sale. They reheated the morning's left-over coffee on a hot plate and sat down for the first time all day. Nate thumbed through the various pieces of reading matter they kept on hand for customers and settled on a recent, much dog-eared Pogo book. The adventures of the irreverent possum had always amused him. This one featured Walt Kelly's illustrated swamp version of the trial from Lewis Carroll's *Alice in Wonderland* with Pogo as Alice and the wildcat character, Simple J. Malarkey, as the King and judge. Simple J. Malarkey bore a striking resemblance to Wisconsin Senator Joseph McCarthy.

The satire on McCarthy prompted Nate to say (which turned out to be an unfortunate issue to raise with his boss), "Look's like Joe McCarthy has taken on a formidable opponent in the form of the US Army. The old blowhard is going to finally get his comeuppance."

"Son," said Harry Bertram, "there's commie pinkos in the army just like in the government. Somebody has to ferret them out. Them Rosenbergs was tried and found guilty and hung until dead. What more proof do you want?"

"They never proved that Ethel Rosenberg was a spy. We hadn't hung spies since the Civil War...and never any women. And they weren't hung...they were electrocuted. Did you know that she wasn't killed by the first electric shock? Or the second? Or the third? They gave her five in all and it is said that her head caught on fire. Is that justice?"

"They were enemies of the US Government. Got what they deserved."

"Loyalty oaths, black lists, suspicion and hatred everywhere now. It's unhealthy. We're better than that."

"And that Supreme Court. Saying the states can't have segregation if they see fit. Next they'll want us to intermarry."

"Say, what are you going to do if that man that bought the Hudson brings it back when he finds out the motor is trashed?"

"Oh, I'll give him a good price for it. Not what he paid for it, obviously."

"You're a real piece of work, Harry. No one will ever accuse you of being a communist."

"Yer darn tootin' they won't! And hey...you're lucky I knew your old man. I wouldn't tolerate back talk like that otherwise. Gave his son a job, didn't I?"

"Just some affectionate ribbing Harry. I got that from my old man. He was a piece of work too!"

On Sunday they parked at Picture Lake, high up the slopes of Mount Baker, nearly to the ski area. It had been a pleasant drive up Primary State Highway 1, along the flood plain of the North Fork of the Nooksack River, past small communities like Welcome, Maple Falls and Glacier. Through the rugged Mount Baker-Snoqualmie National Forest with its stands of silver fir and western hemlock. They were at the edge of the tree line now.

Nate's new (used) car was a dark maroon 1951 Nash Rambler 3-door station wagon. He had selected this particular vehicle from the cars on Harry's lot after studying the acquisition book. The Nash was one of the few entries that listed its previous owner—not a little old lady from Pasadena who only drove it to church, but a man whose name he recognized: Warren Furston, Bellingham's high school mathematics teacher and football coach. Nate had been in Furston's algebra 1 class. He figured the man had taken good care of his automobile. And as far as he could tell, Harry hadn't messed with it.

They walked along the hiking path that skirted the lake. The air was crisp and clear. A Steller's jay scolded them from a nearby pine. The lake had a dark sheen to it like brushed metal; it reflected the mountains like a mirror. There were still patches of snow on the heights above them. Nate took Noreen's hand as they walked.

"Tomorrow," Nate said, "I'm checking her into hospice care. She's had too many episodes that scare me."

"Me too. I think you're right in doing that. I can take care of her most of the time, but she won't eat. I hate to say this, but I think she's slipping away. It's something you need to face, Nate. It's sad, but it's getting near that time."

They walked silently around the lake. Near the end of the trail they encountered a clear area where the sparse vegetation was blackened, as if there had been a recent fire. Even the dirt and the few stones scattered around seemed charred and pulverized. The area was a perfect circle, and slightly indented as if something large and round had depressed the earth and scorched it.

"Nate! Something landed here," Noreen said, squeezing Nate's hand more tightly.

"Look," said Nate, "it's not what you think. Probably somebody's campfire got out of control. Or there was a lightning strike."

"If you say so. Can we go back to the car? I don't like this place."

They continued driving on the Mount Baker Road to Artist Point on the Kulshan Ridge. The road curved, hugging the contours of the mountain, often with dangerous drop-offs on one side and shear rock walls on the other. The road ended at Artist Point. They parked and got out to look at the view. Snow sat on the low areas, rock-strewn crags poked up toward an azure sky. The few trees that stood like sentinels around the parking lot rustled in the chill wind. Nate pointed out a large bird that soared above them: a bald eagle on the hunt.

They could see the snow-covered peak of Mount Baker to the southwest and Mount Shuksan to the southeast. There was a trail. Neither of them had worn proper clothing or hiking boots. Yet this gravel trail was easy. Glacial tarns and ancient gnarled trees lined the landscape. As they hiked they saw wild flowers budding out among the stumps of the old growth forest; new and ancient life in its never-ending cycle. In just under a mile they reached the switchbacks for the trail up Table Mountain.

"Are we going to climb that? It looks impossible," said Noreen.

"It's not far to the summit. I've been here when there was a lot more snow and I'll admit it is difficult...but the view! You'll love it!"

"Oh no, Nate. I can't do it. My shoes..."

"Just watch your step on the loose gravel. You'll be fine."

And up they went. The mountain, a truncated peak with a more or less flat top like a mesa, afforded a steep ascent up lava cliffs along narrow switchbacks. Hundreds of feet below lay Iceberg Lake. In the distance were spectacular views of the Cascades Range, its many mountains, lakes, and glaciers. The trail was only a few feet in width at many points. Nate's leather-soled shoes slipped on the loose gravel. Noreen fared no better and considered taking off her penny loafers. Nate grabbed her arm and pulled her along past rocky outcroppings where tenacious vegetation hung like angry spiders on the smooth basalt. After an ascent of 400 feet they reached the plateau.

They found a flat ledge of smooth granite and sat, exhausted from the climb. From their vantage point they could look out toward

Mount Baker and the Ptarmigan Ridge. Below lay the lakes and the forests and the winding highway they had driven up. The entire scale of things had changed; the world stretched forever before them— they felt like gods. Nate took an orange from his pocket and began to peel it. "Nothing tastes better than an orange at high altitude," he said.

"Oh, Nate, we can't stay long. Your mother…"

"Mrs. McCredie is with her. She'll be all right. Look out there. It's like the whole of the human race has vanished and we're the only people left on earth. Isn't it magnificent?"

The orange consumed, they lay back, watched clouds billowing, found faces and animals in the puffs and wisps, told each other stories of childhood, hinted at future dreams. Noreen told of one day when a neighbor's horse had breached the fence and wandered into the orchard. She knew that she should chase the animal away from the lower trees where it pulled half ripe apples from the branches and gorged itself on the sweet fruit. But the animal was so magnificent in stature! Its strong thighs rippled with muscle, its haunches shook with excitement for the feast. Its smooth brown skin shown in the sunlight. Its long main unfurled as it tossed its head.

Nate told of his disappointment in not making the high school football team. Nor was he suitable for playing basketball or any of the other team sports. He was always the last to be picked in gym class. But then Mr. Furston, the football coach, had created a new sport for after school activities: cross country running. Running? That was for the scrawny kids—but he tried it. And it changed his teenage life in a way that nothing else could have. He had finally achieved something in athletics. He had gained a self-esteem that would see him through life.

When the talk shifted from the past to the future, an inevitable uneasiness surfaced. Nate sensed the importance of the moment: it was now or never. They were lying close together on the rocky ledge. Now he rolled over, lightly pressing down on her, and kissed her lips. Noreen tensed at first, then she relaxed, as if she had melted into the granite, welcoming the weight of Nate's body against her own. For a long while they remained entwined, short pecking kisses alternating with the passionate merging of lips and tongues. Hands explored, buttons popped from button holes. Clothing awkwardly removed was scattered on the mesa. A red-tailed hawk circling above them was the only witness to their love making.

The sun disappeared behind a cloud bank, casting a shadow over the lovers. A chilling wind whipped up from the abyss below. Now cold, they dressed hurriedly. Noreen looked up at the dark cloud. "It isn't going to rain or to snow, is it?" She asked.

"Of course not," said Nate, ever the optimist. "You'll have to excuse me for a minute. I need to relieve myself. I'll be right back."

"Nate! Are there any snakes up here?"

"On the mountain? No snakes allowed."

Nate moved down the trail that circled the mesa top. He came to a thicket of Manzanita bush: scrubby, but it would have to do. As he went about his business he wondered about the future. Was he ready to commit to a life with this woman? It needed more time, surely, to develop. Perhaps they had been carried away by the moment, the setting, the intoxication of nature. Certainly they both were lonely, in need of companionship. Obviously they were attracted to each other. Marriages had been based on much less. Marriage? Now he was getting ahead of himself.

When he returned to their rock shelf the cloud was blocking the sun so thoroughly that a circle of night seemed centered on their special place. Not a good omen, thought Nate. Noreen was standing, waiting for him. He stopped and just looked at her for a short time, savoring the moment. She smiled back at him. They were about ten yards apart. He began to move toward her again.

Suddenly, a beam of light broke through the cloud. Nate looked up, expecting to see the sun in all its glory. The light was too bright, the surrounding cloud too blackened by contrast: it hurt his eyes. He looked back at Noreen to see that a pillar of that light was falling directly onto her, as if the heavens had opened up to become a glorious spotlight, she a human performer on the earthly stage, and he an audience of one, enthralled by the drama. But this fanciful sensation was shattered by an unearthly sound: a high-pitched whistling coupled with a roar like a deluge of water rushing over a falls or the suction of a jet aircraft. Aircraft? Again he looked upward.

The dark cloud now had parted. Above him was a huge disk-shaped object, hovering and emitting the sound and the beam. Flecks of silver and gold swirled within the pillar of light. Where it touched the ground the dust stirred, formed into small dust devils, spun off in all directions. Noreen still stood in the midst of the light. Now it became a vortex; she seemed to merge with it. Slowly she rose, up, up toward the shining circular thing above her. Nate ran toward her, but she had risen too high for him to reach.

"No, you bastards," Nate yelled. "No! Take me too!"

She disappeared into the ship, the beam of light ceased, the cloud again blocked Nate's view. Nate fell to the ground, unconscious. When he awoke it was late afternoon. The sun would soon dip behind the distant mountains. The sky was again clear of clouds…and spaceships. Nate's memory was hazy. What on earth was he doing up on top of a mountain? Darkness would fall quickly up here and descending would become treacherous. He hurried down the path, slipping on the loose gravel. He reached Artist Point and his car. Funny, he didn't remember having driven up here. He thought he was supposed to take Noreen out today. For a drive. In the mountains.

"Oh my God!" said Nate as he began to remember.

---

[2]Fata Morgana: a mirage usually consisting of multiple images, typically of cliffs and buildings that are distorted and magnified to resemble elaborate castles. This atmospheric phenomenon, which can display objects located below the astronomical horizon as magnified and hovering in the sky, is thought to be the explanation for many UFO sightings.

# 7

## Mare Island Naval Hospital, July 8, 1954

25 miles northeast of San Francisco in Vallejo, California, was the Mare Island Naval Shipyard. Dating back over 100 years, it was the oldest US Naval base on the Pacific Ocean. The first hospital on the island, opened in 1864, was a converted granary with 30 beds. Its replacement, a massive, three-story structure designed by architect John McAthur, was damaged by an earthquake in 1898. The current main hospital building was completed in 1901 and built to withstand even the most severe earthquakes. More buildings were added over the years and now, in 1954, there was a wing for "special cases" such as patients suffering from psychological trauma.

Dr. Albert Forstinger flipped through the chart which he had retrieved from the end of Seaman Christian Resnik's hospital bed. After a few requisite "hmms" and the arching of eyebrows, he turned to the day nurse and told her to leave while he examined the man. "I won't need you, nurse. This is going to be a psychological exam," he said. Now, except for the patient (who was sleeping) and the good doctor, the only person present was Ensign Rodney Matthews. Forstinger gave Matthews a stern look.

"What is your security level, Ensign?" he asked.

"Security level, Sir? We don't have levels. I am trained in security procedures. My duty is to provide security for Seaman Resnik while he is hospitalized…Sir. Is there a problem?"

"No, I guess not. What do you know about Seaman Resnik?"

"I know he is here for observation. He is suffering from stress related to…well, they didn't tell me. Combat, I assume. And he is suspected of having been contacted by enemy agents. Sir."

"Well, I have previously interviewed Seaman Resnik, and I can tell you, without a doubt, that he is not a security risk. He never met with any agents."

"Sir. How do you know that, Sir?"

"He is delusional and suffering from what we term post traumatic stress syndrome stemming from an experience which will at this juncture remain classified."

"Sir. Roger that, Sir."

"He is subject to hallucinations and may at times become violent."

"I haven't observed anything like that. He seems pretty normal to me. A bit dopey. Sir."

"He has been under sedation since he's been here. But I need to examine him once he comes out from under the drugs. I need to do that alone, Ensign Matthews."

"Well, I don't know, Sir. You being a civilian doctor and all. I'm supposed to…"

"Would you do me a favor? Could you go down to the nurse's station and ask them to bring us some bed restraints? Just in case."

"Bed restraints? You really think…"

"Who is the doctor here, Ensign? Do I need to call your superior officer?"

"No, Sir. I mean, aye aye, Sir. Right away."

Matthews left the room—against his better judgment, but after all, who *was* the doctor? Once Forstinger was sure the ensign was out of sight down the hallway, he opened his briefcase. He took a syringe he had previously prepared from the case, pulled off the plastic cap protecting the needle, and approached Resnik. "This may sting a little," he told the sleeping sailor.

## San Diego Naval Base, July 12, 1954

Petty Officer First Class Charles O'Bannon opened the communiqué that had been delivered to him during mail call. It was from the base commander and it read: "Your request to visit Seaman Apprentice Resnik at Mare Island during your leave has been denied. No further information is available at this time."

"Well, I'll be damned!" muttered O'Bannon. "Fuck the Navy!"

O'Bannon had been transferred shore-side just as the Cocopa was about to set sail again from the Treasure Island drydocks. He hadn't understood that twist of affairs either—why take him away from his ship? Now he was due for a another leave of absence, with full pay, and he had been counting the days while serving as adjunct clerking staff at the San Diego Naval Base—a desk job! What were they thinking? Then there had been those interviews. First, that Judge Advocate General's Corps fellow with all his questions about Russian spies. Then that civilian doctor. Why was he being examined by a *civilian* doctor? He had no after effects from radiation, he was certain of that. He'd seen a few swabbies with minor burns and such, but he had been tested and given a clean bill of health.

The doctor had asked him more questions about Resnik than he had about his own health. He'd gone over the story again and again. He always left out the part about Resnik's alien visitation, however. He didn't want to get the boy in trouble. He had described the two strangers at the bar. Described them as accurately as he could without making it seem like *they* were from outer space. Now he was beginning to think that maybe they were.

Couldn't visit Resnik! Well the only thing left now was to sign out and hit the bars. This O'Bannon did with due haste. In the Gas Lamp District he found a suitable watering hole: the Tivoli Bar. He sat alone at a table near the back. A couple of shot-and-a-beers and he was feeling better about everything. Still, there was a something that didn't add up that still bothered him. Maybe…

Then, one of those things that only happen in the movies occurred. The smart-ass jarhead they'd met that time in the Frisco bar happened into the very place where O'Bannon was drowning his…not sorrows…his anxieties. First Sergeant Andrew H. Millender wandered into the Tivoli and sat at the bar. O'Bannon strained to see if, indeed, that hulk of a man on the stool was Millender. Finally deciding that the probabilities were in favor of a fortuitous reunion, O'Bannon abandoned his table and approached the Marine. He tapped him on the shoulder and began to say, "Well, if it isn't…"

"Don't say it. Uncle Sam's etcetera and so forth. If it isn't the old sea salt. What's the haps?"

"I'm marooned on this damn dry land. Going crazy."

"Great little bar though, isn't it? Oldest one in Dago. Did you know that Wyatt Earp once drank here? There was a brothel upstairs…no, don't look. It's gone now."

O'Bannon grabbed a handful of peanuts from a bowl on the bar and said, "Come over to my table. I've got lots to tell you."

He hadn't blabbed the story to anyone, as Forstinger had worried he would. But it was bursting inside of him and he had to get it out. He outlined Resnik's bizarre tale in as much detail as he could remember and told of his interviews. Lastly, he complained, "First they boot me off my ship, and then they won't let me see my buddy."

"That's just not right. What are you going to do?"

"I'm going to go to Mare Island anyway. See if they can stop me!"

"Do you want some company?"


# Holloman Air Force Base
## Near Alamagordo, New Mexico, July 12, 1954

Dr. Albert Forstinger is standing on the tarmac a few yards west of the main hanger. He is one of an entourage of less than two dozen non-essential people who have been allowed on the base today. With him are the other members of MJ-12, four CIA operatives, two FBI agents and an assortment of military personnel of high rank and security clearance. Behind them, next to the hanger, is an US Army M-59 armored personnel carrier, an Air Force M43 Ambulance and a jeep carrying four nervous looking men with machine guns.

They are watching as a silver Lockheed C-121 Super Constellation, called Collumbine III, taxis across the runway and, instead of turning toward the hanger, continues out across the expanse of the desert airfield to stop nearly a mile and half away. The airplane, designated as VC-121E, will become known as Air Force One in the coming years. It is carrying President Dwight David Eisenhower and his staff. It is sitting silently, very far away from the view of the control tower and airbase personnel who go about their jobs and ask no questions. Holloman has been the scene of mysterious events before—lights in the sky, unexplainable radar sightings, test flights of strange-looking aircraft. No one on the base is particularly interested in the landing of the president's plane. No one, except the group on the tarmac.

The base radar is ordered to be shut down. An unusual circumstance. Some of the tarmac group raise binoculars to their eyes. So far, no one has emerged from Columbine III. A spotter on an access road calls in a sighting of two circular objects approaching the airfield. They are above Road 12, then Road 7, then they can be seen from the control tower as they hover above the runway. An air traffic controller in the tower jots down some notes stating that the objects, which are clearly not airplanes—having no wings or tails, are between twenty and thirty feet in diameter and saucer-shaped. His notes will later be confiscated and destroyed.

The two craft hover above Columbine III, staying around 300 feet above the surface of the runway. After several minutes, one of the craft lands. A door opens and a ramp extends down to the ground. A man exits Columbine III and walks toward the spacecraft. From his vantage point on the tarmac, Forstinger can not make out whether or not it is the president. He looks at Admiral Hillenkoetter for conformation. Hillenkotter nods. Yes, it is Ike.

Forstinger doesn't like the number of people witnessing this saucer landing. He knows they will be told that Ike is merely inspecting an experimental aircraft flown over from area 51 in Nevada. But someone is bound to leak this one to the press. More work for Forstinger.

This isn't the first meeting Eisenhower has had with the aliens. Earlier this year in February, the president was vacationing in Palm Springs when the aliens requested a meeting with "the head of a powerful government." He was taken to Muroc Field in secret but his absence was noticed by the press—it was rumored that the president had had a heart attack and possibly was dead. Working the cover-up on that one had been a nightmare for Forstinger and the MJ-12. They had come up with a story that Ike had broken a tooth eating fried chicken and been taken to a local dentist for emergency treatment. They had even supplied a dentist who would claim he had treated Eisenhower. It was not their best work, but it had been rushed.

The results of that first meeting had been inconclusive. Some in MJ-12 felt that the aliens had demanded too much in exchange for their non-interference in the affairs of mankind. We were to dismantle and destroy our nuclear weapons. Eisenhower could not agree to that. The aliens had also refused to share their advanced technology stating that we hadn't evolved enough spiritually. They would leave us alone while we thought this over, they said, if we would allow them to "sample" and study our population. They would not reveal themselves to the rest of the world and admonished us to keep their existence a secret. They began abducting humans and animals.

Eisenhower has been inside the alien ship for nearly 45 minutes. The entourage is getting nervous. Forstinger turns to Admiral Hillenkoetter with a worried look. What if?

"If anything should happen to Eisenhower..." he says.

"We'll have that dick-head Nixon for president," finishes Hillenkoetter. "Saints preserve us if that ever happens!"

Eisenhower exits the alien ship, walking slowly, deliberately displaying pomp and a very presidential swagger. The ramp retracts into the ship and the door closes. Once the president has climbed aboard Columbine III there is a stirring of dust around the saucer. It rises swiftly. It and its companion ship dart away and the skies are now empty. Forstinger and the others wait to be summoned by the president. Has there been an agreement, he wonders? Or a surrender?

## Golden Years Home for the Elderly
## Outskirts of Bellingham, July 12, 1954

Nate watched out the window as a fat squirrel hung like a circus acrobat beneath a bird feeder. Several birds, jays and sparrows, flew at the usurper, squawking loudly and beating their wings in a futile effort to dislodge him. Nate sat on the freshly made bed; his mother sat in an overstuffed armchair, wrapped in a colorful crocheted throw. It was, Nate observed, the only source of color in the drab room, save, of course, the flowers he had brought. Flowers that would be spirited away by the nurses once he had left. He already had complained that his mother's wedding ring was missing. "We take the jewelry and keep it safe," he was told, "so there isn't the temptation for sticky fingers. Of course, all our staff are very honest." Of course they are, thought Nate.

Beverly Mirko's evaluation by the nursing staff at the home had determined that she was not ready for hospice care. "She'll outlive us all," had been the comment. All she needed was constant care and pampering and a little physical therapy. It didn't cost all that much, they said. She'll be happier here where she can interact with people of her own age, they said. Nate was skeptical, but willing to give it a try. He had other things on his mind right now.

Like a missing girl friend. He had come home that day, still in a daze, unsure of what exactly he had seen…or thought he had seen. The farther he got away from it the more preposterous it was. He half expected to see her in the kitchen when he walked through the door. Mrs. McCredie had greeted him. Where was Noreen, she wanted to know? Where indeed.

The following morning Nate went to the police station to file a missing person's report. He was told they would wait 24 to 48 hours before investigating. Missing persons usually show up within that time, they explained. Nate was furious. He couldn't tell the police about the…what was it? A flying saucer? However, he could tell that agent who had come out to talk to Noreen that time. What was his name? He had no idea. The agency? A handful of capital letters which he also couldn't remember.

Once back home he had entered Noreen's room. He found her purse sitting on her dresser and opened it. There, stuck into a tear in the lining was a business card. It read:

Second Lieutenant Leon Blackman
4602 Air Intelligence Service Squadron
McChord Field, Tacoma, Washington

There was no phone number. He called information and got the number for the AISS at McCord Field. He dialed. The base operator answered and he asked for Lieutenant Blackman. Was he certain he had the right branch of the AISS? There was no Lieutenant Blackman listed on the roster. Could he speak to someone who took reports of unidentified flying objects? Could he wait a moment? Then followed a series of clicks and buzzes and more clicks. Finally the telephone started to ring somewhere at the other end of the line.

"Hello?"

"Who am I speaking to?"

"My name is Nathaniel Mirko. I need to report a kidnapping...by flying saucer."

The man at the other end of the phone line did not break into peals of laughter. On the contrary. He took Nate's information and told him that an agent would be out to talk to him as soon as one was available. He seemed a bit distant, perhaps bored by the routine of taking down crackpot reports. But once Nate mentioned the name, Noreen Ashley, his interest piqued. He asked for more details and had Nate repeat his story several times. There were more clicks on the line while Nate talked: he had the feeling he was being taped. He didn't care. Just so somebody took this thing seriously.

So far, no agent had called. This weighed heavily on his mind as he watched the birds and the squirrel outside his mother's window. Suddenly there was a rush of wings and the birds flew off; the squirrel retreated into the adjacent bushes. The sun must have gone behind a cloud for the scene outside fell into shadow. It was about then that his mother started talking in a loud, clear voice, unlike the trembling warble more characteristic of her old age and condition.

"Yes...yes I will," she said. She apparently thought she was talking to someone in the room—someone who was not Nate. Then:

"Yes. I do want to. Yes, Noreen, I will. It's so good to see you, Noreen. How have you been?"

She would pause between statements or questions as if she were listening to answers from Noreen. Nate was beside himself. He was used to her delusions and her talking to imaginary people...but this! It struck a nerve that she thought she was talking to Noreen. Well, it wasn't her fault. She didn't realize Noreen was missing. Maybe it was just a wishful delusion. Nate wished he could share it.

Something hit the window from the outside. A bird? A large bird had flown against the glass and broken the window! There were jagged splinters of glass all over the floor. Nate jumped to his feet.

"Stay in your chair, mother. There is broken glass on the floor. I'm going to get someone to clean this up. Just don't move!" he said.

He expected to find the battered body of a bird among the shards of glass, but there was nothing. He ran down the hallway to get some help. When he returned bringing a maintenance man with a broom, his mother wasn't in her chair. The window stood wide open. Illogically, perhaps, he went to the window and looked out, afraid he might see her sprawled on the ground below. There was nothing to see. He and a nurse spent the better part of two hours searching the home and its grounds. She was just plain gone.

There was something else. There had been a faint odor in the room when he had returned. Not the mingling of urine and stale body odor that usually permeated the place. A different sort of smell, like burnt vanilla. He had smelled that before. And now he remembered where and when he had smelled it. It was the smell given off by the disk-shaped craft that had taken Noreen!

Byron Grush

# 8

## July 14, 1954, Hotel Colorado
## Glenwood Springs, Colorado

"It's a damn hotel!" said O'Bannon.

"Well, you knew it might have closed down as a hospital. Most of those Navy convalescent hospitals became obsolete a few years after the war was over," commented Millender.

They were standing on the steps of an elegant brick edifice which had been built, as a hotel, to replicate the Villa de Medici in Rome with its pale-colored brick and twin towers. There was a plaque explaining the history of the place. It had been built in 1891 and had been designed by the famous architect, Edward Lippincott Tilton, a fact that failed to impress either the marine or the sailor. It had been a favorite of at least two presidents, several movie stars and many of the rich and elite of the early twentieth century. It had been here in 1905 that Teddy Roosevelt had been presented with a stuffed bear by the hotel's maids, a classic toy that from that time on would be known as a "teddy bear."

O'Bannon read on. "Ah, here it is," he said. "In 1942, the Hotel Colorado was leased to the United States Navy for use as a hospital.

It was called the US Naval Convalescent Hospital and was decommissioned in 1946. Well! I guess we're a little late."

"What do we do now?" asked Millender.

"I don't know. I think we were given a bum steer."

They had gone to the Navy Hospital at Mare Island. When they had inquired about Seaman Resnik they were told that the sailor had been transferred to another facility. Where? Somewhere in Colorado. The patient had become violent and delusional and a danger to himself and others. Staff here weren't able to cope. Where in Colorado? Near some hot springs. There's no record of the exact place. Checked out to a Doctor Forstinger. Glenwood Springs? That might be it.

Even before the US entered World War II, the Navy had laid plans for the expansion of its hospitals. It realized the need for the extended care of sailors even after their physical wounds had healed. Starting in 1941, the Navy took over hotels and private homes that offered recreational advantages like swimming and hiking, golf and tennis. Climate, rest, diet and psychotherapy were the order of the day. The Navy Convalescent Hospitals included former resorts at Arrowhead Springs, California, Sea Gate, New York, Sun Valley, Idaho, Glenwood Springs, Colorado, and Yosemite in California, among others. They were phased out after the war and most returned to their former venues.

"Look at this place! The Navy sure knew how to take care of their own. Not so much now. Let's go in. Maybe somebody knows if there is a hospital around here." O'Bannon stepped through the doorway into a long hallway lined with arched windows that faced out toward a courtyard where fountains bubbled and gardens bloomed, completing the illusion of a villa in long-ago Rome. "Find the front desk. Somebody's got to know something."

The desk clerk eyed them suspiciously. "Are you guests here?" he wanted to know. O'Bannon slipped a five dollar bill, folded neatly into one quarter of its size, into the man's hand.

"Tell us something about the area. Isn't there a hospital or a private clinic around here? One that specializes in mental problems," O'Bannon asked?

A man came from a room behind the desk and stood for a moment, scrutinizing the clerk and the two "customers." A supervisor. The clerk pocketed the bill surreptitiously and began a rehearsed recitation about the hotel:

"…and we have two tower suites available. One is named after the 'Unsinkable Molly Brown' who was a frequent visitor when she lived in Colorado. Our hot springs have delighted visitors since the days when Doc Holliday bathed here. Although President Taft declined to use them, stating that a man of his girth should not be allowed to bathe in public. Then there is the legend of Teddy Roosevelt and the teddy bear…"

The supervisor walked away, much to the relief of O'Bannon, Millender and the clerk. There weren't any nearby hospitals, private or otherwise that took mental patients, maintained the desk clerk. However, he had once heard of a private clinic up on Lookout Mountain. Where was that? Not far. Was there anywhere to rent a car? There was.

"And," said the hotel desk clerk as O'Bannon and Millender walked away, "we have our very own ghost. When the hotel was converted into a Navy hospital someone murdered one of the maids. People sometimes hear her screams up and down the corridors. We don't rent her room out any more."

O'Bannon and Millender were soon out of earshot.


## Kirkland Air Force Base, Albuquerque, NM, July 12, 1954

The conference room table was a magnificent work of hand-polished walnut. It sat 20 comfortably…26 uncomfortably (which was the number of people around it today). President Dwight David Eisenhower sat midway on one side of the long oval. Two of his aides stood behind him. Around the table were the members of the entourage that had witnessed the encounter at Holloman only a few hours ago. There was no stenographer to take minutes, no tape recorder to document what Ike was going to say. What he did say was:

"Smoke 'em if ya got 'em."

There was a sigh of relief around the table. The members of the Majestic 12 were primed to learn what had transpired between the president and the aliens. The others, not privy to the actual facts, were waiting to hear a report on the efficiency of the new experimental aircraft Ike had inspected. Why he had been in the craft for 45 minutes was not a question that occurred to them. Why he had not been accompanied by his aides or someone from the scientific community was also not questioned: Eisenhower was known to be a loner on important issues.

"The craft," said Eisenhower, "is not ready. You may have noticed the slight wobble when it landed. They hover nicely, but air speed and landing are still concerns. We do expect absolute secrecy, gentlemen. You CIA people will monitor messages leaving the continent to make sure there are no leaks. You FBI people will keep up the close surveillance of all known foreign operatives. You military men are the most important. You must be certain that all personnel coming into contact with the experimental craft are vetted for security. Any questions?"

There were a few. How long would development take? How expensive would manufacture be? Who would receive the contract? Ike shrugged these questions off, saying nothing was set in stone. The whole project might be shit-canned at any time if certain problems couldn't be solved. Keep your fingers crossed. Dismissed.

Forstinger thought to himself, what a great liar the president can be when he has to. That's what makes a great president—the ability to manipulate people with falsehoods—for the greater good, of course. Yes, he thought, I *do* like Ike!

"General Vandenburg," Eisenhower added, "have your group remain for a few minutes. There are some other matters we need to discuss."

Once the room was cleared of everyone but the MJ-12 and the president (even his aides had been ordered out of the room), Eisenhower's very complexion seem to darken. He looked around the table at the Majestic 12. "Gentlemen," he said, "Worry is a word that I don't allow myself to use. Say instead, we must err on the side of caution...if we must err."

Dr. Lloyd Berkener, who headed the Weapons Evaluation Group and was a member of the CIA panel on UFOs (he had steered the CIA toward the notion that flying saucers were not a threat to the national security), rotated the coffee cup in front of him. It left little brown rings on the table. "From what you are saying," he said, "I assume there is some sort of threat from our Grey friends."

"These were not the aliens we call the 'Greys,' Doctor. It was a different group. A different race, I suppose, like our Caucasians and

Negroes. The Greys were unresponsive to any offers we made them, insisting that we dismantle our nuclear weapons. But this different race is on the negotiating scene now. I would suggest we call them the 'Nordics' due to their pale skins. They are very different in terms of temperament. They seem to be somewhat more flexible."

"Still...did they threaten us?"

"Let me tell you what I saw and heard. Oh, this was very different from that meeting with the Greys. Then I never heard them speak...except in my mind. They had a sort of mental telepathy way of communicating, if I have the proper term. Even then, it wasn't the way you'd assume mental telepathy works. Like a magician or a performer in the circus might pretend to do. It wasn't words I heard...more like bits and pieces of knowledge that were undeniably true.

"The Nordics, however, have advanced beyond this form of communication. It was eerie, all right. I heard words...English language words...spoken from the mouth of a being who I would have sworn was a human. But not quite a human. It was as if they used him like a telegraph, sending telepathic signals to his human brain and causing him to generate into words the thoughts they wished to put forth. There would be a slight pause between questions and answers between myself and the Nordics, while this...person...seemed to process the ideas. It was like talking to a ventriloquist's dummy, or a robot."

Dr. Donald Menzel, sitting directly across from the president, was an expert in cryptanalysis. He was unable to control his enthusiasm and interrupted the president to ask, "What about the phrasing, the inflections. Were there any odd combinations of words or reversals of sentence structure, as if the translation was too alien be accurately stated?"

"Yes, Doctor Menzel. But I'm afraid I couldn't remember any specifics that would help you. I wish we had been brave enough to let me carry a tape recording device or a broadcasting microphone of some sort. But..."

"They would detect it," said General Montague. "We saw many things so technically advanced in the ship that crashed at Roswell and the one that crashed at Aztec! I would have to assume they could."

"Let me continue, gentlemen, and then I will try to answer your questions," said the president. "The Nordics reiterated the demands of the Greys, that we dismantle our weapons. They want their share of human experimental subjects, and they want the return of the bodies we have at Area 51. When I presented the same argument about the weapons, that we must stay strong in the eyes of our enemies, well, gentlemen, they hinted that we were not the only nation with whom they are communicating."

There was a general shuffling of chairs and the mutterings of phrases like "My God!" and "Those bastards!" Eisenhower looked around the table, studying each face.

"We may have to act," he said. "But the question is…how?"

"Do we have any idea," asked Dr. Vannevar Bush, "if our weapons would have any effect on the saucers?" Dr. Bush had been instrumental in the development of the first atom bomb. He wasn't what one would call a hawk when it came to actually using such weapons, but he knew their capabilities.

Dr. Jerome Hunsaker, Head of the National Advisory Committee on Aeronautics, spoke next. "Our ground to air missiles are just not accurate enough to bring down a saucer, armed either with nuclear or conventional explosives. We've seen them outrun our F-102 and F-106 Deltas. If we could catch them on the ground…"

"Well, gentlemen," continued Eisenhower, "the aliens are very unhappy that we went ahead with Operation Castle. I think this is where our greater strength lies. They wouldn't be so concerned about our weapons if they were immune to them. We don't have a good stock pile—we keep detonating them. However, this is a show of force that may turn the tide…if there is a tide to be turned. Remember what I always say, it's not the size of the dog in the fight that matters, it's the size of the fight in the dog."

The meeting over, the men left the conference room. Dr. Albert Forstinger would not be accompanying the MJ-12 members boarding the transport plane back to Washington, nor the ones flying to Los Angeles. He lingered for awhile at the Kirkland Airbase, musing to himself. So the Nordics, as Eisenhower called them, were making their own play for the domination of Earth. His counterpart in the Grey forces hadn't told him of this new wrinkle. Maybe their intelligence wasn't as efficient as it should be, or else they had kept him in the dark for some obscure reason. At any rate, he would need to make contact, and soon.

## Lookout Mountain, Colorado, July 14, 1954

They took the bus down Grand Avenue all the way past 27th Street where the street hugged the Roaring Fork River. There they found a series of new and used car lots. The dealers wanted to sell, not rent, but Millender had a "Semper Fi" card up his sleeve. He saw that the owner of the lot had some Marine Corps memorabilia on a shelf in his office. Semper Fidelis, meaning "always faithful," was the motto of the marines and it never failed to elicit favors from those who thought themselves "swinging dicks," comrades in arms. So when Millender spouted the motto, "Semper Fi," the man agreed to rent him a car for the afternoon, provided he would return it by six o'clock closing time.

They also obtained directions from the man on driving to Lookout Mountain although, the car lot owner said, why anyone would want to go up there…well, it was just craziness. Fifteen-plus blocks north they located a twisting country road at Cemetery Gulch and piloted the '49 Ford pickup up out of the tree line, through scrub vegetation and into a maze of dirt roads that crissed and crossed each other and ultimately began to climb up the mountain. Dead reckoning was of no use and no map had been available. The only thing they had to rely on was their own dumb luck.

The two would-be rescuers were discouraged. They had inadvertently backtracked along dirt roads they didn't recognize. Landmarks were nonexistent. They were going in circles, ellipses, trapezoids. Once or twice they saw snow in the shadow areas of small hills of volcanic gravel or the occasional ponderosa pine. Then they saw a house…well, more like a cabin. A hunting lodge, perhaps. No one was in evidence…no car or truck or horse or mule. The door wasn't locked. There was nothing to steal. They continued on.

"Let's give up and go back," said O'Bannon.

"Okay…sure. Which way *is* back?" quipped Millender.

They had begun to descend and entered the tree line once again. All around them there was evidence of a forest fire. This had been, perhaps, a few years in the past, and blackened trunks stood or leaned or were scattered like pick-up sticks where they had fallen. New growth had risen to cover some of the devastation. Young saplings were framed against the charred remnants of a century's old forest. Destruction everywhere. But somehow the road they traveled remained passable. It had been cleared of debris here and a fallen tree had been cut and hauled away there. A boulder had been rolled out of the way. Someone was using this road.

"How in God's name could anyone have a clinic up here?" O'Bannon wanted to know.

The road followed a dried stream bed and wound around and through the burned-out forest, descending—and O'Bannon and Millender realized that although they were now heading down the mountain, they were not going in the direction of the town of Glenwood Springs. Maybe they should turn around.

It was time for the aforementioned dumb luck to come into play. The road ended in a clearing—a well maintained clearing. Ahead were several low buildings with metal sides and roofs. A tractor was parked next to the nearest building. Off to one side was a large circular space that looked for all the world (to their military eyes) like a helicopter landing pad, only bigger. There was activity in one of the buildings. Bright lights were flashing inside and shown through the windows. Someone was taking flash pictures. Or something.

The only vehicles other than the tractor were two late model coupes parked next to the building with the flashing lights. O'Bannon and Millender walked toward the building next to where they had parked and peered through the window. It was dark and it appeared to be empty of people and devoid of furniture. There were two more buildings. They approached the next building but this also proved to be empty. Now they stood contemplating the farthest building—the one with the flashing lights. There was nothing to do but investigate. They had no business being there. They had no story to tell if they were questioned. They had no idea what they were about to discover. But fools will inevitably rush in where angels fear to tread. And they were no angels.

# 9

## Bellingham, Washington, July 19, 1954

It was the day that Sam Phillips of the Sun Records Company in Memphis, Tennessee, released a record single of "That's All Right" backed with "Blue Moon of Kentucky" by an unknown 19 year-old singer with the improbable name of Elvis Presley. Frida Kahlo had died in Mexico the week before, another relatively unknown artist whose influence would last for generations to come.

Operation Wetback, a border control system instigated in May to stop and reverse illegal immigration across the Mexican border, was breaking up families in the Hispanic community: over 170,000 undocumented persons had been rounded up to be shipped back and many others simply fled the United States to avoid persecution. In other acts of national patriotism, we now had a memorial statue depicting the Iwo Jima Flag Raising, and the words, "under God" had been added to the Pledge of Allegiance.

This same month at the Geneva Conference, the 17th parallel was set as the boundary between Communist-controlled North Vietnam and Western-influenced South Vietnam. The war was over—the French had lost—but the Second Indo-China War was looming just over the horizon. The televised Army-McCarthy hearings had ended the month before and McCarthy's approval rating had dropped from 50% positive in January to 45% negative. The senator was on his way out. He would be censured by the US Senate in December.

The news that captivated the country now, however, concerned the investigation of a murder that had taken place in Bay Village, Ohio; it would be called the Dr. Sam Sheppard murder case, and would result in the controversial conviction and imprisonment of the good doctor for the brutal murder of his wife. (In another reality) there would be a second trial in 1966 in which he would be acquitted. Millions would watch a television show loosely based on the Sheppard case called, "The Fugitive."

In Bellingham, Washington, Nate Mirko was not watching television, nor was he reading the newspaper or listening to the radio. He was waiting for the arrival of an FBI agent who had promised (and broken that promise two previous times) to come by and update him on the investigation into the two missing women. Nate had given up trying to convince anyone in authority that Noreen and his mother had been kidnapped by aliens from outer space. That always resulted in long pauses during phone conversations and the transferring of his calls to someone who took copious notes but never got back to him. He had finally called the Feds and insisted that there had been two kidnappings. No ransom requests? We'll look into it. But at least this agent *had* called him back and seemed to be taking him seriously.

The doorbell rang. Good thing. Nate was just about to give up waiting for today and go down to the car lot where his job was in jeopardy because he had missed so much work. Nate opened the door and greeted the man who introduced himself as Agent Daniel L. Fox of the FBI. He was a short man, in his middle thirties (Nate guessed), and was dressed in pale khaki slacks, a ruffled Hawaiian shirt decorated with palm trees, and a pair of soiled, high-topped tennis shoes (Keds). Nate asked to see his identification and Fox obliged, flashing open a wallet where his ID card was encased under a glassine window. Just like in the movies. Nate half expected to see a tin badge obtained from a box of Kellogg's Pep cereal.

"Can we sit out here on the porch?" Fox asked. "It's a nice day and you never know…sometimes the walls have ears."

Nate pulled two wicker chairs close together and the men sat, studying each other for a few minutes until agent Fox said, "I'm not what you expected, am I?"

"Oh, it's all right. I've been a bit nervous lately. I don't know who to trust."

As if on cue, a motorcyclist sped down the street in front of Nate's house. The blaring of the motor, unhampered by an adequate muffler, sounded like the barrage of a battery of machine guns. Nate jumped.

"A bit spooked today, are we?" quipped the FBI agent.

"I would offer you some ice tea or lemonade, if I had any," said Nate. Agent Fox shook his head.

"I have been in contact with your very efficient sheriff," said Fox, "concerning your missing mother. The local boys in blue have done a door-to-door and even rousted some homeless men living in the park, but no one has seen an elderly lady dressed in a bath robe walking or being dragged through the neighborhood. I'm sorry. She has disappeared rather completely. It happens."

"That's hardly encouraging."

"Now, about your girl friend. You say you were up in the mountains and you fell asleep and when you woke up, she had vanished. Why would you suspect a kidnapping?"

"I don't know. It seemed that someone else must have been there and taken her. She wouldn't just disappear like that."

"I know what you aren't *not* telling me, Mr. Mirko. You saw your girl friend abducted by aliens in a flying saucer."

"How did you know…I never mentioned that to the FBI."

"We're aware of many events that aren't public knowledge, Mr. Mirko. My boss, J. Edgar Hoover, is very displeased with the AISS and the CIA and the Armed Forces for withholding certain information about extraterrestrial visitors from the FBI. Apparently we are considered loose cannons. We have informants in various places, however. We are interested in your case because the victims, if I may call them that, haven't resurfaced as is usual in these abduction cases."

"What does that mean?"

"We don't know. I would like you to take me to the place in mountains where you last saw Noreen Ashley. Then we'll see what we shall see."


## Back on July 14th: at Lookout Mountain, Colorado

Andrew Millender, being the taller of the two, was peering into the window of the building where lights were flashing. Chuck O'Bannon waited, not too patiently, for his report. Suddenly Millender jumped back, ducking below the level of the sill.

"What is it? What did you see?" asked O'Bannon.

"I think they might have seen me. We'd better duck around the other side of the building," he answered.

"Who's in there? Any jolly green Martians?"

"Not green ones. At least I don't think so. C'mon…drop your cock and grab your socks…we gotta go!"

They had just made it around the corner to the back of the building when a tall shape appeared and began poking with a long metal stick around the ground on which they had been standing. The stick glowed red, and then green, and then red again. Finally the man, or whatever he was, seemed to give up and walk around to the front of the building. They heard a door shut loudly.

"Holy shit, dammit!" said O'Bannon.

"I quite agree, dammit!" said Millender. "That was a close encounter."

"What was causing the flashing?"

"All I could see was some sort of machine and a lot of tubes and wires. I couldn't tell where the flashing came from. There was a table with a body on it. I couldn't tell you if it was alive or dead…or if it was Resnik. There were maybe three or four people standing or walking around. I couldn't tell you if they were human or not. The flashing made it hard to see."

"We have to go in there, don't we?"

"Yeah. But maybe we wait a bit. Maybe they'll all go beddy-bye."

"Do Martians sleep?"

The aliens, who were not Martians but Greys from a planet orbiting a star called Betelgeuse in the Constellation of Orion, did not go night-night while the sailor and the marine waited. Perhaps their star, now around 630 light-years distant, hadn't set yet on their home planet. As you looked at Orion, Betelgeuse would appear on the right shoulder (some would say in the arm pit) of the figure of the ancient warrior. It was a super red giant of the spectral class M1-2 and one of the brightest stars in the night sky. Astronomers predicted that it would go supernova, expanding in size and brightness, expelling cosmic rays, stellar dust and gases, and sending a gigantic shock wave into the galaxy sometime in the next…oh…one million years. But scientists, at least those theorizing from the comfort of Terra Firma, have been wrong before. The Greys knew the catastrophe would come much sooner.

"Well, this isn't working. We have to get in there somehow," said

Millender.

"Maybe we should just knock on the door."

"Actually, that's an idea! We get them to come out, and we go in."

"But…"

"You have a lighter or some matches? And a rag?"

One of the coupes parked near the building, a grey '49 Plymouth, was to become a sort of beacon for freedom for whoever lay on the examination table. Millender poked the rag, torn from O'Bannon's undershirt, down into the gas tank until it was soaked. They had found a box of farmer matches in the glove compartment of their Ford pickup. Lucky, as neither of them smoked.

"You ready?"

"Let 'er rip!"

Flames climbed the rag like a fuse. They hoped it would continue to burn until the fire reached the tank—was there enough air? There was. Air and gasoline fumes. Just add flame and…boom! The Plymouth became a fireball. Black smoke billowed into the air. They reached the safety of the back of the building just in time to watch as four aliens came out of the building. The Greys gestured wildly and made guttural noises and squeaks that might have been talking or shouting. The desired effect had been achieved. O'Bannon and Millender ran through the door, pulled it shut and pushed a heavy machine against it to bar it. So far, so good.

Now what? They looked at the man on the table. It wasn't Resnik. It wasn't alive. It wasn't an alien but it didn't look altogether human. The Greys were pounding on the door. They were pushing at it and the machine blocking it was beginning to move. It would only be a matter of time before they gained entry. O'Bannon and Millender were trapped. Rats on a sinking ship had fared better. Millender picked up the metal rod they had seen the Grey use to poke at the ground.

"Let 'em in!" he said.


## Then on July 16, in Albuquerque, New Mexico

Dr. Albert Forstinger walked to the barrio just to the east of Albuquerque's Old Town. Old Town and its plaza attracted many tourists these days; it wasn't a good place for a meeting. So Forstinger and his contact had decided on the safe house that was located at the end of a cul-de-sac in a quarter where local Hispanics made their homes in centuries-old adobes—and where tourists did not wander. Ancient cottonwood trees lined the Calle Juan de Dios, their heart-shaped leaves rustling in the hot wind that blew relentlessly through the neighborhood, giving minuscule relief from the heat. It was in the mid nineties that day, but of course, it was a dry heat.

The adobe was unremarkable, looking like all the other brown stucco-covered houses on the street: front door painted turquoise blue, a ristra of dried red chiles hanging from a viga, a flat roof with canales poking through the parapets to drain water, a candelabra cholla cactus in bloom beneath a window covered with wrought iron bars. Forstinger used his key. Waiting for him inside was a boy of nine years of age. Most people encountering this youth on the street or along the plaza would not notice anything unusual about him— unless they looked closely into his eyes.

His name was Hziulquoigmnzhah. He had been among the first of the Grey/Human hybrids the aliens had created. Forstinger couldn't pronounce his name so he just called him Hziul. Hziul excelled intellectually, beyond the capabilities of a normal human child of his age. His specialty was language; hence he became a go-between for the Greys for their necessary interactions with their human agents.

"Hello, Doctor Forstinger. It is good to see you once again," said the boy.

"Hello, Hziul. How are you getting along?"

"Very good, thank you, Doctor. I have received an adequate shipment of my nutrient. I shall be quite well sustained for many days."

"Good for you. Don't you ever eat...uh...regular food? Human food?"

"Why no, Doctor Forstinger. The local food here is too spicy. It gives me heartburn. I do like the pastel de tres leches, however. Apparently my human genes have supplied me with a sweet tooth."

"Don't the people in the neighborhood here ever ask you where your parents are?"

"I tell them they are both working. Or if I am pressed, I say that they are at the INS, waiting to be deported. That is what I think you call a laugh."

"Hziul, I wanted to meet because I have some concerns. First, the sampling program has a serious flaw. The techniques for memory erasure are not always working. Abductees are remembering and I fear that very soon the stories they tell may be believed by the public. This could cause our authorities to have to admit that extraterrestrial visitations have, indeed, taken place. It could cause a general panic."

"I understand. I shall endeavor to communicate this fear of yours to the Circle. What does your own Circle think?"

"The Majestic 12? They are dedicated to keeping knowledge of your race a secret. Which brings me to my second concern. Did you know that the Amine…Amineg…"

"The Aimnegarwfuchee."

"Right. That they have met with out president? This is the first time they have come forth and it is troublesome, is it not?"

"Very troublesome, Doctor Forstinger. I was unaware of such an aberrant event. The hauteur of the Aimnegarwfuchee is unexceptable, to say the least."

"Will there be repercussions, do you think?"

"The Ratiessrvedflynach, my own people…that is, on my non-human side…have a saying: clandestineness is power— clandestineness shared is power lost. That loses something in the translation, but you get the idea."

"You'll be in contact then, with the Rat…Ratie…"

"The Ratiessrvedflynach. Yes. They will be most appreciative of the intelligence you provide. Go now in peace and keep up the good work."

## Table Mountain, Washington, July 19, 1954

Nate Mirko has brought FBI Agent Daniel L. Fox to the site of Noreen's abduction. Agent Fox has been struggling with the high altitude and the stress of climbing the steep mountain side. He sits on a rock and tries to catch his breath. Nate looks around; yes, there is evidence of the saucer having hovered above the mesa: dirt and gravel have been noticeably disturbed in a circular pattern. There are no burn marks or scorching as the saucer never actually landed.

He points out the circle to Agent Fox. Fox strains to get up off his rock and walks slowly to the area. He stands a few yards away from Nate, surveying the site. "This is it, is it?" he asks.

"This is where she was standing when the saucer appeared above. There was this beam of light that sort of sucked her right up."

"It elevated her. There have been reports of levitations...entire vehicles, cattle, people of course. These stories are always discounted as hallucinations or out-and-out fraud."

"Is that what you think, Agent Fox? You think I'm either crazy or lying?"

"Let's put it this way. Either it happened or it didn't. If it didn't, then you need to see a shrink and I need to stop wasting my time. If it did, we may have a national emergency on our hands. I am, of course, concerned about the safety of your girl friend, but think about the ramifications of alien abductions! No one would be safe. There could be panic, riots, anarchy. That's what the Chief is worried about. Civil unrest. Why, we have enough on our hands with the Negroes in the South, now with this anti-segregation legislation!"

"You didn't answer my question," says Nate.

Nate walks into the center of the circle and stands looking upward at the sky. It has been, up to now, a cloudless day, sparkling with the golden sunshine that only comes at the height of summer, and only in the Rockies—those who have experienced that special summer light on the mountain tops will maintain that this is true. Nate tries to regain his former optimism. His outlook has clouded in recent weeks, and rightly so. He watches an eagle circling overhead and marvels at the freedom of movement it enjoys. There is a sense, on a mountain, of kinship to such a magnificent avian. A desire, and a delusion that one can rise upward toward the heavens, to soar, to drift along on the updrafts and swoop down from vast heights toward the waiting earth.

FBI Agent Daniel L. Fox walks to Nate's side. In his hand is a silver globe, about the size of a tennis ball. He holds this above his head and rotates it slowly until it begins to hum softly. Above them, the sky is suddenly obscured by a cloud bank. The clouds are dense and darken the mesa as if night has fallen early. Nate feels a throbbing vibration and wonders if an earthquake is starting. Then he realizes what is about to happen and a chill runs through him, a terrible fear like one might experience when an airplane suddenly loses altitude or an elevator begins to plummet out of control.

Nate tries to move away, to run, but he is paralyzed. He cannot move nor can he cry out. Agent Fox is smiling. The clouds part and a beam of light issues forth—a beam like a pillar, filled with swirling flecks of silver and gold. The two men begin to levitate. They are being drawn upward. Nate is able to move his head now. He looks up at the opening above them as they rise nearer and nearer to the saucer. Maybe now, he thinks…maybe now I can be with them. Mother. Noreen. I am coming.

# 10

## The Dark Side of the Moon, August 3, 1954

Nate Mirko stirred. He lay on a cold metal table, naked, with a light blanket covering him. The blanket had a gelatinous feeling as he pulled it more tightly around himself. Where was his pillow? Why did his bed feel so cold and hard and strange? He didn't remember having gone to bed without donning his pajamas. He forced his eyelids to open; a difficult task as they felt cemented shut. His entire body ached. His mouth felt dry. As his eyes became accustomed to the low level of lighting in the room and its strange, greenish color, he looked for familiar objects: his night stand on which sat an electric alarm clock, the glass of water he always brought to his bedside at night, the paperback book he was reading…what was the title? Something about the sea…*The Sea Around Us* by Rachel Carson…that was it.

This wasn't his bedroom. It was bare of other furniture and windowless. A hospital room? Had he been in an accident? He struggled to remember. He threw off the blanket and sat on the edge of what he now realized was a metal table…the kind they used in the morgue! Had he died? Was this the afterlife? Nate tried to shrug off the bizarre thoughts that clouded his mind. It was difficult to move, as if he had been immobile for days…weeks…who knew how long? He slipped to the floor on weak legs and found he needed to steady himself by leaning against the table. Curiously, he felt light on his feet.

"It's natural to be off balance at first. As you regain your strength you get accustomed to things," someone said. Someone else was in the room, someone he hadn't noticed. He turned to see the short, stocky form of Agent Fox, still wearing that ridiculous shirt (Nate had thought it pretentious) with its colorful palm trees. Nate would not realize, as yet, how ironic the tropical scene was.

"Where am I?" he managed to ask, finding his voice to be squeaky and his throat sore and raspy.

"You won't believe it. We'd better talk later. Now I suggest you take some fluids and lie back down for a bit. I'll get someone to bring you something to drink."

"Wait…wait! Where am I? Is this a hospital? What happened to me?"

"You don't remember…of course you don't. Nate, you were abducted by aliens. Just like your mother was. Just like your girl friend was. You're at…their base of operations. They mean you no harm. You'll see. Just trust me for now, okay?"

"Clothes. Can I get some clothes? I feel…I do feel light-headed. My body feels…I don't know, like I could jump six feet in the air."

"I'll see that you get your clothing back. And Nate? Don't try any jumping. The ceilings are low here." Fox chuckled. Nate wasn't sure what the joke was.

After Fox left, Nate curled back up on the table and wrapped himself in the blanket. For so flimsy a piece of material it supplied him with adequate warmth. He soon fell asleep. He did not dream; he had entered that realm of deepest slumber where all demons and angels are banned. He may even have snored.

Someone was shaking him. He woke to find an angel bending over him. He *had* died! But no, it was a human angel…his angel…his Noreen!

"Oh my God! Noreen! Is it really you?"

"Yep, big boy. In the flesh. Speaking of which, I brought you some clothes. And food. And lots of liquid refreshment…don't ask what it is. I couldn't say. But it will quench your thirst and pep you up a bit."

Nate rolled off of the table and seemed to float to the floor. He exclaimed: "What is this place? Did we die and go to heaven? You're here so I know it isn't hell."

"Get dressed. I'll tell you everything I know about it. And don't worry…we're perfectly safe here. The Ratiessrvedflynach have our best interests at heart…or maybe hearts. I think they have more than one."

"The…who? The aliens? That's what Agent Fox said. I didn't believe him."

Noreen just looked into Nate's eyes, giving him one of those "Oh, you poor sweetheart" looks. "Here," she said. "I'll help you with that clothing. Don't be shy. You know I've seen you naked before."

Noreen and Nate had been brought to large room by Agent Fox. Again there were no windows. There were several cubes about three feet in diameter made of the same gelatinous material of which Nate's blanket was made; apparently these served as chairs. Several humans stood or sat on the cubes. Nate didn't recognize any of them.

Nate had recovered enough to get around, although walking in the lower gravity of the moon took some getting used to. His second shock of the day (the first had been seeing Noreen) was being told that he was in the main complex, the operational and residential center of the Ratiessrvedflynach species, *on the far side of the moon.* Incredible. Yet, with all that had happened, Nate was becoming a believer.

"It's not really the *dark side*," Noreen had told him. "It has full sun during the rotation that angles it toward Sol. We call it that because…well…we don't know what the far side looks like. Because the moon rotates at the same rate that the earth circles the sun…or more or less…it always presents the same face to earth."

"I knew that," Nate had said. "And about the green cheese." This didn't elicit a laugh from Noreen. She had frowned.

"We are on a sort of a mountain in the middle of a crater[3]…a big one, where the Ratiessrvedflynach first landed their mother ship. They built this complex and have used this as a base to explore our planet."

"I'm surprised," Nate had offered.

"Surprised about what?"

"That you can pronounce that Raty-son-thingy name, or

whatever it is."

"You haven't met them, but you will. They look a little like us...taller, paler, with bigger heads and skinnier bodies. Kind of a grey tint to them. And their eyes! Well, you'll see."

Once situated in the large room, Nate did see. Through an opening (Nate couldn't quite think of it as a door—more like a veil of some metallic substance that seemed to pour from the ceiling like a silver waterfall) the unmistakable form of an alien entered. The being was tall, perhaps seven feet or more. His dangling arms ended in shovel-like hands with long, slender fingers. His head was disproportionately large for his body—at least by human standards. He swayed as he walked. His clothing seemed painted onto his body: more silver gel that glistened in the eerie green light. Most of these features were but an exaggeration of humanoid form. In a dark night on earth he would almost pass for human—except for those eyes.

The lids closed down to thin slits when he blinked. When fully open they were like those of a jungle cat: yellow irises that expanded to show dark pupils—so dark you could fall into them, so otherworldly they were like black holes where nothing could exist, so hypnotizing that you couldn't turn away no matter how hard you tried.

Nate tried. But his fascination with this extraordinary creature was overwhelming. The thing stood and surveyed the small group of humans. It began gesturing with those long fingered hands as if it were speechifying. Nate noticed that people in the room were captivated by the being and were nodding. Nate heard no sounds issuing from the alien. He had the sense that something was being communicated to the others—but not to him. He looked at Noreen; she was beaming, her gaze focused on the alien as if she were drinking him in.

The alien left through the silver veil. Nate rushed up to get a better look at the door but it had merged with the wall so thoroughly that there was not a mark or a crack to indicate it had ever existed. Maybe this really is all just a dream, thought Nate. He returned to where Noreen was standing. She was still transfixed. He took her by the shoulders and shook her. "Noreen!" he pleaded. "Wake up! It's me, Nate."

"Oh...hello. Did you like our group leader's speech? It's going to be a wonderful, wonderful world, Nate. We are so lucky!"

There are times in life when circumstances are so overwhelming, so traumatic, that the mind decides to just shut down: surviving a horrendous automobile crash, walking though the ruins in the aftermath of a tornado or an earthquake, the death of a child, seeing the results of a horrific battle—or realizing you've been abducted by aliens, you're on the moon, and your girlfriend has been brainwashed. Nate tried tenaciously to stay lucid and logical. He could sort this all out. Just a few more facts. Something to grab on to as his world swung incongruously out of control.

"We have a little time left before we must return to our cubicles," Noreen told him. "Come and meet some of the others."

He had already met Agent Fox, who was talking with another man as they approached. Noreen introduced them. The other man was Second Lieutenant Leon Blackman, the investigator who had interviewed Noreen and then disappeared.

"What did you think of our group leader's speech?" asked Fox.

"Oh…it's going to be just wonderful," answered Nate. "Just the best." Play along with them, he thought to himself.

They moved to another group. Here Nate met First Sergeant Andrew H. Millender and Petty Officer First Class Charles O'Bannon. These two men, Nate thought, seemed disoriented and not enthralled with the leader's speech. They, like Nate, were new arrivals at the moon base. Was it possible they had yet to become brainwashed like the others? Nate wanted to talk to them alone, but Noreen dragged him away for more introductions.

"Noreen," Nate said at last, "is my mother here?"

"Oh, Nate…how can I tell you? Your mother didn't survive the transport. They were very sorry. They want to help elderly people too, but their…I guess you'd call it medicine…doesn't wok past a certain age. They were able to study her, though. She will help them understand aging in humans much better now."

Study her? Nate's previous submission to the inevitability of his present circumstances was about to shatter. His resistance flared, but logic cautioned him to remain calm, to observe, to plan. Was hope an illusion? Not for the eternal cockeyed optimist.

# Oval Office, White House, August 3, 1954

On the mahogany Theodore Roosevelt Desk sits a brass plaque with the inscription, "Suaviter in modo, fortiter in re," which means "Gentle in manner, resolute in execution." Behind this is a pen and pencil set trimmed in brass and an ordinary ink blotter with a few stains on it. Behind the desk is a credenza on which sits a large clock in a wooden case with extra faces for a barometer and thermometer. Across the yellow carpet from the desk stands a 32-inch world globe on a dark cherry wood stand. The globe rotates around its axis at the poles as well as around its equator.

The mantle of the room's fireplace is the setting for a group of miniature soldiers each representing a different era, selected by the president's wife, Mamie. In the center of the room are arranged two love seats and several upholstered armchairs, in a circle. Upon this furniture sit Dwight David Eisenhower, 34th President of the United States of America, General Curtis LeMay, Commander of the Strategic Air Command (whose nicknames include "Old Iron Pants," "The Demon," and "Bombs Away LeMay"), Captain Edward B. Blount commanding the 6555th Guided Missile Group, and Otto P. Weyland, Commanding General of the Tactical Air Command.

On this same day in Paris, the novelist, Sidonie-Gabrielle Colette, is dying; she will be denied a religious funeral by the Catholic Church. (In another reality) her most famous novella, *Gigi*, will be made into a Hollywood movie four years later. A week ago, Court Marshal T. Perry Lippitt of the US Supreme Court selected 14-year-old Charles V. Bush as the Supreme Court's first Negro page boy, with the blessings of Chief Justice Warren. It is the court's first implementation of the new anti-segregation laws.

Penny uranium stocks are being investigated by the Securities and Exchange Commission. Meanwhile, the joint Committee on Atomic Energy has put through a bill to create a private atomic-power industry in order to end the government's monopoly. The bill, however, has been stripped of President Eisenhower's plan to purchase electric power from private companies. A strike is pending at American Airlines after the company has asked the Civil Aeronautics Commission for permission to boost the maximum flight time for air crews from eight to ten hours. Last winter's plan for the withdrawal of United States troops from the Far East has been revised. Force levels will now be stabilized at 3,070,000 men.

On the coffee table around which the men sit are copies of the New York Times and Life and Time Magazine. The events mentioned above are reported in these news sources. None of the men pay attention to these news sources. None of the men pay attention to anything but what their president is saying. He asks for a brief report from each man, pertaining to the nation's preparedness to retaliate in case of a nuclear attack. General LeMay is most enthusiastic about his SAC bombers' abilities to deliver their payloads over Moscow and other Russian cities. "You build 'em and I'll drop 'em," he brags.

But Eisenhower is more interested in missiles today. The 1st Pilotless Bomber Squadron is being deployed to Bitburg Air Base in Germany, armed with B-61A[4] missiles. These carry W5 nuclear warheads, an improved version of the Fat Man atomic bomb dropped on Japan. The missile is piloted remotely, by radio signals from ground-based radar stations. This guidance system limits the missile's range to about 250 miles.

"Captain Blout," said Eisenhower, "Does the B-61 have the capability to reach the stratosphere?"

Blout had never been asked this particular question. He stammered. "We'd tested them at Holloman as surface to surface missiles, of course," he said. "The range depends on adequate guidance. But I suppose if you shot one straight up…"

"Ridiculous," interjected General Weyland. "They would burn out before they reached that kind of altitude."

"We have had some intelligence," Eisenhower explained, "that the Russians are working on a ballistic missile. Code name 'Semyorka,' which means, 'seven,' but it is as yet not operational."

"Convair has slacked off on development of the XB-65[5]," said Blout. "If we could raise the priority of that project, it would be able to carry an even larger payload than the B-61A, and it would leave the atmosphere briefly, giving it a much longer flight time. Guidance is always a problem, however."

"Gentlemen," said Eisenhower—his final words to the group, "I want us to be able to send a nuclear bomb anywhere in the world. I want to be able to send one to the moon, if necessary!"

# The Dark Side of the Moon, August 6, 1954

Nate found his cubicle remarkably dreary. There was a table of sorts: a low slab of metallic plastic or plastic-like metal (silver). Next to that was a sitting cube, and in one corner of the 10 by 10 foot cubicle was a low platform that served as a bed. This was considerably more comfortable than the metal table upon which he had initially awakened, and it came supplied with the usual gel blanket. There was a sink and a toilet, or at least, something that looked like a toilet. The cubical had all the elegance of a maximum security prison.

There was a daily routine, although Nate's second day of consciousness consisted of a long orientation conducted by his mentor(?), Agent Fox. He gained little knowledge from this and struggled to present a "brainwashed" persona to Fox. Fox either bought it or he didn't care one way or the other. The next day, which was today, Nate participated in the daily routine of "free recreational time" by joining the other humans in the large room. He wandered around, talking to the others, trying to act normal—whatever normal might be for a brainwashed abductee.

Eventually, Nate approached O'Bannon and Millender. He considered attempting to feel the men out, as to whether or not they were looking forward to a happy future under the alien conquest of earth, but he decided instead that a direct approach was warranted…and he had nothing to lose.

"So, have you been brainwashed yet?" he asked.

Millender took his time answering; perhaps he wished to study Nate, to determine on which side of this incredible conspiracy the man stood. On a paranoid scale of one to ten, this question really only rated about a five. He had nothing to lose by trusting him.

"So you noticed that too," Millender said, finally.

"And your friend?" Nate nodded toward O'Bannon.

"As steadfast as my Aunt Petunia's nighty. But we hadn't met anyone…until you, that is…of whom we could say the same. They all have that funny glazed-over look in their eyes."

"Listen. I don't know if they can monitor us or not. We'll have to take that chance. But I have a theory that not all humans 'take' to their brainwashing technique, if I can call it that. We may be immune…or it may just be a matter of time."

"We need to stick together, that's brass tacks stuff. But how…and for what?"

"For now, let's just say a few words back and forth during these rec periods. Don't want to get them suspicious. We need to know if any of the three of us has succumbed to the evil eye of brother alien."

"Roger that."

"Is there anything you've noticed about the others that gives them away, besides that glazed look?"

O'Bannon now put in his two cents: "They never laugh."

---

[3] The crater was probably the one we call Tsiolkovskiy, named for the Russian scientist, Konstantin Tsiolkovsky. It is a large impact crater floored with dark material which may be a form of basaltic lava, much like the vast plains of mare on the visible side. It has high walls and a tall mountain peak in its center.

[4] The B-61A would later be known as the Martin MGM-1 Matador. It was the primary tactical missile for the US from 1952 to 1962.

[5] The XB-65 was the first intercontinental ballistic missile developed by the United States. It is better known by its name "Atlas." It has been used as the first stage for launching satellites.

# 11

## Alien Origins

It is from Hmnogykwaer, a rebel Grey who eventually befriended Nate, that we get the story. It is infused with legend and muddled by age, a strange brew whose factual basis may only be wondered upon, but it is all we have. The planet Klivpokla circled the sun, Twodhlog (the star we call Betelgeuse). At the time the legend begins, some 10,000,000 years ago, Twodhlog was not the red supergiant we know today. It was a runaway star, formed many hundreds of parsecs from its present location. Along the path of its journey it meandered through space, buffeted by the explosions of other stars like a giant stellar billiard ball. The stellar wind preceding the young star created a bow shock. It began to cool and expand.

It pulsed and transformed into a blue giant, then a red giant, then back again. Solar flares sent gases and star dust millions of miles into space. The fusion at its core suddenly ceased and the star began to collapse. But the huge mass of the star would not die without a struggle. Pressures at the core of Twodhlog restarted the fusion process. Its movement slowed. In the greater scheme of cosmic things, it might be said to have settled down. There had formed about it a solar system of planets and moons and fragments of space debris. Where comets collided and deposited ice, life emerged.

4,000,000 years ago the predecessors of the Ratiessrvedflynac and the Aimnegarwfuchee rose to walk the virgin soil of Klivpokla, the fourth planet of Twodhlog. There were similar stirrings of early human life on our own planet about this time but the Klivpoklaians were much advanced and would develop mathematics and scientific technology many millennia sooner than earthlings. By 3,100 BC, during the early Bronze Age on earth, near the start of the Mayan calendar and predynastic Egypt, the Klivpoklaians were learning to harness gravitational forces and to build primitive airborn vehicles. By the late Second Millennium BC, when the City of Troy fell to the Greeks, when the Chinese of the Zhou Dynasty developed the first ideograms and the Phoenician alphabet was invented, the Klivpoklaians had mastered space flight and had visited the other planets in their solar system.

The Klivpoklaians developed not only technologically but with regard to their perception of life and their place in the universe. They had learned through the practice of various formal rituals to amplify their senses, to expand and control their consciousness. They obtained the ability to sense vibrations along the entire electromagnetic spectrum (not just the visible ones) and all ranges of sound waves. With this heightened awareness of the inner and outer aspects of their environment, the Klivpoklaians experienced realms we might think of as mystical or spiritual—but to the Klivpoklaians this was only an understanding of reality that allowed them to evolve as its guardians. Guardians. A monumental arrogance, perhaps, but as they began to understand the mechanics of existence and certain inevitable hazards of the expanding cosmos, they knew that they, and only they, were positioned to preserve intelligent life everywhere. For they suspected other intelligent life existed somewhere in the galaxy, and they felt certain it was in danger of extinction.

The irony of this view was that the Klivpoklaians were, in actual fact, in danger of extinction. This was because that funny old sun of theirs was about to go supernova. Their scientists held differences of opinion about the timing of this disastrous event. Most felt the death of their star was so far into the future as to be inconsequential. There was plenty of time to arrive at the perfect solution: escape to another solar system, for example. One eminent scientist by the name of Zopthmnquiosk, urged the immediate study and planning for such an exodus, but his misgivings about the future were considered extreme and unwarranted by the established scientific community. And these were the folks who had the ears of the politicians.

Their world was populated by four different races, distinguishable by physical characteristics that had evolved from separate branches of a common tree of origin. The Aimnegarwfuchee (the "Nordics") and the Ratiessrvedflynach (the "Greys") were the most alike, the former being of a very pale hue and the latter a slightly darker grey. The other two races were more distinct in appearance. The Matofnblotjuupz had a light brown textured skin that made them look as if they had scales (they did not). On the rare occasions when they were seen on Earth, they were referred to (by humans) as "Reptilians." The fourth race, the Syktijthraxteraq were short, had very large heads, and were of a yellow-greenish coloring. They had given rise to the sightings of so called "Little Green Men" when they appeared on our Earth.

In the early years of cultural development on Klivpokla there was not universal harmony among the races. The Syktijthraxteraq (the Greens), because of their diminutive stature, were considered inferior by the Aimnegarwfuchee (the Nordics), and for several centuries were summarily enslaved by them. The Ratiessrvedflynach (the Greys), more liberal in their thinking but hesitant to take action, opposed the slavery in spite of its economic advantages. Eventually, a civil war broke out. The Matofnblotjuupz (the Reptilians) had attempted to remain neutral in the conflict but were soon dragged into the fighting on the side of the anti-segregationists.

Explosives were unknown. The Klivpoklaians fought with bladed weapons and maces. The Ratiessrvedflynach used a long, straight sword sharpened to needle sharpness at its tip and along its flattened edges which they used for jabbing and slicing. It resembled the Chinese Jian and was also useful for cutting off hands. The Aimnegarwfuchee preferred a saber, also razor sharp, and not unlike the Japanese Katana. Both wielded their weapons with the practiced routines of a dance-like martial art called Rikthijmb. The Matofnblotjuupz were less sophisticated. Their weapon of choice was an ugly mace studded with spikes.

It was a particularly bloody war lasting many years. This was the first great war of such a magnitude that the planet had experienced. When it was over, millions had been killed, the Syktijthraxteraq were freed, and a resolution was adopted to end war permanently on Klivpokla. This marked the end of the Dark Ages and the beginning of the Age of Enlightenment.

Zopthmnquiosk, the scientist who had warned against the coming supernova, began to attract followers. These came for the most part from the Ratiessrvedflynach, his own race, but soon factions who favored the exodus developed among all four races. The wheels of industry were oiled, aligned and set in motion, and within five rotations of Klivpokla around its sun, a fleet of intergalactic ships had been produced, enough to carry away around one tenth of the population of the planet: nearly one million souls.

It was decided that lots would be drawn. Equal numbers representing all four races would go with the first fleet. Those who stayed behind would construct more ships and follow when they were able. An equal number of male and female sexes were chosen. Children made up a sizable proportion of the lucky ones. Lucky, because one month after the last ship left the solar system, Twodhlog belched out an angry tongue of gas and cosmic rays that incinerated every living thing on the side of the planet facing the sun, and doomed the rest to a slow death.

The exodus took place in the early 13th Century AD (as the date would be counted on Earth). On Earth, Boniface I had just led his Crusaders in the Sack of Constantinople, marking the end of the Byzantine Empire. The Mongols had invaded Northern China; the Chinese had tried to fight them off with gunpowder-propelled rockets. English barons forced King John to sign the Magna Carta, severely limiting the power of his monarchy. Jamal ud-Din, a Persian-speaking Muslim astronomer in the service of Kublai Khan, presented the emperor with an astrolabe and a globe; Europeans were still convinced the earth was flat.

Fifteen "mother ships" led the exodus. These were very large, egg-shaped ships that were constructed to carry farms where plants and animals[6] could be raised. A population of one hundred thousand rode on each—small cities with schools and libraries and governmental offices. A fleet of saucer-shaped ships followed. These varied in size and purpose, some being used to ferry officials between the mother ships, others to collect and distribute resources.

Two years out (years measured according the rotation of Klivpokla around Twodhlog—approximately ten times our own year) a meeting took place on one of the mother ships. Khfezfleyomoniu, leader of the Greys, and Wsofekbullhmj, leader of the Nordics, sat as Grand Arbitrators at a table on the top level of a tiered auditorium. Scientists testified. The search for an inhabitable planet was the goal. The location of one was a mystery. Zopthmnquiosk suggested splitting the fleet into five groups, each with three mother ships.

These separate fleets would head in five different directions, toward likely solar systems where planets might exist. It was a gamble. It might result in dooming four fifths of the population.

Of the fate of the other four groups there is no record (as yet). Our narrator, Hmnogykwaer, knew only the legend passed down through generations who lived and died on the mother ship called the Uoigykwosp (after an ancient Klivpoklaian astronomer). Many light years were to pass before a planet was to be found. Fortuitously, the Uoigykwosp and its sister ships were headed for our solar system.

Propulsion of the fleet was not by chemical means in the manner that our own earth rockets work. The Klivpoklaian technology involved the harnessing of gravitational forces, in particular, using the effects of anti-gravity on gravity. Velocities very close to the speed of light were able to be sustained, even without the proximity of a large mass such as a planet or a star. Hmnogykwaer was unable to explain exactly how this worked to Nate, who wouldn't have understood it anyway. But it worked.

"How did you have enough air to last all that time? And water?" Nate wanted to know. It was the only half-way intelligent question he had thought to ask. The answer was simple. They brought it with them, in the form of comets[7]. They could generate a gravitational field to surround the entire fleet which could capture a comet. The saucers would then mine it for its ice and minerals—hence, oxygen and water and other useful substances. When they used up one comet, they would look for others. They might, at times, have three or four of the cosmic snowballs circling them.

Still one hundred light years from their goal, tragedy struck in the form of one such comet. It was an unusually large comet, and it had no magnetic field, a circumstance which confused the astronomers on the mother ships. They failed to calculate its orbit correctly. One of the mother ships collided with the comet, splitting it into fragments. The ship was destroyed along with several dozen of the saucers which were struck by bits of the exploding core of the comet. The two surviving mother ships were greatly damaged. It was necessary to cannibalize one of the ships in order to repair the other. Thus, the Uoigykwosp, now crowded with double its capacity, limped on toward its goal accompanied by several hundred saucers—now the only known survivors of the death of the planet Klivpokla.

Overcrowding took its toll. There were shortages. The animals had been transferred from the scuttled ship but there was not sufficient space to expand the vegetable farms. Without enough feed, many of the animals died or became sick. Fighting broke out...not just racial conflicts or politically motivated quarrels, but strife born of frustration and hunger and fear. Some advocated throwing the Syktijthraxteraq overboard, illogically blaming them for their own dire circumstances. Martial law was declared. It looked like a new Dark Age was beginning.

Then the plague came. Before dead animal carcasses could be jettisoned into space they were stolen...and eaten. There were just enough bacteria still in the air...some exotic strains that hadn't been filtered out by the ship's air cleansing systems...that the carcasses became tainted and the people who ate from them were infected. Soon even those who only ate healthy meat caught it. The lessons of the old planet about cleanliness had been forgotten. They sneezed on each other, drank from common glasses, ate before washing their hands. And they caught it. Living in the supposedly sterile environment of the mother ship had slackened caution. Now even a kiss could be deadly.

But the plague solved one problem: overcrowding. In one month's time, the population of Uoigykwosp had dropped 25%. In another month, in spite of health officials' (a newly created bureaucracy) efforts to curb the sickness, the death toll, especially among those weakened from hunger...and children, had brought the population to under 60,000: well below the original number that had left on the mother ship—and this number included those on the saucers. To add to the devastation was a terrifying fact: around 50% of the females and 75% of the males who had survived the plague were now sterile.

The narrator of our story, Hmnogykwaer, was born (to a female Ratiessrvedflynachian who had not yet been infected) on Uoigykwosp, the mother ship, thirty earth years before it landed on Xmkitosp (their name for our moon). Since Xmkitosp orbited the planet Sjilgezhm (Earth), and kept one side always facing away from this inhabited planet, it was a logical choice for a temporary home. Since Sjilgezhm was populated by 2,700,000,000 Sjilgezhmians (humans), it seemed like a good idea to hide from them. And there was the problem of the diminishing birth rate to be solved.

The great scientists had long ago died. No one had the

intellectual capacity for creative thinking anymore, or so it seemed. Hmnogykwaer had enrolled in the Science Academy and had graduated with honors. His contemporaries specialized in astrophysics or gravity science and few had thought to explore the field of biology. But Hmnogykwaer was not swayed by convention. He located an aging mentor, a male named Klmneezji-aldu who had been a biologist. He was, at the time of the landing, 175 years old—elderly even for a Ratiessrvedflynachian.

Together they worked on cloning as a solution to the growing sterility of the female and the male population. They harvested as many viable eggs as they could and froze these as well as sperm from the males. Their success rate was dismal. About this same time the aliens began sending some of the smaller saucers to Sjilgezhm. Some of the first explorers crashed, alerting the Sjilgezhmians to their existence. It was too soon to reveal themselves, but the Klivpoklaians realized that contact would need to be made with an important Sjilgezhm leader. Plans were set in motion.

Now Klmneezji-aldu, proposed a plan: why not bring some specimens back from Sjilgezhm? They appeared to be carbon-based creatures with a similar metabolism as the Klivpoklaians. And they reproduced with the same system of zygotes from ovum and spermatozoa as they did. They should be studied closely. A program was initiated with Klmneezji-aldu at its head and Hmnogykwaer as his chief assistant.

Klmneezji-aldu and Hmnogykwaer, experimenting with specimens brought back to Xmkitosp, found they could clone the Sjilgezhms with much less difficulty than their own species. They learned many new techniques but still could not achieve a practical success rate to reverse the decline of their exiled brothers and sisters. Then Klmneezji-aldu had a bizarre, but brilliant idea: why not create a hybrid?

The experiments intensified and the need for more subjects from the planet below grew. There were a few successes. Their very first success, the hybrid named Hziulquoigmnzhah, was taken down to Sjilgezhm to act as a spy, a recruiter, and a gatherer of information. They had not been able to achieve the semblance of an adult with the cloning of Hziulquoigmnzhah. It was just as well. He would be perceived as being a nine year-old boy by the planet's inhabitants. All the better to move among them unnoticed. But there was more work to be done. Much more.

Hmnogykwaer would walk through the laboratory's specimen room and look at the glass tubes in which floated the many false starts and dead ends of their experimentation. Fetuses with cloven craniums, shrunken torsos, double the ordinary numbers of limbs or none at all. There began to grow within him a revulsion—not to the physical aspects of these grotesque creations, but to the act of the creation itself, and to its consequences for an entire planet of living beings. What would happen when they achieved success? The Sjilgezhms would be conquered, eliminated and used as a source for seed. What had happened to the great principles of the ancient Syktijthraxteraq? Those guardians of intelligent life? The followers of Zopthmnquiosk, the legendary scientist who had led them into space? Hmnogykwaer began to rebel, silently, secretly. He looked for a way to thwart the plans of his mentor.

He had access to the Sjilgezhms that had been collected and subdued—of course: he needed their eggs and their sperm. He became aware of a few of these who did not respond to the hypnotic mind control that was used to control them. Had no one else noticed? He brought one of these to the laboratory. Nate. He tried communicating through thought transference. No response. He returned the Sjilgezhm to its cubicle. Next he brought one of the initiated ones, the ones into whose minds he could place ideas. A female. Noreen. He probed her mind and began to learn the thought patterns that these Sjilgezhms turned into sounds in order to communicate. Crude. But useful. He practiced making the sounds. He learned about Nate from Noreen's deepest thoughts. He began to learn about humanity.

---

[6] The Klivpoklaians were meat-eaters and raised an animal called an Ahtejiq that, like our earth-bound cow, gave not only different cuts of meat but a nourishing liquid substance, the equivalent of our milk. The Ahtejiq was covered with a thick, wiry hair and sported a nose horn, much like our rhinoceros. The males also had short, stubby horns on the sides of their heads. Another domestic animal raised by the Klivpoklaians was the Fwilhog, a flightless bird not quite half the size of our ostrich. This was kept for its eggs but its meat was inedible. Also on the mother ship was a smaller animal kept as a pet, the Plablikz. It provided companionship for the aliens much as our

pet dogs and cats do for us. It was known as Klivpokla's best friend. It was covered with a soft, curly fur and had six legs.

[7] Comets are mostly composed of ice, dust and frozen gases. They may have a core of rock or an amalgamation of rock and other substances. Their tails are composed of dust and gas. They have eccentric elliptical orbits, usually around a star such as our sun, and this orbit may extend as much as a million miles into space. Comets that have visited our solar system include Halley's Comet and Comet Belize. Belize is thought to have split into two because of some cosmic collision or other catastrophe, perhaps in a similar manner as the comet that was struck by the Klivpoklaian fleet.

# 12

## Cloning Laboratory, Moon, August 15, 1954

Nate had seen the glass tubes containing the fetuses before, but it still unnerved him. He turned away. Hmnogykwaer noticed his distress. He shared it, but didn't let any emotions show on his face—not that Nate would have been able to read them. He gave a whistle, or what passed for a whistle coming from a Klivpoklaian. There was a scurry of padded feet and through an opening at the other end of the laboratory a small shape bounded. Its six feet operated in synchronization like a hipster tapping out a complicated rhythm to a jazz song with his fingers. The low gravity sent it on leaps.

"Brhmph!" called Hmnogykwaer to his pet Plablikz. Brhmph was its name, and also the sound it made when it...barked.

"Aw, isn't he cute?" said Nate as he leaned down to pet the animal. "Who's a good boy? Who's a good boy?"

Brhmph responded by nipping at Nate's outstretch hand. He pulled it back just in time.

"Please not to be foolish, Nathaniel. Brhmph is unlearned of your smell. He recognizes you not," said Hmnogykwaer. "It is good to be unobserved here in this place. We have discussing to do."

"Yes. I have lots of questions," said Nate.

Hmnogykwaer had brought Nate to the laboratory several times in the past week. He had told Nate the history of the great journey and the origin of his race. He had explained that the cloning of hybrids was an attempt to perpetuate his dying race, but had not alluded to the threat that it posed to the people of earth. Nate had figured out that little twist all by himself. Hmnogykwaer found it necessary to placate Nate, to keep him from emoting in his fury and, as a consequence, risking the discovery of his immunity to the mind control technique. Hmnogykwaer needed Nate's cooperation. He had plan.

"I can help you to return to your planet," he had told Nate. "You must continue undiscovered until then."

Brhmph sniffed at Nate's legs. Nate resisted the impulse to bend and pet the creature. True, it looked like a giant, hairy spider, but it acted so much like an earth canine that he expected it to roll over to have its tummy scratched at any minute.

"The woman, Noreen. Can you unblock her mind? I won't leave here without her."

"It is possible. However, I have learned of the emotion of the human which is unleashed at moments of great change. This is a concern. The best strategy is to wait with this until…what you call 'the last moment.' I will promise she will accompany you, if we are successful in the escape."

"And O'Connor and Millender? They could be helpful, couldn't they?"

"This is unknown to me. More entities equals more risk. Perhaps at a later time. I would request you not to share information with them. Are you agreed?"

"It's just that…they are the only humans I can talk to. I would feel guilty about leaving them behind. They are soldiers…you have this concept? Fighters. I need them."

"This is what you call 'a hard bargain.' I am not pleased with this prospect. However, I will interview them. You will not advise them of our plan before this. I cannot probe their minds any more than I can yours, but I must be assured they are not what you call 'loose cannons.' Are you agreed on this?"

"You certainly have picked up the human lingo. I wonder what else you may have gotten from that girl's mind. I would ask…but…"

"A gentleman never asks. Yes, I could tell you but it is not being useful. A distraction we cannot afford. So, again, are you agreed?"

"Yes, I am agreed." And now Nate did reach down to stroke the soft fur of the Plablikz. And now Brhmph did not snap. It purred.

## Meanwhile, Back on Earth, August 15, 1954
## US Naval Research Laboratory, Washington, D.C.

Wernher Magnus Maximilian Freiherr von Braun had a visitor. There were Secret Service Agents standing in the hallway leading to his workspace: a dusty, windowless room with a solitary desk, chair, and a wall-length blackboard covered with much erased and rewritten equations. He turned from the calculation he was making to greet the balding man who always looked so uncomfortable in his business suit. Von Braun felt uncomfortable as well, having been used to seeing the man in military uniform. They were not old friends: more like old acquaintances who had survived the aftermath of a terrible war, each in his own way. Herr von Braun had switched alliances; General Eisenhower had pursued the winning of the peace.

In Germany, on October 3, 1942, von Braun had successfully launched his first V-2 missile. Over 1000 such rockets struck England in the following years. The Professor, as he was known, came under arrest by the Gestapo for his defeatist sentiments. After his release, as the Russian Army advanced on their position, von Braun led his team of rocket scientists in an escape. On May 2, 1945, upon reaching Austria, they surrendered to American troops. Crates of rocket data, 100 captured V-2 rockets, and 115 German rocket scientists, including von Braun, soon found themselves in New Mexico.

Wernher von Braun's conflict with the Nazis stemmed from his almost obsessive preoccupation with space exploration. Indeed, he advocated building spacecraft instead of bombs. This was an unwise attitude to have in a country trying to conquer the world. Ironically, in the United States, the German scientists, cleansed of their Nazi pasts by the US Joint Intelligence Objectives Agency, were set to work developing missiles—to carry bombs. The work on the V-2 led to the development of the Redstone missile which became the first short range ballistic missile this country would produce.

"Herr Präsident," said von Braun, "it is an honor to me that you visit."

"Well, von Braun, it looks like the mountain is coming to Mohammad. I need your expertise. You wrote a book about flying to Mars, didn't you?"

"Ja. *Das Marsprojekt*. An enormous scientific expedition of ten spacecraft and 70 explorers. It was not a science fiction novel, you know. All the specifications, all the calculations are there. Everything ready...except for the ignorant politikers. Sorry, mein herr, I didn't mean you."

"I am," said Eisenhower, "a very ignorant politiker when it comes to rockets. What I want to know is not about Mars, but about going to the moon."

"Much closer. I wrote that we build first a space station in orbit. We use that to reach the moon."

"That would take time. What could we do now?"

"Rockets have limited range and burn up fuel too fast. Of course, we could use a thermal nuclear engine using liquid hydrogen pumped through a reactor. Or create with the reactor electrically charged atoms which we expel..."

"Do we have anything like that?"

"Nein, mein herr. I am thinking you desire this trip immediately. There is one possibility. We use big rocket to escape atmosphere. Put little rocket on top of big rocket and fire once in space. There is only one problem: how do you get back?"

"I'm thinking of a one-way trip, von Braun. A one way trip for a nuclear device."

## The City on the Moon, August 23, 1954

Nate had never been outside of the compound before. The humans and the experimental laboratories were housed in a separate building, a converted saucer, located down slope from the aliens' main habitat. The compound was connected to the habitat by a long gravity tube that acted as an elevator, although it had no moving parts. The walls of this tube had windows of irregular shapes at intervals, so that during the gentle rise up the tube, Nate could look out at the surface of the moon, occasionally getting a glimpse of the distant stars at the rare times when lunar winds blew away the layer of moon dust that hung just above.

Nate knew the term, surrealism, but only now did he begin to understand its meaning. This was a surreal experience if ever there was one. The ascent was slow enough—no blood rushed to his head—but looking down at his feet to see that there was no visible surface on which he stood, made him giddy and apprehensive. Above him he could see the form of the alien. Hmnogykwaer was leading him along the dangerous path he and his companions would have to follow in order to make their escape. This was, Hmnogykwaer had said, what you would call a "dry run."

Not entirely dry, for Nate was sweating. He worried. He had been instructed by the alien on how to exit the tube when they reached the top: a little hop to the side. A small step for a Klivpoklaian, a giant step for a man. If he bungled it he would be stuck hanging at the top of the tube until someone reversed the gravity and he was sent down again. To his surprise, he executed the action flawlessly. Just like stepping off an escalator. Sort of.

They stood on the edge of a broad highway that circled around the horizon as far as Nate could see. There was a domed roof above them, so immense that it functioned as a sky, and like a sky, it reflected light down onto the landscape—that same greenish light that Nate had still not gotten used to. Below were terraces that crept down the sides of the interior space of the city to form a huge bowl, mimicking the domed sky above, as if these were two hemispheres of a globe. An inside-out planet. Once used to the scale of this vista, Nate could pick out sections where vibrant colors indicated vegetation (although not the greens and browns of earth—instead, purples and mauves and scarlets fading to pale pink.) Other sections held cubes and spheres and egg-shaped structures that Nate took for buildings.

There was traffic on the highway. Cars or other kinds of vehicles sped along the road at even intervals. Hmnogykwaer had pulled Nate over onto a shoulder that he took for a sidewalk, although no other foot traffic was evident. The cars, or whatever they were, were perfect spheres. They had no wheels or treads or other visible means of locomotion, yet they moved along, inches above the highway as if suspended by invisible cords. More anti-gravity, Nate assumed.

"Remember how we go now," said Hmnogykwaer.

There were tube openings all along the sidewalk; some of them large enough to accommodate the spherical cars, and some smaller, like the one upon which they had just ridden.

"Look for this symbol," said the alien, pointing out a sort of hieroglyph attached to one of the tube openings. It was shaped like a seven-pointed star, although asymmetrical, and had a textured surface of small red and green protrusions like bumps. "You will be descending this lifting tube to the fourteenth level. You must count the symbols that indicate these levels and at the fourteenth, you will step off. Ready now?"

Nate was not ready. Why couldn't the alien go first and he follow? Just as he was about to ask, Hmnogykwaer pushed him into the tube and he began to float slowly downward. He watched for symbols. There was one…then two…three…and so forth, each with a few minutes of travel between. Don't lose count! Where would he end up if he miscounted?

At fourteen Nate stepped sideways through the opening and found himself on another circular highway. He quickly moved to the shoulder. A few minutes later, Hmnogykwaer stepped from the tube.

"This is an agricultural section," he explained. "Be very certain you don't disembark into a housing section. Although we no longer allow segregation, we do have ethnic clusters something like what you would call 'ghettos.' It can be very dangerous these days to find one's self in the wrong section."

Nate studied the vegetation. It was not arranged in broad open fields as it might have been on earth. Instead, he found himself walking through a labyrinth of high walls upon which plants of a very (to Nate) exotic nature climbed. It reminded him of a picture he had once seen of the hanging gardens of Babylon. It was ancient and alien and astounding.

Silver vines that twisted around each other like ropes made of metallic pipe held fronds the size of elephant ears, some like fine woven lace, some bulging with internal fluids that oozed. Berries of odd shapes and colors competed with the leaves for attention. He saw: purples hues speckled with dark azure; orange and violet stripes that seemed to vibrate in the harsh light that came from…where? He could find no light source; even the sky above was dim compared to the brilliance of the light in those curious corridors. It was as if the very air were made of liquid light. The plants swam in it.

Along the way he saw what he took for fruit hanging from the vines. Here were cone-shaped objects as big as basketballs. Strange clusters of tubes with rounded ends, not arranged in bunches like bananas, but intertwined like writhing snakes. Something that looked comfortingly like an apple, but of a dark blue color with streaks of white. A thick stalk studded with spines like a cactus—this Hmnogykwaer pulled from the wall and devoured hungrily.

"Wherever there is a corridor which crosses you will take the turning to the right. Always to the right. This will lead you out of the maze." Hmnogykwaer spoke, juice from the stalk dribbling down his chin. He wiped it away with a brisk motion.

In the next corridor were blooms. Fleshy petals with hungry looking tentacles that undulated. Blisters that pulsated and spirals of dainty beads that were transparent like glass. Spider-shaped flowers, repulsive at their centers with clusters of what looked like eyes—eyes that followed Nate as he skulked past. And insects. Or something. Winged, big as your hand, buzzing and flitting and banging against things as though they were blind.

"The pollinators," explained Hmnogykwaer. "Don't touch the blooms, it interferes with their sense of smell."

After many right turns they left the labyrinth and emerged onto a gently rolling plain. The ground was covered with spongy moss, orange, yellow, violet, and pink. In the distance Nate could see animals. Familiar looking animals.

"Cattle?"

"From your planet…yes. We are also trying to clone them as hybrids with our Ahtejiqs. We haven't been very successful and so we turn them out to propagate naturally. They are useful…"

"That's where the meat comes from you feed us!"

"Yes. Personally, I find it bitter and chewy. Ahtejiq meat is more agreeable. Now, we cross this field and we find a tube with a symbol which I will show you…you must memorize it. That tube leads down to one of the saucer ports. You will lead your group to that and I will be waiting for you inside a saucer with a particular marking: I will draw it for you…you will also memorize this symbol. This saucer port is unused and there will not be anyone there to stop us."

Once they had found the tube opening, Hmnogykwaer instructed Nate to memorize the symbol marking it. It had an irregular shape that confused Nate. He decided it looked like a three-legged orange amoeba (did they have legs?) and committed the abstract shape to memory. Hmnogykwaer quizzed Nate about getting from the human compound to this tube, making him repeat what he remembered over and over until he was satisfied Nate could find his way on his own.

"We must go back now. Be very careful not to be noticed. Inform your friends only after I tell you the time has arrived for escape."

"Why are you helping us? Aren't you taking a great risk?"

"I am going with you to your planet. I will need your help once we arrive. There are things I must do and say. You will take me to your leader."

## Back at the Human Compound, Same Day

First Sergeant Andrew H. Millender and Petty Officer First Class Charles O'Bannon were in the large room. It was the recreation period when they are allowed to mingle with the other captive humans. At the beginning of each such period the two men would tell each other a joke; this was to test whether or not they had succumbed to the alien brainwashing—brainwashed humans did not laugh.

"A sailor walks into a bar," began Millender. "He has a parrot perched on his shoulder. The bartender says to him, 'Where the heck did you get that thing?' So the parrot says, 'Would you believe it? It started as this little wart on my butt!' "

O'Bannon laughed. "My turn," he said. "This Marine Drill Sergeant is talking to an enlisted man who is a short timer. 'Now that you're getting out of the Marine Corps,' he says, 'I suppose you'll just be waiting for me to die so you can come and piss on my grave.' The grunt looks at the sergeant and says, 'No way! Once I get out of the Marines I'm never going to stand in line again.' "

Millender laughed. The two men now felt secure in each other's company. They could not, however, trust anyone else. They had both been interviewed by the alien, Hmnogykwaer. They were suspicious of this as Nate had not shared the escape plan with them yet. They discussed the possibility that the alien had seen through their pretense—but if so, why hadn't there been any repercussions? Something, as usual, didn't add up.

As they talked, the alien group leader, Utskolggvjiyz, entered leading a human behind him. The man was limping, barely able to walk, and looked as if he had been dragged along a gravel road and rolled into a muddy ditch.

"Ah," said Millender, "a new recruit."

"Holy shit, Millender...do you see who that is?" exclaimed O'Bannon. "It's Resnik!"

Seaman Apprentice Christian Resnik, the sailor they had thought to rescue, whose location had eluded them for so long, was now being brought into the common room. He had a dazed look about him. He didn't seem to recognize Millender or O'Bannon. He slumped down onto one of the sitting cubes.

"What do we do?" O'Bannon asked.

"We do nothing. Wait until the alien leaves, then think of the funniest joke you can to tell Resnik. I have a bad feeling about this, though."

# 13

## The Narrative of Seaman Apprentice Resnik

O'Bannon and Millender waited until the following day before talking to Resnik. The man still looked like death warmed over, still was disoriented, and seemed to stare off into space instead of looking at whoever might be speaking to him. There was no acknowledgement on Resnik's part of their previous friendship...not at first. O'Bannon talked to him about going down to the sea in ships, about the USS Cocopa and the South Pacific. At the name of the ship Resnik's eyes widened just momentarily—a good sign, thought O'Bannon.

Two days later, Resnik looked O'Bannon squarely in the face and said, "Well, Cap'n, when do we weigh anchor?" O'Bannon was so happy that he neglected to scold Resnik for calling him Cap'n.

"Chris," he said to Resnik, "I'm going to tell you a joke now. It will cheer you up. I heard this one around the waterfront in Dago. Stop me if you've heard it."

Resnik sat on his cube, all smiles, attentive to O'Bannon for the first time in the several days that the Petty Officer had been trying to communicate with him. This was the test, of course. If Resnik failed to laugh they would have to exclude him from their conversations. O'Bannon got ready to do stand-up comedy. He began:

"A priest, a rabbi and a minister walk into a bar. The bartender says, 'Is this some kind of a joke?' " There is no reaction from Resnik.

"A sandwich walks into a bar. The bartender says 'Sorry, we don't serve food in here.' " Still Resnik just stares into space, unmoved.

"Okay, how about this one: A woman gets on a bus with her

baby. The bus driver says, 'That's the ugliest baby that I've ever seen.' The woman goes to the rear of the bus and sits down, angry and humiliated. She says to a man next to her, 'That driver just insulted me.' The man says, 'You go right up there and tell him off! Go ahead, I'll hold your monkey for you.' "

Resnik broke into howls of laughter. He slapped his thighs. Others in the room turned to look at him. O'Bannon and Millender looked at each other and smiled.

Little by little, for their time in the common room was limited and often inhibited by the presence of the alien, Utskolggvjiyz, they told Resnik of the circumstances of their tenure at the moon colony. At first, Resnik could hardly believe he was on the moon. When that sunk in he became severely depressed. It took another series of bad jokes to snap him out of it. He learned that he, O'Bannon, Millender and a man named Nate Mirko were the only humans unaffected by the alien brainwashing. Because they were four, united against overwhelming odds, there was a feeling of camaraderie and hope. Resnik took notice of the fact that Nate seemed the most hopeful of the four. Nate had still not told the others of the escape plan, however. He was stalling for time and understandably cautious.

"Escape," Millender said at one of their bull sessions. "Every prisoner of war is obligated to escape."

"Are we at war?" asked O'Bannon. "Are we even prisoners? They don't lock us into our rooms."

"Yes, but where could you go? There are the cubicles, the halls and this room. We can't get out of here except when they take us to the lab to fiddle with our gonads."

"True. But we could jump the alien in the lab."

"We are only in there one at time. And where would you go from there? Do you have a space ship? Could you fly one if you did?"

Conversations like this one alternated with stories they told of earth, particularly how each came to be abducted. Of extreme interest was the narrative of Seaman Christian Resnik. Although it was given in sporadic episodes during the brief conversation periods, it is presented here in continuity:

"I've told you about being taken up in the space ship by aliens. Nobody believed me. I was in the hospital somewhere. They kept me pretty well drugged up 'cause I guess I was babbling at lot.

Then…well, I started seeing things and hearing things. Monsters made of red smoke flew around the room. The chairs got up and danced. The walls melted and flowed like lava, filling the room with colors like you'd never seen. I heard laughter and screams, laughter and screams, then more laughter and more screams. I guess I screamed too. They came and tied me to the bed. I think…I think that one doctor gave me something that made me see all those things.

"This doc…he wasn't Navy or Army or any kind of Armed Forces…he took me away. He didn't use an ambulance like you would have thought. Just his personal car. I was still tied up like a prisoner. This wasn't the normal way you treat a sick person. I knew something was wrong, but I couldn't move, being trussed up in the back seat like livestock or something. He took me to an airport…not military…one of those private ones with all the piper cubs and small planes people fly as a hobby. I always wondered how rich you had to be to afford your own airplane. Well, this doctor, he had his own chopper! And a pilot to fly it. I always wanted a ride in one of those whirly-birds. This wasn't exactly what I had in mind.

"We were up in the mountains somewhere when we landed. I was still pretty drugged up…oh, not hallucinating anymore, but numb. He had untied me but I couldn't have run away…I could barely move my legs. He took me into some kind of a metal shed or building. I collapsed onto a cot and lost consciousness. Slept…for I don't know how long. Might have been days or weeks or only a few minutes. It wasn't the same day when I woke, though.

"The doc was gone. There was this guy that brought me food and water and then left. The door was locked. The windows were locked. I tried them. A good swabbie always tries to escape, like you said. But no go. I sat there trying to puzzle things out. This wasn't a Navy op…that was for sure. CIA maybe. Russian spies? What would they want with me? The only thing that made sense was that the doc, and his buddies, they believed me. Believed I got taken up in a space ship by little green men…only they wasn't little or green. They was big and sort of grey.

"Well, it was just me and this food guy for days. I tried talking to the son of a bitch but he wouldn't say nothing. Just came with food and left. It was like I was in the brig, all right. But I wished I could be back in a *normal* brig, where there were people to talk to. Then one day the doc came back.

"I could hear them talking outside the building but I couldn't make out just what they were saying. I could see out the window, though. That's when I saw the space ship land. It was shaped like a saucer...just like in the movies. I'd been inside one, but I'd never seen the outside of one before. It was unreal...smooth like a baby's ass and shiny. You couldn't see any doors or windows, but a doorway opened up just like magic. And these aliens came out. I saw the doctor and the other guy start to walk over to meet them, then they all of a sudden stopped, like they'd seen ghosts or something. These weren't the grey ones I'd seen before. They were different...pale, almost translucent skin and bigger eyes than the Greys. The doc and the other guy were clearly scared of them. They turned and ran.

"One of the aliens pointed a kind of a long rod...it wasn't exactly a gun...and it glowed all kinds of colors. The doc and the other guy just collapsed. Just fell straight down like they were marionettes and someone cut their strings. I never seen anything like it before. I was scared shitless. The aliens picked up the bodies like they was made of straw and took them to another building. I tried to find someplace to hide but there was nowhere. Then they came for me.

"I got behind the door as it opened and ran outside before they could grab me. I was afraid of that rod thing and I ducked around behind a car that was parked there. I looked but there wasn't a key in the ignition...damn! That would have helped. I ran into the woods. This wasn't much help either: the trees was all burned. No where to hide. I just kept running. My breath was burning in my throat. I thought I would die from exhaustion before they could zap me. Maybe that'd be better.

"But these aliens, they don't run very fast like you'd think they could with those long legs. Or maybe they was lazy or they just knew they would catch me sooner or later anyway. I made it down a slope and ran along a dried-up creek bed. I didn't know if they could track...you know, like hound dogs. Finally I came to where the trees gave way to rocks. There were crevasses and places to hide. I looked for a cave and I found an overhang that was covered with vegetation. I crawled under it and tried to stop my heavy breathing...I thought maybe they had really good ears...I didn't know.

"Darkness fell. I was still safe, as long as I stayed hid. I guess I slept some. I awoke at the dawn. There was birds singing. I felt safe as long as I could hear birds singing. Maybe they weren't looking for me. Maybe they didn't care. But I was to find out that they did care…a whole lot!

"I had to piss. I peeked out from my hidey hole. Nothing. I found the little stream bed and did my business. Then I noticed that the birds had stopped singing. Boy did I run! Back to my hiding place. But it was no use. They were waiting for me. They had me cornered. I put up my hands, like…you know, I surrender. That didn't make no difference to them. They clobbered me with that rod thing and I was out like a light bulb when you don't pay the 'lectric bill.

"Well, I woke up on the space ship, but like last time I wasn't naked on a table with tubes up my butt. I knew it was a space ship…it had those same kind of curved floors and walls and a sort of low hum that I remembered from my last trip into outer space. I really was hoping I was either dreaming or crazy, but no such luck. I was in a small room and I wasn't alone. There was the doc sitting right next to me. I could have punched him right then. I should have!

"He tells me his name is Forstinger and he's really sorry he got me into all this. He tells me they were just trying to isolate me so I wouldn't tell about being abducted. A matter of national security, he says. Well, I could identify with that. I'm Navy, ain't I? I wasn't going to blab around something I wasn't supposed to. Then he tells me the scary part.

"These aliens…he calls them the Nordics…are sort of at war with the other ones…the Greys, he calls them…and we're caught in the middle. The Greys have a deal with our government to abduct a few people now and then to study them. This is so they don't just conquer us outright. The Nordics want their share of the deal too, but the Greys don't trust them as far as they can throw them. It's not like a war with guns and bombs…more like intrigue and stealth. Like the CIA was fighting the FBI.

"They took us to their base of operations. I didn't know at the time it was on the moon! I didn't see Forstinger after that. This was, I don't know…weeks ago maybe. I kept waiting to get probed and have needles in my balls but they just let me sit. Man, that is the worst! Not knowin' what's going to happen…nobody to talk to.

"Then one day the door bursts open and these Greys come in. They don't say nothin'…well, they never do, do they? They just jerked me up and walked me down a bunch of corridors and put me in this tube which was like an elevator but different, and bingo…I'm here. I don't get it exactly. But if what the doc said is true, they was fighting over who gets to keep the humans. It's like we're in their little zoo or something."

Nate Mirko was conflicted. Each session with O'Bannon and the others made him increasingly nervous that the three were planning an escape which ultimately would fail and which would therefore endanger his own attempt. He should tell them. But if Hmnogykwaer found out he might abandon the plan or refuse to take the others along. He had to wait. What if Hmnogykwaer never released Noreen from her mind control? He tried to dissuade Millender and O'Bannon from planning. He told them to be patient. He hinted that he was working on something, something he needed to keep secret…because who knew if the aliens could hear their conversations? This reasoning didn't convince them; they continued to plot:

"We jump the alien who comes into the common room before that weird door closes."

"We make our way to the saucer airport and kidnap a pilot…force him to fly us to earth."

"We'd have to take one of the others along. Somebody whose mind the aliens can read, so we could communicate with them."

"Could they shoot us down? Do they have weapons like that?"

"How many people could we take with us? Would they even come? They're brainwashed."

Nate considered all this, considered that O'Bannon and Millender were determined to try, at least, to escape. The other fellow, Resnik, didn't say much through it all. He still seemed distant, as if he were shell-shocked. There was something about Resnik that bothered Nate. He had been through a lot, that much was true. But he didn't seem as though he was wholly recovered from his ordeal. He didn't seem to Nate to be all together stable. If Resnik were to be included in the plan, Hmnogykwaer would need to interview him.

## Meanwhile, Back on Earth, September 13, 1954
## Air Force Missile Test Center, Cape Canaveral, Florida

On launch pad LC-5 sat the huge MX-1593 missile, the predecessor of the Atlas (in another reality). Ground crews had checked the linkage between this first stage rocket and its hitchhiking second stage, a PGM-11 Redstone ballistic missile with an improved engine and a payload which weighed the same as a W5 warhead with a 6 megaton yield, but without any explosives or fissionable material. (This was only a test.) Fuel was being pumped into the two missiles and the scene was one of controlled chaos of men and machines, billowing vapors, and flocks of concerned pelicans. No press had been allowed on the site.

Wernher von Braun and his team were busy reading dials, testing switches and plotting trajectories—only this trajectory was unlike any that the team had plotted before. Usually, at the Joint Long Range Proving Ground, as it was called, missiles were launched out over the Atlantic Ocean. There was a 5,000 mile range between Canaveral and the Ascension Islands and there were tracking stations all along the Bahamas, the Dominican Republic and St. Lucia in the Caribbean. Today's test, however, was headed more or less straight up.

A red telephone rang. Someone answered it, waved at von Braun. "He wants you," the man said.

"Das ist voll nervig!" said von Braun. "Annoying as hell!" But he hurried to the telephone, knowing full well who was on the other end of the line. He answered:

"Ja? Ja. It will be as perfect a launch as is humanly possible under these rushed circumstances. We should be sending a monkey or a dog into orbit, Not this…"

The ex-German scientist stood listening and shaking his head— both in the affirmative and in its opposite. He carefully placed the phone in its cradle.

"Das macht mich verrückt!," he said loudly. "That drives me crazy! Das Arschloch! Die Arschmade!"

The pretend warhead weighed almost 3,000 pounds, a payload that gave von Braun much concern. The first stage would lift the composite missile above the atmosphere and then success was up to the degree of accuracy with which they could control the separation of the second stage and guide the Redstone toward its lunar goal.

Too many factors, thought von Braun. Why the idiots didn't see that his plan, the building of a space station, was the only practical one...was zur hölle! "They can leck mich am arsch!" von Braun muttered beneath his breath.

There had been a delay because of the report of a front of bad weather building off shore. There was still much nervousness about this heretofore never attempted launch of a veritable exquisite corpse of a rocket, whose parts were like a Rube Goldberg assembly of odds and ends that shouldn't go together, shouldn't work, shouldn't be tested without more study, without further calculations. But if it succeeded...

The launching area was cleared of personnel, the gantry was retracted and countdown begun. The president had sent General Holger Toftoy, Director of the Ordnance Missile Laboratories, to observe, and to keep a watchful eye on von Braun. Von Braun's previous links to the German SS and his use of slave labor in the building of the V-2 rocket made the scientist controversial at best. His brilliance made him indispensible, but he had to kept on a short lease. General Toftoy now stood behind von Braun as the countdown neared its dramatic final sequence:

"Five...four...three...two...one...lift off!"

A rush of super-heated vapor erupted around the base of the rocket, nearly obscuring the blinding inferno of burning rocket fuel that pushed the enormous bulk of the missile away from Mother Earth. It rose slowly in the first minutes, only inches, then a few feet. A great monster rising from the depths of hell, suspended impossibly, raging with an ear-shattering roar, then gaining momentum, shaking and scorching the earth as it shot upward—it was off! There arose a cheer from the control room staff. Cameras were angled to follow the vehicle up through the clouds; a diminishing flare still visible to the naked eye. A glorious sight.

Then, the Redstone buckled and fell, striking the first stage. The fireball lit up the Florida sky like a second sun. Burning rocket fuel and shrapnel rained down, falling into the ocean and sending up geysers of steam.

General Toftoy snapped at von Braun: "Werner, why did the rocket explode?"

"It exploded," answered von Braun, "because the damn sonofabitch blew up!"

# 14

## The Vicious Circle

There was little need for a governing body among the aliens. Centuries of confined travel had necessitated mutual cooperation, division of labor, and strict adherence to protocol. This diverse society of multiple races could only have survived the hazards of space as a unit with a logical social order whose primary aim was that survival. Yet, the seeds of racial vanity and conceit had been planted deeply in those long-ago days of the civil war over slavery; megalomania was sprouting in a fertile soil of narcissism. The realization that they were on the brink of extinction, should they fail to acquire the life-giving resources of the planet below, had fostered an arrogant desire for power among many—especially the restless Nordics who mistrusted the Greys and were irked by their apparent assumption of authority.

No central government, no dictatorial leaders, no dynasties of rule by divine right: these were concepts unknown and unthinkable to the Klivpoklaians. But disagreements did arise and so the Circle was formed to act as a sort of Supreme Court in matters affecting the survival of these beings, the last members of a dead planet. The Circle was composed of three representatives from each of the four races. Their given names were not used during meetings in order to achieve an anonymous and ordinary status; to give them an "everyman" persona in an attempted elimination of political bias. They believed they realized fairness in all considerations, but of course, the very structure of equal representation presupposed that the ideal of fairness was not predestined. There would always need to be negotiation and compromise. And therefore, politics.

The Nordics (the Aimnegarwfuchee) were known as Aim/1, Aim/2, and Aim/3. The Greys (Ratiessrvedflynach) were designated as Rat/1, Rat/2, and Rat/3. The Reptilians (Matofnblotjuupz) were called Mat/1, Mat/2, and Mat/3. Which left the Little Green Men (Syktijthraxteraq) as Syk/1, Syk/2, and Syk/3. This system of nomenclature greatly simplified things as the representatives were regularly replaced in a rotation chosen by lots; the concept of elections was alien…to the aliens.

Even the Circle member who was to run the meeting was chosen by chance. As they sat together in, of course, a circle, before them was a low table upon which two objects were spinning, much like an earth child's toy top; one with three sides, the other with four. The symbols etched on the sides of the objects would be meaningless to describe here, but the combination of the sides facing upward, once the tops ceased their rotations and fell over, indicated the name of the Circle member to be chosen. On this particular occasion, the honor fell to Syk/2, a "Little Green Man" of slight stature but determined bearing. The Nordic delegation shifted uncomfortably in their seats, but did not object. Perhaps a thought passed among them that was shielded from the others. This was not apparent, but it would not have surprised anyone as the animosity that the Nordics held for the Green Men had never been disguised.

Languages of the races, those of ancient origins, were supplanted by a universal amalgamation of word-thoughts similar in purpose to Earth's Esperanto. Verbal communication was frowned upon, even considered crass and rude. Certainly, words were open to interpretation and easily misunderstand, especially given the undertones of emotion with which they could be delivered. Therefore, the Circle only communicated by thought patterns. These could be shielded, blocked, and directed at specific individuals but these techniques were usually discouraged in high-level confabs.

The table was cleared away and replaced by three seating cubes to be used by the witnesses that the Circle would interview. These were soon occupied by three Greys: the aged scientist, Klmneezji-aldu, his ward, Hmnogykwaer (the rebellious Grey who was helping Nate to escape), and Utskolggvjiyz, the group leader and overseer of the human unit. Syk/2 addressed the other members of the Circle, blocking his thoughts from the witnesses:

"We have come together to consider the program of cloning of hybrid Klivpokla/Humans. There are doubtless other issues here, which we will discuss in all due course, but I urge you to focus now on evaluating the prospects of success, failure, cost of resources, and consequences to the purity of our races."

"Yes," interrupted Aim/1, an unusually tall Nordic who had been fidgeting throughout the introduction, "indeed the purity of race is at stake. When Ratiessrvedflynachs are given sole authority over the process, is it not apparent that results will be skewed in their favor?"

"This was determined by random as is our custom," answered Syk/2 sharply (if a thought pattern can be said to be sharp). "It was fortuitous that the eminent scientist, Klmneezji-aldu was chosen, for it was he who originated the hybrid cloning theory. He sits before us now, so you, Aim/1, will have ample opportunity to question him about your concerns."

"We have similar concerns," said the Reptilian, Mat/3, one of only three female aliens in the Circle. "How is it that the few successes have involved the mating of human and Ratiessrvedflynachian genes, and the many failures have been with samples taken from Matofnblotjuupzs?"

"And from Syktijthraxteraqs," echoed Syk/1.

Rat/1 interjected the following in support of the Greys: "Klmneezji-aldu and his staff have taken over the burden of collection and conservation of the human samples as has been their assigned duty. They have acted fairly in the testing process, as I am sure these witnesses will attest. We must point out that the Aimnegarwfuchee have embarked upon their own project of collections, without the authority of this Circle. This seems at best to be counter-productive, and at worse, a politically motivated ploy to gain power."

Syk/2 now raised his hand with two slender fingers arched in the symbolic gesture that signaled an end to the private discussion. "Let us now inquire for facts from these witnesses," he said. "Aim/1, you may begin the questioning as you have voiced the strongest concerns."

"He means inquisition," said Rat/1 sending his shielded thought to the other Ratiessrvedflynachs.

Hmnogykwaer had observed the subtle facial gestures of the Circle members which betrayed their otherwise masked conversation.

He could not know what the content of that conversation was, but he could guess. He feared, not unnecessarily, that his collaboration with the human called Nate had been discovered. That circumstance, however, would have been dealt with directly—and drastically. It would not have entailed the convening of the Circle. For the moment, Hmnogykwaer tried to relax and wait to learn exactly why the three of them had been summoned.

"Klmneezji-aldu," Aim/1 addressed the scientist, "we acknowledge the excellent work you have done in fertility and cloning. Without the strides you have made, meager though they are, our races would surely be doomed to extinction. We have asked you here with reference to the hybrid program and we wish you to give us reasons not to curtail what some perceive as a dead end and a waste of resources. Can you comment on this?"

Klmneezji-aldu flinched noticeably. His extreme age had endowed him with the ability to read between the lines, so to speak, of word-thoughts and glean hidden agendas therein—although the inference in Aim/1's statement was hardly hidden. He shook any thoughts of intrigue from his mind and answered:

"The only 'dead end' that has appeared in our researches has been in the area of fertility. We have been unable to achieve viability in the great numbers of those who are sterile. We have harvested, as you know, the sperm and eggs from the few who can still produce them and have stored these to produce future generations…but this is inadequate to insure the survival of our species. Hence the cloning program was instituted.

"Our success rate has been discouraging although any day now there may be a breakthrough. It so happened that in experimenting with human subjects from the planet below we discovered we could clone them from artificially fertilized zygotes…something we had not been able to do with our own stored material. This suggested that something in their genetic makeup was significant. We attempted to develop a hybrid and were eventually successful.

"Statistically, cloning success rates are as follows: about 3% from fertilized eggs produced by non-sterile Klivpoklaians, only 1.5% from artificially fertilized Klivpoklaian embryos, and nearly 25% from human embryos. When we create hybrids of both sexes and harvest from them sperm and eggs to create zygotes we are able to achieve a cloning success rate of 9.75%. And we can do better. This is the reason to continue to pursue this program of hybrid research."

"But there are two issues here," said Aim/1. "First, you are talking not about extending the future of the Klivpoklaian races, but of an impure, half-breed, artificial creation. Second, you have been working almost exclusively with Ratiessrvedflynachian genetic material…your own race. I would maintain that this practice smacks of racist imperialism. How do you answer this charge?"

"With all due respect, there would never be a circumstance in which a Ratiessrvedflynachian would foster the survival of his own race at the sacrifice of the others. Perhaps an Aimnegarwfucheeian…"

At this, the Circle leader, Syk/2, held up two fingers in a gesture indicating that all discussion be ended. Political bickering would lead nowhere, he knew. Yet Aim/1 had raised a valid question…two in fact. Why create a race of half-breeds? And why were the results of the experiments primarily Ratiessrvedflynachian/Human? He pressed Klmneezji-aldu for the answers.

"As to the first question," said Klmneezji-aldu, "there are genetic differences between our four races which contribute to the success or failure of hybrid production. It is perhaps ironic that the humans, who have many races, are yet compatible genetically such that their mating interracially is possible, while we are incapable of this. It turns out that the humans and Ratiessrvedflynachians are much more compatible genetically than are humans and our other races. Thus we have concentrated our studies accordingly. This is not politically motivated…it is only practical.

"As to the second question, our ultimate goal is not to sustain a hybrid race, but through successive interbreeding to filter out the human genetic elements to the extent that a nearly pure Klivpoklaian will result. This will take many generations. It is my view that this is the only solution to the survival of our planetary lines."

Hmnogykwaer smiled broadly at his mentor. Good answer, he thought…maybe too good. There was no way to predict how the Circle would vote, but the logic, and the facts, pointed to the continuation of the hybrid program. Good for Klmneezji-aldu…bad for Earth. That answer had confirmed what Hmnogykwaer had suspected all along: that the human race was destined for extinction once the Klivpoklaians got a foothold on their planet. Why he had a soft spot in his heart(s) he didn't know. He just did.

"We will consider your testimony and will let you know our decision all in good time," said Syk/2. "Now we turn to another issue. For this we would like to hear from the Head of Human Conservations, Utskolggvjiyz." He addressed the overseer: "Please give us your report on the mental controls of the humans."

Head of Human Conservation, thought Hmnogykwaer? When did that happen? Utskolggvjiyz was now the one to squirm in his seating cube.

"We are able," he began, "to place thought images in the humans' minds and to retrieve a certain amount of sensations and word-thoughts from them. Using this technique we can convince them of their safety and happiness and of our benevolence toward them. This seems to work in almost all cases."

"Almost?" queried Aim/1. "This has been a concern ever since our attempts to influence the human leaders failed. The one called 'Eisenhower' was particularly difficult to work with, according to our ambassador."

"It is crucial that we improve our mind control over these beings," added Syk/2. "The humans have developed weapons against which we have no defense. Worse, they appear to be on the brink of destroying each other with these devastating weapons and contaminating the planet with radioactivity. Even if they manage to refrain from self-destruction in this manner, they are well on the way to polluting their planet and bringing about environmental chaos. It is unlikely they will develop intellectually and emotionally soon enough to avoid what amounts to species suicide. We must intercede if we are to inherit a useable planet. What can you tell us about these humans you seem unable to control?"

"That's just it. I can't tell you anything. This is why I requested that you summon Hmnogykwaer. He has been working closely with one of the humans whose mind is blocked from us. Ask him your questions."

Oh boy, here it comes, thought Hmnogykwaer. Syk/2 now directed his thoughts at Hmnogykwaer:

"You have been working with this human? In what way? With what success?"

"I have not been able to probe his mind, nor to place thought images in it. I have been trying to communicate in other ways," answered Hmnogykwaer. Now he must tread ever so carefully. "I believe I can learn his verbal language or at least enough of it to make a case for his cooperation."

"But would this work on someone like the Eisenhower being? Haven't we tried verbal language with him?"

"To answer your question," interjected Aim/1, "our ambassador communicated in this way using a human as a sort of an interpreter, by placing thoughts in the human's mind and causing him to verbalize them to the Eisenhower. It was not effective."

"There is a thing," said Hmnogykwaer, "that the humans call 'psychology.' This can be used to control them, but it takes some time to implement. We need to study this more. That is what I have been trying to do with the human."

"And how will you proceed?" Syk/2 wanted to know.

"There is something the humans like. They follow it like a religion, but a religion which gives them pleasure. It is called 'baseball.' I think it can be used to control them if it is offered, and taken away…in the same manner you might train a Plablikz to sit up or roll over."

"And how will you get this baseball? Can we bring it up from the planet or create one in our laboratory?"

"This will require more study. I am doing my best, but it will take some time. These humans are very intelligent, you know. Not just stupid Ahtejiqs as we once thought."

"Very good, Hmnogykwaer," said Syk/2. "You are to proceed with your study of this human. You three will leave us now as we need to discuss all that we have heard today."

As Hmnogykwaer left the Circle chamber he breathed a sigh of relief. Had he really pulled it off? Perhaps. But this Utskolggvjiyz, with his new title of Head of Human Conservation…he seemed suspicious. Time to watch one's step. Time to move the time line up a bit. Time to give Nate Mirko his next instructions.

Nate was in the laboratory with Hmnogykwaer a few days later. Hmnogykwaer was anxious to bring the human up to date with his new plan. He described what had occurred at the Circle, at least so far as it concerned Nate and their escape plan.

"Baseball? You told them about baseball?" Nate asked.

"I had a sort of stroke, as you call it," Hmnogykwaer began.

"A stroke! Hmno! That's awful. Are you okay?"

"No...no...I mean I had a stroke of genius, as you call it. The baseball...don't you see? I needed something to extend my time working with you and the others who are mind-blocked against us. You don't know how disastrous the consequences might be if they decide to terminate the program! So I remembered a part of Noreen's memories that I had scanned. She was at baseball...a huge arena with many humans in a sort of religious gathering complete with an obscure ritual that nobody on the Circle would ever understand. It was perfect."

"I still don't get it. How does that help us?"

"I've gotten permission to allow you to do baseball. It is like a form of training we use with pets...offer a treat, take it away...and so forth. And if I have an accurate picture in my mind of baseball...it happens out of doors, correct?"

"Ah! We go out to play baseball and make a run for the saucer!"

"Almost. Don't get ahead of me, please. There are many details to be worked out. Tell me more about baseball. What would you need to do it?"

"Well, there are two teams each with nine players on the field and waiting to bat. We need a ball, a bat. We need a big park..."

"No. Too many. Too complicated. Can you not do baseball with just the four we have said we will take?"

"Um...I guess so. Pitcher, catcher, batter and fielder. Could we have a first baseman? Five? We could work with that. There is another man who came here very recently who appears to be blocked. His name is Resnik. Do you know this one?"

"I will examine him, but I can't promise anything. My idea is to find a suitable space on one of the levels...it will have to be a city level, not a garden level which has no such space, and this complicates matters considerably. I'll have to devise a plan to take you across it to the saucer port. For the time being, we will go do baseball for several days, always returning to the compound. It is essential that you control the others. Keep them from thinking about running once they are outside. It must look innocent."

"And Noreen? Will you unblock her?"

"I will need her to act as an interpreter. This will be a subterfuge so that no one suspects you and I can converse in spoken language. I will put thoughts into her mind which she will communicate to you and visa versa. So we cannot unblock her until the very last moment."

"I don't like it."

"I can put a post-hypnotic suggestion in her mind which will unlock it upon hearing a code word. You can use this code word when I tell you it is time. I will use the word, 'rutabagas.' "

"Rutabagas? Why rutabagas?"

"I gleaned from her that this is a vegetable that she dislikes. Also, it is unlikely anyone will use that word in a conversation with her."

"Ha. Rutabagas!"

# 15

## Buy Me Some Peanuts and Crackerjack
## (I Don't Care If I Never Get Back)

Hmnogykwaer had found a small park near the gravity tube outlet on level 12. He had brought the five aliens down one by one as the tube wasn't large enough for more than one passenger at a time. To his dismay, Utskolggvjiyz, the overseer, accompanied them and stood guard over the first ball players as the rest slowly joined them. Utskolggvjiyz would undoubtedly be an impediment to the plan and would make communicating verbally with Nate an impossibility.

Nate had specified the equipment they would need, beginning with a ball about the size and weight of an Earth softball. No gloves would be available so this seemed the logical choice to avoid injury when catching the ball. The ball was fabricated in one of the aliens' laboratories, as was the equivalent of a hickory wood bat—carved from one of the exotic plant vines—and complete with a decal which read "Louisville Slugger," a detail whose significance escaped the aliens.

Home plate, the pitcher's mound, and first base were marked out on the moss-covered ground. Noreen, using thought images, explained the rules of the makeshift baseball game to Hmnogykwaer and Utskolggvjiyz. The players would rotate through the positions, each getting an opportunity to bat and score a run to first base. Three strikes would be an out; four balls would be a walk, just like in a real game. If the fielder caught the ball, that would constitute an out. If he or she fielded the ball on a bounce but was able to throw it to the pitcher before the runner reached first base, that would also be an out.

The aliens had no team sports of their own, nor any athletic activity involving balls. The chief exercise regime for the Klivpoklaians was the practice of Rikthijmb, a solo sword form not unlike Tai Chi on Earth. This had a spiritual aspect, reminding them of their connection to nature—ironic during the eon-long space journey during which nature had become a vague memory—yet symbolic and meaningful for the practitioner. Each movement represented something: the passage of clouds across the mountains, the flight of Zlthmogs (airborne creatures similar to Earth birds but reptilian), the rush of water falling from great heights, and so forth. Although this was not a competitive sport, there was always the image of an invisible opponent before them with whom the practitioner fenced. The two aliens, as they watched the humans playing, were both confounded and fascinated by the human's strange game.

Nate, being the catcher during this rotation, approached the pitcher's mound where O'Bannon was warming up his underarm throw. Noreen had explained to the aliens that this type of personal conference between pitcher and catcher was a common game strategy, and Nate was able to take advantage of this fact to talk to the Navy man privately.

"It is essential," Nate said, "that you and the others make no attempt to escape during these game sessions. Don't even give the appearance of thinking about it. We have to get the aliens to trust us out here. Our time will come...but not now."

"Roger that. I'm worried, however, about my little buddy, Resnik. I think he may try to bag ass out of here. See how he's scanning the horizon like he's on watch spotting enemy ships?"

"Talk to him. And trust me on this, O'Bannon. This may look like a golden opportunity, but it is only half a plan. Let me work on it. Tell the others to keep a cool head and just enjoy the outdoor recreation while they can."

Nate returned to his position as catcher. The batter was Noreen.

Her first swing missed the ball. Strike one! How he wished to whisper the word in her ear that would release her from her mind-control! He couldn't just now. Her reaction might give the plot away. He threw the ball back to O'Bannon. The pitch, a swing and a miss. Strike two! His heart ached for the days before all of this abduction business had so changed their lives. He missed his mother. He missed the blossoming romance with Noreen that had brightened his days. He even missed Harry Bertram, his cantankerous boss at Honest Harry's Deluxe Used Cars. How much simpler life had been!

The pitch. The swing. Noreen connected! The ball arched up over O'Bannon's head, over Millender's head in the outfield. She reached first base easily before the ball could be returned to O'Bannon. One point for Noreen. Everyone rotated, Nate moving up to bat, Noreen to pitch, O'Bannon to field, Millender to first base and Resnik to catch. Nate couldn't help being reminded of his childhood days playing sandlot ball back in Bellingham. How bizarre, he thought…we're playing baseball on the moon!

The game continued. A short distance from the park was an apartment building, seven stories high, shaped like a truncated pyramid and speckled with balconied widows. On the balconies, residents of the building were emerging, curious about the goings on below. Most had never seen a human and were only vaguely aware of their existence. No one was as yet brave enough to venture outside and observe the spectacle up close. In the days that followed, however, as the baseball game became a common daily event, children from the building began to approach the outskirts of the park—cautiously at first, then boldly seating themselves on the ground along the periphery of the playing field.

Most of the children were of the Grey race, a few were Nordic and one was Reptilian—no Greens were among the onlookers. They were transfixed by the game and soon caught onto its rules. It was only a matter of time before one child approached and stood staring at Nate, who was playing first base at the time. After a few moments, Nate realized the child was "thinking at him." He called to Noreen:

"See what this child wants, will you?" he asked.

Noreen did so and faced Nate with the kind of smile on her face that Nate had been missing since their days on Earth. "They want to know if they can play," she said.

This was going to complicate matters even further, Nate realized.

He looked at Hmnogykwaer for some sort of decision. Hmnogykwaer gave the Ratiessrvedflynach equivalent of a shrug and sent a thought image to Noreen. "Let them play," he instructed.

## Bellingham, Washington, October 15, 1954

Mrs. Laura McCredie was worried about Hazel—Hurricane Hazel, that is. Hazel had begun ten days ago in the Lesser Antilles as a tropical storm and had developed rapidly into a tropical cyclone. She had maintained a small "eye" as she streamed across Grenada and entered the Caribbean Sea. But by October 8 her eye had expanded and she presented winds of 125 miles per hour. On the 10th she turned and made landfall along the northwest coast of Haiti. Flash floods destroyed several villages and hurricane-force winds ripped through cities. As many as 1,000 people may have been killed by the storm; 100,000 were made homeless. Hazel strengthened as she rolled across the Gulf Stream and headed for the coastal regions of North and South Carolina.

Yes, Mrs. Laura McCredie was worried about Hurricane Hazel. Her daughter, Lynette, together with her husband Ralph and their two year-old daughter Elizabeth, were vacationing at Myrtle Beach. Hazel was headed directly toward that resort area. Mrs. McCredie telephoned the hotel to try to reach her daughter but was told that all the lines were busy. She was frantic.

Things had been strange and confusing for Mrs. McCredie ever since her neighbors, Beverly Mirko and son, Nathaniel, had disappeared. That nice live-in nurse was gone too—although Heaven knew that she, Laura McCredie, had been more than able to take care of Beverly Mirko by herself. Land o' Goshen! Beverly had been a bit addlebrained, it was true, but never presented a problem that she couldn't handle—no need for extra help. Well, the boy, Nate, had had a roving eye where the nurse was concerned, that was plain as day. But now the empty house was just eerie. Spooky. And sad.

Why wouldn't the phone lines open up? She had to get through. The television news was already reporting that Hazel was throwing ten-foot waves up along the coast. She had destroyed two piers at Myrtle Beach. Numerous residences, including a 3-story hotel, had been washed out to sea! Not the hotel Lynette was staying at, thank

God…that was further inland. Couldn't afford the fancy places. And now that it looked like God was punishing the rich (for what sins Mrs. McCredie didn't know—but that didn't much matter), why it was a blessing to be poor—or at least not to be rich.

The films on TV showed palm trees bending over double in the fierce torment. Sheets of water cut like knives through flimsy buildings, flinging metal signs and roofing material aside like leaves. Electric lines fell sparking into flooded streets. The reporter stated that 75 homes had been destroyed at Cherry Grove Beach and another 40 at Pawleys Island. North Carolina was the next to be accosted. At Long Beach 352 buildings virtually disappeared beneath raging sea and devastating wind.

President Eisenhower declared it to be a major disaster and pledged immediate aid. The American Red Cross was already assisting the Haitian Red Cross with donations of money, but a typhoid fever epidemic was about to ravish survivors on that once idyllic island. It looked like Hazel wasn't going to dissipate any time soon. She would, in fact, charge across Virginia, West Virginia, Maryland, Delaware, New Jersey, Pennsylvania, and New York maintaining her hurricane strength winds and dropping heavy rains which would flood the Canadian city of Toronto. The damage and death toll was so high that her name, Hazel, would be retired and no future storm could use it.

Yes, Mrs. Laura McCredie was worried.


## Project Blue Book: Unexplained Sightings
## September and October, 1954

In Butler, Missouri, on September 4, a CAA communications specialist named J. Faltemeier witnessed 23 lights in the sky, arranged as if on a string, flying straight and level for one and a half minutes. On the following night he observed "one silver or white object with a slightly swept-back leading edge and a following exhaust" flying straight and level, then veering off south to southwest after 30 seconds. A private pilot, J. N. Williams, along with E. J. Ash, in Marshfield, Missouri, on September 22, said they saw "a thin, translucent tan asymmetrical boomerang-shaped object" which revolved, then tumbled down behind the trees. It left visible marks.

Two California policemen, four US Marine Corps Policemen, and one California Highway Patrolman in Barstow, California, witnessed a red-orange ball giving off sparks, along with a smaller lighted object. This occurred on September 21. As they watched, the objects descended, zigzagged, then hovered during the 20 minute event. In Gatlingburg, Tennessee, on September 23, David Owenby saw two bright silver, wheel-shaped objects fly north to south with one trailing the other. On the nights of October 15, 16, and 17 in Kingfisher, Oklahoma, witnesses reported seeing 50 objects with illuminated bottoms flying quite fast in a V-formation.

There were other unexplained UFO sightings during that two month period: in Kimpo Air Base, Korea, at the Santa Maria Airport in Azores, in Nouasseur, French Morocco, at the Miho Air Base, Japan, and again in the Azores. Captain Charles Hardin, in command of Project Bluebook was not happy. He and his two-person staff were stretched much too thin to adequately debunk every report that came across their desks.

Hardin's objectives were premised on the recommendations (read orders) of the Robertson Panel. This panel of physicists, missile experts and nuclear scientists had been formed in 1953 under the auspices of the Intelligence Advisory Committee and the CIA in order to review the Air Force's UFO files. They had reviewed, among other things, two motion pictures: the Mariana UFO Incident taken in 1950 in Great Falls, Montana, and the 1952 Utah UFO Film taken by naval photographer Chief Warrant Officer Delbert C. Newhouse. The panel concluded that 1) there was no evidence that the objects were related to space travel, and 2) that there was no evidence of any direct threat to national security by the objects.

The panel stated, however, that dangers did exist in the *reporting* of such UFOs such that actual enemy artifacts might be misidentified, emergency reporting channels might be overloaded with false information, and that the public, subject to mass hysteria, could become vulnerable to enemy psychological warfare. Therefore they recommended that debunking, to result in a reduction of public interest in flying saucers and other such phenomena, should be undertaken with great zeal. The panel suggested "That the national security agencies take immediate steps to strip the Unidentified Flying Objects of the special status they have been given and the aura of mystery they have unfortunately acquired."

However, there was just not enough swamp gas to go around. Several sightings every month went unexplained. The newspapers picked up on the ones involving pilots, military personnel, or civilian police, who were assumed to be dispassionate witnesses. Harding was continually under fire from some very important people. It was just too bad there wasn't something to take the public's minds off of UFOs for a while. Maybe a nice hot war…like the one brewing in Southeast Asia.

## Back on the Moon

There were now two baseball teams on level 12. Each had either two or three humans and a few Nordics mixed in with the Grey children who made up most of the roster. The single Reptilian child was eagerly sought after by the captains of the two teams. He was apparently a switch hitter and able to send the ball out of the small park when he connected. Now, with adequate creature-power, the game was expanded to three basemen, three outfielders, and a short stop. After a day or two of confused play, the alien children began to understand the concept of team sports and the cry of "Batter! Batter! Batter!" could be heard (although in the thought-transferred Klivpoklaian language). Moms and dads came to watch and cheer for their offspring. It was as American as zlthmog pie.

"Too bad we can't take some of these little buggers back to Earth," said O'Bannon to Nate as they waited to bat. "They'd soon be in the minors. That lizard, especially. He'd give Ted Williams a run for his money."

"Maybe," answered Nate, "we're doing more for human-alien relations than all the diplomats in the world could ever do. There's something universal about our national past time."

A sudden nostalgia overcame Nate. His thoughts harkened back to this year's season: Stan Musial hitting five home runs in the doubleheader between the Cardinals and the Giants; White Sox pitcher Jack Harshman striking out 16 batters to win against Boston; the Milwaukee Braves' no-hitter against the Phillies—the greats: Joe DiMaggio, Bob Lemon, Willie Mays, Yogi Berra, Hank Aaron, Bob Feller, Roy Campanella, Ernie Banks!

The game was going well. There were base hits on both sides, pop flies were fielded expertly, bases were stolen; all in all the alien kids played energetically and seemed to be having the times of their lives. There was none of the distracting banter or booing that sometimes characterized a Little League game on Earth...no antagonism among the parents. Only a shared joy at the novelty of this new thing, this gift from the humans, this diversion from the monotony and pointlessness of living in an artificial world. Living in a bubble that could burst at any moment should the fragile ecosphere fail. Living with uncertainty sustained only by the slim hope that the humans' world would become their own—but how, and when?

Andrew Millender, the Marine, was pitching. The Reptilian, a boy named Hfvueqroztina, was up to bat. Chris Resnik was in center field. Noreen played catcher. Nate and O'Bannon were in the batting lineup. There were two outs and two "men" on base. The score was tied, 8 to 8. It was the top of the ninth inning. Millender considered walking the Reptilian. Still, that would load the bases and a hit by the next batter would bring in at lest one run, maybe more. He decided to try his fast ball, something he had been famous for back in the day...*way* back in the day. Well, it was worth a try. He wound up, and let fly what he hoped would clear the strike zone before the "lizard" could complete his swing.

Hfvueqroztina connected. There was sharp crack as the bat, hewn from a pflematap vine, split length-wise. The ball arced up, up, up, and over Resnik's head. The centerfielder turned to run after it but it was clearly headed out of the park. The park, so called, was defined by the limits of the moss-covered field which was surrounded by apartment buildings and, at the furthest edge of center field, a high fence of some synthetic material resembling dull metal but soft like gel. Resnik approached this fence, running a bit too fast to stop, and collided with it. It gave and toppled over, spilling Resnik out into an alley that ran along one of the buildings.

At first he looked around for the ball, then (had he been a cartoon character, a bright light bulb would have appeared above his head) he ran up the alley. This led him to a series of crossings of narrow alleyways and streets like a maze with no discernable solution. But Resnik was undaunted. He took the first turning that offered him a path that stretched into the distance; others were cul-de-sacs or dead ends. In no time at all he was far from the ball field. With nowhere to go. With no prospect for a successful escape. But the adrenaline pumping through his veins and the idea that at long last he was *doing something*, spurred him on.

Noreen had seen him take off up the alley. Apparently neither of the alien overseers had noticed, being more involved in cheering on the Reptilian, who was leisurely trotting around the bases. Noreen pulled Nate aside, a worried look on her face.

"Nate!" she said. "Resnik has run off. We have to go and tell Utskolggvjiyz."

"I'm still amazed," Nate answered, "that you can pronounce that name. But no, we don't have to tell him anything."

"But Nate, it's our duty. If you won't come with me, I'll go alone. Resnik is getting further and further away! Please come with me."

"Noreen, please wait a moment. This is wrong. You won't believe me, so...I have to say something to you."

"What? You want to tell me you love me? I know that. So what? We..."

"Noreen, listen carefully." Nate said one word: "Rutabagas."

# 16

## Resnik's Run

He had taken a wrong turn and now found himself staring at a blank wall which rose up many stories above him and blocked the narrow avenue. The buildings on both sides of the street looked abandoned, their once shining walls seemingly corroded with a dull grey stain. Yet from open windows on the floors above waved torn cloth which he took for curtains. Perhaps these tenements were occupied by some disenfranchised elements of the aliens' races…much as the slums of Earth housed the poor, the desperate, the sick, the elderly. And the criminal? Had he unknowingly wandered into a quarter where danger lurked on every corner?

Resnik retraced his steps back to the last junction where alleys crisscrossed and twisted through the canyons of the city. He had no goal but to keep on the move, certain that *they* were pursuing him. He had been a captive of both the Nordics and the Greys. He wasn't going to return to those circumstances if he could help it.

The streets and alleyways he had traveled since leaving the baseball game had been deserted. But now, as he followed a new route, the avenue broadened, and he could see ahead of him aliens walking or standing in doorways. These creatures noticed him, but made no move toward him. In fact, it seemed to Resnik that they were ignoring him. They seemed oblivious to his presence. It was as if seeing an Earthman wandering through their neighborhood was a common occurrence, one that had no particular significance to their lives.

Nervously, he passed along the crowded street. A Grey turned away from him, perhaps repulsed by his appearance: his slight stature relative to theirs, his ruddy complexion, his small eyes—what? He wasn't *that* different from them, was he? He had two arms, two legs, he walked upright. But his mind was blocked to them...perhaps that was it. He was like a deaf, dumb, and blind person to them. An imperfect entity to be shunned. Well, on Earth such an outcast might be ridiculed or bullied. Being different was a cause for intolerance back home. Here you just turned your head.

Presently he came to an intersection of three major roads. At its center was a park, not with trees and grass, but paved with fine gravel and lined with low bushes. All around the park were aliens with hand carts and larger wagons heaped with what Resnik assumed were fruits and vegetables—by the variety of colors and shapes, it was difficult to tell. Some aliens were approaching this market carrying long sacks while others were leaving, their sacks stuffed with goods. Resnik watched but he could not see money changing hands. The aliens simply walked up to a cart and picked out what they wanted. This was fortunate for Resnik as he was getting hungry. Could he also take what he wanted?

There were two problems with his plan: he had no way to communicate with the vendors as his mind was blocked and they shared no verbal language; and as he observed the shopping more closely, he became aware that, although no money changed hands, the alien shoppers bared their arms to reveal what appeared to be tattoos—this must have been their method of showing their credit or the degree to which they deserved to receive the fruits and vegetables. To test his theory he walked up to one of the smaller carts and gestured at a piece of fruit (or vegetable). The vendor stared at him. Resnik tried to indicate that he could not mind-speak. He rubbed his forehead and shook his head. The alien vendor just kept staring. When he became so bold as to reach for and grab one of the items, the vendor came around the cart and wrenched it away from him. Then the alien pushed him away. This clearly was not going to work.

For the first time in his life Resnik felt like a bum...a street person with no means of support. He lingered, hoping that someone would drop a piece of fruit. The afternoon was waning (soon this would be indicated by a change in the artificial lighting from the usual sickly greenish tint to a darkening mauve—inside the habitat there was no sun to rise and set, no moon, of course, because they were standing on it). Vendors began packing up and moving their carts and wagons from the park.

There had been aliens of all four races at the market either providing goods or acquiring them. This was the first time Resnik had seen members of the Syktijthraxteraq, the race of aliens Earthlings called the Little Green Men. One such creature pushed a hand cart past where Resnik stood. As it bumped over a curb at the edge of the park, a wheel fell off and the cart tipped over. The diminutive Syktijthraxteraq jumped up and down and began uttering growls and other noises that indicated his extreme displeasure with the spilled cart.

Resnik didn't hesitate. He retrieved the wheel, which had rolled down the avenue, and affixed it to the axle of the cart. He pulled a piece of woody material from one of the bushes and thrust this onto the axle at the point where the wheel sat, achieving a temporary repair. Then he began picking up the vendor's wares and replacing them in the cart. The Green watched, stunned that anyone would help him in his predicament. Resnik was aware that the Green was "thinking" at him. Again he mimicked his brain-block with gestures.

The Green took a fruit from his cart and offered it to Resnik. He took it and bit into it. Sweet juices gushed forth and spilled down his front. It was the most delicious thing he had ever eaten; he attacked it eagerly. He finished the fruit as the astounded Green watched, then Resnik looked into the alien's face with a smile on his own and said, "I know you can't understand what I'm sayin' but I just want to thank you for this."

Then something happened that would change Resnik's prospects for the better, at least for a time. He felt thoughts enter his mind…word thoughts and picture thoughts, vague, but real. He would certainly have discounted this under ordinary circumstances, but he knew about the aliens' ability to place thoughts in human minds. Had he suddenly become unblocked? He uttered, "What the…" and a more comprehensive thought took hold of him:

"When you speak in sound patterns I am able to probe your mind for meanings. This is astounding to me as I have never experienced anything like it before. I can sense that you are unable to send thought images back to me, but if you speak in your verbal language I will understand you. This effect allows me to target the area of your brain you use to form word symbols and manipulate them. This way we can talk to each other."

Of course, Resnik only sensed the concepts presented above—not in human language—the Green was not good enough—yet—to articulate detailed thoughts. But it was a beginning. Resnik replied:

"I see. I need to speak to you out loud so you can read my thoughts. Hot dog! This is the coolest!"

"I don't understand your last images, but I will work on learning. Please come with me. I will take you to my home. We will eat. We will speak. We have much to share with each other."

Resnik followed the Green as he pushed his cart through the narrow alleys that led off from the square like spokes of a wheel. The wheel he had fixed wobbled as it turned; Resnik kept one eye on this, the other on the curious tenements they passed—each a harshly geometric structure with little grace or charm or evidence that life lived happily within. As they progressed further from the market, the condition of the buildings worsened. The grey rust or mildew-like coating on the walls suggested a lack of maintenance and surely indicated extreme age. Yet there was no litter in the streets, no graffiti or other attempts by the denizens to counter the drabness of their environment as would have been the case in an Earth slum.

The Green pulled his cart into a small side alley and collected the remaining fruits (vegetables?) into a sack which he hefted over his shoulder. He led Resnik to a door with opened magically like the parting of a veil. He motioned for him to step into a gravity tube just inside of the building. Resnik did so and soon found himself ascending swiftly to the heights of the tenement. There was only one place to step off from the tube and he did this, and waited for the alien to appear.

"I am on this level," said the Green when he arrived. "My rooms are this way."

The rooms were, as Resnik had suspected, sparse and rather sterile with a lack of decoration and few furnishings. There were no bookshelves, no vases filled with blooms, no pictures on the bare walls. Resnik found a seating cube and settled down onto its gel-like softness. He could have fallen instantly into a deep sleep, so exhausted from his flight was the ex-sailor, and so awed by all he had seen. Ex-sailor...yes. And nearly an ex-human. Did the Green read the thoughts he was now having? Did it understand how utterly alone and frightened he was? How deep was his despair?

"My name," came a thought pattern into Resnik's consciousness, "is Tmptolzogykmn. I get the feeling that you are not from around here. This is all new to you."

"Oh yes," answered Resnik. "I am a (here, although Resnik vocalized the term, 'human,' the alien perceived 'Sjilgezhmian'), from the planet around which this moon circles. My name is Christian Resnik. I was a Seaman Apprentice in our Navy before I was abducted by your (Resnik said 'Nordics' and Tmptolzogykmn translated the thought as 'Aimnegarwfuchees'). I appreciate your hospitality as I am afraid I have wandered off from my group and am somewhat lost."

"I wondered how you came to be at the market. We know so little of what goes on in the (here, the obscure term, 'Glrovaktres,' was assumed by Resnik to mean 'laboratories')."

The Green placed his hand on a certain spot on the side of Resnik's seating cube and it extended to twice its length. "You look tired," he said. "Nap while I go to the food preparation area. Later you may tell me about your world."

Resnik leaned back onto the cube that was now a daybed and closed his eyes. It was the first time he had felt relaxed in a very long time. He slept. Dreams came—not the troubled dreams that had monopolized his captive nights, but tranquil visions of earthscapes that entranced and revitalized the weary dreamer. Vast valleys carpeted with purple aster and golden blanket flower. The cool mirrored surface of a mountain lake reflecting snow-capped peaks like jagged teeth—like the open mouth of Mother Earth turned upward toward the blazing sun. Pine forests of juniper, spruce and yew, singing in wind that gusted and darted and pounded like invisible fists against the ancient growth.

Then came the aroma of roasted meat. A perfume to entice the dreamer to awake; not abruptly, but slowly, happily rested. Hungry. Resnik rose and wandered toward the delightful smells. Kitchen. Table. Small green alien with what must have been an alien smile (square, lipless mouth with thin, needle-like teeth). Resnik sat, took in the presentation of smoldering chunks of…what?

"Eat," said Tmptolzogykmn.

Resnik ate with a relish that seemed to have waited for this moment, hidden away in memories of Mom and apple pie. The flavor of the meat was somewhat akin to chicken with a slightly gamey accent. The texture reminded Resnik of pork bellies: rich and fatty with melt-in-your-mouth goodness.

"This is delicious! What do you call it," Resnik asked.

"It is the very last piece of Gklenmgoeq. I've been saving it for a special occasion."

"Gklenmgoeq? Is that some kind of a bird?"

"Oh no. Gklenmgoeq was my last wife. She died one year ago. You see, we honor those who are deceased by ingesting them. It perpetuates their spirit and completes the cycle of life and death."

Resnik promptly threw up.

"You don't have this custom on your world? No wonder you are spiritually impaired."

"Jesus! I'm sorry. It's just…I haven't eaten anything in a while and my stomach couldn't deal with the richness of the food."

"Christianresnik, you forget I can read your thoughts. I am very much aware of the repulsion you feel about eating a sentient being. While I understand your race does not so honor their dead, I cannot forgive you. You have offended me deeply. This was my wife you splattered all over the table! You must leave my rooms. Now."

"Oh, Gawd! Oh…I'll go. But could you at least point me in the direction of the nearest gravity tube? Oh, crap…I don't even know which level…"

"I will do better than that, Christianresnik. I have sent a thought image to our neighborhood patrol. They will be here any minute to take you…I don't know where. Somewhere dark, cold and cramped…I hope."

"You have a neighborhood patrol? Holy shit!"

Moments later the veil door parted and a Green entered the room. He stood, exchanging thoughts with Tmptolzogykmn, then he approached Resnik. Resnik moved back and instinctively took a defensive stance. The Green stopped, apparently communicating again with Tmptolzogykmn. Tmptolzogykmn mind-spoke to Resnik:

"Don't be afraid. You are in luck, it appears. There has been a notice out about you…they have been looking for you. You are to be returned to the Glrovaktres where you will rejoin your fellow Earthmen. Go with this man. Go in peace and may you someday learn the meaning of dignity."

Resnik followed the Green guard down the gravity tube and out into the street where one of the alien vehicles was waiting. It was a transparent globe just large enough to accommodate two or three individuals of the stature of the Green men. Resnik found himself squeezed into the back of the bubble car as the Green guard took a seat in front. The mechanism by which the Green piloted the car consisted of a spherical object about the size of an orange fastened to a slender post. As the Green pushed or turned the sphere, the car glided along the avenue, inches above the surface. The Green raised the sphere and the bubble car rose up above the level of the buildings.

"Kind of tight quarters here," Resnik commented, but the pilot gave no indication that he had heard, or cared. He can't read my mind, Resnik thought to himself. That's a good thing.

As they gained altitude and swung out over the wide expanse of the habitat's interior, Resnik looked down at the concentric levels built there eons ago: the drab-looking residential and business levels with their narrow streets and geometric buildings; the grazing levels spotted with what looked like cattle, brown against the yellow-green moss; the intricate labyrinth levels of the vegetable gardens, with garish hues of azure and crimson, spots of pale ochre, bloated, dripping purples and the ever twisting stalks of thick vines hung with impossible shapes.

There were other spheres navigating the airspace. They sailed past each other like soap bubbles floating in a gentle wind. Resnik saw a globular shape rear the apex of the habitat—a glowing, sickeningly green blotch that he realized must be the chief light source for the artificial world. Unlike our sun, it could be looked at directly without injury. Unlike our sun, it seemed to cast no shadows, filling every surface, every corner with an even radiance.

This world, sculpted from the metal/plastic/gel substance that everything here seemed to be made from, was shaped like an egg. Its large end contained the varied levels that maintained its ecosphere. The empty space above, thought Resnik, was an afterthought…a nostalgic reference to the long-ago sky of a barely-remembered lost world. He had a sudden inspiration. What if these alien beings could coexist with our own world? They, on the moon, sustained by a technology which had succeeded for centuries to support them; we, on our own planet, aided by the wisdom and the technology of the Klivpoklaians, ending war, ending poverty and hunger, ending pollution; together, creating a diverse inter-culture—what couldn't we achieve together?

\*　\*　\*

It was the end of a not-so-perfect day. Seaman Apprentice Christian Resnik was back. His attempted escape, the others knew, had negated the possibility of a more orderly escape—one that Nate had hinted at but not yet revealed. As Resnik narrated his bizarre experiences with the Green, O'Bannon glared disparagingly. At the end of the tale O'Bannon drew near to him, whispered in his ear: "You sure stepped in the shit this time!"

Nate had spent hours with Noreen, dealing with her shock at awakening from the severe mind-control under which she had been living since being brought to the moon colony. She was like a new born infant, encountering the blinding light of the world for the very first time. She now remembered her enthusiasm for the aliens' plan of conquest of her own world; her rapture at the transformation of humanity…its absorption, its corruption; her joy in the unthinkable partnership whereby her very genetic structure gave hope to the conquerors…she remember all this and she was horrified.

Hmnogykwaer was furious with Nate for having awakened Noreen. Her mind could be probed by other Greys, he told the Earthling, and the secret plan discovered. Utskolggvjiyz, the overseer, was already suspicious. It was premature, but the escape plan would now have to be executed as soon as possible. Hmnogykwaer was still searching for a pilot for the saucer they would steal, someone sympathetic to their cause. A difficult proposition. Nate thought about O'Bannon and Millender, about what they would say. Had it not occurred to the alien to kidnap a pilot and force him to fly the thing to Earth? Sometimes these extraterrestrials had tunnel vision when it came to problem solving.

"Let me bring the others into the plan," Nate told Hmnogykwaer. "Find a qualified pilot and let us do the rest."

Hmnogykwaer was incredulous. However, human ingenuity might yet offer success if he trusted the animal instincts of these pale pink creatures. He thought about the horrific weapons their race had developed. Yes, their propensity toward violent action could be exploited. Risky it was, but he was desperate. And so:

"Give me two sleep-period's time. I will locate a pilot and lure him to the laboratory where you and your fellows will be waiting.

Then we will go."

"One thing…can you procure weapons for us?"

"Can you handle a sword?"

"I'm a fast learner. And I'm sure the others can make do with a sharp blade."

"It is well. I will procure weapons for you. But understand that we…all of us…study the sword form from early childhood. We are experts at rikthijmb."

"No ray guns, I suppose," said Nate, envisioning something that Buck Rogers or Flash Gordon might use.

"Nathanielmirko, there is no such thing as a ray gun!"

# 17

## The Nordic Raid

As Robert Burns once said, "The best laid plans o' mice an' men gang aft agley," or as Hmnogykwaer might put it, "Zheldse baidk qpnals naecen ngatf hajliy pmim." There was a contingent among the Nordics who refused to accept the Circle's ruling that allowed the Greys' dominance over the cloning project. These rebels had done unauthorized abductions and conducted their own experiments, but their pool of human specimens had dwindled due to death and disease. They desperately needed new material.

Just before the hour of the sleep period that would have been called midnight, had there been clocks on the moon, a band of Nordic raiders slipped into the human compound intent on procuring the egg-producers they needed for cloning material—the Earth women.

They had a long metal rod that glowed in the darkness. This was not carried for its illuminative properties, but for its ability to produce vibrations that stunned. With this they were able to subdue Utskolggvjiyz who had been standing guard against just such a dastardly event as this raid. Quickly they went from cubicle to cubicle. Women that they found were wrenched from their beds and herded into the common room; men that woke and fought against them felt the wrath of the stunning rod.

There were six women corralled and shivering in the room, dressed only in the light sleeping clothes they had been issued by the aliens. They clung to each other for warmth as the heat in the common room was turned down during the sleeping periods…down well below the human comfort zone. They clung together in fear for the actions of these aliens, pushing, "yelling" at them in mind-speak, clearly indicated peril.

Among the six were Sally O'Neil, a former private secretary from Indianapolis, Indiana, Sandra Knight, the daughter of a United States Senator whose disappearance had been a major news story earlier in the year, Anita Gonzales, a teacher from the Indian School in Santa Fe, New Mexico, Andrea Goodwin, a high school girl who had disappeared after wandering off during a cheerleading rally for the East Peoria High School Devils' homecoming football game, Iris Walker, a retired librarian from Poughkeepsie, New York, and our own Noreen Ashley.

"What do they want with us?" asked Andrea Goodwin, her usual youthful vigor now eclipsed by trepidation.

Her answer came soon as the Nordics forced them down dark corridors toward a gravity tube and one by one, shoved them into it. After exiting on another level, the women were led to a large, open-topped, barge-like vehicle. Defying gravity, and suspended a foot or so above the floor, it swayed like a moored boat as each woman settled onto its bench-like seats. The aliens followed, sitting on the edges of the barge. One took a seat at the bow, presumably the pilot's seat. Up the impossible airboat rose and out it swung across the vast open space above the living levels of the habitat.

"Where are you taking us?" Noreen mind-spoke to the alien nearest to her.

"Silence!" came the answer. "You will not be harmed…if you cooperate. You are to take part in the glorious reseeding of the Aimnegarwfucheeian Empire."

Glorious reseeding? That didn't sound good to Noreen. Cautiously, she peered over the edge of the airboat. They were skimming several hundred feet above a plain covered with verdant moss and a few scruffy plants that looked like flattened pineapples. Here and there were grazing animals that definitely were not earth-type cattle—they were ahtejiqs, the aliens' meat animals. She could also see a pack of smaller animals on a low hill. She thought of wolves or coyotes, but of course, they were not from Earth. They were akin to the spider-like plablikz that some of the aliens kept as pets. They were phamleblikzs, the ancient ancestors of the plablikz—undomesticated, vicious predators. She saw the pack descend the hill and begin to stalk the grazing ahtejiqs.

The pilot of the air-boat dipped its prow and swooped down toward the pack of phamleblikzs in an effort to scare them away from the ahtejiqs. "Fool!" one of the other Nordics thought at him. "We haven't time for this."

The air-boat suddenly faltered. Had it been an earth-type airplane one might have said the engine stalled. As it was, the anti-gravity generator momentarily failed just long enough to send the airboat plummeting toward the ground. They were spiraling wildly and the airboat began to tip. Two of the Nordics fell from their seats on the side rails and were dashed to the ground. Noreen and the other woman held tightly to the built-in benches. Noreen felt her grip loosening as the airboat swung and tipped and jostled her relentlessly.

The airboat struck the ground on edge. The impact hurled Noreen out across the mossy ground. She was rolling, curled into a protective ball—an instinct gained by her years of doing tumbling and gymnastics in school. When she came to a stop she was dazed, but managed to raise her head and look back toward the crashed airboat. The others had also been thrown from the flying barge. Luckily, because the twisted and broken remains of the vehicle indicated that it too had rolled; fragments were strewn hither and yon and beneath of the bulk of it she could see the limbs and torso of the alien pilot.

The women gathered to assess their situation. Sandra Knight had a badly twisted ankle and needed help walking. Noreen, Anita Gonzales and Andrea Goodwin were shaken and bruised, but otherwise uninjured. Iris Walker had a deep cut along her left leg. Sally O'Neil had ripped a length of cloth from her night clothes to bind the wound and stop the bleeding. Sally seemed to be the least disoriented and, much to Noreen's relief, instantly took charge of the group.

There was one other survivor: a Nordic. The alien was in shock and, Noreen thought, might have some broken bones or internal injuries. It only took a few minutes of discussion for the women to decide that they could not leave the alien. Wherever they managed to go from here they would take him with them. It was the human thing to do.

And go from there they must—the pack of phamleblikzs, at first frightened away by the crash, were now beginning to overcome their fears. The prospect of fresh meat and the smell of blood lured them away from the ahtejiqs and set them on a course toward the women. Slowly they came, flanking out to the sides. Careful, crafty hunters they were. This prey would not escape their wiles.

"Run!" screamed Andrea Goodwin. The teenager leaped to her feet, only to be dragged back down by Sally O'Neil.

"Wait. Don't run. That will only make them charge us. Wasn't there some kind of a weapon these aliens had?"

She shook the injured Nordic. He opened his eyes briefly, then clamped them shut. He would be of no help. Sally crawled to the wreckage of the air-boat. She averted her eyes from the bloody remains of the pilot. There it was: the long tube that could be used to stun. Could she figure out how to use it? Would it be enough against the pack?—there were at least five of the animals. At the very least she could swing it like a club.

The women were huddled together. The phamleblikzs now circled them. They were the size of large dogs but there the resemblance ended. Six hairy legs with barbed talons made them look like giant spiders. Their heads were bulbous and seemed to be all mouth. Their mouths bristled with needle sharp teeth and had loathsome purple tongues that dangled and dripped gruesome saliva on the ground. Their most frightening aspect, however, was their cluster of red, beady eyes that burned with anger and lust.

Sally ran her hands all over the weapon but could find no way to activate it. Slowly the circle of predators tightened. "Damn this thing!" she shouted and slammed the rod against the ground. It lit up, flashing red, green, red, green. The phamleblikzs stopped suddenly, growling.

Sally brandished the weapon now, swinging it at the nearest of the phamleblikzs. The animal snarled and crouched as if to spring. Sally thrust the rod against the beast's head. Miraculously, it collapsed. One down…four to go. The other phamleblikzs backed away, still facing the women with fangs bared.

"Now," said Sally, "might be a good time to run!"

Sandra Knight and Iris Walker needed help to walk and certainly would not be able to run. Noreen and Andrea Goodwin each supported one of the injured women and the four limped slowly away. Noreen looked back over her shoulder, hoping to see the others coming. But Sally and Anita Gonzales stood their ground, protecting the Nordic. Sally had felled another phamleblikz. The other three animals now stood close together and began to advance.

"I can get one more," said Sally. "Then what?"

Anita Gonzales was working on reviving the alien. She made an attempt at artificial respiration, pushing down on the alien's chest and raising his arms. The snarls of the animals grew louder. Anita pounded on the alien's chest with a clenched fist. Suddenly, he coughed. Something liquid and green spurted from his mouth. His eyes opened and he struggled to sit up.

"Oh, help us," Anita thought at him. "Those animals..."

The alien blinked; saw the advancing phamleblikzs; saw Sally brandishing the stun rod. He quickly grabbed the rod from the woman and pointed it at the phamleblikzs. The rod flashed red, orange, yellow. One by one the animals fell, sinking slowly as if they were melting. They lay on the ground twitching. Then they were still. The effort had been too much for the alien. He lay down, breathing in short gasps. His body jerked in spasms. A long, low wail emerged from his mouth; the sound sent shivers up the women's spines. One last jerk and...

"He's gone," said Sally.

There were flying things in the air around the bodies of the dead phamleblikzs. Sally and Anita folded the alien's arms across his chest...absurd, perhaps, but a gesture of respect for the bravery and sacrifice of the Nordic. There was no time to bury him. The two phamleblikzs who had only been stunned were stirring. Clutching the rod weapon to her, Sally took Anita by the arm and hurried to join the other women who were making their way across the moss to...where?

They had gone about one half of a mile when Iris Walker collapsed. She had lost a great deal of blood. The six women sat on the moss, back to back, looking out over the landscape, fearful of the approach of the predators.

"We have to get word to Utskolggvjiyz," said Andrea. "Signal him somehow...maybe we could make a fire..."

"With what?" quizzed Sally.

"Rub two sticks together," said Andrea. "Weren't you ever a Girl Scout?"

"Andrea," she answered, "I was *never* a Girl Scout!"

Nate, O'Bannon, Millender and Resnik faced Hmnogykwaer in the alien laboratory. They had awakened to discover that six of the women had been kidnapped by the Nordics. Nate knew that Noreen was among the victims. He was frantic.

"We must get the women back," Nate told the alien. "I won't leave without Noreen."

"Our escape plan must proceed…whether you accompany us or not," replied Hmnogykwaer. "I can't risk being found out. It could mean my death. You all…you can live your lives out here in relative comfort. You have nothing to lose. I have everything."

"But…can't we storm the Nordic stronghold and rescue the women…bring them with us too?" Nate was adamant. He looked to the others for support.

"Yes," said Millender. "The Marines never shy away from a fight, especially where the fairer sex is concerned. You can get us weapons. Say…don't you guys have a death ray or something we can use?"

"Don't be silly," answered Hmnogykwaer. "There is no such thing as a 'death ray.' Anyway it's too risky. We'd never be able to get in and out again, swords or death rays not withstanding."

"You get us in," O'Bannon said, "and we'll get us out."

Resnik was shaking his head. "Where is Buck Rogers when you need him?" he mused.

Noreen was studying the stun rod. It no longer glowed or flashed, but she had an idea that it might be used as a signaling device. If only they could figure out how to turn it back on. There were no apparent buttons or switches on the smooth surface. She was very afraid that it was activated by mind-control, which meant they would need an alien—and the aliens all were dead. She tried banging it against the ground as Sally had done, but to no avail. It was simply just a fancy stick, a useless artifact of this mystifying world.

Iris Walker poked Andrea. "You wanted to know about making a fire?" she asked the girl. "Well, look out over there."

The grazing level was far from actually being level; there were rolling hillocks and a rise near the horizon that cut off the view of whatever might be off in the distance. The underside of the next level up was evident—that would be just above at the edge of this one, but with no other point of reference, there was no clue as to how far this level extended. Now, as Andrea focused her attention in the direction indicated by Iris, she thought she could see the faintest wisp of something…something which could very well be smoke! So she said:

"Smoke! I see smoke!"

"Where?" everyone said, almost in unison.

Six pairs of eyes now scanned the horizon. Six heads nodded in the affirmative. It surely looked as if someone…or some thing…had lit a small fire. Just over the rise.

"Can you walk?" Sally asked Iris. In answer, the woman stood, still shaky on her injured leg, but determined to try. She took a few steps, stumbled, but continued to limp in the direction of the smoke. She was unwilling to let the pain that traveled up her leg show on her face.

"Here, lean on me," offered Noreen.

"How's your ankle?" Sally now asked Sandra Knight. "We could come back for you…if…"

"I'm fine. My ankle is better. I won't drag you down."

The location of the rising smoke was farther away than it had appeared at first glance. The women stopped to rest more than once but persevered until at last, just over the next rise, they saw something unexpected; they marveled at its incongruity and rejoiced in their own good fortune. There, in a shallow indented space surrounded on two sides by a cluster of low bushes, was a campsite.

It might have leaped from the pages of "The Deerslayer" or "The Last of the Mohicans." Next to a smoldering campfire was an array of cooking utensils: a crude clay pot, a spoon or spatula which appeared to be carved from bone, a basket containing chopped bits of some purple substance, several sharpened sticks, and a flat stone on which a slab of raw meat sat, attracting a swarm of tiny, gnat-like flying things. A few yards away from the outdoor kitchen stood a hut or tent made from stretched animal hides hung over the hardened stalks of the nearby bushes. There was no person or creature in evidence although it looked as if someone had been busy preparing a meal.

"Hello! Is anybody here?" yelled Anita. Cautiously the women crept down the hill toward the campsite.

"He's out there somewhere," said Sally. "Hiding from us. At least we now have a fire. We should heap some more brush on it…create a signal fire. Maybe someone will see it."

"Yes," said Noreen. "But who? The Greys or the Nordics? Who do you want to have find us?"

There was a rustling in the brush nearest the campfire. Two eyes stared out at the women. The creature in the brush was fascinated, afraid, and furious that the women stood between himself and his meal. His fury overtook the other emotions and he stepped defiantly out of the brush.

"Oh my God," said Noreen when she saw the creature. "He's just a boy!"

"Or a girl," added Sally. "How can you tell?"

"But...what is he?" asked Anita.

She had seen Greys and Nordics during her captivity, but never this. Before them, trembling with anger—and perhaps fear—stood the figure of a young Matofnblotjuupzian, one of the race humans called the Reptilians. He was dressed in ragged animal skins and he carried a long spear which he used to menace the intruders, pointing its wicked looking barbed end at them. Now a thought-image appeared in the minds of the women:

"Go away!"

Hmnogykwaer had brought the men to another room in the laboratory where, in anticipation of the escape which now seemed imminent, the Grey had hidden a bag containing several short swords. He handed each of the four men a weapon.

"If you meet any guards," Hmnogykwaer told them, "be aware that they will be armed also. And very versed in the arts of rikthijmb. You will need all the skill you can muster to defeat them if it comes to that."

"Say, there was a thing that the Nordics had...a long rod that could stun," said O'Bannon. "It was sort of like an electric shillelagh. Couldn't we get some of those?"

"Once again," Hmnogykwaer said, "your language eludes me. But perhaps you mean a gfelpodzex. It has many uses, primarily as a prod for ahtejiq. I suppose it could be used to stun someone. I never thought of it as a weapon."

"Get us a bunch of those shillelaghs. We'll keep these pig stickers for good measure."

"There is a phrase you humans have that I never understood until now. It is: 'I should have my head examined.' I will try to procure some gfelpodzexs, but it won't be easy. Meanwhile, you will go back to your cubicles and wait. Hide the swords well. I go to have a conference with Utskolggvjiyz. He knows I have gathered you together here but he believes I am evaluating the effects of the psychological indoctrination we began with the baseball games. He will know where the Nordics have taken the women and what measures, if any, are being taken to retrieve them. Whether he will share that information with me I can not predict."

"When do we leave?"

"During the next sleeping period if all goes well."

Nate and his fellows had no way of knowing that the women were not being held by the Nordics, but were lost somewhere on the veldt-like level where the ahtejiqs roamed. They also had no way of knowing that Hmnogykwaer had no intention of leading them in an attempt to liberate the women from the Nordics. The alien wanted to leave the moon colony swiftly and without unnecessary complications. He needed the Earthmen, or at least one Earthman, to accompany him to the planet and help him to communicate with Earth's leaders. Nothing could interfere with his mission…nothing like a senseless rescue attempt.

# 18

## Toho Theater, Tokyo, Japan, November 4, 1954

Flickering shadows dance across the movie screen. The film's opening scene shows a fishing boat moving slowly through the water. Suddenly, there is a flash of light. The crew is bathed in brilliance; they attempt to shield their faces from the radiation. Their screams are horrific. The boat bursts into flames and sinks. There is a shot showing the fishing boat's life preserver: it has a number 5 on it.

In the audience, a man named Oishi Matashichi, is shaken with emotion by the scene. He has experienced something similar, for he had been a crew member on the Daigo Fukuryu Maru—the Lucky Dragon #5—the fishing boat bombarded with radioactive fallout from the Castle Bravo tests—the fishing boat whose radio operator, Haruo Nakajima, has just died from radiation poisoning.

The film, whose advertising poster proclaims "mightiest monster...mightiest melodrama of them all...a monster of mass destruction," is the brain-child of director Ishiro Honda. The mighty monster is Gojira, a sleeping sea demon who has been awakened by atomic testing. Later, the director will admit that the monster is intended to be an analog for "a living atomic bomb," and that the movie is intended to make Japan, and the rest of the world, "experience the bombings of Hiroshima and Nagasaki all over again."

Gojia, spelled Godzilla for the watered-down version later released in the United States, rises from the sea, breathes radioactive flames, and rampages through Tokyo, incinerating people and knocking down buildings. He destroys the Toho theater (where the movie is being shown—some people in the audience panic and run from the theater). Oishi would like to run also, but he will stay to watch as the movie's characters struggle to find a way to stop the monster.

It's only a movie; the monster is just a man, actor Haruo Nakajima, sweating inside a rubber suit, knocking over cardboard buildings—but this depiction of the destruction, the suffering of woman and children, the futility, the impending apocalypse—are all too familiar to the audience who less than ten years ago watched bombs fall and set fire to their cities.

Japan had been occupied by United States forces until late 1952. The Americans had imposed a ban on information relating to the bombings of Hiroshima and Nagasaki and about the radiation sickness that resulted. Then came the Bikini tests and the Lucky Dragon tragedy. When the crew returned to port they were covered with burns and were bleeding from their gums. The Japanese government quarantined the men, but somehow the tuna they had caught found its way to market. The government frantically tried to retrieve the unsafe tuna. It was subsequently found that 856 Japanese vessels had been exposed to radiation from the hydrogen bomb tests. 75 tons of tuna were destroyed. The fishing industry was crippled. And then the Soviets began nuclear testing. The fear of radioactive rain falling from the sky spread throughout Japan.

Oishi Matashichi had been attending meetings about the concerns. Housewives, now unable to purchase tuna for their families, had organized the Chifuren (the National Council of Regional Women's Associations), and the Shufuren (the Housewives' Association). These and other groups began protesting the proliferation of nuclear weapons. In May, in the Suginami-ward of Tokyo, one of the first "ban the bomb" demonstrations had taken place. Chifuren helped to collect signatures on a petition to ban the H-bomb. Within a month 260,000 signatures were collected. One year later, there would be 20 million signatures.

Oishi watches the film. Is there no way to stop the living atomic bomb, Gojira? A scientist has developed an oxygen destroying weapon. He is conflicted: what if this new weapon should fall into the wrong hands?—the hands, for example, of the United States military? But it must be used. The noble scientist gives over the weapon to defeat the monster, but destroys all his notes…and himself…so that it can never be used again. This is the message of the movie: mankind must not rise above nature and try to control it.

Something bigger than us is always out there.

Oishi wanders out into the street after the conclusion of Gojira. He looks up at the buildings, colorless and grim in the dull, overcast afternoon. A single bird, a dusty and bedraggled pigeon, floats by on the gust of cold wind. Oishi notices other people emerging from the Toho; they instinctively look up toward the sky, as if to watch for the return of the monster. Oishi shakes his head and ambles down the street. He is thinking of the bowl of rice and vegetables flavored with miso he will make for his supper.

## University of Oslo, Norway, November 4, 1954

The tall, white-haired man with the bushy mustache standing at the podium is Albert Schweitzer. The 79 year-old humanitarian wears an out-of-date black suit coat, a wing collar and a meticulously tied four-in-hand necktie. He had been awarded the 1952 Noble Peace Prize for literature, but was unable to accept the award at the time because of his duties in Africa. Now, gold medal dangling around his neck, he is presenting a lecture to the Noble Prize audience entitled, "The Problem of Peace." He speaks in French (we translate):

"Let us dare to face the situation. Man has become superman. He is a superman because he not only has at his disposal innate physical forces, but also commands, thanks to scientific and technological advances, the latent forces of nature which he can now put to his own use. To kill at a distance, man used to rely solely on his own physical strength; he used it to bend the bow and to release the arrow. The superman has progressed to the stage where, thanks to a device designed for the purpose, he can use the energy released by the combustion of a given combination of chemical products. This enables him to employ a much more effective projectile and to propel it over far greater distances.

"However, the superman suffers from a fatal flaw. He has failed to rise to the level of superhuman reason which should match that of his superhuman strength. He requires such reason to put this vast power to solely reasonable and useful ends and not to destructive and murderous ones. Because he lacks it, the conquests of science and technology become a mortal danger to him rather than a blessing."

Schweitzer's wife, Helen, sits in the front row. She has been his partner and inspiration during his missionary work in Lambaréné, French Equatorial Africa. She knows her husband's views on atomic warfare well, and she knows it will be only a short matter of time before he gives up his reluctance to being more active in his opposition to nuclear tests and the stockpiling of bombs. She knows he will join with Albert Einstein, Bertrand Russell and Otto Hahn to speak and publish and bring others into the movement to abolish nuclear weapons. But will his fame and the strength of his character be enough?

"...the essential fact which we should acknowledge in our conscience, and which we should have acknowledged a long time ago, is that we are becoming inhuman to the extent that we become supermen. We have learned to tolerate the facts of war: that men are killed en masse—some twenty million in the Second World War— that whole cities and their inhabitants are annihilated by the atomic bomb, that men are turned into living torches by incendiary bombs. We learn of these things from the radio or newspapers and we judge them according to whether they signify success for the group of peoples to which we belong, or for our enemies. When we do admit to ourselves that such acts are the results of inhuman conduct, our admission is accompanied by the thought that the very fact of war itself leaves us no option but to accept them. In resigning ourselves to our fate without a struggle, we are guilty of inhumanity."

Schweitzer talks for nearly an hour. In the back of his mind as he reads his paper there are fond thoughts of his music room in Lambaréné where his pedal-piano sits, old, but still as tall and sturdy as Schweitzer himself, and still fundamental in the aging musician's study of Bach, Mendelssohn, Reger and Franck. His love of music, and the skill with which he executes pieces for organ, are linked to his philosophy of the Reverence for Life, his belief in spiritual rationalism. He will take the money from his Nobel Prize back to Lambaréné and build a hospital. Reality, he would say, is neutral— neither good nor evil. It is only in our own good practices that we can find meaning. Now he finishes his address with a reference to Paul, the Apostle, a favorite topic:

"May the men who hold the destiny of peoples in their hands, studiously avoid anything that might cause the present situation to deteriorate and become even more dangerous. May they take to heart the words of the Apostle Paul: 'If it be possible, as much as lieth in you, live peaceably with all men.' These words are valid not only for individuals, but for nations as well. May these nations, in their efforts to maintain peace, do their utmost to give the spirit time to grow and to act."

## White House, Washington, D.C., November 4, 1954

Dwight David Eisenhower is at his breakfast table in the residence. The glass of cold orange juice in front of him is as yet untouched. The President has had a sleepless night. Yesterday was mid-term election day and the results are now trickling in. It looks as if the opposition party, the Democrats, are going to take over the House of Representatives. The country is now weary (and wary) of Senator Joseph McCarthy of Wisconsin. The stigma of McCarthyism falls on the Republicans. Although Eisenhower's landslide in the election of 1952 had brought many Republicans along on his coat tails, his popularity is not translating back to incumbent representatives and senators. His party is about to lose 18 seats in the house and 2 in the senate, giving power back to the Democrats.

What will this mean for the programs he will pursue in the coming two years? If he brings a proposal to congress, will they take it up, consider it, pass it? Things were much simpler in the military where the chain of command was the rule of the day! Paramount among his concerns is the proposal he made in his "Atoms for Peace" speech last year before the UN General Assembly: to create an International Atomic Energy Agency under the aegis of the United Nations to which contributions of uranium and fissionable materials would be made by the significant players in the nuclear game; to make this agency responsible for impounding, storing and allocating such material only for the peaceful pursuits of mankind. But will congress see the necessity for diminishing the world's stockpile of bombs? Will it support the development of peace-time uses of nuclear energy? Will Russia?

Ike knows Mamie is still wrapped in a pink blanket in her bedroom. She maintains that anyone over the age of fifty should be allowed to stay in bed until noon. She often conducts her correspondence and other duties from the softness of pillows and comforter. Ike wishes she were here now as he values her opinion and always likes to run things past her—although she seldom takes an interest in politics. She supports him in his decisions, and that is the important thing. She often says that she does have a career, and it is Ike; Ike runs the country and she turns the pork chops.

Ike's gaze drifts to the windows. It is cold today, and windy. It has not snowed for winter is yet far off, but the world seems frozen, dead. He wishes he had gone to the farm for the week, or to Palm Springs. Washington is so stark and friendless sometimes. His thoughts also drift—back to the months just before D-day. Back to the warmth and kindness of his secretary, Kay Summersby. Because of the war he hadn't been with Mamie for almost three years. He had been in need of feminine companionship. His affair with Kay had been mostly platonic—but it was a deep and tender refuge for the hard-boiled Supreme Allied Commander of the European Front. He could talk to her, lay open his innermost thoughts, doubts, fears. She understood. She was there; Mamie was not.

There will be a press conference in a few hours and Ike will be asked by reporters if he thinks that he and the congress will be able to cooperate. He isn't sure. Then there is the problem of the flying saucer aliens. The tall grey ones are insistent about eliminating nuclear armaments. But Ike knows he can't stop stockpiling as long as the Russians are building and testing their own weapons of mass destruction. Having the bombs is a deterrent—the old "two men in a small room with hand grenades" idea. It is a risk of mutual suicide of course, but it is also a race to see who can amass the most overkill—be the biggest bully.

He sips his orange juice. God! Mamie is buying frozen concentrate again to save money! Maybe, he thinks, I'll start a new painting today. A self portrait would be nice. The President back in uniform, perhaps. And maybe, he thinks, I should get a dog.

## Moon Colony, November 4, 1954

The Circle is meeting in its chamber. The four races are equally represented. Mat/3, a Reptilian woman from the Matofnblotjuupz quarter of level 1, has drawn the lot and will officiate the meeting. She smoothes the gel fabric tunic she wears and looks around the room at the other members. This meeting has been called because of complaints from Ratiessrvedflynachian leadership that experimental material, the human women, has been stolen from the Glrovaktre by renegade Aimnegarwfucheeians. There are ripples of unrest rolling through the population.

"For the first time in six hundred ktanyos," Mat/3 begins, "our civilization is becoming divided. Where there may have been deeply seated resentments between the races in the past, these obscure emotions have remained buried because of our common understanding that our survival depends upon cooperation and the adherence to our long standing rules of order which we must follow willingly.

"Now there have been actions taken by a small group which fly in the face of order and tranquility. These extreme actions are, perhaps, not universally sanctioned by the Aimnegarwfucheeian race, but there is sentiment being expressed, even by other races, as to the necessity of opposing what is perceived as a monopoly in the advancements in scientific experimentation so crucial to our survival...a monopoly held by the Ratiessrvedflynachians.

"Whereas we can't condone theft or violence, must we not recognize that frustration arises from unfairness? Is not our society based on fairness and the equal sharing of burden and reward? Do we maintain peace and order at the expense of the individual who feels left behind? Or can we move forward without strife, without malice, and achieve our goals by coming together as a civilization? That is what we must decide today."

"Coming together," says Syk/2, the Syktijthraxteraq who had officiated at the previous meeting of the Circle, "generally means compromising. It seems to me that in this case, there is no compromise that will satisfy both sides. Either the Ratiessrvedflynachians are to be allowed to continue their single-minded approach to cloning...or they're not."

"There is certainly a danger," adds Rat/1, one of the three Ratiessrvedflynachian representatives, "in not addressing the illegal actions taken by this small group of Aimnegarwfucheeians. The cloning experiments are following a logical direction by pursuing areas in which success, or at least partial success, has been achieved. If this appears to discriminate against one or another race...well, that is just the natural order of things. Criminal acts only serve to ignite the flames of racism."

"Maintaining the status quo without addressing the real problem," replies Aim/2, an Aimnegarwfucheeian, "stifles the evolution of ideas and creativity. It leads to desperate acts. Look at the tragic results: five dead and the experimental material lost. This happened because we were excluded from the process."

"If the criminals had not stolen the humans they would not have died. It was because of their own foolishness," says Rat/1.

"We are not getting anywhere," says Mat/3. "You have only to look at the planet below us to see what happens when a people become divided. While we argue among ourselves, these human creatures may very well destroy themselves and the planet we need for our own survival. Can't we learn from them what path we should *not* be following?"

"We are not like the humans," says Syk/2. "They have something called 'religion.' It stems from their primitive state of development as sentient beings. They became aware of the inevitability of death and this reality was too painful for them to accept. They developed the technique of denial—refusing to believe the truth and inventing myths to reinforce their denials. But as they became more diverse in the varieties of these denials, they began to blame each other for their own failures and short comings. Race, religion, politics…these gave rise to quests for power over others. This gave rise to universal fear. No…we are not like the humans. We abandoned war long ago. We must not go down that path!"

"Here is a horrible thought," interjects Mat/1. "What if this divisiveness and bigotry that resides in the human psychic is *genetic* in character? Will our interbreeding with them carry that tendency over to our children?"

"We have not found a gene for hate in the human genome. It is a psychological state which is learned at an early age. If only the humans would listen to us, we could steer them toward the realization that they are all of one common nature. That cooperation is superior to competition. That the needs of the many…"

"Surpass the needs of the few. Yes. But what do we do about our own little dilemma?"

"We vote. Anyone want to propose a resolution?" Mat/2 is now losing her patience with the discussion. She points to Aim/1. "You?"

"I propose," Aim/1 says, "that we censure the perpetrators of the theft...posthumously, as they are all dead...and open up the scientific experiments to all qualified persons. To include representatives of each race, just as we do with the Circle."

"I agree," says Rat/1. "This may mean slowing down the work as we attempt to follow a multitude of hypotheses, but in the long run, it will avoid conflicts."

"And what about the human women? Should they be recovered?" asks Syk/2.

"Time and resources are limited for such an endeavor. This is the law of diminishing returns. Their survival is their own problem," answers Mat/3.

# 19

## Escape!

"We mean you no harm," Sally O'Neil thought to the alien child.

The young Syktijthraxteraq still held the barbed spear out in front of him. He was poised as if to hurl the weapon at any moment. Sally placed the stunning rod on the ground before her. She held out her hands to show they were empty, hoping this would placate the child enough to get a dialogue going. But the Reptilian glared back at her in anger.

"You won't take me," he thought to the Earth woman. She and the others were creatures he had never seen before. At first he had thought them to be the pale Aimnegarwfuchees, the Nordics. But the more he examined them the more their strangeness became evident. They were small, but not children. Their eyes were tiny dots on faces that had too much of the hue of pzotyklo fruit…a pinkish orange color that no Klivpoklaian had ever exhibited. Perhaps they had some illness.

"We are lost. We need to get back to the city level. Can you help us?" Sally was considering whether or not she could rush the alien and disarm him without being gored by his spear. He was very nervous. What could she do to distract him long enough…

"Go away," he thought to the women again. It was a loud thought, nearly a scream.

"I think he must be a runaway," Sally said aloud to the others. "He thinks we are here to bring him back to civilization or to his parents or to whatever he is afraid of. Try to put him at ease. Back away a little."

The women backed away, still facing the alien boy. Sally inched forward. The boy brandished his spear. It was a Klivpoklaian standoff. Then, the unexpected happened. From the brush behind them, a small furry creature emerged. A plablikz! The spider-like animal that was a pet to many on the moon colony. Obviously, this was the boy's pet and its curiosity had brought it forth from hiding. It scurried on its many legs past the boy and straight at Sally. Some of the women gasped. But Sally instinctively knelt and extended a hand out to the plablikz.

"Here, boy. That's a good boy. Come to Sally," she said.

It paused. It sniffed. Then it jumped into Sally's arms. She rose, cradling the little animal and cooing to it as if it were, in fact, an Earth puppy. This was difficult for Sally to do, given that the plablikz resembled a giant spider, but its reaction, and the reaction of the alien boy gave her the confidence she needed to overcome her initial revulsion. The animal snuggled against her and made a sound not unlike the purring of a happy kitten. The boy dropped his spear and stood gaping at the sight of his pet in the arms of this strange female.

"What's your pet's name?" Sally asked. "He's a real sweetheart."

The boy was hesitant. But seeing how the animal had taken to the female he softened. "He's a she," he finally answered. "Her name is Fagryumo, and she's a plablikz, not a 'sweetheart,' what ever that is."

"What's your name? Mine is Sally. And this is Noreen, Sandra, Anita, Andrea, and Iris."

"Those are very peculiar names! Oh...sorry....I am being rude. But it is true!" The boy now was more curious than frightened. "My name," he thought to them, "is Ghyrikkanmo."

By now the other women had surrounded Sally and the plablikz and were petting it and talking to it in baby talk. The boy, Ghyrikkanmo, was even more curious about the sounds the women were making. This prompted him to ask:

"Why do you make those sounds? It is not plablikz language."

"No," Sally responded, "but she understands the feelings behind the sounds we make. Don't you make sounds to her sometimes?"

Sally placed the plablikz on the ground and it scurried to the alien boy, jumping up into his arms. Good, now he can't pick up his spear, Sally thought to herself.

"You still must go away. You won't take me. You won't tell about me. I will (here the alien boy used a word that the Earth women translated as 'curse') you if you tell."

"No, we won't tell about you. But please, can you help us? We are lost. We need to find a gravity tube to return to some city level so we can go…home." As soon as Sally had uttered the word, "home," Noreen grabbed her arm and pulled her aside.

"We have to talk," said Noreen. "You don't realize…you and the others have been brainwashed to believe the aliens are helping us. It isn't true. They want to take over the earth. They will kill all of us to do it! We have to find a way to get back home…home to Earth…and warn them."

"Noreen, you are deluded. Of course the Greys are our friends. Brainwashed? Ha! I can't be brainwashed. I'm too intelligent."

"Doesn't the word, 'rutabagas,' mean anything to you?"

"Rutabagas? It's kind of a turnip or something, isn't it? What's that got to do…"

Ghyrikkanmo was looking at Iris Walker's leg which had begun to bleed again. "You come and sit here," he thought to her. "I have ointment and leaves of blgiiktmnas tree to fix your leg. Rest. Then go. I will show you where to find gravity tube."

Once Ghyrikkanmo had attended to Iris' leg, the women settled down by the fire, exhausted from their trek across the veldt. It was pleasant here, protected in the shallow basin from the harsh, rolling landscape beyond. The surrounding brush added to the feeling of enclosure; just what the women needed after an uneasy journey through the wild prairies, pursued, they believed, by predators. Ghyrikkanmo now overcame his shyness and, even without prompting from the women, related something of his background:

"You wonder how I came to be here, living like a wild phamleblikz. I was only three ktanyos old when my parents took sick with nhuddetkiosos. It is a rare disease and has no cure. When they died I was taken to a pfsedariotmne, a house for orphans. This was a horrible place. We, even the youngest of us, were forced to work in the tunnels harvesting mkehfutwess. These only grow in absolute darkness so we had to feel our way through the dirt and the slime that drips from the mkehfutwess. The tunnels were narrow and low, hence the use of children.

"Once I was older I could no longer tolerate this indignity and I formed a plan to run away from the pfsedariotmne. I joined with another child, Hichikloodze by name. Together we plotted. One day when the workers were returning from the tunnels we dropped back to the end of the line. There was one particular alley through which we were led that afforded us some cover, as it had a sharp turn and the overseer couldn't see us. We broke into a run and soon were blocks and blocks away. Where could we hide? What would we do next? We didn't know, but the taste of freedom was tantalizing; the very air sparkled with expectancy and good prospects.

"We lived on the street, hiding from the authorities who we knew were looking for us. We drank water from ditches and ate discarded food scraps. You would be surprised at how much good food people throw away. It was during that time that I found Fagryumo. The poor little plablikz was trying to reach the top of an open receptacle in which garbage was deposited. She was weak…starved. I took her with us and nursed her.

"We knew we had to abandon the city or it would be just a matter of time before they caught up with us. We located a gravity tube and I slipped into it holding Fagryumo in my arms. I emerged on this level. That was many llopikms ago. I waited and waited for Hichikloodze to follow, but he never arrived. My fear is that he was taken as he waited his turn at the gravity tube. I am guilty for having gone first. And now Fagryumo and I live in this wilderness, knowing that someday they may find us also."

As Iris rested, her leg wrapped in a blgiiktmnas leaf, she and the others sat around the camp fire listening to Ghyrikkanmo's story. Their turn came. They tried to make him understand exactly who they were, where they were from, and how they came to be in this place. Some of the concepts eluded the boy, but gradually he came to understand that an entire world existed beyond his own, peopled with creatures similar, but different than himself.

It was a matter of about an hour later that the one-person observation sphere flew overhead. It floated like a soap bubble and began to descend toward the campsite.

"Quickly! Run!" yell-thought Ghyrikkanmo. He bounded into the brush, Fagryumo close on his heels. Noreen followed, ducking down below the brambles, not daring even to peek out to see if the sphere was landing. Sally, however, began jumping up and down, waving her arms and calling to the sphere: "Here we are! Come and get us!" This was fruitless as the sphere only had room for one person. But its operator saw them. The sphere dipped down and skimmed across the basin only a few feet above the women's heads. It suddenly gained altitude and flashed away.

"Aw, nuts," said Sally.

"He's going to get a bigger ship," said Anita. We should wait here. We'll be saved."

Noreen saw that Ghyrikkanmo had other plans. He crawled on his belly through the brush until he had reached the side opposite the campsite. Noreen followed. "Where are we going?" she thought to the alien.

"We? You'll come with me? I'm not sure that is a good idea."

"I help you…you help me. I don't want to be captured either. Those other women…"

"Are fools! But this world of ours is small. Eventually they will catch us, I think. Still, I would rather run than surrender."

"Do you see what I grabbed before we ducked into the brush?" Noreen held out the stun rod which she had kept hidden behind her back until now.

"A gfelpodzex! Are we going to be herding ahtejiq?"

"You know how to use this, don't you? We can use it as a weapon in case someone tries to get at us. Only…only, we need a plan. I have some friends. They are going to escape from this moon colony. Fly back to my home planet. If we could get to them…"

"This seems even more foolish. Fly to the planet? How can you even do that?"

"Oh, Ghyrikkanmo, you don't know much about the universe, do you? Is there a saucer port on this level?"

"There is a place where the ahtejiq that are brought back from your planet arrive. I hadn't thought about it, but yes, they must use ships capable of 'flying' to your Sjilgezhm. We can go there, but what we do next…I surely don't know."

"Oh please, take me to the saucer port. I want to go home. I'll think of something once we get there."

*   *   *

The short sword Millender swung made a sound like the song of an injured bird against the stale air in the antechamber of the saucer port. When it struck flesh it made a dull thunk. Green blood flew in droplets; the droplets sank slowly in the reduced moon gravity. The great pale form of the Nordic guard slumped to the floor, his precious life's fluid pouring from his wound. Millender slipped in the sticky fluid, but regained his balance in time to parry a chop from a second guard. The strength of this attack nearly knocked the sword from Millender's hand. His wrist numbed and he switched the sword to his left hand. He turned to face the guard.

Before the guard could bring his bade down on Millender's neck, Resnik had thrust his own sword through the guard's back. Its point, glistening with green gore, emerged from the alien's chest with a pop. Just like sticking a pig, thought Resnik. He jerked the sword out of the alien's body and watched it sink to the floor.

Nate's opponent held a straight thin blade not unlike a Chinese Jian. He moved this in slow circles looking for an opening, the point inches from Nate's chest. Nate rested the blade of his sword against his enemy's, following it instead of resisting it with effort. This confused the Nordic. When the alien reversed direction, Nate followed. When the alien raised the sword upwards, threatening Nate's neck, Nate stooped down, disengaged his sword with a swift arcing movement, and thrust upward at the alien's unprotected chest.

"Touché!" Nate shouted.

There were now three dead guards and a pool of green blood on the floor of the antechamber. Hmnogykwaer, who had been watching from a distance, now rushed to open the door that led to the saucer port. Once they had entered, and Nate saw where they were—not in quarters where the women were kept as prisoners as he had thought, but at the saucer port—he turned to Hmnogykwaer.

"What is this? Where are the women? You know I won't go without Noreen," he said, accusingly.

"We have to go. The women will not be here," answered Hmnogykwaer. "I didn't tell you this before, because I didn't want to worry you, but the aircraft carrying the women prisoners crashed. All were lost. She's gone, Nathaniel. Now it is time to save yourself and your companions. I'm sorry."

Anguish overtook Nate. In his despair he swung his short sword wildly at the empty air. "No! No…no…no!" he cried. O'Bannon tried to console him, wrapping his arms around Nate's shoulder. Hmnogykwaer gave them a moment, then:

"Come quickly before any more guards come. We must find a pilot and commandeer a craft!"

Nate, although he had ridden in a saucer during his abduction, had never really seen one from the outside. He had an idea what one looked like of course, but this was based on a movie he had once seen: the large, sleek, smooth disk of *The Day The Earth Stood Still* stuck in his mind. At this port were docked several saucers and each had a slightly different configuration. None of them were smooth with unbroken lines and hidden doors like the one in the movie. The largest was a long, cigar-shaped vessel studded with small domes which might be windows or antennae. Another was disk-shaped but topped with a smaller cylindrical cabin with a cone-shaped roof. It sat on four spherical legs. There were two of the transparent one-person spheres and a medium-sized saucer with a flattened rim around which were a series of narrow, slit-like windows.

There now remained two problems: capturing a pilot they could force to fly a saucer, and finding a way to open the port doors to allow the saucer access to the outside. Obviously, once the port doors were opened, air would escape from the room and the severe cold of the moon would freeze any unprotected creature not in the ship. This procedure was normally done by a port worker throwing a switch from a control room near the big door. That person couldn't emerge from the control room until after the door was again shut tight and pressurized air was reintroduced into the port.

The pilots' quarters were near the antechamber. Hmnogykwaer entered this while the others stayed back out of sight. Inside he found a Grey sleeping on an expanded cube chair. He shook the man until he awoke. "You are needed to pilot a htyopker. It is an emergency. Come quickly," he told the pilot.

When the pilot saw the group of humans brandishing swords he tried to run. Millender grabbed him in a bear hug and O'Bannon pointed a bloody sword at his throat. Still the Grey struggled. Millender had to drag him the full distance to the medium-sized saucer which Hmnogykwaer had indicated would be their Noah's Ark of escape.

"Now we have a decision to make," said Hmnogykwaer once the Grey had been deposited in the pilot's seat and there were four sharp blades surrounding him. "Someone will have to stay behind in order to open the door. I am needed to communicate with the pilot...and to talk to your world's leaders once we arrive. I need Nathaniel because...and he doesn't know this yet...I have been able to penetrate his mind to a certain degree; this will become useful for me in order to have private conversations with him during negotiations on your planet. This means one of the three of you must decide among yourselves who will open the door. That person won't be able to return to the ship."

"I'll stay," Resnik said immediately before anyone could object. "If I go back to Earth I'll just end up in the brig again. I've been AWOL...what'll I use for an excuse? Aliens abducted me in a flying saucer and held me captive on the moon?"

"Chris...you don't have to do this. Let's draw straws," said O'Bannon.

"Hey, I'll just go into the city and find a nice Greenie family to live with. They taste like chicken, you know."

"Good," said Hmnogykwaer. "Come with me and I'll show you which switch to throw."

*   *   *

On another level, at the entrance to another saucer port, Noreen and Ghyrikkanmo were hiding behind a stack of crates. Fagryumo, the pet plablikz, was rubbing against Noreen's legs and emitting sounds that were a sort of cross between a kitten's purr and an electric blender.

"Hush, Fagryumo!" Noreen whispered. "We don't want them to hear us."

There were several Greys in the saucer port, attending to the maintenance of a large saucer. They were readying the space vehicle for a flight to the surface of the planet where there would be an abduction of cattle. The port was one of the largest spaces Noreen could remember ever having seen—larger than a football stadium. The saucer itself was larger than a jet liner. It had an ovoid shape. At one end of the saucer was a gaping opening which was the doorway through which the cattle would be herded when it landed on the planet below.

Ghyrikkanmo explained to Noreen that once the maintenance crew left the area and the flight crew arrived, she would have only moments to run to the saucer and enter it through that large door. The saucer would be sealed and the port door would open, rendering the space around it uninhabitable.

"Come with me," Noreen thought to Ghyrikkanmo. "You would love Earth."

"No," he answered, "I will remain here and live simply until they find me. I will remember you. Watch now, as the crews are changing over. You only have a few minutes…"

Noreen waited until the maintenance crew had left the area. She then saw five Greys approach the saucer and enter it through a smaller doorway at the front of the ship.

"Now!" Ghyrikkanmo told her.

She ran as fast as she could toward the large opening. An overhead door was descending just as she stepped inside. She turned to wave at Ghyrikkanmo and saw a small furry shape crawl through the opening behind her. Fagryum had followed her! Close behind the plablikz was the Matofnblotjuupzian youth. He leaped into the saucer and grabbed up his pet but before he could exit the saucer, the heavy door clanged shut. The saucer began to rumble and vibrate as it energized for the flight that was about to begin.

# 20

## The Journey Home

As the saucer rounded the "dark side" of the moon, Nate watched the bright blue globe of Earth come into view. It shimmered in the direct light of the sun. Swirling clouds partly obscured the continents. A deep blackness surrounded the globe; the sun's brilliance made seeing the stars behind Earth impossible. The grey surface of the moon, barely illuminated by earthlight, fell away as the saucer began to accelerate. Soon, as the saucer came out of the moon shadow, Nate watched the sun's fierce corona emerge; followed by the edge of that golden disk; followed by the blinding light of super-heated plasma.

During interstellar flight the aliens' ships generated gravitational waves from engines of dark matter which bent time-space and allowed them to achieve near light speed (around 670,616,629 miles per hour, as the photon flies). The distance from the moon to the planet was only around 238,855 miles on an average. The saucer could easily travel this distance in a few hours without accelerating much beyond 100,000 miles per hour, but it would need to slow to enter an earth orbit before it could land. Thus it began decelerating at the mid point of its journey.

They entered the Van Allen radiation belt, a torus-shaped collection of charged particles trapped in the Earth's magnetic field.

A decade later (in another reality), when the American and Russian space programs were sending men farther and farther into space, there would be some concern over whether passing through the Van Allen belt would expose astronauts to fatal radiation levels. Someone would propose clearing the belt by detonating nuclear bombs there. America, in fact, would detonate a 1.4 megaton bomb at 250 miles above the planet as a test, but would only succeed in adding radiation rather than dispersing it. As the saucer entered the belt (its hull was impervious to radiation), tiny particles of charged matter sparkled as they ricocheted from the saucer's outer surface.

Nate could now identify the various continents. It was like looking at a paper globe, but without the grid lines and place names and national boundaries denoted by different colors. Hmnogykwaer was also watching out of one of the saucer's many windows as the world below them filled their view.

"You didn't seem bothered," Nate said to Hmnogykwaer, "by the fact that we sliced your people up into chowder."

"Again your colorful language eludes me. But if you mean by dispatching those guards, who would surely have prevented us from escaping by any means necessary…then yes, I was not bothered. We all die. It is just a matter of when and how. There is nothing tragic about it."

"What do you hope to accomplish by revealing the true nature of the cloning project to Earth officials? Doesn't that put your people at risk? It could start a war, you know."

Hmnogykwaer turned away from the bank of windows. "I've considered this," he replied. "*Your* people do tend to solve conflicts by killing each other…somewhat needlessly, I think. My hope is that logic will prevail over fear and hatred. Your scientists are very clever. All they lack is an understanding of some of the basic principles of the universe which *we* have discovered. Together we might solve the problems of both our worlds."

"I don't know, Hmnogykwaer. Humans don't have a great track record at being logical. There was a poet once who said, 'Where ignorance is bliss, 'tis folly to be wise.' Truth has never been worshiped by the masses. And we'd rather kill each other than accept each other's differences."

"I must at least try, Nathanielmirko."

As the saucer entered the atmosphere, heat from friction ignited gases; flames enveloped the saucer. As the atmosphere thickened beneath the Kármán line, the saucer presented itself in an oblique angle to lessen the drag. Anti-gravity was increased by the pilot to slow the descent; the flames of entry disappeared abruptly as the saucer sailed silently into the stratosphere. Now, slowly, she descended into the troposphere, into banks of cloud where heat lightning crackled. Nate strained to see through the murk and brume of the unfriendly environment outside.

The oppressive opacity began to brighten and thin; became wispy like a mist over a stagnant pond, then parted to reveal a dark, rolling expanse of ocean. There was no frame of reference by which Nate could judge their height above the peaking waves; their speed was such that the ocean blurred below them. Nate had to look away from the windows as nausea gripped him.

"The land mass you call the North American Continent is just ahead," said Hmnogykwaer. "Our reluctant pilot is familiar with an area you know as New Mexico. Apparently he has been there before. We will find a remote place to land and then make our plans."

Landfall came quickly. The saucer soared at 20,000 feet. Nate saw a tapestry of fields and forests, farms and cities, unraveling below them as the saucer sped inland. The citizens of Philadelphia, if they had looked upward, would have seen a bright silver speck shooting across the sky. In Cincinnati and Saint Louis people on the streets did look up, did see a flying disk which now had descended to 10,000 feet. No one reported the sighting—there was too much of a stigma attached to witnessing UFOs these days. A housewife in Vinita, Oklahoma, was hanging laundry on a line in her yard when the saucer went over. She ran screaming into the house to fetch her husband who was watching a ball game on their black and white television. She received a beating for her hysteria and the disruption. Because of electromagnetic interference from the passing saucer, the television never worked properly again.

Skimming over the vast empty plains of the Texas Panhandle was a dizzying experience. Pale greens changed into dull browns. The rolling llano of New Mexico was now below them. Had he known his geography better, Nate could have picked out the sparkling ribbon of the Pecos River. In the distance, Nate saw mountains. Their speed decreased as they neared their goal, an isolated mountain top on the edge of nowhere.

The saucer hovered above a ridge in the Manzano Mountains, just south of Tijeras, New Mexico. Slowly it descended until it sat on the rocky outcropping of a castle-like peak where nearby, scruffy cedars, twisted by years of heavy wind, stood like crippled sentries. The mountains, named for the groves of apple trees on its slopes, were the southern most leg of the Rocky Mountain Range. To the west lay the great rift through which the Rio Grande now flowed— an ancient rift where two continental plates had pulled apart and filled with sand and rock and basalt flung from the ferocious eruptions of New Mexico's volcanoes.

And nestled in a valley between there and here was the town of Albuquerque. The travelers opened the door on the side of the saucer and went out to look at the vista. The city sprawled before them. Behind it were low mountains and three peaks that had been ancient volcanoes. Hmnogykwaer gestured toward the south side of the city. "There is Kirtland Air Force Base," he said. "That is where we go."

"How do we get there?" asked O'Bannon.

"We walk," came the answer.

As they stood looking out over the brown cityscape with its low brown buildings from which brown smoke rose in tendrils, the pilot, now unsupervised, emerged from the saucer and began to run.

"Look!" shouted Nate. "He's escaping. Shouldn't we go after him?"

"It does not matter," said Hmnogykwaer. "We don't need him now."

"What if he comes back and takes the saucer?"

"He won't be able to start it," explained Hmnogykwaer. He held out a sparkling sphere about the size of a grapefruit. "This is needed to make the ship work. It is something like the key you use to start your automobiles. As long as I have it, that ship is going nowhere." He slipped it into a cloth bag which he hung over his shoulder.

They followed the ridge line along Cedro Canyon and into the small town of Tijeras. There they found Highway 66, part of the old route that stretched from Chicago to Los Angeles. They would follow that west to Albuquerque and the Kirtland Air Base. There wasn't much to the town of Tijeras—a store with a weathered, hand-painted sign, a school made of adobe bricks and white-washed stucco, a few small adobe houses. The road out of town led through the canyon. On either side of it foothills rose gradually upward against an azure sky. Reds and browns of coarse dirt and gravel met the eye; scattered boulders of shiny black basalt and dwarfed green junipers with ripened purple berries added a few color accents.

"What do you think of our world?" Nate asked Hmnogykwaer as they walked along the road.

"Reminds me a little of the moon we just left," he answered, "except for the vegetation."

They had been walking for half an hour when they came upon a truck parked along the side of the highway; they could hear angry words in Spanish: "Hijo de tu puta madre!" A man was kneeling by the rear of the truck. As they drew closer they could see that the truck leaned to one side. It had a flat tire. Nate approached the man, digging deeply in memory for the high school Spanish he had studied—and passed, although not exactly with honors.

"Hola, Señor.," he said. "Necesitas ayuda?"

The man got up from his examination of the flat tire. "Sí," he answered. "No tengo…um…jack."

"He hasn't a jack," Nate told the others. "Look around for a tree branch or something."

This was easier said than done, but soon O'Bannon came back from searching with a long piece of wood—perhaps some building material which had fallen from another truck. "This will have to do," he offered. The three humans placed the board under the back of the truck like a lever and managed to raise the truck up just enough roll a large rock under the frame. Now the wheel could be changed— except for one small problem:

"No tengo la rueda de repuesto. Troca pendejo!"

"He doesn't have a spare," Nate said. "We'll have to repair the inner tube."

"How are we going to do that?" asked Millender. "We have no repair kit. We don't have a tire pump. It's useless."

"Wait," said Hmnogykwaer. "Let me have a look." The Grey alien bent over the wheel, ran his hands over it, and turned around holding a large rusty nail in his hand. "This is what caused the tire to deflate," he said.

"Yeah, so what?" said Millender.

Hmnogykwaer tore a bit of the gel cloth from his tunic. He stuffed this into the hole that the nail had left. The material expanded once it was inside of the tire. Now all they needed was a way to get air back into the tire. While they pondered this problem, the Hispanic man rummaged around a tool box on the bed of his truck. He extracted a red metal cylinder and held it up to show the others.

"A bicycle pump!" exclaimed O'Bannon. "He hasn't a spare tire, but he has a bicycle pump!"

"This may take a little while," said Nate, grabbing the pump and attaching it to the tire's valve. "The tube is not going to hold air, but the tire should. We should take turns pumping."

It wasn't working. Air filled the tire but no matter how hard they worked the bicycle pump's handle up and down, they could not create enough pressure to adequately inflate the tire.

"It's no use," said O'Bannon.

"Let me see what I can do," said Hmnogykwaer. He reached into the cloth bag where he had placed the sparkling sphere that controlled the saucer. This he brought out and placed against the side wall of the tire. His long fingers manipulated invisible switches on the surface of the sphere. Immediately, the tire began to expand.

"There. I've accelerated the atoms in the small bit of air we forced inside. This thing should remain inflated for several qwerkls. The man is a bit dumbfounded, by the way. He is thinking we are supernatural beings and is becoming afraid. You should reassure him."

"You can read minds thinking in Spanish?" asked Nate.

"Of course. Thoughts are images. Language is just a poor attempt at transforming those thoughts into sounds. You depend upon sounds to communicate. I do not."

"Well," said Nate, "maybe he is right about *you* being supernatural." He now addressed the man:

"Señor, como se llama? Mi nombre es Nate. Mis amigos son llamados Chuck, Andy y…Hmnog…uh, Hermano."

"Ellos me llaman Paco, pero mi nombre es Rubén Sandoval. Soy de Moriarty. Voy a Burqué y vender chiles."

"Okay," said Nate, translating for the others. "His name is Rubén Sandoval but they call him Paco. He is on his way from Moriarty to sell his chile harvest in Albuquerque. I'll ask him to give us a ride."

They climbed up onto the bed of the truck and settled down among the canvas bags of fresh picked green chiles. The highway was paved, but out of repair so that pot holes occurred periodically along the way. These caused the bags of chile and the travelers to bounce and bump each other. The road now entered the fringes of the city. Rows of motor courts lined both sides of Route 66 (which here was called Central Avenue). Adobe casas that looked like castles made of brown sugar were clustered among the motels. Bright red ristras of dried chile peppers were hung from vigas. The sweet aroma of cedar and piñon smoke reached them and mingled with the spicy chile smells from the bags.

"We must practice communicating with thought transfer," Hmnogykwaer told Nate. "I must have your input when I talk to the leaders."

"I don't know if we'll find any leaders at Kirtland...any that can help. But maybe we can arrange to talk to someone higher up."

"The Eisenhower would be the one I would wish to see. But now, concentrate for me on some vivid memory. I wish to probe your mind."

Nate complied. His thoughts went to those days back in Bellingham when he had first met Noreen. Emotion welled. She sat in the rocker in the front room. They talked of ordinary things. He sniffed back a tear. The alien nodded.

"You are thinking of the girl. You miss her. Excellent. I got that very clearly. Now you try to read me. Empty your mind and become receptive. It might help if you stare at the center of my forehead."

Nate focused his attention on the alien. At first, nothing happened. Then, gradually, he began to get little flashes of images— just colors, then indistinct shapes. Then he saw a picture of a female alien, her large, smiling face occupying the entire frame of the image. A wonderful warm feeling came to him upon seeing this. Excitedly, he told Hmnogykwaer what he had seen.

"Yes," said the alien. "That was my mother. Very good. Now we must attempt to send word thoughts back and forth. This is more difficult because you must let loose of your dependency upon language."

By the time they reached Kirtland Air Force Base, Nate and the alien were conversing by thought transfer. Nate was thrilled by his new ability, yet fearful of its potential. Now the alien could read his innermost thoughts. Nate wasn't yet skilled enough to be able to close off certain portions of his mind the way alien could. He would have to trust him...but could he?

At the entrance gate a sentry approached the truck. O'Bannon said to Hmnogykwaer, "Millender and I had best stay with the Spanish guy and wait out here. We are both AWOL, technically. Technically we could end up in the brig."

"I agree. Take the sack with the sphere in it. I don't want it to fall into the wrong hands and we don't know how we will be received here," said Hmnogykwaer. "Be very careful how you handle it. It has a great deal of energy inside which if released improperly..."

"Roger that. Good luck to you."

Now Hmnogykwaer focused on the sentry. He placed a thought in the man's mind that it was imperative that he and Nate be brought to the base commander...with all due courtesy. They climbed off of the truck and followed the sentry through the gate and into the military base. So far...so good, thought Nate.

The sentry brought Hmnogykwaer and Nate to the offices of the commander of the Air Force Special Weapons Center at Kirtland, Major William Lorring. While Lorring was not the base commander, nor the highest ranking officer at the base, he was at the time entertaining an important visitor, General Nathan Twining. Twining had been commander of Air Material Command at Wright-Patterson Air Base when the bodies and the debris from the saucer crash at Roswell, New Mexico, had been taken there for study. Twining was also a member of the Majestic 12.

"Major Lorring," bellowed Twining, "what is the meaning of this? Who are these civilians and why have they been allowed access to the center?"

"General Twining, Sir, I can only tell you that I have a strange feeling that you should talk to them. Logic tells me I should summon the MPs but this sensation is so strong..."

Nate and Hmnogykwaer stood silently in front of the two Air force officers. The alien was thinking to Nate: "There is something about this general...I'm getting a peculiar sense of recognition from him when he looks at me."

Nate thought back: "I haven't a clue as to how to proceed. We may be in big trouble."

Twining turned to Hmnogykwaer. "Who are you?" he demanded. "Where are you from? What do you want here?"

Hmnogykwaer to Nate: "He knows I'm an alien. He has some special knowledge."

"I need to communicate something of extreme importance to

your President Eisenhower," Hmnogykwaer said to Twining. "I think you understand who I am and where I am from. It is a matter of what you call 'national security.' Will you take me to your Eisenhower?"

"Eisenhower? You don't know?" Twining said. "President Eisenhower has suffered a severe heart attack. He is in the hospital in critical condition. The Vice President, Richard Nixon, has been sworn in as acting president."

# 21

## Somewhere in the South of France

Ghyrikkanmo, the Matofnblotjuupzian youth, Fagryum, his pet plablikz, and Noreen, the human girl, slipped out of the saucer's big door before it was completely open; there was just enough space to wriggle through. Before them was a field where cattle were grouped together closely, staring dumbly at the huge saucer that had just landed. Beyond these was a cluster of hawthorn trees. Noreen and her companions made for this as fast as they could run.

From the cover of the thicket they watched a number of Greys carrying gfelpodzexs—cattle prods—as they moved toward the herd of cattle.

"Oh shoot," Noreen thought to the alien boy, "I've left mine back in the saucer."

"No time to get it now," replied Ghyrikkanmo. The plablikz was purring loudly. "Hush, little one," the boy said out loud.

"You can talk! I didn't understand what you said, but those were definitely words," Noreen thought to Ghyrikkanmo. "I wonder if I could teach you English. You understand me when I think in it."

"You think in mind images. Words are unnecessary abstractions."

"We're in my world now. You should learn the spoken language. You are going to stand out a bit more than will be comfortable. Still, we need to get to a village or a farm house. We'll take things as they come."

After the saucer was loaded with the purloined beef-on-the-hoof, it shot straight upward into the clouds and was gone. Noreen and the alien boy started walking. The little plablikz scurried along behind them making noises not unlike a small puppy demanding its supper. Presently they came to a dirt road and this they followed, not sure of which direction would prove fortuitous. The road wound through a landscape of rock-strewn hillocks and low bushes. Magpies circled above them, scolding with staccato insistence. In the distance a mountain peak rose up against a sky piled high with dense clouds.

Over the next hill was a small cottage constructed of the field rock they had seen along the road and surrounded by a low rubble wall of the same stone. "Better put Fagryum inside your tunic," Noreen thought to the boy. "I can maybe explain you, but that big spider is going to startle whom ever we may meet."

"He isn't a spider, but yes, I will secure him in my clothing."

"And stay behind me, out of sight as much as possible."

Noreen knocked. The door opened a crack and someone peered out, hesitated, then opened it wider. A woman stood on the stoop, a stained dish rag in her hands, her hair mussed and falling into her eyes. "Qu'est-ce que tu veux," she asked?

"Oh-oh," thought Noreen. "we're definitely not in Kansas!" Then to the woman she asked, "Madame, parlez-vous Anglais?"

"Oui. A little. You are Américaine? You miss your tour bus?"

"Yes, um…we are a little bit lost. Can you tell us where we are? How far it is to the next big town?"

"This is the Pays d'Aix. Very rural. You are nearest to Aix-en-Provence. The main road is about a kilometer north of here. You might find transportation by the hike-hitch. Walk across the field behind the house and keep the mountain on your left. You can't miss it. By the way, don't mind me asking but what is the matter with your son?"

"Oh, he has a rare skin disease. Don't worry, it isn't contagious."

"And…what is that he has? Is that a monkey?"

They reached the road after trudging through an open field where dried stalks of heather lay, late of the harvest and early of the plowing. The road itself was no super highway: just a country road in dire need of the filling of its ruts. There was no traffic in sight. Noreen had a vague idea that Aix-en-Provence was situated on the slopes of the mountain so it was in that direction that they hiked. Ghyrikkanmo had placed Fagryum on his shoulders—the little tike, he said, was tuckered out from their hike across the heather field.

A car sped by, coming from the wrong direction and so they did not try to flag it down. Dust flew up as the automobile passed. Why didn't that vehicle hover, Ghyrikkanmo wondered and he sent this thought to Noreen for an answer. Thus began a sketchy explanation of the workings of the world called Earth and its (Ghyrikkanmo decided) primitive technologies.

The vehicle that had passed consumed fuel made from the bones of ancient creatures who once had ruled this planet. The byproduct of this energy consumption rose as smog to choke away the sun and fowl the air. Soon the bones would be used up. The Earth would heat up. Oceans would rise to swallow cities. An ice age would begin. The humans would not have advanced enough in their technology to escape. Ghyrikkanmo deduced all this from the undertones of Noreen's narrative of the cities and nations of her planet.

"It is no wonder," thought the alien to Noreen, "that my people desire to take over your world before you destroy it."

A car was approaching from behind them. Noreen led the alien off to the side of the road and stuck out her thumb. "Put Fagryum back inside your tunic, she thought to Ghyrikkanmo." The car went past them, slowed, then pulled off to the side of the road and stopped. They hurried toward the vehicle.

A man got out of the car—a man wearing a uniform. It was too late to turn back. It was too late to run. Was it illegal to hitch hike in France? Noreen didn't think so. There were stories of ex-pats hitching all over Europe. She tried to relax, to clear her mind of the anxiety she felt welling up. She sent a quick thought to Ghyrikkanmo: "This man is a policeman. He might be helpful…or he might not. Keep Fagryum hidden."

"Bonjour," she said. "Nous avons fait de la randonée…" The policeman held up his hand to stop her.

"I speak better English than you do the French," he told her. "You are vagrants, n'est pas? You will please show your papers."

"We don't have them with us. We were out for a hike and…"

"And you needed a ride. Perhaps you will come in the auto with me to the poste de police. There have been many what you Américains call the cattle rustling. What do you know of it? Is this the wild west? Je ne pense pas!"

Noreen to Ghyrikkanmo: "We have to go with him. Can you…do you remember how I told you how the Greys controlled our minds when I was their captive? Can you do that to him? We don't want to end up in jail."

Ghyrikkanmo to Noreen: "I am probing. He is a cadet officer, just started active duty this week, and he is trying to make an impression on his superiors. He is from Marseilles originally and just recently married. He is worried that his wife in cuckolding him with another man. He…"

Noreen to Ghyrikkanmo: "That's more than I need or want to know. Any chance he might be sympathetic to us?"

Ghyrikkanmo to Noreen: "I don't think so. I will try to place a suggestion into his mind, but this is very difficult for me to do. There are many, many things cluttering his mind. Perhaps if you could distract him in some way."

The policeman was now staring at Ghyrikkanmo, perhaps noticing for the first time that the boy was not normal. The scaly-looking skin, the large, slanted eyes, made the officer suspicious. At first he had thought the boy was wearing some sort of costume. Now…

"Does your young friend have some sort of condition?" he asked Noreen.

"Yes. A rare skin condition…I can't pronounce the name. We were going to the city to find a clinic for treatment. You would be very helpful if you could take us there instead of to the station. We would be very grateful."

Noreen turned on her most seductive smile—which was to say, her *idea* of what a seductive smile might be like, having had very little experience in that area.

Ghyrikkanmo to Noreen: "Good. I am having some success. I am giving him the suggestion to help you. I have to warn you, however, he is attracted to you in a vaguely sexual manner. You may have to fight him off at some point."

Noreen to Ghyrikkanmo: "Only vaguely? I guess I'm not doing this seduction thing so well."

The policeman held the car door open for Noreen and Ghyrikkanmo. "Entrer s'il vous plaît," he said. "I know of a good clinic. Perhaps we can drop your companion there and go for a glass of wine? I know a great little place along the river."

Ah, thought Noreen…these Frenchmen!

## Kirtland Air Force Base, Albuquerque, New Mexico

"Let's go get in the cab with the Mexican," said O'Bannon. "There's plenty of room and these chiles make me sneeze."

"I think he is a *New* Mexican, not a Mexican. They are very sensitive about that. You speak any Spanish?"

"Not a bit. You?"

"Uh-uh. We'll have to hope he is friendly enough to let us hang out with him until Nate gets back. It's a long way back to town."

They hopped from the bed of the truck and opened the door of the cab on the passenger side. O'Bannon gestured—would it be all right if they sat in the cab? The man named Paco nodded in agreement. As they were climbing in, the bag containing the saucer sphere swung against the door jam with a clunk. It started to vibrate.

"Oh-oh," exclaimed O'Bannon. "I hope this thing isn't going to explode!"

The sentry had returned to his post. Now he approached the truck and spoke to Paco:

"Amigo! You have to move your truck out of here. Com-pre-hendo? You speak any English?"

Paco shrugged.

"Come on...andale! Vamos. Adiós. Move the fucking truck!"

Paco still shrugged. O'Bannon took the sphere from the bag and began to examine it. "Maybe there is an off switch," he said.

As O'Bannon turned the sphere over and ran his fingers over its surface the thing began to glow. O'Bannon raised the sphere up to look at it more clearly and in doing so, must have activated the ability of the sphere to produce an anti-gravity field because the truck began to float several feet above the ground.

The startled sentry backed away. Paco let out a string of profanities which included, "Puta Madre! Mi cago en Dios! Mierda! Que te jodan come mierda! Hijo de puta!" The truck rose higher. O'Bannon tipped the sphere; the truck rolled onto its side, cascading the bags of chiles onto the pavement below. O'Bannon kept manipulating the sphere, running his hands over it, frantically trying to turn it off. The truck began to fly erratically. It soared out over the airfield, tipping and rolling as if controlled by an aerial acrobat flying a biplane in a 1920s air circus.

"I think I'm getting the hang of it," shouted O'Bannon.

He found that the rotation of the sphere determined the bearing and slight movements up and down increased or decreased altitude. Moving the sphere forward or backward, to the right or to the left, started the flying truck moving in that direction, until the "pilot" executed a new manipulation of the sphere. Soon O'Bannon had smoothed out the flight of the chile truck and was circling the air field in ever widening spirals.

"Hey…I should have joined the Air Force instead of the Navy!" he declared.

Down on the tarmac a worried Nathaniel Mirko and his alien companion were being led by two MPs to a waiting C-119 "Flying Boxcar" which would take them to a secret location in Nevada (which later in another reality would be commonly known as Area 51). As they walked along the landing field, Nate noticed that Air Force base personnel had ceased their work duties and were gesturing and looking upward. He too looked to the sky. The incredible sight of a flying truck had stunned all who witnessed it; Nate instantly understood what must have happened—he sent a thought to Hmnogykwaer:

"Do you see that?"

Hmnogykwaer to Nate: "Those idiots! They've activated the sphere. It is not only the power source for the saucer, it generates the gravity/anti-gravity function and can lift any object that surrounds it. If they are not careful…"

## The Moon, Shortly After the Escape

Resnik watched the saucer slowly leave the port. He lost sight of it once it entered the terminator where sunlight no longer illuminated the moon's surface. Never had a man felt so alone. He operated the lever that would close the saucer port's door and waited while the chamber pressurized and filled with breathable air. He had only one recourse at this point: to get as far away from the scene of the crime as possible. No doubt an alarm had been sent by the opening and closing of the big door.

He discarded his short sword. It would only draw attention to him once he entered the city proper. He remembered his previous sojourn through the city streets. He had been ignored by most of the populous. But…where to go? He would need to find some alien who would befriend him, shelter him, keep him safe. But the odds were not in his favor and he knew it.

He found a gravity tube and took this to a lower level where there was an urban environment. Again he wandered through narrow streets cut like caverns through the massive housing structures. Here and there he saw small parks with children playing and a few adults, possibly their nannies, seated on outdoor cubes. He was in a Grey neighborhood. But he remembered the initial kindness of the Green he had met and wished he could locate that community again. He would not make the same mistakes he had made before.

Another street, another park. Resnik was good and lost. Those children…were they some of the ones that had played baseball with the humans? It was unlikely. He decided to investigate anyway. Again, there were the nannies on seating cubes…did alien children have nannies? As he drew closer, one of the female Greys rose and watched him. It appeared to Resnik that she was smiling. He had never actually seen an alien smile before. The smile and her attention to him were intriguing, alluring, suggestive. Too bad he couldn't communicate with her. Sometimes having one's mind blocked was a disadvantage.

He came closer to the female. She was, he thought, strikingly beautiful in her alien way. Once you got over the grey cast to her skin (which was very smooth and unblemished), you noticed other things: her almond-shaped eyes—large, dark and placed so symmetrically over high cheek bones; her long flowing hair—delicate and wispy and moving like weeping willow leaves in a light wind when she tossed her head; her figure—lithe, yet fully sculpted; and, of course, that smile!

She was as tall as he—still petite for a Grey alien. He believed she wouldn't be able to read his mind and yet he couldn't resist talking to her. He moved closer. "Hello, you big beautiful creature," he said, not dreaming that she would understand.

"I am not thought to be so big," she answered with thought images that appeared very clearly in his mind. He was startled.

"You can read my thoughts! Not many of your people can do so."

With a slight toss of her head the female answered: "You talk of males, no doubt. We females have better abilities…in many things." Her smile broadened.

"I can see that. What's you name? Mine is Christian…Christian Resnik. I'm not from around here."

"Well, Christianresnik, I am called Rkohtealnaq. You are not Ratiessrvedflynach, and you don't seem to be Aimnegarwfuchee either. What are you?"

"I am a human, from the planet this moon is orbiting. I was a somewhat reluctant visitor at first, but now I guess you'd say I'm an immigrant, looking to settle down. Are you here with your son or daughter today?"

"My niece. I am not coupled. That is she over there playing on the tpiroleaw."

"How old are you?"

"I am almost sixteen ktanyos."

"Oh my God! I'm robbing the cradle!"

Rkohtealnaq paused to consider the meaning of the expression Resnik had used. Then: "Christianresnik, that is most insulting. We come of age at fourteen ktanyos. I am almost too old for coupling!"

"I'm sorry, Rkohtealnaq. On my planet you'd be underage and it would be inappropriate for someone like me to…uh…court you."

"Court? This is a concept I do not grasp. It means…what?"

"It means I'd like to see more of you. Maybe go to a movie."

"A what?"

# 22

## The Bisti/De-Na-Zin Wilderness

The chile truck had flown in a north-westerly direction. The landscape below them was particularly barren. It was high desert, spotted with chamisa and ribboned with ravines through which arroyos ran; these raged with rain water only once in a blue moon. The sparse vegetation disappeared as they approached the badlands. Occasional patches of grass appeared on higher levels of plateau—a deception by nature to hide what lay below. The truck was losing altitude, the result of pilot O'Bannon's fatigue in holding the sphere steady. It swooped over the edge of the plateau and descended toward a fantasy landscape of rock formations of crimson, tan, ochre, and dusty grey.

The Navajo called the place Bistahí, or "place among adobe formations," and De-Na-Zin (which alluded to the crane-like shapes of some of the eroded rock). Totem-like hoodoos and tent-shaped rocks carved by wind and water rose from clay-colored mudstone and grey shale canyon floors. Here a stone arch casting weird shadows against a jagged ridge; there a forest of slender pillars and impossibly balanced table-like rocks atop rainbow-painted spires; ravines cluttered with petrified wood; hidden caves; a maze of narrow canyons; a desolate, other-worldly, nearly lifeless place which jack rabbits shunned and where tarantulas and scorpions sought shade under a matrix of broken rock.

The truck dipped lower and lower. O'Bannon was looking for a suitable area to bring the vehicle to the ground: how do you land a flying truck? He saw a dry wash and angled the truck toward it. O'Bannon had somewhat mastered direction and altitude in his use of the sphere and usually managed to keep the truck more or less level. What he lacked in flying technique was the ability to control the truck's speed. Thus it landed in the center of the wash but slid across this, scattering clinkers of broken rock in all directions, and finally came to a stop against the wall of a mesa.

The collision shook loose several good-sized boulders which fell onto the truck, caving in the hood and narrowly missing the cab. Three very frightened men sat watching an avalanche of rocks and dirt beginning to bury them. Paco wrenched open the driver's side door and leaped from the cab. O'Bannon and Millender followed.

O'Bannon examined the sphere from the saucer: it was silent and dark; apparently the crash had jarred it enough to terminate its generation of antigravity. It had been one hell of an off switch.

"Now what?" asked Millender. "Where the hell are we? Back on the moon?"

Paco stared silently at his truck, now immobilized by half a ton of debris that had slid down the side of the mesa. "Madre naturaleza," he muttered, "ella es perra dificil!" He began walking up the wash.

"Should we follow him? Does he know where he is going?" Millender asked O'Bannon.

"I think we'd better keep our distance, whatever we do," answered O'Bannon.

The badlands had evolved from a fertile delta that had bordered an inland sea; this stretched from the Arctic Ocean to the Gulf of Mexico over 100 million years ago, splitting the North American continent into two great land masses. The rivers of the delta in the area that would become New Mexico supported prehistoric life in abundance; the skies were filled with Ichthyomis, the ancestors of our modern birds, and Pteranodon, flying reptiles which soared over the waters in search of fish; the shore line teamed with small mammals who would survive the approaching Cretaceous-Paleogene extinction event (dinosaurs such as Triceratops and Velociraptor were doomed by the collision of a massive meteor with the Earth).

Waters receded; the land was filled with ash from volcanoes and formed layers of sandstone, coal, clay and sediment; an ice age carved out a huge plane; mountains rose as continental plates moved away from each other; the coal caught fire and burned; water from melting glaciers began to erode away the softer ash; winds sculpted sandstone into fantastic shapes. A labyrinth of crevices formed as rain waters found the easiest path along the soft sandstone bluffs. A spider's web of tributaries fed a stream bed that etched its way into the shale: this became the dry wash the stranded men now followed.

A fine dusting of snow covered the bizarre landscape—not

unusual for the high desert this time of the year. It would melt off by noon under the naked New Mexican sun. For now it gave a strange rendering to the hoodoos; they looked like giant mushrooms sprouting from the undulating sandstone plateau. The much needed moisture brought forth an ocean scent; the fragrance of ancient shells that composed much of the khaki-colored terrain.

Millender stumbled through a scattering of fist-sized clinkers, crimson shards of lignite coal burned into bricks by ancient fires. The dome-shaped remnants of limestone tubes sat like a forest of giant eggs at the edges of the wash. O'Bannon pointed these out as if he were a tourist guide: "Look how artistic nature can be!"

"It would be nice if Mother Nature had created a pretty little lake. I'm thirsty," Millender said.

They sat for some minutes in the shade of a siltstone wall. They could still see Paco in the distance but the wash was wide here and so they were afraid of losing sight of the one man among them who might actually know the way out of the badlands. They would not linger here long. They watched the striped body of a whiptail lizard flash across a piece of petrified wood, chasing after a large brown spider. It caught the spider and sat happily ingesting it. A bit of trivia surfaced in O'Bannon's memory, previously lost in the muddle of half-attention he had given to his high school biology studies. But something, the hot sun perhaps, prompted him to say:

"Did you know that the whiptail lizard is a female-only species? They reproduce by laying eggs which don't require fertilization. No daddy lizards! I knew some gals back in Frisco that would be into that sort of thing."

"You're a wealth of information today."

"The reason I remember this stuff is because of Sister Sophia Maria, who taught biology. She once hit a girl student with one of those wooden pointers...you know, the ones you use with the big pull-down maps? The girl's parents sued the school but, of course, they lost."

"Why did she hit the girl?"

"She wasn't paying attention. It sort of makes me remember certain things...but not others. Funny, huh?"

"Paco is getting way ahead of us," said Millender. "We'd better shake a leg."

## Room 8002, Fitzsimons Army hospital, Aurora, Colorado

The President wore a set of maroon colored pajamas. On the pocket were embroidered the words, "Much Better Thanks." Finally the cumbersome oxygen tent had been wheeled away and he could carry on with the business of the nation, meeting with members of congress, his staff and distinguished visitors. Mamie had moved into an adjoining suite and redecorated it in pink (including a pink toilet seat).

The Eisenhowers had been vacationing in Colorado, staying with Mamie's relatives, the Douds, in Denver. Ike had been playing golf at the Cherry Hills Golf Club when he began to feel ill. Later that night he awoke with chest pains. At the hospital, he was diagnosed as having suffered a myocardial infarction. The doctors ordered him to stay in bed and not return to work for several weeks. He was exhibiting the affects of a left ventricular aneurysm according to Doctor Paul Dudley White. There was worry of a possible stroke.

Cabinet meetings were being conducted at the White House, officiated by Vice-President Richard Nixon and Secretary of State John Foster Dulles. They communicated with Ike on important issues. At first, the particulars of the President's condition were withheld from the press, but Ike soon directed that a full discloser be made. Although two former presidents, Franklin Roosevelt and Woodrow Wilson, had kept their health problems secret from the public, Ike believed honesty was essential in a world leader. He hoped to set a new standard in this regard. A president should never be perceived as dishonest.

One day Ike had a visit from General Twining. The General told him that an alien had been captured and was being detained at Area 51. He had been in the company of an Earthman. Both had been interrogated, but neither would give up any real information. The alien was demanding to speak with the President. It was a matter of world importance, he had said. General Twining doubted this was so, but the fact that the alien was allied with a human was troubling.

"I told them that you had been hospitalized and that the Vice-President was acting in your place in all matters of diplomacy," said Twining. "I said that I couldn't authorize a meeting with Nixon. What do you want to do, Mr. President?"

"Oh hell's bells, Nathan, I don't want that idiot Nixon mucking things up. If I survive this heart attack…and it looks very much as if I shall…I'll be running for a second term and I'll be asking Dick to step down…take a post in the cabinet or something. I don't want him negotiating an intergalactic peace treaty while I'm being held prisoner by the pill-pushers in this dreadful place! Did you know that they are billing me $51.75 for my meals?"

"He won't talk to anybody but either you or Nixon. What should I do?"

"Aw, stick 'em both in a cell until they're ready to talk through channels. Make that clear to them. World importance…my Aunt Hattie's hairbrush!"

## Aix-en-Provence, France, at the Place de la Rotonde

They had driven up Avenue Victor Hugo to the large, circular Place de la Rotonde at the very center of Aix-en-Provence. At the center of the park was the Fontaine de la Rotonde, a three-tiered fountain over 100 feet wide and 40 feet tall. Around the rim of the basin of the fountain sat six pairs of bronze lions. At the top pedestal were three female figures, each facing in a different direction and representing Justice, Agriculture, and Fine Art. There were also assorted swans, angels riding the swans, dolphins, and jets of water arcing from the top two tiers to fall elegantly into the basin below where Noreen half expected to see mermaids swimming or, at the least, fairies dancing and flitting across water lilies.

The policeman had pulled into a parking lot at the side of the rotunda and stopped the car. "I wanted you to see this," he said. "It dates to 1860. The three women at the top were sculpted by three different artists. My favorite is the one you see facing us…and facing, by the way, toward Marseilles. She is called 'Agriculture' and was made by the famous sculptor, Louis-Félix Chabaud. He also did the Fontaine Saint Louis in another part of town. We are called, you know, 'ville de mille fontaines,' the city of a thousand fountains."

"It's beautiful! I've never seen anything like it. I'm so happy you thought to show us this."

"I am, of course, having to take you to the poste de police. For a while I had…another idea. But, no, I must do my duty. So I like to show you the beautiful sights before you are maybe sent away to somewhere, I don't know where. They will not be lenient with undocumented foreigners. Your friend has some animal concealed in his clothing. I can hear it and I can smell it. It is also illegal to transport animals. I am afraid you are, as you say, in for it."

Noreen thought to Ghyrikkanmo: "What has happened? Have you lost control of the man?"

Ghyrikkanmo to Noreen: 'I told you he had many things floating around in his mind. It is too difficult to control him. Right now he is thinking about his wife. There is something...oh...a feeling of guilt. He still desires you. He mistrusts his wife. But he cannot quite bring himself to be unfaithful. He is quite conflicted."

Noreen spoke to the policeman: "I'm sorry. Of course you have to do your duty. But I would have enjoyed that glass of wine. There are so many things we could...talk about."

"I'm sorry too. But..."

A call came over the radio. It had the quality of being transmitted by a tin can and a string. It was garbled and too fast for Noreen to understand. The policeman:

"I have to answer a call. There has been a robbery. You will have to come with me." He started the engine and pulled out of the parking space. The siren blared.

Noreen to Ghyrikkanmo: "This may be our chance to escape. Watch me when he comes to a stop...we'll run for it. And keep that spider quiet, will you? He's getting on my nerves."

Ghyrikkanmo to Noreen: "I told you, he is not a spider. He is a plablikz."

## Room 8002, Fitzsimons Army hospital, Aurora, Colorado

Ike opened his eyes. He wasn't able to identify exactly where he was. There was a kind of mistiness in the air. He was in a bed, in a room. There was the smell of antiseptic and urine—a field hospital? No, this didn't look like a tent. There were no sounds of battle. He had been at the front, of course. Supreme Commander of the Allied Expeditionary Forces in Europe. Five Stars. He must have been wounded, taken to a station hospital far from the fighting.

A woman approached. Was it Kay? Kay Summersby? Was his

jeep ready? Was she here to take him…somewhere? Was there a meeting? He sat up in bed. With an effort, he managed to raise his arms, to beckon to Kay. Then the world went black.

The nurse who had entered the President's room hurried to the bed side. She didn't like the look of her patient. She felt for his pulse. There wasn't one. Quickly she hurried back to the nurse's station to summon the doctor on duty. This was terrible! She had witnessed patients dying before, but this was the President of the United States!

## Service Road near The Bisti/De-Na-Zin Wilderness

It was a beautiful sight: cherry red, a great chrome grill grinning above a spotless chromed bumper, white walls, moon-shaped hub caps, the split windshield that gave this 1953 Chevrolet 3100 pickup its "five-window" designation. A little bit of road dust, to be sure, but otherwise, the vehicle that was speeding up the gravel road was as clean and shiny as if it had just emerged from an automobile showroom. O'Bannon and Millender stepped into the middle of the road to flag it down.

The driver slowed, stopped short of the two men, and appeared to be contemplating what action to take. The engine revved. It seemed likely he would drive on, leaving the men to their fate. He wore a straw cowboy hat with a bright-blue beaded hat band. His hair hung in two braids tied with red ribbons. His wool shirt seemed stained with sweat: incongruous in the coolness of the day. There were bales of alfalfa in the bed of the truck.

O'Bannon and Millender walked toward the pickup. O'Bannon waved. "Hello," called O'Bannon. "Yah' eh-the'," replied the man.

"What is he saying?" Millender blurted.

"I speak Diné Bizaad…the language of the people," answered the man. "I can also speak in Anglo if I must. You enjoying your walk today?"

"We are not. Where is this place? How far is it…"

"To civilization? This is what we call 'the Big Rez.' Navajo country. You, bilagáana, are deegize…loco…touched in the head to be out here like this. I suppose you want a ride, aoo'?"

"Please. And there is a Spanish man up ahead who needs a ride as well. We can't pay…"

"T'aa shoodi! This is not necessary. I help my brothers, bilagáana included. Get in back and we will pick up the other da'alzhin that walks in the heat."

Paco was seated in the cab, with the Navajo man. O'Bannon and Millender were uncomfortably perched atop some prickly alfalfa bales, bouncing every time the truck hit a rut—which was often. They came to a section where the road exhibited the washboard pattern of tiny hills and valleys that originated from too many cars traveling too fast for conditions. The Navajo man, instead of decreasing his speed, accelerated to what must have been, O'Bannon figured, at least 60 miles per hour. The truck, at this speed, seemed to glide over the rough surface. Of course, braking would be impossible, but the occasional road runner or errant jack rabbit that strayed onto the road would not be missed.

Paco kept glaring at O'Bannon and Millender through the back window. O'Bannon clutched the canvas bag that held the anti-gravity sphere. One good bump, he thought, and we're airborne again. As it turned out, activation of the sphere, accidental or otherwise, would not be necessary for elevation of the Chevy. The vibrant blue New Mexico sky suddenly clouded over. A dark round shape emerged from the cloud bank, just above the speeding pickup. Forward motion of the truck ceased abruptly, nearly catapulting the two men from their alfalfa bales and slamming them against the rear of the cab. An intense beam of light suffused with silver flecks fell upon them. Slowly the truck rose, up, up, and into the saucer.

## Parc Jourdan, Aix-en-Provence, France

Noreen and Ghyrikkanmo scrambled up the grand staircase which connected the two levels of the park. Broad lawns with wide sandy walks had offered no concealment from pursuers who, they were certain, followed closely behind. When the police car had stopped at the site of a robbery, the policeman had suggested to Noreen that if she and her companion remained in the car while he performed his duty, he would be pleased to sit with her later over glasses of the region's good wine and perhaps, change his mind about turning them in. Ghyrikkanmo sent a thought to Noreen: "He's lying." Thus once the policeman was out of sight, the two—now fugitives—sprinted across the road and into a cluster of walnut trees on the fringes of Parc Jourdan.

They had found the entrance to the park, a gateway into a classic French garden complete with lime trees and a pond, and had kept running into the open area beyond. Now half way up the double staircase, they paused to look back. A few children playing in a play area. A man and a woman strolling up the walk, hand in hand. A boy playing fetch with his dog. No police…yet. They continued to the upper level of the park. There they found a series of terraces filled with people: revelers relaxing in the cool air and the bright sunshine, enjoying the last vestiges of late autumn as it unfolded into early winter.

On a side terrace a crowd of children were watching a puppet show of Guignol and Polichinelle (the original French version of Punch and Judy). At the top of the steps there were a juggler, a mime, and a young man playing the accordion, also surround by onlookers. They walked away from the crowds. At the far end of a second terrace stood a large red-and-white striped tent. Along side of this stood a man dressed in a traditional Pierrot costume: white smock with baggy sleeves and pom-pom buttons, wide white pantaloons, black skullcap, whitened face with the drawing of a tear below one eye.

A clown! A circus! Sanctuary for a frightened boy with lizard-like skin who appeared much too unusual to sunder down the avenue unchallenged. Well, weren't you supposed to run away and join a circus when you were a child? Weren't circuses filled with disenfranchised people…odd balls…freaks? Even the strange, spider-like plablikz might find a home here. Noreen approached the Pierrot.

"Bonjour," she said.

# 23

## Groom Lake, Nevada

The ancient salt flat lay in the valley of the Tonopah Basin in southern Nevada, some 80 plus miles from the glitzy city of Las Vegas, and adjacent to the vast Nevada Test and Training Range where, occasionally, mushroom clouds sprouted over the desolate terrain. The disused airfield on Groom Lake originated as the Indian Springs Air Force Auxiliary Field in 1942 but was abandoned after the end of World War II. An old aircraft hanger there was still used for storage—storage of unusual artifacts not intended for public viewing. Like the wreckage of an alien spacecraft retrieved from Roswell, New Mexico, and another from Aztec, New Mexico.

The CIA was becoming interested in the remote site as a testing area for the spy plane Lockheed was proposing: the U-2. Soon the air strip would be expanded, new structures would be built—windowless and hulking under the harsh Nevada sun—and tunnels would connect the various facilities so that materials and secret constructions could be moved out of the sight and out of the mind of any evil enemy observers who might be lurking in the surrounding hills.

It would be called "Dreamland," "Watertown Strip," "Paradise Ranch," or just "the Ranch," and eventually would be designated as "Area 51," although that number seemed to have no particular significance, at least none that could be known without fear of imprisonment...or worse.

Already there were a few newer structures. Already the perimeter was being patrolled by men wearing camouflage uniforms and carrying rifles. Already Air Force personnel assigned to duty at Groom Lake were sworn to secrecy. Already a team of medical experts were busy taking samples of blood and skin, measuring blood pressure, listening to double heart beats, poking and probing and x-raying a grey-skinned being from another planet—a long-gone planet from a long-gone solar system, far far away. Already a human captive was being interrogated by special operatives whose names never appeared on the rosters of any agencies known to the ordinary public.

Nate had considered being entirely open and honest with his interrogators, telling them details about the moon colony and its alien inhabitants. But Hmnogykwaer had warned him to be guarded in his narration. For one thing, the story of his capture and imprisonment on the dark side of the moon lacked credibility, although the incident of the flying truck hinted at the existence of some bizarre reality. Trick or hallucination though it might be, *that* required an explanation.

Hmnogykwaer still insisted on talking to the President and this, he was told, was impossible. Nixon was much too busy with the transition; A vice president needed to be appointed, cabinet members replaced, and the oval office redecorated (Mrs. Nixon would pick out carpeting and draperies, and order the repainting of the pink bedroom and bathroom walls).

There were things going on in Southeast Asia that Dick Nixon didn't like. And there was the embarrassment of the censure of Senator McCarthy—Nixon had been a member of the House Un-American Activities Committee years before it fell into the hands of the virulent Senator from Wisconsin, and had been a silent supporter of McCarthy, distancing himself, but remaining a confirmed believer that the Red Peril existed within our own society and was a threat to our democracy. Yes, the Communists both at home and abroad should be dealt with in a manner that demonstrated the determination and the strength of the new leader of the free world!

In a small room at Groom Lake Nate played mouse to the interrogator's cat:

"How did you come to meet this Martian?"

"He's not a Martian. We met on the road. I was hitch-hiking."

"You were just walking along the highway and met a space alien."

"I didn't know he was from outer space at the time. You told me that he was an alien. I just thought he was a normal person."

"And that is why you accompanied him into the Air Base to talk to the President. Aren't you in collusion with an enemy combatant? Don't you know that is a treasonable offence?"

"I'm not in the army, he is not a combatant, and we are not in collusion, as you put it. I just thought he was a swell fellow and I went along with him."

"Talking to the President. What was that all about?"

"I don't know. Maybe he has delusions of grandeur. Maybe he is a fan."

"And what about the flying truck?"

"What flying truck? Now you are pulling my leg. I don't know anything about a flying truck or spacemen or talking to the President. You have to let me go…you can't hold me here without letting me talk to an attorney."

"Oh, can't we?"

Hmnogykwaer wasn't faring any better:

"Why do you want to talk to the President?"

"He is the only one who can prevent the end of your world as you know it."

"Can't you be more specific?"

"You would not believe me if I told you."

"Try me. I'm a good listener. Tell me what this great tragedy is all about. The end of the world?"

"See? You are skeptical. And powerless. Take me to the President."

"No. That can't be done. You tell me and I'll relay the information."

"I doubt that. Take me to see the President. It is the only way."

## White House, Washington, D.C.

Snow flurries outside the floor-to-ceiling windows behind the President's desk foretold the coming of winter in earnest. Those who had hoped for a white Christmas would not be disappointed. The 41 year-old president, Richard Milhous "Tricky Dick" Nixon, was getting ready for his daily briefing, laying out the lined yellow paper pad upon which he liked to take notes and arranging in perfect alignment with the pad his Waterman Stateleigh Taperite fountain pen with its gold-filled cap, a present from his wife Pat on his fortieth birthday. Maybe he should get one of those tape recorders for the Oval Office, he thought to himself. It would save a lot of note taking.

He didn't much like the winters in Washington—he was, after all, a California boy—and he was considering establishing a winter White House in Yorba Linda in Orange County where he was born, or perhaps Key Biscayne in Florida where Pat had suggested they buy a house. He could do whatever he wanted to do now that he was the most important person in the entire world.

Nixon relished the briefings, especially when they centered on international affairs. Domestic issues bored him—he was content to perpetuate Eisenhower's policies, quasi-liberal though they might be, so that he could focus on world politics and the struggle against Communism. The Soviet Union had detonated a thermonuclear bomb for the first time in September. Now the race was on to stockpile a greater collection of death-dealing devices than one's enemy. Like two naked men wagging their members at each other, the USA and Russia would persist in courting the apocalypse in order to one-up one another.

The Soviet Union and China had recognized Ho Chi Minh as Vietnam's leader and supported the Viet Minh in their effort to take over South Vietnam. Nixon would not be outdone. He would increase the number of "advisors" that Ike had sent to South East Asia. As yet, he could see no point in directing the troops into active combat. That time would come, however, and soon. Perhaps a series of atom bombs along the 17th parallel…

Toward the end of the briefing, Gordon Gray requested a private meeting with Nixon. He was a former Secretary of the Army under President Harry Truman and had recently been appointed Assistant Secretary of Defense for International Security Affairs by Eisenhower. And he was a member of Majestic 12. After discussions of the Chinese threat to the people of Formosa and the need to support the Nationalist Army against the Communists (Nixon again fantasized about a few well-placed nuclear bombs…if we've got 'em, why can't we use 'em?), the briefing broke up and Gray remained in the Oval Office, seated across from Nixon on the striped davenport.

"Mr. President, we've got an EBE under lock and key in Nevada."

"EBE?"

"Extraterrestrial Biological Entity. A spaceman. He walked into

Kirtland Air Fore Base and demanded to talk to the President. We've isolated him along with a human companion he was with."

"A human companion, you say?"

"Yes. This represents something new along the lines of extraterrestrials. We may have a ring of humans in collusion with the aliens...traitors."

"Communists?"

"Who can say? It wouldn't be out of character for the Soviets to use the aliens against us. The crucial issue is that of the alien technology. What if they have some sort of devastating weapon...and Russia gets their hands on it before we do?"

"I thought we had made a treaty with the aliens. Of course, Ike never let me in on the details. Asshole didn't trust me."

"The discussions were ongoing. There were two distinct factions...the Greys and the Nordics. We achieved a period during which they agreed not to interfere in world politics if we let them study us...take random humans to their base. It was just a tactic to stall while we came up with a plan."

"Their base? Where is it?"

"Apparently on the dark side of the moon. We haven't been able to observe it. Eisenhower accelerated the space program but we haven't the ability to reach the moon as yet."

"I know. I was going to cut back on that...a waste of money. Better to put it into the spy plane program. What do you suggest?"

"You may need to talk to this alien. He seems to want to cooperate, but he won't talk to anyone but you. It's a pain in the ass, I know, but..."

"Set it up as soon as possible. And this human traitor...have you gotten anything from him? Will he name names?"

"He has been extremely uncooperative. There is a new drug we are going to try. The army has been experimenting with it...lysergic acid diethylamide it is called. Results are sporadic, even dangerous. But in this case..."

"Do what ever you need to do, Gordon. But get results!"

"Yes sir, Mr. President. I'll see to it."

After Gordon Gray had left the office, Nixon looked down at the yellow pad where he had been taking notes during the meeting. It was covered with doodles: flying saucers, atom bombs, and a nasty-looking hammer-and-sickle design.

## Somewhere in the New Mexican Sky

They were in a large chamber near the bottom of the saucer, sitting next to the red truck. They could feel the motion of the saucer as it lifted toward the upper atmosphere. Millender looked at O'Bannon quizzically. "You really don't know how to turn that thing on?" he asked, referring to the anti-gravity sphere O'Bannon still had in the cloth bag slung over his shoulder.

"Not really, no. It apparently needs a knock at the right angle. Do you want me to try?"

"I was thinking, if you started that thing up, it would interfere with this flying saucer that is most likely going to transport us back to the moon. I don't fancy a visit to that place again."

"It could crash us. Or take us farther out into space...to Mars or Venus. It might not be strong enough to counteract this saucer. There are a lot of maybes involved."

"But, what do we have to lose by trying?"

"Maybe we should get back into the truck...along with the others. The extra mass might make a difference. It might help protect us if we crash."

"I'll tell the Indian and he can tell the Mexican."

"*New* Mexican."

All four men squeezed into the cab of the truck. O'Bannon began turning the sphere over and over and pressing every indentation, every minor bump on its surface. He shook it. He battered it. He dropped it onto the floor of the cab. He banged it against the dash board. Finally, discouraged, he let it sit on his lap while he pondered the problem. All at once the sphere began to glow. Flashes of different colors danced across its surface; violets, pinks, greens. It hummed. The truck began to vibrate.

"Gravity," said O'Bannon, "is the attraction that one mass has for another mass. The greater the mass, the greater the attraction. It's why Earth rotates around the sun and the moon rotates around the Earth—it's a balancing act of big and little masses. I would assume that anti-gravity would work much in the same way."

"So are we going to be orbiting the saucer?"

"We are inside of the saucer and therefore part of its mass. Our sphere will affect the truck, which has less mass than the saucer-plus-truck. I can probably fly the truck around inside the saucer, but we will still be captive by the saucer's superior anti-gravity."

"What if the sphere produced a field of *positive* gravity?"

"I suppose the saucer would push against that…maybe it would cause it to wobble…maybe to crash. But I don't know how this thing works!"

"It might be like a woman," said the Navajo, "giving birth. Push, push, push! Out she pops!"

O'Bannon raised the sphere slightly; the truck rose a few feet above the floor. He raised the sphere higher and the truck rose up until it touched the ceiling of the chamber. Quickly, O'Bannon inverted the sphere. The truck plummeted downward, hit the floor. There was a surge of pressure against the top of the truck; the roof of the cab began to buckle. They felt heavy. It was difficult to move, to breathe. The Navajo said a silent prayer.

The floor beneath them gave way and the truck fell toward the greater mass and gravity of the Earth. O'Bannon inverted the sphere again just as the truck neared the ground. They floated above a dusty plain speckled with candelabra cactus and juniper. A curious coyote stood watching as O'Bannon set the truck gently down. They were back on Terra Firma. No one was happier than Rubén "Paco" Sandoval who vowed silently never to drive or ride in a troca again.


## Area 51 at Groom Lake


The CIA had been testing the drug secretly by dosing GIs without their knowledge and then observing the results. The results fell short of expectations. Most subjects hallucinated. Some experienced euphoria. Some had elevated episodes of anxiety. Some became violent. There did not seem to be any value to the drug as a chemical weapon. Perhaps, like sodium pentothal, it could be used for interrogation purposes. Now they had a subject upon whom they could experiment.

Nate Mirko, meet LSD-25. LSD-25, meet Nate Mirko. The introductions were by a green-garbed male nurse via syringe. The dose was ample. The precautions taken included restraining straps which held Nate's arms securely to a metal chair—a cold metal chair in a small, windowless room. A single lighting fixture mounted on the ceiling gave forth only enough light to chase shadows into the corners of the room where they hid behind metal file cabinets. There was a metal table at which sat (on a metal chair) a man who might have been a scientist or a doctor—except that he wasn't. Before him on the table lay a clip board and a fountain pen.

The man seemed to be talking to Nate; he wasn't quite sure, but the undertones of his voice, like the rumbling of an elevator, persisted in entering Nate's conscious mind no matter how hard he tried to avoid hearing them. He had reached a plateau as his senses heightened, where he had climbed out of the dull grey cubical by exiting through the ceiling light and entering a multi-colored universe of sparkling gems and wispy strands of golden stuff like the wind-blown hair of some ethereal angel.

No one else occupied Nate's universe, hence it was extremely irritating that the oily, earth-bound utterance that issued from some metal monster still below in the grey room could percolate up into his glorious domain. Nate pulled at his ears: they detached from his head with two subtle pops. He tossed the ears away and silence came to him like a wall of emerald colored bricks, like a cocoon spun of finest verdigris—no, it was a savannah of prairie grass and he, the last buffalo, grazed in contentment as a purple dawn brightened into pinks and oranges and a swarm of black ravens rolled through the sky like the unfurling of a quilt—a crazy quilt.

The prairie became the ocean; the flock of ravens became flying fish, leaping and floating above a churning azure sea flecked with neon foam. Then everything began to melt. Colors swirled but did not mix. Sea and sky became one great kaleidoscope of sensation; Nate merged with fragments of pure light broken off from an impossible and unearthly spectrum. He *was* light. He refracted. He super nova-ed. He big-banged. He broke up into a wave of particles. He maelstromed, swirling ever downward in a vortex of pure energy.

There was a metal bed with a clip board hanging at one end. Grey-green sheets tightly made with hospital corners so precise one could cut a finger running it along the crease. A glass bottle of some clear liquid hanging from a wire stand, a dull brown tube connecting it to his arm. Nate blinked open eyes that had seemed crusted shut like barnacles on a ship's bottom. Too bright. Window light filtered through a dusty shade. Silhouette against the light. That rumbling, grating, ugly sound again! A voice? Voices?

The male nurse had called for the doctor once he had seen that his patient had regained consciousness. They talked, the nurse and doctor, but the words didn't resolve beyond noise for Nate—a painful noise like the screaming of a semi's air brakes descending a steep hill too fast. Nate pulled at his ears: no result. Contorted face. Soundless scream. Writhing and flaying of arms. The covers mussed, no longer precise, not regimentally correct.

"Hold his arms," the doctor directed. He injected.

Nate felt a welcome calm seep through his body. There was a brief flash of memory as he faded back into oblivion: something about a buffalo.

Byron Grush

# 24

## Cirque d'Renard Agile

Tent canvas flapped and ruffled in a jealous wind. Crowds who had stood in line for tickets to the afternoon show in previous weeks were no longer in evidence. The entertainment season had waned as the days had shortened. The traveling circus would be heading for warmer climes soon, perhaps to the south of Spain.

Guillaume Clément Monette, manager of the Cirque d'Renard Agile, ran his fingers through his closely cropped goatee. What was he going to do with these two—the girl who, although pretty, seemed to have no natural talent like singing or dancing or acrobatics, and the boy—the boy who in a sideshow (which the Cirque d'Renard Agile didn't have) might be passed off as "the lizard boy," but who also lacked any ability of interest to an audience? He spoke:

"Years ago, when I was with the Cirque d'Hiver in Paris, we had 'Ferry the Human Frog.' He was a contortionist who dressed up in a frog costume and hopped around the stage. Very effective. If your young friend could do something like that…"

Noreen knew it was useless. Ghyrikkanmo wasn't about to perform. And she couldn't swing on a trapeze or ride bareback on a painted pony. She hadn't even been able to housebreak her first puppy, much less train a lion to jump through a flaming hoop. Maybe…maybe…

"I could be a clown," she said. "I'm good with makeup and costumes. Give me a chance to work something up."

"I don't know. Now I *could* find a use for that giant spider you have with you. Would you be willing to sell it to me?"

Guillaume Monette and his circus were part of a long tradition dating back to the days of Antonio Franconi, the founder of the French circus. Before the days of touring, the big circuses, the Cirque Olympique des Champs-Élysées, the Cirque d'Été, and the Cirque d'Hiver, had established permanent residences in large buildings (designed by famous architects like Jacques Hittorff) which could accommodate equestrian shows. These elegant stadiums featured a central ring, or circle…hence the name "Cirque" was given to those establishments.

Monette's tenure at Cirque d'Hiver under the Bouglione brothers had been an early education into showmanship: parades and pantomimes with wild animals, clowns, and acrobats. He became expert at horseback riding, standing up on the animal's back as it trotted around the ring. He could jump through a hoop or do a somersault as the horse broke into a gallop and the crowds cheered. Then one day he slipped. The fall broke both his legs. He never again performed as a horseman.

He found a job as a régisseur, a kind of all around administrator, manager, and producer, for a traveling circus, the Cirque Maxime. It was there he met Francette Justine, a 16 year-old tight rope walker with luxurious auburn locks, and fell in love. Jean-Baptiste Cheval, owner of the traveling circus, suggested that the marriage between Francette and Guillaume would make a spectacular tableau if conducted inside the tigers' cage during a performance, but Monette rejected this idea. Instead he agreed to a lesser publicity stunt: he and his bride-to-be rode through town on the way to the court house on the back of an elephant, she in a bridal gown and he in top hat and tails.

The young couple stayed with Cirque Maxime until the tragic day on June 14, 1940, when the Nazis marched into Paris. Guillaume felt compelled to join the underground resistance. He insisted that Francette go to live with her mother and father in Saint-Août, a small rural town well away from the invading army. Of his adventures during that period much could be written. The valiant work of Monette and his compatriots advanced the time of the liberation of France. It left, however, many scars on the people who had resisted, and on those who hadn't.

Monette reunited with the love of his life and Cirque d'Renard Agile was born. Influenced by Moscow Circuses which began touring through France after the war, Monette decided to add a dancing bear act. He had a trained Airedale who could walk along parallel tight ropes carrying a monkey on its back, and a pony which could do math problems by stamping out answers with its hoof, but these paled against the spectacle of a great lumbering bear raised up on hind legs and put through its paces by a pretty young woman.

Thus it was that Francette stood in the center ring one fateful August afternoon, a Siberian Brown bear nearly twice her height swaying awkwardly in front of her as the odd couple performed their dance. Although the bear wore a leather muzzle and its claws had been clipped to dull stubs, his immense bulk presented a grave danger to the girl. He was small for his species but weighed close to 600 pounds.

Midway through the act, Pipo, the clown, was mimicking the dancing bear to the delight of the crowd—but not of the bear. His antics infuriated the bear who saw the clown, dressed in a bear suit, as a competitor. Suddenly the animal dropped to four legs and bounded across the ring toward the hapless clown, dragging Fancette by the chain lease she held which attached to its collar. The bear trainer managed to subdue the bear, but not before Pipo lay bleeding in the sawdust and Francette had received internal injuries that would prove to be fatal. Monette had the bear shot.

"I *could* find a use for that giant spider you have with you. Would you be willing to sell it to me?" Monette said to Noreen.

Here Ghyrikkanmo winced—it isn't a spider, he thought to Noreen.

"If you want the spider," she replied, "you must take the two of us with it."

"Hmph. Well, maybe you can work in the kitchen. Can you cook?

"Um…I…yes, of course. And I'm a good dish washer."

"And the lizard boy…I'll think of some kind of an act he can do that doesn't involve much talent. He could work with the clowns. So. It is settled. Tomorrow we leave for Spain. You can stay in the red wagon with Madam DuBois, the mind reader. I'll arrange it."

Oh, oh, thought Noreen…another mind reader!

Noreen had not expected the circus wagon to be quite so vintage. Arched top, painted spokes on the wooden wheels—it could have emerged from a gypsy caravan. At least it wasn't being pulled by horses or mules—or elephants! The ancient truck that did pull it might have pre-dated the wagon. It seemed constructed more of rust than of metal. There were six such wagons in their cavalcade as Cirque d'Renard Agile wound its way through the mountain pass and down the main road toward Girona, Spain.

The ancient city, once protected by high walls, had suffered over two dozen attempts at invasion since the Romans were driven out by the Moors in 715. Seven of these succeeded—most recently there were conquests by the French. Girona then became part of Catalonia under Charlemagne in 785, a nationality which the region has preserved proudly. Its large Jewish population was expelled or absorbed during the Spanish Inquisition but the city remained rich in diversity. Two languages were spoken there: Spanish and Catalan.

The circus set up just outside of the town in an open area along the banks of the Riu Ter. Roustabouts pounded stakes and raised the canvas tent high upon twin poles. Hawkers walked through the town with leaflets announcing the show. It was a small circus without a great menagerie of exotic animals—just three ponies, the tight rope walking dog, a monkey, and now, a giant spider-like creature from another planet. Noreen had misrepresented the plablikz as a specimen found in a Brazilian rain forest by her deceased father, a botanist and explorer (also a gigantic fib) who had traveled extensively collecting oddities. He had, she said, discovered Ghyrikkanmo (who was now being touted as "the alligator boy") on an excursion to Equatorial Guinea, and had brought the boy back to civilization.

Like most fabrications, Noreen's deceitful history became more and more complicated. Her presence in France, she claimed, resulted from having accompanied her father to a conference in Marseille. The man unfortunately had contracted trypanosomiasis when in Africa, and the parasitic protozoa had by that time reached his nervous system. He had died, stranding Noreen, the alligator boy and the giant spider in the south of France. No one at the Cirque d'Renard Agile really believed her story, but then, no one really cared if it were true or not. Everyone had a story.

Madame Dubois, for instance, claimed to be descended from an Egyptian princess. She had actually been raised in an orphanage near the Passage d'Enfer in Paris and had run away at the age of ten. Six years later she married a juggler named Alexander DuBois who worked in the Pinder circus. There she originated her mind-reading act. This depended, since her psychic abilities were bogus, upon planting an accomplice in the crowd whose "secret thoughts" she would reveal to the amazement of the audience. Alexander left her for a knife thrower's assistant, a young girl he had gotten pregnant. Madam Dubois' popularity dwindled and the Pinders let her go. She moved from small circus to small circus. The low point of her career was her present position in the Cirque d'Renard Agile.

Madame DuBois was a woman of considerable girth, having put on the pounds as depression led her to food as a panacea for her descent into melancholy. She hefted that weight with authority when the need arose. Now she squeezed through the door of the circus owner's wagon, coming to Guillaume Monette with a fantastic story: she *could* indeed read minds, she told the circus owner. Just the other day she had felt an unusual presence as if someone were probing her inner most thoughts—not maliciously, but as a sort of introduction. She concentrated and discovered she could hear…hear was not the proper word…realize the thought images from this other persona. After some experimentation she discovered that it was the alligator boy who was attempting to communicate with her. And she could answer him! She had discovered why the boy never talked. And something more: he was from another world, another universe. He was an outer space alien! Monette was incredulous.

Two days of under attended shows in Girona convinced Monette to pull up stakes and head south. The following day saw the circus on the outskirts of Barcelona. Barcelona! Ciutat Comtal! Capital of Catalonia, ancient Roman city, jewel of the Mediterranean, site of Gaudi's Sagrada Familia, birth place and home to Joan Miró, early home and inspiration for Pablo Picasso, city of ornate balconies draped with Catalonian flags, city of stubborn resistance to Francisco Franco and his Nationalism, city of tapas and sangria—Barcelona!

"I hope we do better in this town than we did in the last," Monette said to no one in particular as the last bit of canvas was tethered.

There had been some changes in the last few days. Ghyrikkanmo was no longer relegated to being a foil for the antics of the clowns. Now he had been promoted to assistant to Madam DuBois. The mind reader had taken him under her ample wings and suggested that he probe the mind of someone in the circus audience during her act, relaying information to her that she could then use to astound the mark. The advantages to Ghyrikkanmo should be obvious, she told him. No one liked to work with clowns.

Ghyrikkanmo had taken to his new status as an entertainer gleefully. It was exciting for the boy to be a center of attention in this strange new world. The thoughts he fished from the simple minds of the crowd were delectable morsels; he became fascinated with the earth peoples' problems, their desires, and their fears. Madam Dubois had proven to be a magnanimous boss, so appreciative of the leverage he gave her for her act that she doted on him, even teaching him card tricks in their spare time.

Noreen, on the other hand, was not at all happy with her new roll at the Cirque d'Renard Agile. She had been made into a performer, and that was better than washing dishes. However, she had replaced a former snake charmer who had left the circus months ago (taking her anaconda with her). Noreen was now a spider charmer. It was humiliating. She was dressed in a skimpy outfit, all veils and sequins, and had to parade before the crowd while Fagryumo, the plablikz, crawled across her shoulders and up and down her arms.

She had been thinking. Yes, she was responsible for the alien boy. But hadn't he adapted nicely to life in the circus? Hadn't that fat mind reader lady more or less adopted him? He would be safe here. No one would be afraid of him or take him into custody to be questioned and probed. She was homesick for Bellingham—and for Nate. Was Nate still on the moon or had he managed to escape? She needed to know. There must be an American embassy in Barcelona. She just needed to get into town…

No embassy, just narrow streets with open bays piled high with melons, limes, mangoes, or trays of ice holding sardines, prawns, crabs and lobsters—still moving (but slowly), or racks where glistening hams were hanging, or shelves of cheeses and bottles of olive oil, barrels of wine—and all this on the side streets. Now they ventured down the broad La Rambla, a divided avenue which would lead them to the larger market, La Boqueria. The circus cooking staff was shopping for Jamon, the dried ham so unique to Spain, and fresh fruits and vegetables, cheeses and olives—Barcelona offered a variety of seafood caught daily, meat grown locally and spirits slowly aged in old wood that had seen the many conquerors of Catalonia come…and go.

Noreen had volunteered to help with the shopping. It was a way to get into the city where she hoped to find help to return to her own country. She had taken Ghyrikkanmo aside and explained her plan to the boy, expecting reluctance or at least some form of sadness at the separation. She was surprised to find Ghyrikkanmo completely ambivalent. The emotional mechanisms of the alien being were sometimes impossible to decipher. At least she didn't have to worry about the boy's well-being: he would be safe and secure in the circus.

She strayed toward a side exit of the massive steel-roofed market building. Tables of colorful and exotic fruits lined the aisles. At a meat station a butcher was slicing paper thin pieces of Jamon from a ham hock. Next to this sat a fresh calf's head, grinning grotesquely. Fish mongers were piling their tables with sole and mullet, turbo and grouper, anchovy and bream. In vegetable bins were rows of artichokes, leeks, asparagus, peppers, onions and potatoes. Men carried wooden crates of all manner of edibles, some of it still squirming. Noreen squeezed past a man whose white apron was stained with blood and soon was outside the Boqueria. Out on the busy street. Out, with no where to go.

La Rambla was a long, tree-lined parkway where people strolled past stalls selling flowers or tables set up by nearby restaurants. Vehicle traffic was kept to one way streets on either side of this. At the southeast end of the street was a statue of Columbus that stood on top of a high pedestal and just beyond that, the Mediterranean. At the opposite end was the Plaça de Catalunya, an enormous plaza surrounded by large buildings, some of which were occupied by various aspects of the government. Noreen might have found the help she sought in the direction of the plaza, but of course, she wasn't aware of this. Instead some instinct led her in the other direction: toward the sea.

The Mirador de Colom was a towering Corinthian column over 130 feet tall. Its pedestal was covered with sculptures of griffins, their wings raised skyward, and encrusted with medallions representing Spaniards related to Columbus. Additional statues, historical bas-reliefs, and broad staircases flanked by lions completed the monument's base. At the top stood the valiant Columbus holding a scroll in his left hand while pointing with his right. Pointing. Some said the explorer pointed toward his ancestral home of Genoa, Italy, although the direction was wrong for this. Perhaps he simply pointed to the sea which had been his home for so many years once he had won the support of Ferdinand of Aragon and Isabella of Castile, the rulers of Spain. Or perhaps he had just been positioned thusly to await the coming of the Klivpoklaians.

Noreen's gaze moved up the monument to the figure of Columbus. She, like many others, wondered where it was that the discoverer of the New World (not counting the indigenous peoples who already had lived there) was pointing. She looked out at the sea and saw that a strange dark cloud bank was rolling in toward the city, although the sun was shining and there was no hint of storm in the air. It rolled and expanded and began to thin.

As the cloud parted there arose from the crowd of people surrounding the Mirador de Colom a gasp of astonishment. Noreen also gasped. From inside the cloud came a fleet of saucers—many saucers. They approached slowly and in formation. She counted at least a half dozen of the disks. They flew over her head and shortly thereafter hovered ominously above the city proper. The invasion had begun!

# 25

## The Saucers are Real!

There were saucers in the sky above every major city. The greatest numbers hovered over Washington, D.C., New York City, London, Paris, Berlin, Rio de Janeiro, Mexico City, Sidney, Moscow, Beijing and Tokyo. They appeared simultaneously and hung in the sky like great silver birds riding updrafts. There were no signals from the saucers, nothing that gave an indication as to their intent. Attempts to communicate with the visitors were in vain. All that the people of Earth could do was to wait.

United States Air Force F-80C Shooting Star fighter planes were scrambled over Washington, circling the invaders. Royal Air Force Hawker Hunter jets flew over London, keeping tabs on the saucers. Soviet Migs littered Moscow's airspace like murderous crows. Every government filled the air with their best and fastest and most deadly. Presidents, prime ministers, chairmen, chancellors, government officials and commanding generals ran for the bunkers. Antiaircraft missiles were put on the ready. So far, not a shot had been fired.

In Denver, Colorado, a corporal at the Nike missile base got nervous and fired off a ground-to-air at the closest saucer to his station. The missile got within 30 feet of the saucer, came to an abrupt stop, then shot away at a perpendicular angle, finally plummeting to the ground in a suburban parking lot where it exploded, destroying a dozen cars and killing six shoppers. Over Moscow, a Mig pilot emptied his wing guns at a saucer with a similar result. The bullets bounced back, perforated the airplane and killed the pilot. The Mig cashed into Red Square where a crowd of people had been watching the saucers. There were many deaths.

Numerous incidents of attempted defense, all ineffective and disastrous, occurred around the world as governments, frustrated by the aliens' silence, flung bombs and bullets at the ubiquitous saucers. The spaceships had some kind of invisible shield, likely some form of anti-gravity, which universally repelled anything within their proximity. The major powers, the United States and Russia, debated using the ultimate weaponry in their arsenals: the atom bomb. A special session of the United Nations was convened, in part to forestall such drastic action. It was unknown if a nuclear weapon could penetrate the saucers' shields, or what effect a bomb being repelled back to the earth might have on the population. The saucers, after all, were all over major cities. It was an alien standoff.

Meanwhile, scientists attempted to communicate using every language and every known wave length of radio, as well as visually signally with powerful beacons in Morse code (hoping the aliens would be able to decipher this). For three days nothing happened. The barrage of bullets finally ceased as its futility was now painfully apparent. Then the saucers began to move.

Several events had led up to the arrival of the saucers. Of significance to many of the Christian faith was the sighting, on Christmas Eve, of the light from the supernova of Betelgeuse, the one-time sun of the Klivpoklaians' planet. Traveling for over 640 years, the brilliant light from the explosion of the red supergiant would remain visible for over two months, giving rise to numerous cults both with and without the Christian mythos of a second coming. X-rays and ultraviolet radiation from the gamma-ray burst had dissipated before reaching Earth: there were no ill effects. There was only the spectacle of the star shining brightly even in daylight—an ever present beacon both for faith in a supreme being, and as an ominous sign of a coming apocalypse.

President Richard Nixon had finally given Hmnogykwaer the interview he requested. The meeting had taken place at Camp David, in a cabin far away from the prying eyes and ears of the press corps. Nixon had listened patiently while the alien espoused his concern for the safety of the planet. His own people, he told the president, were a dying race whose only hope for survival was to assimilate the human species, siphoning off genetic material and combining this with their own. They would do this ruthlessly, resulting in the eventual extermination of the human race. They considered humans less than animals—this, they said, was evident in the manner in which Earth nations warred with each other and polluted their environment. The development of the atom bomb was an example of the suicidal mania humans possessed in their struggle for dominance over one another. The passing of the human race would be no great loss.

Hmnogykwaer suggested that the major governments of Earth demonstrate to the Klivpoklaians that they could live in peace and become good custodians of the world, foregoing the greed and lust for power which caused them to rape the land and kill one another. For starters, they should destroy all their nuclear weapons. Earth scientists should collaborate with the aliens in an effort to perfect the genetic cloning that would save the Klivpoklaians. This was the only path toward survival of the human race, said Hmnogykwaer. Nixon just blinked, astounded and outraged at the arrogance of the spaceman.

What sort of weapons did the aliens have, Nixon wanted to know. Would they share their technology freely if humans welcomed them with open arms? Hmnogykwaer was silent on these points. The President was frustrated and left the cabin to think and stroll among the pines while the alien remained guarded by Secret Service men. A light snowfall had dusted the landscape and capped the nearby peaks of the Catoctin Mountains. Nixon turned the collar of his trench coat up. There must be something to be gained from the spacemen, he thought. Some weapon that would trump the arms race. The ability to travel into outer space—what a strategic advantage that would be! Certainly we must make an agreement with the saucer people before the Russians do!

An incident that preceded, and in a way fostered the coming of the invaders, took place in New Mexico. The Navajo had dropped O'Bannon, Millender, and Paco Sandoval off in Farmington and put as much distance between them and himself as possible, driving toward Shiprock at a speed that challenged the structural integrity of his '53 Chevy. Paco wandered off down Main Street past pawn shops and boarded-up store fronts until he found a suitable bar where he could wash away the frightful memories of flying trucks with cheap beer. O'Bannon and Millender stuck out their thumbs. It seemed a good idea to keep moving, although to where, and to do what, eluded them at the moment.

A trucker driving an eighteen-wheeled Kenworth picked them up outside of town. The semi-trailer-truck headed south to Gallup and turned east on Route 66. Hours later they were approaching the Pueblo of Acoma where the Pueblo people lived high on a mesa top known as "Sky City." It was one of the oldest continuously inhabited communities of indigenous people on the North American continent; the oldest in the United States.

The mesa rose 357 feet above the flat, nearly barren New Mexico desert, a craggy sandstone mountain truncated like a giant broken tooth, cluttered with adobe dwellings and an old Catholic church, the San Esteban del Rey Mission. In 1598, the Spanish, under Juan de Oñate, were colonizing throughout the region with, in most cases, dire results for the Native Americans living in the Seven Northern Pueblos. The Acoma killed eleven of Oñate's men. Oñate retaliated, burning their pueblo, murdering over 600, and enslaving the survivors. As punishment, the right feet of all males over 25 years of age were amputated.

O'Bannon and Millender sat in the front seat of the semi next to the driver, a man whose face, pale from lack of sun, was smudged with road dust and streaked with little rivulets of sweat that seemed to mimic the arroyos in the desert outside. The cloth bag containing the anti-gravity sphere sat on O'Bannon's lap. It felt heavier than usual to O'Bannon, and it was beginning to hum softly. He shifted his legs out of discomfort, causing the bag to slide from his lap and hit the floor of the truck with a loud thump.

"Whacha got in there," asked the driver, "a bowling ball?"

The mesa of Sky City was within sight just ahead when the truck suddenly stopped. No amount of pumping of the gas pedal or jerking of the shift lever could coax the semi even an inch up the road. Millender stuck his head out of the window and looked up. Sure enough, as he had feared, there it was: a shining silver disk hovered just above them—the saucer people had found them!

"Oh shit!" Millender uttered. Quickly he grabbed the bag from the floor, pushed open the door and began running into the desert.

"Get rid of it," yelled O'Bannon. "Throw it far away from you."

But it was too late. A beam of light fell from the saucer onto the running man. Silver and gold flecks swirled within the beam as sand from the desert floor, bits of cholla buds, and the helpless man rose up so swiftly they were gone in the blink of an eye—a sailor's eye, fearful and soon to be tearful: O'Bannon watched his buddy disappear into the saucer.

This time, the sphere was wrenched from Millender's grasp before he could try to manipulate it. He had no idea how to work it, at any rate. He was taken back to the moon colony where he soon found himself appearing before the Circle. Twelve telepathic minds were aimed at his inner thoughts and memories. The Circle learned about Millender's escape in the stolen saucer and of the traitor, Hmnogykwaer, and his intent to reveal the truth of the inevitable alien invasion of Earth. The time table for the invasion was about to be altered.

The saucers that had lurked in the skies began to move away. As suddenly as a spring rain storm, they were gone. A few theorists with remarkable insight said that the parade of the disks had had the purpose of alerting the world, not only to the presence of the alien beings, but to their intention to negotiate—or possibly to make demands. Yet there had been no formal communication between humanity and the invaders.

Nixon was frantic. He desperately needed the aliens on his side. He summoned Hmnogykwaer once more, this time to Oval Office. He would agree to cooperate with the aliens, he told Hmnogykwaer. He would offer them sanctuary, their own space, a sort of alien reservation…maybe a whole state (how about South Dakota?—nothing much happened there anyway). He would begin talks with the Soviets about reducing nuclear weapons. He would assign the best scientists to develop a cure for the dying…what should he call them? Moonmen?

Hmnogykwaer just shook his head. "I have no way to contact my people," he replied. "You will just have to wait until they come to you."

They came the very next day. A lone Grey appeared as if by magic in the foyer of the White House. Secret Service men scrambled, drew pistols. The alien focused his thoughts. The men lowered their weapons, led the alien to the president's office. The Grey, the spokesperson for the Klivpoklaians, made it clear to the president that his counterparts were simultaneously visiting First Secretary of the Central Committee of the Soviet Union, Nikita Khrushchev, Chairman of the People's Republic of China, Mao Zedong, Prime Minister of India, Jawahar Lal Nehru, Prime Minister of Japan, Ichiro Hatoyama, President of France, Ren Coty, Prime

Minister of the United Kingdom, Sir Winston Churchill, President of Mexico, Adolfo Ruiz Cortines, and Chancellor of Germany, Konrad Adenauer.

Richard Nixon was sufficiently awed by the experience of communicating by thought transfer that he agreed to the alien's demands without bothering to negotiate for an exchange of technology (i.e., weaponry). While he couldn't actually turn over the state of South Dakota to the aliens, he could set aside a large area of Federal land which was already under the jurisdiction of the National Park Service: Grand Teton National Park at Jackson Hole, Wyoming.

"It's a great little place. Pat and I took the kids there a couple of summers ago. Beautiful broad valley with the Grand Tetons on one side…fantastic peaks, a big lake, National Forests on all sides. Over 300 acres in the park and millions of protected lands surrounding it. We'll move the few people out that live in Jackson and you can have the whole place to yourselves."

Yes, the alien thought (to himself), a nice isolated place where a couple of ten megaton bombs could fall without endangering any humans. "I don't think so," he thought to Nixon. "I don't trust you. I don't think you are honest."

"I am not a crook!" stammered Nixon. Blood rushed to his face. "Well, where do *you* want to settle?" he managed to say, barely able to conceal his anger.

"We don't need your permission. I am only here to inform you that it is in your interest to aid us in our assimilation of your people and your planet. Do you want to stay in your position of power? If so, you will make a case to your people that we come in peace. We will cure the ills of your planet, stop your wars, rid you of the threat of annihilation by your science of destruction. Make your national boundaries obsolete."

"Do you guarantee not to wipe us out like rats once you are finished exploiting us?"

"Of course we have only the best of intentions toward the human race. We will live in harmony together."

Worse than the damn commies, thought Nixon (to himself—or so he thought).

The alien, whose name was Xilhmekrol, had been authorized by the Circle to attempt to reason with his assigned world leader. He and the other "ambassadors" were told to determine if it were indeed true that the commonly held belief that humans were too possessed of a willful stupidity to honestly cooperate. And if this proved to be reality, which Xilhmekrol had now affirmed, to use their superior powers of mind control to accomplish their mission. Thus Xilhmekrol probed the grey matter of the POTUS until he had made the necessary adjustments to turn Nixon into a dutiful puppet.

"Of course I will make it known to my fellow Americans," Nixon told the alien, "that welcoming you to our world is in our best interests. I will go on television and give a fireside talk. I'm very good at convincing people...especially over the television."

It was the same all around the world. The heads of state of the most powerful nations were now accompanied by aliens who operated them like ventriloquist dummies. When other government officials bulked at their leaders' actions, additional mind-controlling aliens were dispatched. The conquest of Earth took place without a single shot being fired.

Little by little the general public became aware of the chicanery employed by the aliens. Small pockets of resistance sprang up like early spring crocuses poking through melting snow, but they had little impact. In certain authoritarian countries, like the Soviet Union, those groups were squelched, snuffed out, eliminated. In the United States they were simply ignored. There would be great benefits in embracing the influx of alien immigrants to come, the public was told—and it believed. It had pressed the "I Believe" button.

If someone had thrown a dart at the absolute center of a map of the 48 contiguous states of the U. S. of A. they might have hit the spot where the Klivpoklaians decided to land their mother ship. In west-central Kansas, in Trego County (the middle, some said, of nowhere), the Cedar Bluff Reservoir had been created by damming the Smokey Hill River. This action, finished in 1951, was part of a response to the severe droughts of the 1930s in an effort to provide water supplies for irrigation and municipal drinking water. The basin was lined with high sandstone bluffs and filled with bluegill, walleye, bass, and catfish, making it a popular spot for boating and fishing. It was about 90 miles north of Dodge City and about 200 miles northwest of Wichita. Between here and there, was pancake-flat land with a scattering of farms and not much else.

Thirteen miles south of the reservoir was the tiny hamlet of

Brownwell. About 4:00 PM on the afternoon of February 13, 1955, Mrs. Elton Chester was looking out of the kitchen window of her two-story home to watch a pair of bald eagles circling in the sky. The sky began to take on a stained appearance, as if a clod of mud had been thrown into a crystal clear stream and its murky obliteration had expanded. Was a winter storm coming? She wrapped a knitted shawl over her shoulders and went to the back porch where she could see better. Kansas was plagued with tornados, even, sometimes, in winter. There had been no warning on the radio, but it was best to be alert to changes in the weather.

A teenaged boy named Dwayne Sheehan was pushing a Schwinn Red Phantom bicycle with a flat rear tire up a hill near the edge of town. His hair was slicked into a "duck's ass" in back and piled up into a pompadour over his forehead. His Levis hung low on his hips, the red tag removed from the back pocket as an indication of coolness. He wore a red leather jacket, inadequate against the cold Kansas winter, but nonetheless also real cool. When the sky darkened he looked up. A bright spot of light pierced the gloom, grew larger. He covered his eyes against the blinding orb.

Neighborhood dogs began to howl, channeling their wolf ancestors. Birds took wing and disappeared from sight. A roaring like the rushing of water over a spillway or the freight train sound of a tornado caused mothers to call their children to come into the house, and into the basement; caused grown men to abandon their cars and lie down in the ice and snow in nearby ditches; caused the town's siren to wail its banshee warning.

The brilliant glow from the undersurface of the mothership, still red hot from entry into the atmosphere, threw tall black shadows across the land behind the houses of the town; paint peeled on the clapboard sides that faced the descending ship. Snow melted. Trees burst into flame. The great, egg-shaped space-traveling city, the mothership that the Klivpoklaians called Uoigykwosp, touched down not so gently and settled into a crater it had made in the earth where the town of Brownwell had once stood.

# 26

## The Assassination of President Richard M. Nixon

The coupling of the female Grey, Rkohtealnaq, and (the former) Seaman Apprentice Christian Resnik had taken place weeks before the descent of the mothership to Earthside. Being nothing like the sometimes extravagant rituals of the marriage of humans, the silent ceremony involved the private meditation of the participations in separate spaces for the better part of a day, the breathing of cleansing fumes from smoldering blgiiktmnas leaves, a shared bath in warmed water scented with pflematap oils, and the deep melding of minds that would forever bond them. There was no audience, no official signing of contracts, no registering with local government—only the mutual understanding of duty, loyalty, and affection toward one another. As a coupled entity, they took the name Knuuplhcanika, which in the Klivpokla language meant "wondrous fusion."

Resnik went to live with his new bride in the apartments of her extended family. Nieces and nephews, grandmothers and grandfathers, brothers and sisters, spouses (coupling–mates), and household pet plablikzs were crowded into a tenth floor living space in the Grey ghetto of level ten. Resnik expected some animosity toward himself—it was, after all, a "mixed marriage," but at worst he was simply ignored. At best he was followed around by the children who were intrigued by the human's strange habits, especially the shaving of his face and the brushing of his teeth which, because of the lack of the appropriate implements for these daily tasks on the moon colony (the aliens performed their sanitizing operations by the use of a strange device which Resnik never could master), he had to make do with items he found in the food preparation area: a knife he sharpened almost adequately, and a sort of bottle brush he trimmed to size to fit his mouth.

The children wanted to ask him a million questions but unfortunately Resnik's mind still resisted telepathic communication except where his mate was concerned. He was working with Rkohtealnaq to learn to relax his mind to become receptive to thought transfers but as yet was basically a deaf mute to the rest of the family. This contributed to their seeming indifference to him. Klivpoklains flaunted neither pity nor scorn, preferring tolerance to engagement with problematic situations involving individuals who were different. He was just another mouth to feed. So he professed a desire to "earn his way," and contribute to the family, perhaps to get a job (a concept that was lost on the Klivpoklaians, at least in the sense Resnik meant it).

The Klivpoklaian society worked because everyone cooperated in the task of survival, doing whatever was required to procure food and living space for each other. There were rewards for extraordinary efforts and a scale of deservedness that was strictly adhered to, but no one ever starved or became homeless. There was no currency. There was no symbolic token that could gain the ugly importance that money had on Earth. There was only mutual service and unabashed sharing.

Resnik expressed an interest in the farms. He had been raised on his grandfather's farm in Iowa where his mother, a single parent, had taken him to live from the time he could barely walk. He had fond memories of chasing sleepy-eyed cows from the apple orchard and playing in hay piled high in a loft in the barn...hay that scratched when it got under his shirt and made him sneeze when it got in his nose. He remembered watching his grandmother lopping off the heads of chickens that flopped onto the ground and sometimes continued to run, headless, spraying blood from their necks. He remembered gathering eggs and removing dead rats from traps and pumping water from the well and running to catch the school bus on many a snowy morning. He would like to work on one of the farms, he told Rkohtealnaq.

"Your duty," Rkohtealnaq responded, "is only to be my coupling-mate and to produce offspring, if possible. We don't choose the way in which we contribute to society."

"But I would be good at farming. I can milk the cows and slop the hogs and dig turnips and..."

"I don't know what those things are, but I will mention your wish to Kza-Tza (an endearing term for grandfather). Kza-Tza may decide to take it to our Circle[6], or he may not. Now tell me again that I am a 'big beautiful thing' as you once did."

Rkohtealnaq did speak to her Kza-Tza and the old man consented to take Resnik's case before the family's immediate Circle. It took some time for the proposal to travel up through the layers of governing bodies but consent was given, due in part to Resnik's professed experience in farming, and in part in order to hide the embarrassing fact of his undocumented alien status by spiriting him away to an agriculture level where he would be out of sight and mind.

Resnik and Rkohtealnaq took up residence in a small farming community on level eight and it was there they were living the idyllic life of fruit and vegetable growers when the mothership landed in Kansas.

Noreen Ashley, lately of the Cirque d' Renard Agile, had been standing across from the Mirador de Colom at the end of La Rambla in Barcelona watching the sky fill with flying saucers. She felt a bit faint, but soon, as the saucers moved off to hover over the city center, a resolve came to her that perhaps she *could* make a difference—she would go to the authorities and tell her story. With all that obvious corroboration in the skies they would have to believe her.

"Dónde está el edificio del gobierno?" she asked a bystander. The woman pointed up La Rambla. "Uno y medio kilómetros," came the answer. Only about a mile. Another nice stroll up the tree-lined boulevard.

But, partly because her Spanish was even worse than her French, and partly because the arrival of the saucers commanded the immediate attention of the officials, she ended up waiting, sitting in the antechamber of one of the City Councilors of the Ajuntament de Barcelona, nervously thumbing through a copy of the Boletin CF Barcelona, a news magazine featuring Club de Futbol Barcelona, in which she had little interest. Her anxiety was rising by the second.

Finally she gave up and approached a woman sitting behind a high counter at the front of the waiting room, probably a secretary, she thought. Noreen opened up to the woman in fragments of English, Spanish, and French about her plight: she was homeless, stranded, and practically a pauper. She tried, and failed, to hold back her tears. The woman scribbled the address of a hostel in the old Gothic Quarter onto a piece of paper and handed it to Noreen. They would take her, she said, until she got back on her feet. If that didn't take too long.

"Muchas gracias," Noreen said, still sobbing. She hadn't broken down like this since she was a child. But then, she had never been quite as overwhelmed as she now was. It felt good to let it out.

The first thing Noreen did once she was settled at the hostel was to write to Nate in Bellingham. She could only hope that he had been successful in escaping from the moon colony and that he had made it back home. She told him in the letter of her own escape and her current plight. Could he send her the money to come home? She had no way of knowing that Nate believed her to be dead. All she had now was hope—blind, desperate, irrational hope.

Nate had been released by his interrogators at Area 51. They had gotten nothing from him except giggles and descriptions of wild colors: the use of LSD as a truth serum was destined to be discontinued. Nate had nowhere to go and nothing he might do made any sense to him any more. He went home to a lonely house, made lonelier now with his mother gone and his—what had she been to him: girl friend, lover, companion?—she had died on the moon, or so he had been told. He would now and forever look up at that great silver orb with tears in his eyes.

Her letter came several days after the mother ship landed. He rushed to wire her enough money to buy an airplane ticket and to pay her debts to the hostel. He was jubilant. The fact that an entire world of space aliens now occupied Western Kansas seem trivial to him as he anticipated his reunion with Noreen. Perhaps he should have been more concerned about the aliens. Perhaps he should have offered his knowledge of the aliens to the authorities. But all he could think of was Noreen.

In the upper reaches of the continental United States, spring presented itself with a nip in the wind and with lazy sunshine which had difficulty awakening to its full warming power. Deep in the heart of Texas, however, spring asserted itself with cruel ambition to chase away whatever pleasant winter weather still lingered. Texans never sweated until it got really hot and so they went about their daily tasks with the knowledge that the burning sun meant only that crops would grow and cattle would breed and mosquitoes would be abated with DDT. And hopefully, the drought would not return again this year.

In Dallas, Texas, the Texas and Southwestern Cattle Raisers Association was preparing for its annual convention. This year's speaker would be none other than the President of the United States, Richard M. Nixon—a great honor indeed! Nixon had been asked to address the convention in order to quell the cattlemen's fears that the introduction of the aliens' version of the cow, the ahtejiq, would devastate the American cattle industry. It was a reasonable fear.

It was a sunny afternoon in the fair city of Dallas. The presidential motorcade proceeded down Main Street. As it neared Dealey Plaza the motorcade jogged over on Houston Street and made a sharp left turn onto Elm, where throngs of people lined the grassy, triangular-shaped plaza. Some waved small American flags. Nixon and his wife, Pat, sat in the back seat of an open convertible, waving at well-wishers. In the front seat sat Texas governor Robert Allan Shivers, a staunchly conservative politician, although a Democrat. In 1952, the Governor had actually backed Dwight Eisenhower for president against his own party's candidate, Adlai Stevenson. Shivers also waved at the crowd. The Secret Service men who walked along side of the car scanned the crowd with worried looks.

Across the thoroughfare there was a slight rise in the landscape: a sort of grassy knoll bordered by live elms and a tall, solid picket fence. If anyone in the cheering crowd had bothered to look over their shoulders at that grassy knoll they might have seen an ominous puff of smoke that coincided with a sharp crack like a firecracker going off. Governor Shivers slumped over in the front seat just as another shot rang out. Nixon's head exploded in a shower of blood and brains, staining Pat Nixon's pink suit.

His name was Leonard Sprange, his friends called him Lenny. Only he didn't have many friends. He was born and raised in the small Texas town of Groesbeck, about one hundred miles south of Dallas. The town was near Old Fort Parker where in 1836, during a raid and massacre by Comanches, a nine year-old girl named Cynthia Ann Parker had been abducted. The girl lived for over 25 years with the tribe, marrying Chief Peta Nocona. Their offspring, Quanah

Parker, was the last Chief of the Comanches. Cynthia was recaptured by Texas Rangers in 1860 at the Battle of Pease River where whites retaliated in a massacre of the Native Americans. Such was the turbulent history of the Texas in which Leonard Sprange grew up.

He was not particularly interested in school and his grades showed it. He would often skip a school day to play in the fields outside of town, penning a note of excuse, purportedly from his mother—although how his atrocious penmanship could have fooled his teachers remains a mystery. He was a dull, unimaginative boy. He dropped out of high school, undoubtedly embarrassed, having been kept back a grade his junior year. He worked on his uncle's small ranch until the army came calling.

If he had played cowboys and Indians as a youth he would soon see very real conflict as an eighteen year-old draftee sent to South Korea in September of 1950. On New Year's Eve the Korean People's Army and the Chinese People's Volunteer Army launched a brutal offensive against the UN Forces near the 38th Parallel. Night attacks were accompanied by the disorienting clamor of gongs and trumpets—a real Chinese celebration of the Anglo New Year. The overwhelming surprise attack resulted in the retreat of the demoralized Western troops. Among them was Private Lenny Sprange. It was a humiliating experience he would not soon forget. He would never get the opportunity for revenge in another major battle. The retreat took him to Samcheok where only minor scrimmages with the enemy alternated with random mortar bombardments. Then came talk of a cease fire.

When Lenny returned home after the Armistice of 1953 he was bitter and disillusioned. His hero, General MacArthur had been relieved of duty in 1951 by then President Harry S. Truman. MacArthur had taken it upon himself to cross the 38th Parallel, thereby emboldening the Chinese and irritating Truman. He had also advocated the use of nuclear weapons. Lenny thought he had been right. Nuke 'em, said Lenny, nuke 'em to Hell! The Armistice and the withdrawal of US Troops from Korea was the fault of that new president...the old general...Dwight D. Eisenhower. Lenny took a disliking to Ike that would fester and grow like mold on a rotting orange.

There were no welcoming parades or cheering crowds for the returning army man. And worse, there was no job. His uncle's farm had failed because of the severe drought. He migrated north to Dallas. There he obtained a job pumping gas in a filling station in a seedy section of South Dallas. And there his hatred of the government that had sent him into harm's way and then had taken away any possibility of heroism intensified. He now focused his anger on the governor of Texas, Allan Shivers. He saw Shivers as a dangerous demagogue, a corrupt politician intent only on personal power (Shivers had run for reelection in 1952 on *both* the Republican and Democratic party tickets). It was then that Lenny sent away for a 6.5mm caliber Mannlicher-Carcano Model 91/38 rifle with a 4x18 Japanese telescopic sight. The Italian-made carbine cost $19.95 plus $7.00 shipping from a sporting goods store in Chicago.

Lenny learned of the visit of the president in an article in the Dallas Times Herald. Governor Shivers would also be riding in a motorcade from Love Field to the Trade Mart with the president. The route to be taken by that motorcade was described in the article in detail. They would pass Dealey Plaza. He knew the area around Dealey Plaza, knew it was an open space, not obscured by many buildings (there was only one tall building—the Texas School Book Depository). He would have a clean shot. He selected a vantage point behind a fence at the top of a grassy knoll on the far side of the plaza. The motorcade would pass just before him and the height of the knoll would allow him to shoot over the heads of the crowd without any problem.

People had gathered along the motorcade route early to see the President and the First Lady. Lenny waited patiently in the parking lot behind the fence. The Carcano was oiled and loaded and hidden in a canvas bag in case any bystanders should notice him. He was alone—everyone else crowded together along the curbs and on the grassy areas of Dealey Plaza. The first car, after the motorcycle police, was an unmarked white police sedan. Following that was a midnight blue 1954 Lincoln convertible carrying President Nixon, the First Lady, and Governor Shivers. Lenny Sprange pulled the Carcano from the bag, adjusted the sight, and propped it on the wooden fence where two pickets came together in a V at the top.

He squeezed off one round. Governor Shivers jerked backwards, then slumped down on the seat. There were cries from the immediate onlookers. A second shot rang out and President Nixon was hit. He lunged forward and fell across Mrs. Nixon's lap. By this time Lenny had abandoned the rifle and run across the parking lot.

It just so happened that an off-duty policeman, Officer Marvin Trivet, was walking hurriedly up the street as he was late in getting to the plaza to see the motorcade pass by. He heard the shots and saw Sprange fleeing the scene. He called out for the man to halt, identifying himself as a police officer. When Sprange kept running, Officer Trivet pulled his police issue handgun from under his jacket and shot twice at Lenny. The second shot felled him. In a matter of minutes, Leonard Sprange bled to death.

There were conspiracy theories, of course. Some claimed the Russians had assassinated Nixon. Shivers, who survived the attack, was hit by accident, it was said. No one suspected it might have been the other way around, that Shivers was the target and that Nixon was the accidental victim. There were others who blamed the aliens for the killing. Why the aliens would choose an earth-type weapon to eliminate someone was not explained—it just fit the profile people had of the alien invaders.

Then there was a Mr. John McGiver who had been watching the motorcade from the plaza and saw, he said, a glint of metal reflecting the sun in one of the open windows high up in the Texas School Book Repository building. His claim was investigated but no evidence was found. It was concluded, ultimately, that Sprange had been the single shooter and not part of any conspiracy to murder the president. Still, there was the curious fact that Sprange's rifle was shown to have fired only one bullet.

---

[6] We have previously noted the existence of the Circle, the group of twelve Klivpoklaians, three from each of the four races, who make decisions for the entire population. To presume that this body is dictatorial or without feedback from its constituents would be a mistake. In fact, each set of three interacts with a sub-circle within its own race, also consisting of twelve persons, and also chosen at random and periodically replaced so that no one person can perpetuate an ideology or be influenced in their judgments. Each of the twelve members of the sub-circle represents a district, and within each district there are another twelve circles of twelve who represent various family groups (the Klivpoklaians are highly interrelated). The family groups, if they are extensive, are then broken down into another set of twelve circles of twelve, and so on.

# 27

## The Resistance

Would the people of the world learn to live in peace and cooperation with their alien visitors? Certainly, the ability of the aliens to apply mind-control to public officials and military leaders was insurance that governments would not use military force against them. The structures in place for propaganda, the newspapers, radio, and television, had done their jobs well in placating the population with promises of peace and prosperity. But the aliens had not counted on the tenacity and fierce intolerance of certain groups of ordinary humans who were, perhaps, not so ordinary in their tendencies toward action and their strong, unreasonable and illogical animosities toward those of a different race or religion, class or philosophy.

The grand-daddy of all hate groups[7], the Ku Klux Klan, was founded in 1866 by Confederate veterans in Tennessee as a "hilarious social club," to "have fun, make mischief, and play pranks on the public." Pranks—like lynching Negroes and burning crosses on people's lawns. The racist 1915 film by D. W. Griffith, "Birth of a Nation," glorified the Klan. The KKK traditionally targeted African-Americans, Roman Catholics, Jews, immigrants, and organized labor. Now they had new "strange fruit" to hang from the poplar trees: the Greys, the Nordics, the Reptilians, and the Little Green Men.

In the Deep South certain pastors had preached for years that non-whites were soulless mud people, no better than beasts. Now they pointed to the aliens as being the minions of Hell, the devil's spawn intent on enslaving the white race and raising up the Negro. This appealed to the lower class "neo-Confederates" who saw the government's acceptance of the aliens as a threat to their own imagined superiority. Their actions were more deadly than their words when they encountered a solitary Grey on the street.

But these retaliations were sporadic and often ill-fated. For one thing, the aliens learned to avoid areas where attacks had occurred. For another, human authorities, now under mind-control, identified and monitored many of the hate groups. When anti-alien demonstrations formed the police showed up in riot gear and quickly dispersed the rabble. In response, the number of anti-alien groups increased. The aliens now put suppressing or eliminating these groups on their "to do" list.

Paramount on that list was the destruction of the world's nuclear weapons. This was proceeding slowly. Neutralizing of radioactive material was time-consuming and needed to be done carefully. The amount of dark matter necessary for the job meant that in all probability, the mothership would never take to the cosmos again. But then, there were no plans for space flight now that the Klivpoklaians had a new home. Securing that home for the future generations of Klivpoklaians, should there be any, must be accomplished at any cost.

Humans had a different view of things, of course. The new acting president, a man named Dwayne Peterson, who Nixon had picked as his vice president from a roster of arch-conservatives, a man who had served on Senator Joe McCarthy's Communist witch hunt committee, a man whose father had once been a member of the KKK, a man whose mind resisted control by aliens to a degree that concerned the invaders, this man, the new leader of the free world (a term now anachronistic), this man had escaped to a bunker.

Vice President Peterson had been at Camp David meeting with members of the Majestic 12 and various chiefs of staff, White House aides, and intelligence officials when the news came that President Nixon had been assassinated. Immediately the Secret Service men assigned to the Vice President whisked him and his entourage away through the underground tunnel that connected Camp David to Site R, a massive underground facility at Raven Rock Mountain.

Raven Rock functioned as an underground Pentagon, a command center and bunker where the executive branch of government and the commanding generals and admirals could be sheltered in case of nuclear attack. It was sometimes known as "The

Rock" and sometimes as "Harry's Hole"—having been planned as a Cold War facility as early as 1948[8] under then President Harry S. Truman. The complex was located just under 9 miles east of Waynesboro, Pennsylvania, and about 6 miles north-northeast of Camp David, Maryland.

Once the solid steel blast-proof doors were closed and secured the facility was "buttoned-up" and safe even from a direct hit from a nuclear bomb. Site R could generate electricity and filter air. A tall radio tower enabled communications with the outside world. In a conference room, Peterson and several of the Majestic 12 sat around a large, oval-shaped table of hand-rubbed oak. Coffee cups and pads of paper sat on the table in front of them.

Admiral Hillenkoetter sat across the table from General Twining. The two leaders had just finished a heated argument concerning the possible deployment of nuclear weapons against the aliens while at least some of those weapons still existed. The aliens would not be so intent on destroying our nuclear capability if they didn't fear our bombs, Admiral Hillenkoetter had insisted. The bombs might have little effect and thus anger the aliens and cause them to retaliate, General Twining had argued. The aliens must have some kind of secret weapon…something that could wipe out all of humanity, he had added. General Hoyt Vanderburg entered the argument pointing out that numerous attempts at interrogation of captured aliens had failed to indicate any weapons beyond swords and sabers.

"Ridiculous," said President Peterson. "Swords and sabers…it is a ruse to divert our attention from their real weapons. Gas? Chemicals? It need not be a bomb to be lethal. After all, they are…inhuman. We won't be safe until we eliminate the alien peril. The only good alien…is a dead alien!"

"You would order a bomb attack against their city in Kansas?" asked Vanderburg. "I wonder…you haven't been officially sworn in as president, you know. You may not have the executive powers necessary to do so."

"And," added Dr. Lloyd Berkener, who had been silent up to now, "you don't have the codes to enable the bombers."

"There are ways around that," said Peterson. "A rogue pilot can be found. All we need is one bomb."

"You know what we have out at Area 51?" asked General Twining. "A saucer. We found it abandoned in the mountains near

Albuquerque. Only thing…we can't figure out how to work it. It doesn't seem to have a power source. There was an alien wandering around up in those hills…we have him too. But it is a long shot to think we could get it running again."

"Maybe we could use it like a Trojan Horse. Place a bomb inside it and give it back to the aliens," said General Robert Montegue.

Suddenly there seemed to be a new enthusiasm for the idea of exterminating the aliens. Creative ideas flowed. The most bizarre of these involved contacting the Russian shadow government—those comrades who had not succumbed as yet to alien mind control. They would be in a bunker somewhere beneath the streets of Moscow or out in the country (too bad our intelligence services hadn't located these bunker sites yet). Send them the coordinates of the Kansas site and…bang!

About 50 miles south of Moscow at Sharapovo was a substantial underground facility designed to relocate the Russian Defense Council in the event of nuclear war. It was linked by underground railway to a similar facility at Chekhov where the General Staff could be housed. At the advent of the alien takeover of the Soviet Union, only a few of the most important officials had been successful in reaching these bunkers. Among those at Sharapovo was First Deputy Chairman of the Komitet gosudarstvennoy bezopasnosti, or KGB, State Security General Ivan Alexandrovich Serov. The 49 year-old Serov had been Ukrainian Commissar of the People's Commissariat for Internal Affairs, or NKVD, in 1939 and allegedly had been responsible for the deaths of hundreds of thousands of Ukrainian peasants. He had two nicknames coined by western journalists: "Ivan the Terrible," and "The Ukrainian Butcher."

Accompanying Serov to the bunker was Yulia Borisov, his current mistress. Miss Borisov acted as the general's secretary but it was well known that her real function occupied those few hours of relaxation Serov could afford during the crisis. At the moment, Serov put the release of tension she would bring out of his mind—his friend and mentor, Nikita Khrushchev, and most of the Central Committee, were effectively prisoners of the mind control enacted by the alien invaders. The aliens were methodically dismantling and neutralizing the nuclear arsenal so important to the Soviet Union's intended supremacy in the Cold War now waging with the West. Retaliation was required.

Serov, in his position as head of the KGB, was privy to many aspects of his country's nuclear weapons program. He knew, for instance, that a super bomb had been under construction at the immense facility beneath Yamantau Mountain known as Mezhgorye. The super bomb, "Tsar Bomba," was believed to be able to yield a 50 megaton detonation, more than three times the explosive power of the American's Castle Bravo test at Bikini. Plans were also underway to produce a 100 megaton bomb. If the Tsar Bomba could be deployed against the alien city located in the middle of the United States, would the Americans consider that an act of war against themselves? Serov didn't know…and didn't much care.

The real problem was how to deliver the bomb to the center of the North American continent. The Russian ICBM program was in its infancy: no missile could travel the distance accurately let alone carry the heavy 50 megaton device. Russian bombers would be shot down well before reaching their goal. Serov looked into Yulia's dark eyes as if to find the answer. She smiled. The woman was extraordinary, thought Serov—beautiful on the outside and possessed of both instinct and intelligence on the inside—multi-layered like a matryoshka nesting doll. Often it seemed she could read his mind. And so she said:

"Call the American president on the red phone and tell him what you wish to do."

Petty Officer First Class Charles (Chuck) O'Bannon, still reeling from the shock of witnessing his good buddy First Sergeant Andrew H. Millender once again abducted by the aliens, had been dropped off in downtown Santa Fe by the trucker who had given them a lift. The semi-tractor-trailer rolled off along the Paseo De Peralta leaving a cloud of fowl-smelling diesel smoke in its wake. The driver was also in shock, having just seen his first flying saucer. O'Bannon moved up the street toward a group of men who congregated in front of what appeared to be an official government building.

As he watched, a pickup truck stopped by the men. The driver pointed at several of the men who climbed onto the bed of the truck. O'Bannon approached a man who stood a little off from the crowd. "What is happening?" he asked the man.

"They are all waiting for work…day labor if they are lucky. Not so much work these days. Many will be hungry tonight."

"Who are they?"

"Mostly Mexicans. Here illegally. Some from South America even. They come a long way to cross the border for a better life. Too bad they don't find it. It's funny, you know. They say we have the tres culturas…the three cultures. The Pueblo Indians, descendants of the ancient Anasisi; we Hispanos, descendants of the Spanish Conquistadors; and you, the Anglos, the new conquerors of New Mexico, from California and Texas…buying up our lands, raising the values so that we cannot afford to keep our ancestral properties. But there is a fourth culture: these wetbacks who take our jobs. Praise be for President Nixon who is deporting them!"

"I had no idea. I'm not here to take your jobs or your lands. I'm a traveler, at the moment at odds with my own survival."

The man pushed his Stetson hat back on his head; sweat glistened through the crown. He studied O'Bannon. Presently his natural dislike of Anglos relaxed and a curiosity about this newcomer took its place.

"Your clothing, Senor, seems most inappropriate for the coolness of the day. You seem to be dressed still in your pajamas."

Indeed, O'Bannon still wore the gel-like clothing he had been given on the moon colony by the aliens.

"These are very warm. I am lately discharged from the navy where I was stationed for a time in Tokyo. I acquired these pajamas, as you call them, at a very high class establishment where there were Geishas and other entertainment." (O'Bannon could see that the man was intrigued by his lie…he would continue.)

"I have been hitchhiking my way across the country but I lost my kit bag somewhere outside of Gallup."

"So you have no where to stay?" asked the man.

"No, none."

"I tell you what. I take you to a place I know. It is on the way to my own village of Agua Fria. It is some abandoned buildings where squatters live…many former soldiers like yourself who return from war to find they have no jobs. By the way, mi nombre es Raymundo…Raymundo Herminio Villanueva."

"Chuck O'Bannon. Glad to meet you. Ah…muchas gracias!"

"De nada. We go now."

Villanueva led O'Bannon west on Alameda, a road that followed the Santa Fe River. Small farmsteads lined both sides of the river. Villanueva pointed to one small compound having a corral filled with sheep. "Mi primo, my cousin Jesus' place," he said.

About one mile and a half later they turned up a dirt road. A battered wooden sign read "Camino Las Crucitas." They followed this up a steep incline until they reached an open area where O'Bannon could see tumbled down tar-paper shacks and the remnants of a barbed-wire fence. Beyond the disintegrating shacks there were more substantial structures, also in disrepair, but apparently occupied. Clothes lines were stretched between buildings on which flapped faded flannel shirts and worn trousers. Men were clustered around a camp fire, passing a bottle. It reminded O'Bannon of a hobo camp straight out of the Great Depression era.

"What is this place?" O'Bannon asked Villanueva.

"It used to be the internment camp[9], where they put the Japs during World War II. It was closed down in 1946. Squatters took it over little by little. Oh, there's even an old Japanese couple living here who refused to leave when it closed. No place to go, I guess."

How ironic, thought O'Bannon as he stood looking at the not-so-abandoned camp. Here I am, Navy personnel gone AWOL, escaped from captivity on the friggin' moon, prepared to hunker down with the dismal dregs of our national defenders, themselves displaced and disenfranchised, holed up in a former concentration camp created for an imagined enemy, American citizens whose relatives were fighting abroad for the USA even then, ostracized because of their race and mistrusted as possible spies. And now, he thought…he feared…an even larger and more brutal war was about to begin.

---

[7] The term "hate group" has emerged to designate so-called social groups formed to advocate hate and hostility and often violence against members of a race or nationality, those of certain sexual orientations, religion, politics, or other differences. In 2014 the Southern Poverty Law Center, in their list of hate and supremacist groups, anti-Semitic and anti-government groups, identified 784 active hate groups in the United States including:

*72 Ku Klux Klan (KKK) groups, 142 neo-Nazi groups, 115 white nationalist groups, 119 racist skinhead groups, 113 black separatist groups, 37 neo-Confederate groups, 21 Christian Identity groups, and 165 "general hate" groups (subdivided into anti-LGBT, anti-immigrant, Holocaust denial, racist music, radical traditionalist Catholic, anti-Muslim, and "other")*

—Goldstein, Joseph (November 20, 2016). "Alt-Right Exults in Donald Trump's Election with a Salute: 'Heil Victory' ". New York Times. November 21, 2016

In a report published in 2016 the count rose to 892 and it has been estimated that in the first year after the election of Donald Trump as President of the United States, anti-Muslim groups tripled in number. Not all of these groups advocate violence, but they do create a climate in which individuals with criminal tendencies, whether members or non-members, are prompted to act out on their hatred.

[8] Raven Rock Mountain Complex is one of several relocation sites designed to assure the Continuity of Government (COG). These include the Cheyenne Mountain Complex nuclear bunker at Colorado Springs, the underground facilities at Mount Weather in western Virginia, the congressional housing project called Greek Island under the Greenbrier Resort in White Sulphur Springs, West Virginia (now defunct and never used). Raven Rock, or Site R, was acquired in 1950 and work on the underground command center began in 1951. Three 3-story underground buildings were completed by 1953. More would be added. In 2013 the Department of Defense reported that RRMC had 69 buildings totaling 640,000 square feet on 716 acres. It has four portals descending 650 feet below the summit, living quarters for over 3,000 with a barber shop, a chapel, a fitness center, a medical facility and a convenience store. The dining room supposedly has fake windows painted to show outdoor scenes. There is an underground reservoir holding millions of gallons of water. And a War Room that may have inspired the one in the movie, "Dr. Strangelove or: How I Learned to Stop Worrying and Love the Bomb."

[9] After the attack by the Japanese on Pearl Harbor in 1941, persons of Japanese ancestry living in the United States were collectively

suspected of espionage, although there was never any proof of such activity. President Franklin D. Roosevelt signed Executive Order 9066, which declared that the west coast, primarily California, was a military zone. Anyone suspected of collusion with the enemy was to be removed. The War Relocation Authority (WRA) which was a civilian organization created for the purpose, opened ten relocation centers where Japanese-Americans and their families were imprisoned for the duration of the war. There was a camp in Santa Fe and another in Lordsburg, New Mexico. The Santa Fe camp opened in 1942 to house 826 Japanese men from California who were later transferred to other facilities. German and Italian internees lived in the camp until 1943. By 1945 the camp had expanded to accommodate 2,100 Japanese-American families. Some had been farmers or fishermen but included in the internees were college professors, doctors, journalists and other professionals. The federal government considered them to be undesirable enemy aliens and treated them as prisoners of war. The Santa Fe camp was surrounded by a 12 foot fence topped with barbed wire. There were eleven guard towers equipped with search lights. The guards were armed with rifles, side arms, and tear gas. Compared to other camps, the prisoners at Santa Fe were well treated (by contrast, two men were shot and killed while allegedly escaping at Lordsburg), although tensions arose. When news of the Bataan Death March reached New Mexico a mob of locals armed with shotguns converged on the encampment. Luckily, they were turned away before there was any violence. A group of 366 Japanese-born first generation immigrants who had renounced their American citizenship were relocated from the Tule Lake War Relocation Center to Santa Fe. They had shaved heads and wore white headbands, white shirts adorned with the Rising Sun. There were two groups calling themselves the Sokuji Kikoku Hoshi-Dan, which meant "the Organization to Return Immediately to the Homeland to Serve," and the Hikoku Seinen-Dan, "the Organization to Serve Our Mother Country." There was trouble. The guards confiscated the militants' uniforms. Rocks were thrown and the Border Patrol agents who were the camp guards fired tear gas grenades into the crowd. Four men were injured and hospitalized. The camp closed in May of 1946. Over 4,500 innocent men, women and children of Japanese ancestry came through the camp. Today it is the site of a subdivision called Casa Solana.

Byron Grush

# 28

## O'Bannon's Raiders

A dull day…monochromatic, as if all color had been leached away by the morning's sudden monsoon rain. An unusually dull day for New Mexico, the land of endless blue sky. The mood in the encampment matched this cruel reversal of climatic values—dark, grey, numb despair saturated the men, washing away much of what little joy of living had remained for them. The meager hope of surcease of fear, pain, guilt, loneliness and hunger (those horsemen of the apocalypse of war)—that hope they had held onto in a desperate fight against the insanity of their situation (the horrors of war)—this hope now slipped away in dribbles as the daily struggle for survival, even in this beautiful land, became their new reality.

War was hell but returning from battle was worse than the fierce fires of that precarious pit. The image of the enemy was imprinted on every rock, tree, and cactus. A hazy image, an illusive ghost impression like a barely remembered dream stared back at them. A daymare at which they could not return fire…no bullet could vanquish an imaginary demon.

As it is often said about our fighting heroes, they had been children when they had been shipped to the shores of Korea to fight for freedom and the American way. They were old men now, the decency they were forced to abandon in order to do the job of killing had been buried along with their youth…and many of their buddies. Their esprit de corps had decayed. Their steadfast patriotism had been rotted away by the futility of the endeavor to preserve democracy where it had never existed. They felt the guilt of surviving. When they returned to the states they saw no marching bands, no fresh-faced girls waving flags, no ladies' aid matrons with chocolate cakes, no employers who held open the jobs they had left to go soldiering. The enemy may have disappeared but fear had not.

O'Bannon understood all this and empathized. He had been living in the former Japanese internment camp now for months. Many of the ex-GIs who were ensconced there were friendly enough although few were willing to talk about their experiences. They had listened with interest as O'Bannon related his tale of the Bikini tests. But his mention of alien abduction seemed to either elicit blank stares or a faint nervousness that threatened to escalate into fearful episodes. O'Bannon ceased telling his story of imprisonment on the moon colony. There was no point in convincing the incredulous or in frightening the paranoid.

When the fleet of saucers had appeared in the skies above the world's largest cities their opinions varied. Some said, just as they had always suspected, it was the end of the world. Others held that the aliens must be a benevolent race who would put an end to war. O'Bannon kept quiet. It wouldn't do to relate his knowledge of the alien's true intentions. When the mothership landed in Kansas, the ex-soldiers exhibited a renewed interest in the saga of Chuck O'Bannon. They quizzed him about the environment inside the huge spaceship, about the social structure of the aliens, about their weapons.

"Swords," answered O'Bannon.

"No stun guns? Disintegrator rays?"

"Just swords."

They had taken the news of Nixon's assassination in stride; they harbored no great love for politicians. Politicians, after all, were the cause of wars. Wars were the cause of their disenchantment with the land of enchantment, with their distrust of the rest of humanity…and of themselves. One less politician was just fine with them.

There were seven of them, including O'Bannon: all ex-Army, ex-Marine, and now ex-Navy. Veterans, all. There was a small vegetable garden although it was still early for planting. Mr. Martínez, who ran the food co-op up on West Alameda, sometimes stopped by with a gift of a bag of dried frijoles, some day-old bread or the odd potato. Yesterday he had brought fresh tortillas made by his wife, Josephina. When the rabbit traps produced the occasional skinny jack rabbit, there would be stew. There was talk of getting a goat, but no money to pay for it.

Sergeant Don Jones was busy pouring a bucket of boiling water on a hill of red fire ants which had erupted at the edge of the camp. He saw Martínez driving his truck up the access road and waved. The others gather around, eager for any news the grocer might bring. Yesterday he had told them that a saucer had been seen hovering above the Capitol. Now he parked the truck next to the still untilled vegetable garden. He was flustered.

"The Martians," he said, "they are south of the city digging up the old mining areas. It is just like the old days when the Spanish searched for El Dorado, La Ciudad del Oro. They look for gold in the hills of Los Cerrillos."

"I doubt that they have any use for gold," said O'Bannon. "My thought is that they need to renew some mineral which they use for producing anti-gravity. I don't know what you would call it…anti-matter?"

"No," answered a young ex-soldier named Stuart Feldman. Feldman had been studying physics at the University of Denver when the Korean War had called him away. He knew a lot about Einstein and about challenges to Einstein's theories. "I would call it dark matter[10]," he continued. "The universe is filled with dark matter and dark energy. We think dark matter is what makes gravity work."

"Why mine for it in Cerrillos?"

"Dark matter may not be distributed evenly everywhere. Perhaps it is concentrated next to certain kinds of regular matter…heavy metals or maybe coal. There is an old ghost town down that way where they used to produce coal for the railroads."

Later that evening, the boys-who-now-were-men sat around the camp fire watching hundreds of sparkling stars appear in the jet black sky. Besides Sergeant Don Jones, and Private Stuart Feldman, there was Howie Clinton Green from Little Rock, Arkansas, an ex-marine, Bruce Forrester whose home town girl had jilted him while he was abroad, Danny Fortuno who had been playing stickball in the Bronx when he was called up, and Tyrone Jackson, a young black man from the South Side of Chicago. And Chuck O'Bannon who felt very old and not very wise.

"If only we could do something," said Forrester.

"We could rejoin the army if only the government wasn't controlled by the aliens," commented Green.

"There is this bunch of aliens down at Cerrillos. We could take them out. A mission, like at the Parallel. We'd need weapons," said Jones.

"Didn't you say," Green asked of O'Bannon, "that these Martians only use swords?"

"They aren't from Mars," answered O'Bannon. "And yes, that's about all I ever saw them use as weapons. They have these energy rods, though, that they use with their cattle. They can zap you with them, but I don't believe they are lethal."

"Well, I for one vote we go down there and mix it up with them," Green insisted.

"You would need a plan. I was on their mothership and I escaped, but we had help from one of the aliens. There is one possibility...with the element of surprise we could steal their saucer. I think I could fly one of them."

"Then what would we do?"

"We'd gain access to their mothership and rescue my good buddy, Andy Millender who is a prisoner there." Yes...Millender. And Seaman Resnik as well. O'Bannon was determined to strike back against the aliens.

"That's just crazy," said Danny Fortuno.

"Crazy...maybe. But it gives us a purpose, doesn't it?"

"Oh man! Can I un-volunteer for this mission?" asked Feldman.

Tyrone Jackson looked through the scope mounted on the Marlin 336 .30-30 caliber hunting rifle that Martínez had loaned him. A beauty of a weapon, clean and well kept. Jackson had won medals for marksmanship during his stint in the army and he appreciated this powerful rifle. He had checked to see that the scope was aligned properly. He had slipped six rounds into it and cocked the lever, bringing a shell into the firing chamber. Now he scanned the scene below him in the shallow valley.

There were four alien males loading bags of something heavy into the saucer. How many others were there, Jackson wondered? The seven men had this Marlin that Jackson was holding and a battered looking old Winchester shotgun of dubious reliability—that was the sum total of their arsenal. Jackson could easily pick off one or two of the aliens but the rest would scatter or retreat into the saucer once they heard the shots. The men needed a plan.

Here in the Cerrillos Hills...no, that was wrong because Cerrillos was Spanish for "little hills." You didn't say, "the little hills hills," did you? These little hills had been the scene of a gold rush years before the more famous one in California. Thousands had swarmed the area digging for gold. Towns had sprung up—and soon had died out once the miners left. The Native Americans who lived in large pueblos nearby had mined as well, but for lead, which to them was more precious than gold. They used it to paint their pottery and their faces. And it poisoned them.

There was still the semblance of a village at the foot of the hills. It was called Los Cerrillos. It had an old opera house, now abandoned, a few adobe houses and a bar. Its once stately hotel had harbored Thomas Edison for a time while he attempted to separate gold from ore using electricity. He had failed technically and financially. Down the road a piece was the coal mining town of Madrid, now practically a ghost town. Dilapidated miners' cabins lined the dirt streets. Slag heaps of coal sat at the edge of the town.

Tyrone knelt on a stone outcropping behind a wind-twisted juniper that tenaciously held on to the edge of the mountain just at the ridge. Down in the valley the activity continued: the loading of the saucer with dark matter, or so he supposed. Tyrone watched as O'Bannon and Feldman emerged from a stand of tamarisk along a dried creek bed a few yards from the saucer. He watched as the aliens turned toward the men. Were they communicating by thought projection? Did they demand to know what the humans were doing at their work site? Were they warning them off? To get a better look Tyrone used the rifle-mounted scope.

He swung the scope toward the opposite end of the saucer where three more of the humans approached, as yet unseen, flanking the aliens. Five on the ground, Tyrone on the ridge with the rifle, and Howie Green hidden somewhere close by with the shotgun. Two more aliens came out from the saucer. Was that their full complement? O'Bannon was gesturing with his hands while speaking to the alien closest to him. The tall Grey seemed not to understand human vocalizing. There was some agitation among the aliens. Heads were bobbing. Suddenly they noticed the other men. O'Bannon sprang upon his Grey, knocking him to the ground. The other men rushed the remaining aliens.

From inside the saucer came yet another; this one carried a long, ugly-looking saber. He swung this in wide arcs as he ran into the fray.

Tyrone didn't hesitate. He calmly centered the cross hairs of the scope on the alien's head and squeezed off two rounds. Another blast echoed from Green's Winchester. Two aliens were dead. Three were wrestling with their human combatants. The superior size of the Greys seemed to give them the advantage. O'Bannon picked up the fallen saber and went to work.

Tyrone was unable to get a clear shot: bodies tumbled and entwined. O'Bannon had dispatched another alien but out from the saucer now came three more, all wielding swords. The shot gun roared. One fell. Feldman struggled out from under the dead body of the Grey whose head O'Bannon had neatly severed from its body. He grabbed up the sword of the shotgun victim and now two furious sword fights ensued—fights which would determine the outcome of the battle.

Centuries of study of the art of the sword were on the side of the aliens. The martial art they called Rikthijmb was instilled in them from early childhood. O'Bannon was holding his own against his opponent but Feldman was in trouble. A vicious swoop of the alien's long sword sliced a scarlet gash across Feldman's chest and shoulder. He stumbled. The alien went in for the kill but Tyrone stopped him with a .30-30 slug into his brain. The alien didn't fall immediately but continued running for several seconds, a grey zombie splattering green blood as it sailed past Feldman and landed in a juniper.

Now it was between O'Bannon and the remaining alien. Green raised the Winchester, watching for a clear shot. But O'Bannon warned him off:

"I want to take him alive," he called out.

The alien swung his saber over his head and brought it swiftly down in the manner of a Samurai swordsman. O'Bannon sidestepped. Short jabs with his blade were keeping the Grey at bay but parrying the saber was impossible due to energy of the alien's intense chopping.

"Oh hell," said O'Bannon. "Maybe we could just wound him." He called up to Jackson who was still on the overlook above. "Can you wing him, Jackson?"

He could. The sharp crack of the .30-30 echoed as the alien spun around, hit in the shoulder.

The Grey had shown them where the medical supplies were kept on the saucer. From a cabinet built into the curved wall of the ship they procured several "healing strips" which were made from the same ubiquitous gel cloth that functioned as clothing for the aliens. When placed upon the wounds of the alien and of Feldman (two were needed due to the length of the gash across Feldman's chest and shoulder) they provided pain relief, were antiseptic, stopped the flow of blood, and promoted rapid healing.

Communications with the Grey, whose name was Wrkanquoigmis, had been tedious due to the fact that O'Bannon was not susceptible to thought transfers and that the others were too inexperienced to protect themselves against possible mind control. Added to this was the stubborn defiance of Wrkanquoigmis. Little by little Bruce Forrester, who proved to be the most adapt at thought transfer, was able to convince Wrkanquoigmis that the humans had one goal only, and that was to rescue two human individuals who were trapped on the alien mothership, the Uoigykwosp. Wrkanquoigmis finally agreed to aid the humans in their quest with the condition that he would be allowed to deliver the saucer's cargo of dark matter and that they would release him once this had been accomplished. The humans accepted his apparent cooperation, secure in the belief that they had the upper hand (and all the swords).

No one thought it strange when Wrkanquoigmis placed a sort of half-helmet on his head just as they approached the mothership; it was a thought amplifier, he explained, with which he would contact the landing crew, essential to docking the spacecraft. Huge doors opened in the side of the mothership and the saucer landed gracefully in a large, empty area—empty of the aforementioned landing crew or any other personnel. Still no one suspected intrigue or betrayal.

It was with caution, however, that the seven human war veterans exited the saucer. With them they brought as many weapons as they could carry, including the rifle and shotgun. Wrkanquoigmis, their reluctant pilot, scampered away, leaving the landing area through one of those nearly invisible doorways the aliens used—a doorway that instantly disappeared into the flat, smooth wall's surface after his departure. The large outside door closed with a loud metallic clang and the humans were left standing in the vast room whose walls offered no apparent exits. Then the area began filling with a bluish vapor which smelled sweet and intoxicating.

[10] Scientists estimate that the universe is made up of 4.9% ordinary matter, 26.8% dark matter and 68.3% dark energy. Ordinary matter, also called Baryonic matter, is made up of protons and neutrons—the stuff of stars and planets. Dark matter, so called because it cannot be seen, is most likely composed of non-baryonic elements. It interacts with ordinary matter through gravity but is unaffected by electromagnetic radiation such as the visible spectrum. It should be noted that dark matter is hypothetical as no particle of it has ever been observed or proven to exist, however, its presence explains certain cosmic anomalies (such as the fact that the expanding universe is accelerating instead of decelerating as conventional physics would expect). Dark energy is distinct from dark matter and theoretically exists in so-called empty space, supplying one of Einstein's gravitational theories with a needed cosmic constant.

# 29

## The Big Bang

In the secret Russian city of Sarov, by late 1953, the Soviet scientists, Igor Tamm and Andrei Dmitrievich Sakharov, had completed their theoretical work on the Tokamak system of confinement for nuclear reactions which involved the use of a toroidal magnetic thermonuclear reactor to control super-hot ionized plasma. It was the culmination of research begun in earnest in the 1940s into the development of the atomic bomb; research which was accelerated after the United States dropped atom bombs on Hiroshima and Nagasaki in 1945. Aided by stolen US documents of thermonuclear weapon design, in particular a classified paper on lithium-6 lost by American theoretic physicist John Wheeler on a train trip in 1953, Soviet tests of the hydrogen bomb proceeded along the lines of a "layer cake" design of fission and fusion materials.

The first true hydrogen bomb that achieved the megaton range for the Soviets was a multi-staged implosion device developed by Sakharov. Although concerned about the morality and consequences of nuclear proliferation, Sakharov joined a team of scientists led by Yulii Borisovich Khariton (Order of the October Revolution, Order of the Red Banner of Labor, Hero of Socialist Labor, etc.), and set to work on increasing the yield of the weaponry.

At Mezhgorye, the research facility deep beneath Yamantau Mountain, the team had put the finishing touches on RDS-220, code named Vanya, a three-stage hydrogen bomb expected to yield 57 megatons—the equivalent of 1,570 times the energy of the Hiroshima and Nagasaki bombs combined. The first stage of the bomb would be a fission device which would compress a thermonuclear secondary stage, then the explosion which resulted would compress the larger third thermonuclear stage. By including a tamper of U-238 it was thought Vanya could achieve 100 megatons, but the problems with a device of such magnitude were monumental—nuclear fallout would be devastating and the airplane used to drop the bomb would be unable to escape the expanding fireball.

Sarharov had argued for a lead tamper for Vanya, in order to reduce the amount of fallout, pointing out that radioactive dust was certain to drift over populated areas. The plan was to explode the device in the atmosphere rather than on the ground, further reducing the effects of fallout. Attaching a parachute to the bomb to slow its decent would theoretically allow the airplane to fly to safety before the fireball reached its altitude. The group had selected a site in the Novaya Zemlya archipelago for the test.

Then the alien mothership landed in Kansas.

First Secretary of the Communist Party of the Soviet Union, Nikita Sergeyevich Khrushchev, had risen to power after the death of Joseph Stalin. Although earlier, as a commissar in the Ukraine, he had supported Stalin's purges and arrested thousands who were sent to their deaths, he eventually denounced the purges and began a series of reforms along with Georgy Malenkov, then First Secretary and Premier following Stalin's death. These contrasted sharply with the ideas and practices of Malenkov's rival for power, Lavrentiy Beria, and led to Beria's downfall. Next, Malenkov was accused of atrocities and Khrushchev slipped neatly into control of the Soviet Union. That was, until a Grey took mental control of him and other members of the Soviet Presidium.

There would be no test of the Tsar Bomba, code named Vanya. Khruschev was cooperating with the aliens in turning over the country's limited resources of fissionable materials to them and in dismantling an existing nuclear device waiting to be tested at the Semipalatinsk test site in Kazakhstan. No doubt they would be coming for Vanya very soon. Khariton, Sarharov, and the other scientists were disappointed at the thought that their crowning achievement would never see fruition. Then the phone call came from State Security General Ivan Alexandrovich Serov.

"Secure the blast proof doors at your site and don't let anyone in," the KGB Chief told them. "Get your device armed and ready."

## Level Eight, Uoigykwosp (the Mothership), Kansas

Resnik and Rkohtealnaq, the coupled entity called Knuuplhcanika, lived in a small structure just yards away from the rows of vegetable growing walls that Resnik tended. Resnik liked to call their home structure "a cottage," and attempted with little success to project the meaning of the term into Rkohtealnaq's mind, but what usually transferred to the confused female Grey was the image of an English country home complete with stone fence, climbing wisteria in bloom, and drooling mastiff dog, directly out of a romantic 1940's movie. There was little similarity between that and their cube-shaped house with its smooth, shiny, nearly windowless walls that caught the artificial sunlight in the morning and reflected the surrounding area (Resnik thought of this area as a "yard") where were stacked the tools of Resnik's trade (wheeled cart, implements vaguely resembling rakes, and long pincher-like devices for plucking the strange fruits and vegetables from the vine-covered walls).

Lazy afternoons were few; the Knuuplhcanika took advantage of the rarity of this one. The current harvest had been taken to market and the vines now hung with still unripe fruit. Resnik and Rkohtealnaq sat outside on a pair of gel cubes and watched the strange bat-like birds circling above them. Rkohtealnaq was the first to send a thought:

"Christianresnik, my mate, my love, have you not thought of venturing outside to revisit the world from which you came?"

"Rkohtealnaq, my mate, my love, I would never leave you. The life we have here is satisfactory. I have no desire to return to a place that courts its own destruction. If your people succeed in changing the world of humans for the better…well, maybe then you and I might explore that world together. For now, we should wait to see."

There followed a lengthy silence. One aspect of the Uoigykwosp which Resnik found rewarding was its unique quietude; in contrast, no place on Earth was devoid of some sound—the miniscule scratching of insects or rodents, the whistling of wind through brush or bush, the distant wailing of predators—these were always just apparent, just at the fringes of one's notice. Here there was, at times like this one, an absolute absence of sound—unless you counted the throbbing of blood in your veins or the hissing of breath through your nose. These ordinary physical noises were easily ignored. So Resnik had found a quiet, peaceful world and a kind and exotic soul mate with which to share it.

"Christianresnik, I have something to tell you...something wonderful. I am carrying our issue! We will produce prodigy in three llopikms from now."

"You're pregnant! Rkohtealnaq, I am so happy...so proud! We will have a son or a daughter!"

"You are not worried that she will be neither human nor ratiessrvedflynachian, but both?"

"She will be half you and half me. She will bring us even closer together. I could not be happier."

This blissful domestic scene was being duplicated—more or less—in another earthly location, by another happy couple.

## Bellingham, Washington

Noreen and Nate had spent the months since their reunion getting to know each other again. The sum total of old traumas they shared was not insurmountable, but it did require a constant effort to shed the effects of those experiences and to "live in the present," as the Buddha would have said. The Buddha would have said the young couple had made excellent progress in letting loose of anxiety about the future, of ceasing to dwell on the frights of the past. Of embracing the promises of each unfolding day.

And yet there were issues small and large which also unfolded— like the petals of poisonous plant-life. These were things surely connected to future fears and past regrets, although Noreen and Nate either didn't recognize the connections or were so seeped in denial (a technique for living in the present?) that an argument over trivialities became augmented and painful.

In their better moods they had talked about marriage. But the outlook for the social structure of America seemed uncertain since the aliens had invested themselves in governments and institutions whose impact on the social order was significant. Those (other people) who were deeply religious, of course, plunged more deeply into dogmas and denials and balanced this descent with a rising acid-like intolerance—an intense prejudice against the beings from another world they held responsible for the erosion of society's values. Differences in people's attitudes had sharpened. For Noreen and Nate, marriage seemed to belong to a concept of commonality which was disappearing.

And what was the purpose of formal, legal, institutional marriage anyway? To bind two people together artificially; to insure a stable environment for child rearing; to meet the approval of one's social class, one's church, one's relatives? Noreen and Nate discussed these things and this too added to schisms and spats. The tensions, however, inevitably lessened and a renewal of their mutual concern for each other returned. The trouble that haunted their paradise was unable to conquer the love they ultimately felt and shared. Most of the time.

Noreen was harboring a secret. This situation hadn't helped her relationship with Nate: perhaps he suspected, or worse, was not only ignorant but disinterested in this coming event which would certainly become a milestone of dubious worth—a make or break circumstance. Even before her return to the United States Noreen had become aware of the change in her body. She thought she knew what was causing her to feel nauseous in the mornings. A doctor confirmed it and added that although he could not accurately determine any abnormalities about her pregnancy, he still intuited something unusual about it. Was it the size of the developing life in her womb that seemed overly large for this stage? Was it the slight oscillating movement which should not be evident? It was beyond his experience and skill to interpret.

She would be showing soon. It was time to inform her partner and lover. There was a further aspect to consider: it was not possible that the child was Nate's. And he would know this instinctively. He would believe that her adventures in Europe, in the circus perhaps, had led to an infidelity she was too immature to avoid. She would not at this time dissuade him from such a belief. The alternative was too bizarre, too dreadful to acknowledge. For she had not had an affair in France or Spain or anywhere else. She had been, she was afraid, impregnated when on the moon colony. Artificially, of that she was sure, but nonetheless raped by aliens! Aliens with test tubes and syringes.

And now she must tell him.

## The Skies over Kansas, May 25, 1955

Major Andrei Durnovtsev had left an airfield in the Kola Peninsula early in the previous day. His aircraft was a modified Tupolev Tu-95V bomber—modified to carry the immense Tsar Bomba. The bomb was 26 feet long and over 6 feet in diameter. It weighed 27 metric tons. Attached to the bomb was a 1,700 pound parachute. Accordingly, the Tu-95V had its bomb bay doors and fuselage fuel tanks removed to create more space. Extra fuel needed to reach its target was supplied by a Myasishchev 3M strategic bomber (known to the West as the Bison-B), which had been adapted as a tanker for aerial refueling.

The initial version of the Tu-95 had a maximum air speed of between 400 and 500 mph and a range of 8,100 miles without being refueled. Its four turboprop engines had double counter-rotating propellers, giving it more power than conventional jet engines. It was, however, extremely noisy. Its swept-back wings and tail gave it a futuristic look when viewed from the ground below—the inhabitants of Wichita, Kansas, barely recovered from the shock of the alien mothership's landing, would watch it in awe as sunlight flashed from its silver body.

Major Durnovtsev held the bomber's altitude at 35,000 feet. As the Tsar Bomba was attached to its parachute it would be subject to the wind; this would make a direct hit on the target almost impossible. But just as in the original proposal for the test detonation, barometric sensors attached to the bomb would initiate the blast at a height of around 13,000 feet; the fire ball would easily reach the ground even at that height. It was estimated that damage would extend at ground level for a diameter of at least 25 miles.

Approximately 200 miles southeast of the location of the alien mothership was the small town of Udall, Kansas. Around 9:00AM that morning, near the town of Blackwell in Kay County, just across the Kansas/Oklahoma border, a magnitude F5 tornado struck that town, killing 20 and injuring 200. It headed into Kansas. Another F5 tornado, spawned from the same supercell, slammed into Udall at about 10:30 AM. At least 80 deaths occurred: about half of the town's population. Buildings were smashed and vehicles flung through the air to wrap around trees. The school was demolished.

There had been no warning, even though the Blackwell F5 had preceded the Udall tornado. These were the worst of the 46 tornados that hit the Great Plains in that two-day period.

Wichita, only 10 miles northwest of Udall was spared the severe devastation of that town, but heavy winds and rain battered the city, bringing down trees. Weird electrical effects were seen including St. Elmo's fire which crawled up utility poles. 6 other tornados also struck parts of Kansas, varying from forces of F0 to F2. But weather wasn't going to be the biggest problem for the people of Kansas.

Later that afternoon, citizens were venturing from their homes to clear fallen limbs and debris from their yards when the Russian bomber appeared in the sky overhead. The noise, in spite of the airplane's altitude, was so loud some people thought the tornado had come back; they ran for their cellars. Major Andrei Durnovtsev, the pilot, was unaware of the extraordinary weather conditions below. His copilot had observed the heavy cloud cover, the increased electrical activity, and the turbulence, but had not registered alarm at these conditions. All systems were preuspevat (go).

Major Durnovtsev began to reduce his air speed due to a headwind. He was entering an area of vertical wind shear where sudden downdrafts could shake the giant airplane as if it were a child's cardboard glider. As he passed through the turbulence, the headwind reversed into a tailwind and the airplane began to drop suddenly. In the early days of aviation, pilots flying light, open-cockpit airplanes often experienced this phenomenon which they mistakenly called an "air pocket." The effect was as if they had sailed into a vacuum but in fact, the tailwind simply reduced the lift which kept the airplane aloft. Major Durnovtsev struggled to compensate, pulling up the nose of the Tu-95V. It was a tragic mistake.

As the tornado had moved away from the Wichita area, a new thunderstorm formed from the collision of two opposite weather fronts. Instead of spawning another tornado, extreme downdrafts pulled rain from the clouds in a microburst which spread outward hitting the cooler ground in swirling curlicues of furious wind. As the Tu-95V dropped it encountered the edge of the microburst and flipped upside down. The pilot was helpless to correct the aircraft.

Having anticipated reaching their target in a very short time, technicians had armed the Tsar Bomba and had set the barometric sensor to detonate the device at an altitude of 13,000 feet. The Tu-

95V was plunging earthward directly over the city of Wichita, Kansas. It soon reached detonation altitude.

On a bulletin board near the end of a hallway at the Mapleton Elementary School in Wichita is a tattered yellow poster showing the cartoon character Bert the Turtle exclaiming, "Oh my! Danger!" He's smart, the poster says, Bert ducks and covers. It has been over three years since the educational film, "Duck and Cover" has been shown here; its popularity has dwindled since the Bikini hydrogen bomb tests have shown the absurdity of the possibility of survival at ground zero. In that film, a young boy named Tony is seen riding his bicycle when a bright flash causes him to jump from the bike and run for cover. Today no one will even see the flash much less have time to duck and cover.

Miss Alexander is showing a film to her third grade class today which has a different approach to the subject of atom energy. It is called "Your Friend, Mr. Atom." It tells the story of the scientific discoveries which led to the development of all the wonderful things atomic energy can do for humanity: generating cheap electricity, powering our atomic submarines, curing diseases, understanding the universe. Where "Duck and Cover" warned against the dangers of atomic power, "Your Friend, Mr. Atom" suggests instead that science is "the new frontier of our time, capable of leading mankind along the peaceful paths of progress, and that man's recent mastery of atomic energy holds a most exciting promise for the future."

On the screen is an animated sequence of an atom of uranium, its electrons swirling in orbits around its nucleus. A lone neutron enters from screen left and bombards the nucleus, splitting the atom apart. The camera zooms back to show the chain reaction as free neutrons from the split atom bombard other atoms in the fissionable material. Cartoon flashes illustrate the energy released by each event. On the soundtrack, a tired-sounding narrator explains the process. In the sky above, the plummeting Tu-95V reaches 13,000 feet and this process, which is fascinating to only a handful of the children in the class, begins for real.

The fission bomb unit of the Tsar Bomba detonates releasing X-rays and heat which compresses secondary fuel components and begin a fusion reaction. The process continues and the secondary stage ignites the third stage. The crew of six in the Tu-95V are the lucky ones as they are vaporized instantly. The children in Miss Alexander's third grade class are flattened as the school building collapses from the impact of the shockwave preceding the descending fireball, then the building and everything in it is incinerated from the heat.

The fireball itself does not reach the ground but is reflected back by the shockwave. It has a diameter of 5 miles and reaches a height of 6 and one half miles. The mushroom cloud rises to an altitude of 40 miles. Its base is over 25 miles wide. Nothing remains alive in Wichita or the small towns surrounding it. Udall is now totally destroyed; there will be no one to remember the tornado. People outdoors up to sixty miles away from ground zero have sustained third degree burns. Windows have been broken in Dodge City, Kansas City, and Oklahoma City. The same winds that drove the tornados carry radioactive fallout across Missouri, Iowa, and Illinois. 170,000 people perish in Wichita alone; many more will die from radiation poisoning along the path of the fallout.

Further west, the Uoigykwosp, the Klivpoklaian's mothership, is being shut off from the surrounding environment. All outside entrances are closed and the ship is now as secure as it had been during its flight through deep space. Saucers are being recalled. The Circle had early on devised an emergency plan in case of human nuclear war. Although the Tsar Bomba was probably the last weapon of its kind remaining since the alien's neutralization of the US and Russian arsenals, it was always possible that they had missed one or two bombs. Conventional weaponry still existed and no doubt the humans would use these against each other. The Klivpoklaians therefore duck for cover within their own turtle shell, and they wait.

# 20 Ktanyos Later
## (more or less)

Byron Grush

# 30

## A New Beginning
## 1974, Somewhere over Chicago

The airboat hovered over a bombed-out building in a north side neighborhood of the once thriving metropolis of Chicago. Trees of heaven and scraggly mulberries poked soiled leafy branches through broken stone and twisted steel, providing a canopy of protection for small, furred animals; yet hawks and turkey vultures swirled endlessly above, waiting to make a fresh kill or to feast on left-overs. The female Grey, Fhigheobtakl, leaned over the open edge of the airboat and took readings from a globe-shaped device, a sort of spectroscope, which measured wave lengths of electromagnetic radiation invisible to the alien eye. Or to the human eye, for that matter, for Fhigheobtakl was only half Ratiessrvedflynachian. Her father was a human.

"There are no life signs strong enough to indicate human life," she communicated to Klikthmougjidt, a Grey male, one ktanyo her junior, yet ranking above her in this endeavor.

"We wait until we are certain," he answered. (The Klivpoklaians, of course, communicated by thought transfer instead of verbally.) Then added: "These humans must have been crazy to destroy themselves so utterly. Well, they were always fools."

"You forget, Klikthmougjidt, that I am half human. And if not for the human genes that mingle with ours and mitigate our inability to procreate, our race would be as doomed as was theirs."

"There are still plenty of humans left on this planet. We will find some adequate specimens, good readings or no good readings." Then he said, somewhat gruffly to the pilot, a young Reptilian named Mziqroafvuent: "Drift due floutb (roughly south) to the next sector.

Proceed quietly so as not to alert the humans."

They were now near what had once been known as the Gold Coast. A strange (to the Klivpoklaians) castle-like building remained seemingly untouched by the destruction; this was the Chicago Water Pumping Station known simply as the Water Tower. The building had survived the Great Chicago Fire of 1871, and now it had survived the disaster of the long war (see Appendix A, Chronicles of World War III for details). A neighboring building lay in ruins, twisted steel and glass shards heaped in disarray. Dark shapes moved among these heaps, scavenging for anything useful. The indicators on Fhigheobtakl's spectroscopic device flashed with multicolored intensity.

"Humans," she exclaimed.

Below, near what had been Michigan Avenue, the human forms ducked to get out of sight of the hovering alien airboat. Kurt Mirko, a stout youth of 19—the same age as Fhigheobtakl, and, ironically, also a Human/Ratiessrvedflynachian hybrid, gestured to his three companions (all fully human—one of Native American decent and the others of mixed European heritage). His gesture was a form of sign language developed by the human survivors for stealth and avoidance when the aliens were hunting them. It meant "scatter." They scattered.

Kurt sprinted across the road with the Native American close on his heels. His companion was of the Oneida People and was named Fitlanká, which means "fiddler" in the Oneida language. The two young men entered the Water Tower through an open window. The others had headed east, toward the lake. There was ample vegetation in that direction which would serve as cover. However, those in the airboat had spotted them and followed.

After a time, Kurt braved a look outside. The airboat had vanished. "I think they're gone," he said to Fitlanká.

Kurt and Fitlanká left the Water Tower and headed toward the downtown area called the Loop where their commune occupied the collapsed ruins of an elevated train terminal and the tunnels under it which connected to the old underground street system. They went carefully, ducking under vegetation and darting through a maze of steel girders, the rusted bones of the city. It would not do to lead the aliens back to the commune.

There were still gangs of former Russian soldiers roaming the city. The danger was not that the battle for world dominance might still be being fought with these stragglers; it was, instead, that the stranded soldiers also foraged for food and supplies among the ruins—competition for survival often resulted in what amounted to tribal warfare. Kurt and Fitlanká crossed the Chicago River on a crude ramp made of timbers lain across the remains of the Michigan Avenue Bridge which still protruded here and there from the now shallow and polluted water.

Along the river's south side, Upper Wacker Drive had collapsed unto Lower Wacker Drive, effectively closing off access to the tunnels nearest the river. However, the humans had discovered a passage through the broken concrete and had hidden this entrance behind a large piece of gilded metal that had fallen from one of the art deco buildings nearby. Kurt and Fitlanká slid this aside and entered the dark, twisting underground passage.

"They used to call this the 'Emerald Tunnel,' " Kurt told his companion. "The lamps down here were sodium vapor and emitted a harsh green light."

"Too bad there's no electricity," answered Fitlanká. "That would have been interesting to see…and helpful for getting through this darkness."

Here and there a shaft of sunlight found a crevice in the crumbled street above them and illuminated suspended motes of dust to add an eerie glow to the tunnel. By now they were familiar with the turns and obstacles of the way to the commune. Still, they stumbled and tripped over unseen objects. Large river rats ran away at their approach, the sound of their tiny claws reverberating in the hallowed-out cavity of the injured city center.

The huge steel girders that had supported the Loop elevated train as it ran down Wabash Avenue had toppled and the old tracks were scattered among the debris of bombed-out store fronts. The Lake Street Transfer Subway Station lay somewhere under all the rubble and had survived nearly intact—but no trains had run there in the last two decades. It became the perfect hide-a-way for the disenfranchised noncombatants whose post war existence depended upon isolation and stealth.

The commercial center of the large city, although in ruins, still offered adequate pillaging—if one knew where to look. Of course, food was a problem and required the establishment of a hunting class to provide meat, but vegetables could be grown on what remained of the roof tops by dredging dirt and hauling water from the nearby river. If someone needed a bed or an easy chair, Marshall Field's department store was just down the street, a shell of its former glory, but well stocked. Nearby, the bookstore, Kroch's and Brentano's, had not burned as so many of the Loop stores had. It provided ample reading material for those who still felt inclined to read.

Kurt Mirko liked to read. He had worked his way through the classics (Penguin paperbacks with boring covers) and had attempted more contemporary fiction by Huxley, Faulkner, James Baldwin and Kingsley Amis. One novel in particular struck a chord with him: William Golding's *Lord of the Flies*. Although his companions—his tribe—were not the preadolescent British schoolboys of Golding's narrative, they were young people without adult guidance, and were similarly forced by dire circumstances to establish a social order and to evolve tactics for survival.

They had banded together in rejection of the so-called adult world which had resulted in war and waste and an empty future. At 19, Kurt was among the oldest; most were between the ages of 12 and 16. They totaled an even dozen, boys and girls, Black, white, Native American and Asian—although there might now be two less in their number.

"Where are Thom and Dupree?" asked Becka, a sandy-haired girl of 14, when Kurt and Fitlanká arrived at the commune. The girl could be a pest, thought Kurt; she often followed him around, moon-eyed and insistent upon acknowledgement. Kurt would have none of that.

"We separated when an alien flyer appeared. We don't know if they escaped," replied Kurt.

In fact, at that exact moment, Thom and Dupree, the two human youths who had fled toward the lake front, were being led to the alien airboat under mind control. They had been cornered on the beach which was strewn with dead fish and debris washed up from the lake. There had been no place else to flee. Capturing humans, once they had been run down, was an easy task for the aliens, if the humans were among the majority who were susceptible to mind control; only occasionally did the aliens encounter a resistant human.

Klikthmougjidt, the Grey male, held the two humans under a virtually hypnotic mind control, a task which required earnest concentration. The airboat was sitting in a clearing a few yards up a bluff. The path to this wound through some aging sycamores and dense, bush-like mulberries which scratched against the aliens' and the humans' legs. Dupree tripped over an exposed root. The Grey was momentarily distracted as Dupree fell, and his concentration no longer focused on Thom. Thom crouched and sprang at the alien, shoving him into the brush.

The female Grey, Fhigheobtakl, and the Reptilian named Mziqroafvuent turned to rush to Klikthmougjidt's aid, but just at this moment, a shrill cry was heard and out from the bushes came a half dozen humans waving clubs. Their dirty brown uniforms identified them as an errant Russian kill squad. Thom and Dupree stood as little chance of surviving this attack as did the aliens.

"Thom!" shouted Dupree. "Run!"

"The girl!" answered Thom. "Get the girl."

Dupree grabbed Fhigheobtakl by the arm and dragged her along as the human youths darted through the brush along the top of a ridge. Behind them they could hear the sounds of a battle—sounds that didn't last long and which ended with the sharp report of clubs against skulls and agonizing wails. They ran as fast as the terrain allowed. They would certainly be followed.

It was the next day before Thom and Dupree showed up. Morning had arrived to the Loop and with it, three species of animal life that seemingly could never be extinguished by war and pestilence: the cockroach, the pigeon, and the rat. Pigeons were edible; rats— well, things weren't quite *that* bad yet. Roaches were too repulsive to be used for their miniscule protein. One very fat rat scurried away as the two humans and Fhigheobtakl approached the passageway to the commune. They waited before using the secret entrance to be sure they hadn't been followed. The zigzag route they had taken seemed to have fooled the Russians…but you never knew.

The alien girl had been reluctant to come with them, yet she was unsure of how to contact anyone to rescue her. The threat of roving Russian packs was enough to keep her close to the humans who knew the territory and who might protect her. Therefore Fhigheobtakl did not resist when Thom and Dupree pulled back the metal hiding the doorway and beckoned her to come along.

"Why did you save me?" she asked, verbalizing instead of using thought transfer. The humans had been surprised the first time she had spoken to them out loud during their flight from the Russians. "My father taught me to speak English," she had told them. She had held back the information that she was half human.

"You're a girl," answered Dupree. "Those Russians would have killed you. We don't stand for that."

"You wouldn't kill a Russian woman?" she asked.

"No…no, of course not. We aren't like them."

"Well, I don't understand. Women warriors are still warriors. Most I've known[11] were very fierce and skilled in attack. You are probably foolish to spare the Russian women."

"Quickly. We must go now."

The counsel met later that evening. Thom and Dupree were called upon to explain why in hell they had brought an alien woman into the secret habitat. The talking stick was passed from hand to hand and recriminations abounded. It was eventually determined that they could not let the woman leave the commune. She knew where the hidden entrance was and would be sure to lead others back with the intent of capture and enslavement. Was there any truth to the rumor that the aliens ate humans? No one knew for sure but it seemed likely. What to do? They could terminate her, but no one wanted to take on that responsibility. That would be inhuman.

"Since you have brought this dilemma upon us," said Steely Peter, the leader of the counsel, addressing Thom and Dupree, "you are hereby assigned duties as care-takers of the alien woman. She will be your charge and woe be to you if she ever escapes!"

Steely Peter was a mere boy of 17 but of an imposing stature due to his height (nearly six feet tall) and weight (easily 250 pounds). Positions of authority in the commune were determined by election, but girth and pomposity, qualities held in abundance by Steely Peter, tended to tip the scales in his favor. Wisdom and insight were typically less of a factor in the group's choice of leadership.

Fhigheobtakl had been locked in a room since entering the commune. She was furious but she bore no malice toward the humans. Her interests in them stemmed from the possibilities of interbreeding. It was the only way to insure the survival of the

Klivpoklaian culture. She was aware, however, that humans were reluctant to copulate with Klivpoklaians; they seemed to insist upon an emotional attachment to their mates. How impractical!

Thom unlocked the door to the temporary prison and entered. He would explain the situation to the alien girl. Surely she would see the necessity of her remaining in the commune, incommunicado with her own people. She would be treated well and given what meager amenities the hideout afforded, if only she would promise not to try to escape. What were the chances that she would agree, Thom wondered?

"What was your name again?" he asked.

"It is Fhigheobtakl. Human tongues have difficulty with our names, I know. You can call me Freda. That is the name my father used for me."

"Freda. That's a nice name. Freda, I have to tell you that the counsel insists that you remain with us. You can see that if we let you go…"

"I would bring destruction upon you. That is not true. We wish you no harm. On the contrary. We wish to form an alliance between Klivpoklaians and humans. Can you not see this?"

"Then why do you hunt us…capture us?"

"Because you hide from us. You do not come to us in friendship. You still war with each other. It will be many long ktanyos before you reach enlightenment. So we bring you to us one by one. Instruct you and nurture you. Join with you to create a new race. We have much to offer…why do you not let me bring you back to the Uoigykwosp with me?"

"No! And don't try to hypnotize me into believing you."

"I could do that, of course. But I would rather convince you by words. That way you will understand. My world is one of great wonders…much technology and a richness of vegetation and animal life. We have survived for hundreds of ktanyos within our Uoigykwosp. But we need the mixture with humans to complete us. And we can save you from all this desolation."

"I don't believe you. But…tell me more about your…Ugh…Ugkee…"

"Uoigykwosp. Our mothership as you would call it. Our home."

Kurt Mirko was annoyed. Try as he might, he could not evade the girl, Becka. She followed him everywhere. The crush she had on him was beginning to become embarrassing as well as being irritating. He went to Fitlanká and suggested they go to the counsel and request to embark upon another foraging expedition. After the last one, which had resulted in an alien girl being brought to the commune, he doubted whether their request would be granted, but it was worth a try. Anything to get away from Becka!

Steely Peter told them he need not convene a counsel meeting and would give them permission to forage, admonishing them not to return with any more aliens. "It wasn't us," protested Kurt. Nevertheless a stern warning was given to the two young men. They immediately went to their rooms to acquire their kit bags and hiking boots (Kurt had recently obtained a pair of Vibram soled Timberlands, a bit clunky and warm for the season, but essential for traversing broken rubble laced with shards of glass). Fitlanká packed his hunting knife and a small leather bag containing...something sacred. He would never reveal what was in the bag to anyone not of the Oneida People.

Fitlanká had been born and raised on the Oneida homelands near Green Bay, Wisconsin. His people came from the Iroquois Nations of upstate New York and had been among the first Native Americans to encounter Europeans in that region. Although the Iroquois Confederacy of the Six Tribes had maintained political neutrality at the outset of the American Revolution, the Oneida eventually joined with the rebelling colonists and fought the British at the Battle of Oriskany. They were given six million acres of land for a reservation, the first of its kind in the United States. This, like all other treaties made by the government with indigenous peoples would soon change. Some Oneida moved to Wisconsin during the so-called Indian Removals that followed in the early nineteenth century. Their land holdings there began to be reduced as well.

The boy had become separated from his family when the battles of World War III spread up into the farm lands of the Midwest. The ever increasing need for food to support both sides threatened the stability of the peaceful countryside of Wisconsin; cattle and grain were stolen and farms were burned. The Oneida scattered. Fitlanká had been hiding inside an old mill along the waterway called Turtle Creek when the group of his people, including his father, mother and various aunts and uncles, were attacked by a roving band of Russian soldiers. He escaped without learning the fate of the others and eventually found himself wandering through the bombed-out streets of Chicago.

He had been adopted by the commune about the same time as Kurt Mirko. Kurt had been raised in Washington State by his parents, Nate and Noreen Mirko. Nate wasn't his natural father—there hadn't been anything natural about the "fathering" of the boy. He almost never knew that there was something different about him. Almost, that is, until he was six years of age and he began to "hear" the thoughts of other children. The truth of his origin came out after much tearful pestering of his mother. As he grew older, Kurt began to explore the aspects of his psyche that he had inherited from his alien side. Because of public animosity toward the aliens, he hid these things from other people. But he became proud of his difference.

The war came early to the Northwest. The Mirkos, like many Washingtonians, migrated eastward. In Salt Lake City they had taken refuge in a third floor walkup flat near Temple Square. At first settled by the Mormons fleeing persecution in 1847, the city was now seeing an influx of refugees from the West Coast with a range of diversity that had the potential to change the holy city of the Church of Jesus Christ of Latter-day Saints to a homogenous mixture of creeds and beliefs. It might have evolved along those lines had not the war finally come to the Great Salt Lake.

A new migration began, ironically, following the Oregon and Mormon Trails in reverse. Just east of Kansas City, Missouri, the Mirkos stopped in the small town of New Franklin. The historic town, relocated after severe flooding in 1826, had been the gathering place for wagon trains embarking upon the Santa Fe Trail. The party of migrants with whom they had traveled, took over a small hotel at the corner of Merchants and Howard Streets. It was struck by Russian bombs. Remarkably, Kurt was uninjured. His parents, whatever remained of them, were never recovered from the wreckage of the building. As he searched in vain among the bodies laid out in the street he determined to continue on and to survive whatever lay ahead. What lay ahead was the Chicago commune.

Now Fitlanká and Kurt crossed the Chicago River and headed back toward the (former) Gold Coast. They darted along the skeletal remains of once tall buildings, keeping out of sight. They were not aware, therefore, of the small shape that followed them from the commune: the girl, Becka. They also did not observe the Russian kill squad that marched defiantly up State Street. Thus it was that the three, Fitlanká and Kurt and Becka, were not present when the Russians attacked the commune.

---

[11] Although the Klivpoklaians were traditionally peace-loving, once the war started among the humans and the long, twenty year isolation in the mothership began, it became essential to prepare for any eventuality. Young people were conscripted into a standing army and given training in the arts of combat. Women warriors were considered the best of the trainees.

# 31

## The Battle for the Lake Street Transfer Station

It had taken the Russian recon team months to locate the American commune which was hidden well below the streets of the Loop. Finding an entrance to the stronghold had been even more difficult. By chance, a squad patrolling up State Street had noticed two American boys scrambling across the Chicago River and scouts were sent to investigate. When Becka emerged from the hidden doorway she was spotted. At last Mother Russia was to acquire a strategic outpost in the heart of the Windy City!

Isidor Grigori Petrov, former Komdiv, or Division Commander for the remnant of Soviet Ground Forces in the Midwest, now reduced to commanding a rag-tag regiment of a dozen misfits, was cautious. Certainly the Americans would have defenses. He ordered his aide, a soldier named Aleksey Yakovlev, to reconnoiter. Yakovlev chose Borya Maksimov and Leonid Antonov, two skilled observers, to accompany him and soon the three were exploring the area where the America girl had been seen. Discovering the makeshift door, the piece of gilded metal fallen from the facade of the Carbide and Carbon Building, the three men slipped quietly into the underground passage that led to the commune.

Darkness surrounded them. The tunnel presented multiple crossings where the path could not be accurately determined. At times, the three split up to explore alternate routes, and finding dead ends, returned to report their failures. Antonov, gifted with a nearly photographic memory, was tasked to remember the twists and turns they had taken as they forged on. Soon a glow appeared at an intersection before them. Approaching this carefully, they could see that light issued from a corridor just beyond this crossing. Yakovlev braved a look and saw that they had reached the commune.

Yakovlev sent Antonov back to report to the commander. They had found no booby traps, trip wires, or sentries. Obviously the Americans were secure in the belief that their fortress could not be found. Now the element of surprise would lead to their downfall as the squad would sneak up to this entrance—was it the only entrance? If this were true, escape would be impossible. The Americans were trapped like rats.

There were rifles and pistols, of course, but there hadn't been a bullet in many years; no missiles or bombs and no petroleum products to run tanks or armored cars. No centralized command, no radio communication. The roving squads of soldiers now stranded in the United States were on own. Fighting was by personal combat: hand to hand, club to club, knife to knife. The goal—territory, supplies, and vengeance.

Petrov's squad had to traverse the tunnel one by one. They would have to enter the commune one at a time as well. This was a clear disadvantage for the Russians. But they lined up just outside the commune entrance, each holding a club in one hand and a long knife in the other, and waited for the signal to spring into action.

The room just on the other side of the doorway was a kitchen. Only two persons were present, stacking dishes and pots and pans that had been recently washed. Beyond was a sort of dining room with long tables and beyond that was a common room where several of the commune dwellers sat reading or playing cards. The element of surprise was going to be tenuous. By the time the Russians reached the inner rooms an alarm would be given and resistance would surely be ferocious.

Petrov tapped Yakovlev on the shoulder and motioned, "Go!" Yakovlev rushed into the kitchen swinging a heavy club which struck one of the two Americans on the side of his neck. He went down without a sound, certainly unconscious and, Yakovlev thought, probably dead. The other American, startled by the attack, shouted "Russians!" and fled from the kitchen. With this warning given, there could be no delay on Yakovlev's part. He gave the signal and the squad filed into the commune like a column of army ants, spreading out to encounter the enemy.

The Americans grabbed up anything they could find to use as a weapon: chairs, iron pots from the kitchen, kitchen knives—even books which made excellent missiles. They were not outnumbered, but they were in trouble. Fhigheobtakl, also known as Freda, being adept at rikthijmb, the aliens' martial art, looked around for something which might serve as a sword. She found a mop with a long wooden handle. This she wielded like a staff, thrusting it into a Russian's solar plexus or swinging it against heads, necks and shoulders. She brought several of the enemy to their knees but it was not a weapon which could easily kill.

The Americans were being forced back deeper and deeper into their lair. Half a dozen lay bleeding. Thom and Dupree fought back to back, dodging the Russians' clubs. Dupree battered a Russian with a broken chair leg. Thom had a kitchen knife and was standing off a Russian who also brandished an evil looking combat knife. The Russian lunged at Thom and would certainly have slashed his juggler, but Freda swung her mop handle at the Russian's neck. There was a crunching sound as the man's neck broke.

"Let's get out of here," yelled Dupree at Thom and the girl.

"But how?" Freda asked. "They control the entrance."

"There is another way out. Follow me. Quickly."

The three ran down a long, dark corridor past living areas not yet occupied by enemy soldiers. They reached what appeared to be a dead end. Dupree pushed at a panel on the wall. This opened onto yet another dark corridor. They slipped through the opening and Dupree replaced the panel.

"We won't be safe until we come out of the other end of this tunnel," he said.

"Where does it lead to?" Freda asked.

"You'll see. Follow me and try not to trip over anything. This passage is full of debris and the bodies of dead rats."

"It's awfully dark."

"Keep your hand on the right side wall. If there is a turn, follow it. It isn't far."

Meanwhile, Kurt and Fitlanká entered a collapsed building on Michigan Avenue near the Water Tower. If either of them had been familiar with Chicago from the days before the war, they would have recognized the stark, blackened skeleton as the Allerton Hotel. By the time of the beginning of the bombings, the Allerton was already a landmark, having been completed in 1924 as one of the first buildings with a setback from the avenue. It had featured a bar on its 23rd floor called the Tip Top Tap. Some of the structure still remained as pinnacles of masonry thrusting upward from the deep rubble of stone, as pieces of the floors of marble bathrooms, as rusted iron pipe and the occasional artifact that attracted scavengers like Kurt and Fitlanká.

A twisted banister of brass lay covered by fallen bricks. Its length made it impractical for recovery. There was value in brass, however. It could be used as barter with other communes. They looked for lamps or scrollwork from elevator doors or ashtrays or silver from the dining rooms in these old hotel ruins. There had been a jewelry store across the street which Kurt told Fitlanká had been quite famous in its day. It had been so picked over by scavengers that nothing remained as a monument to its lustrous renown. This hotel, however, still had bits and pieces of its former glory, albeit mostly buried, burned and bruised. They continued looking.

Fitlanká thought he saw a shadow dodging behind a free-standing pillar of marble, a fragment of lobby wall that hadn't yet toppled. He nudged Kurt and put his finger to his lips. After a few hand signals, Kurt walked deeper into the ruins while Fitlanká ducked down behind what had once been the lobby's front counter. He waited. Becka crept forward, following Kurt at a distance. As she passed Fitlanká's location, he jumped out and grabbed her—somewhat more roughly than was necessary. Becka pounded him with her fists as best as she could given that her arms were trapped in a bear hug. The entrapment didn't stop the outpouring of swear words alternating with a high-pitched screeching that issued from her mouth.

"Becka! What do you think you are doing? We thought you were a Russian. I was going to hit you with a brick."

"Well I'm not a Russian, am I? So let go!"

When Kurt saw that their stalker had been Becka he was angry, but he was also concerned. "You shouldn't be out here alone," he said.

"I'm not alone now, am I?"

"You are going back to the commune. Right this instant!"

"But wait," said Fitlanká, "she can't go back alone. There are Ruskies out there. We'll have to take her back."

"I'm not going," answered Becka. "I'm staying with you. I can forage too. I'm good at it."

"What are we going to do, Fit?" asked Kurt. "If she won't go she'll have to stay with us. I'm not ready to go back. I want to make a find."

"Okay, but you stay close and keep watch," Fitlanká told Becka. "And don't be a pest."

When the boys and Freda emerged from the tunnel they were standing on the north bank of the river, next to the shattered remains of a building that covered over two city blocks. Freda glanced down. At her feet was the broken stone statue of an Indian, with feathered headdress and arms crossed as if in defiance of the ultimate destruction of its masonry world. They had crossed the river beneath the Wells Street Bridge through one of the underground rail tunnels that linked Chicago's buildings, crucial to commerce for many of the years before the war.

"What is this place?" asked Freda.

"It was the Merchandise Mart, the world's largest building, or so it was said. There is so much rubble piled on rubble here that it is almost impossible to forage for goods. Anything on the surface has long since been taken way."

"And where are we with regard to the place where we were first attacked by the Russians?"

"Just over in that direction," replied Dupree, pointing north. "Why?"

"Well isn't it obvious? We will go now to recover my airboat. Do you have a better suggestion?"

Kurt and Fitlanká had moved on toward the east with Becka trailing behind. They hadn't found much: a broken candle stick which was definitely not brass—more likely pot metal painted gold, a spoon which was silver plate, and a fragment of stained glass that looked like a jewel (worthless, but pretty). They had kept only the spoon. There had been some fancy residences in the direction they were heading. Probably picked over by other scavengers, but still worth a look.

Here the semblance of a forest had taken root in the ruins...and then had died. Ugly blackened, leafless trees and low bushes with webs of dead branches sat upon a carpet of twigs and bark so deep one had to watch their step for fear of stepping into a crevice between buried bricks. Closer to the lake, vines had claimed territory and wound around the trunks and limbs of the dead trees. Closer yet, young vegetation had taken root in the form of sycamore and tree of heaven, mulberry and a variety of weeds: thistle, pig weed, nettle and fleabane. Fitlanká pointed out poison ivy, warning the others to avoid it.

They found a townhouse: remarkably it was nearly intact. The windows had been blown out and the roof had burned and fallen, but through the open door they could see stairs that led to the upper stories. These were weathered and splintered and one or two steps were missing, yet it seemed they would support the weight of the explorers. Becka bounded up the stairway. Kurt yelled at her to be careful…slow down…watch your step. Up she went, bold and unconcerned. At the first landing she peered over the banister at her companions.

"Wait 'til you see what's up here," she called down to them.

On the second floor they found a room that just couldn't exist in the aftermath of the bombing and pillaging. Neat and furnished with modern furniture including table and chairs, bed, dresser and an occasional table upon which sat a chess set. In one corner was a makeshift kitchen complete with washtub sink and charcoal-burning grill. Shelves were stacked with canned goods. On the table was a loaf of bread, the most impossible of the impossible things in the room.

"Someone is living here," said Fitlanká.

"I wouldn't mind having a piece of that bread," Becka mumbled.

"I don't suppose any of you play chess. Do you?" a voice called out from behind them.

They turned to see the figure of a man, elegantly dressed in period costume of…what was it? The 1920s? Waistcoat of green silk with pearl buttons, a smoking jacket (was that what it was called?) with leather patches at the elbows, pin striped trousers, a highly starched shirt with paper collar and expertly tied four-in-hand tie (also silk). And—no, they must be imagining this—patent leather shoes *with spats*! He appeared to be in his mid-sixties, but had only a single streak of gray in his otherwise light brown, curly hair. No mustache or beard. No walking cane or top hat. And no, it wasn't an illusion.

"Welcome to my modest lodgings. You may have a piece of bead, young lady, if you wish. I would join you but I have already eaten."

His name, he told them, was Alexander Henley. He lived in the townhouse alone and had taken up residence some ten years previous, having arrived in Chicago with a caravan of Spiritualists who left their camp grounds in Wisconsin when it was destroyed by a stray bomb intended for nearby Madison. The others were appalled by the devastation they found in Chicago and continued on, seeking adequate living conditions in the lower Midwest. Henley stayed in the City of the Big Shoulders, putting together a domicile from bits and pieces he found in the surrounding area. He was quite happy, he maintained, living alone with the ghosts of the Gold Coast with whom he attempted, so far unsuccessfully, to communicate.

"Aren't you afraid of the Russians?" asked Becka.

"No. I have been friendly with them, telling them where they could find a warehouse filled with canned goods. They were grateful and never bothered me."

"Gee! I wish you'd tell us where that warehouse is," blurted Becka.

"Too late. It has been cleared out by now. I managed to put up a fair amount of food here before they got to it. I don't know what I'll do after this runs out."

"You could come back with us to our commune. We grow vegetables and hunt. You could tell us stories…that would earn your keep."

"And the canned goods would help, I suppose. No, I think not. I'm happy here, and here I'll stay…until the end."

"The end?"

"The End Days, of course.

"It looks like they tried to get it started, and then got frustrated and tried to wreck it," said Dupree as the three fugitives from the battle stood examining the airboat.

"They could not harm it sufficiently to disable it," said Freda. "We build them really well. The Russians did not understand the principles of its operation…luckily for us. Now if only they haven't taken the globe…"

"Is this what you're looking for?" called Thom, who had been poking around in the tall grass with a stick. He held up a shining sphere about the size of a grapefruit.

"Mziqroafvuent must have dropped it when the Russians

attacked us. It is keyed to his aura, but I think I can retune it to mine." Freda took the globe from Thom and turned it over and over, pressing hidden buttons on its surface. "There! I think…yes. We can operate the airboat now."

"Freda, I could kiss you," said Thom.

"That would serve no useful purpose," she answered. "Come. Let us get on the airboat."

"Wait…where are we going?" Dupree asked.

"To the Uoigykwosp, of course. To the mothership."

"What? Why don't we go down south…Florida or somewhere…somewhere it's warm in the winter?" said Dupree.

"Can we at least try to find out if any of the others are still alive?" asked Thom. "If they are, they would have escaped out the way we did. And, remember? Kurt and Fitlanká are out here somewhere. They don't know about the attack."

"All right. We look for your friends. But no Florida. Get into the airboat now. Time is wasting."

Becka was thinking, what a nice man Mr. Henley was. It would be fine to come to live with the old gentleman, cook for him, clean. He could be just like the father she no longer had. Becka wasn't a runaway, not really. She had been abandoned by accident when her parents moved from the encroaching war zone in Milwaukee; she had been six. They had traveled south and reaching Chicago, they had huddled together in a burned out three-flat west of the Loop. Becka went to sleep that night dreaming of a life without turmoil or strife. Country gardens with butterflies. Cool breezes along a babbling brook. Fairies dancing at twilight. When she woke they were gone: mother, father, younger sister. Gone.

Alexander Henley was telling a story about the days before the war. Becka was fascinated and hung on every word. Kurt and Fitlanká were less enchanted. Kurt walked to an open window where a faded, torn piece of fabric provided the only protection from wind or rain. He pulled this aside and looked out.

"Fit!" he called. "Come look. It's an alien flier. Are they tracking us somehow?"

"I don't see how. Stay back from the window. Maybe they will pass by." Fitlanká was curious, however. He peered around the edge of the window to look up at the airboat. Then: "What…is that? Is that Thom up there?"

Indeed, Thom was hanging over the side of the airboat hoping to catch a glimpse of any humans from the commune—any humans who weren't Russians. He saw Fitlanká waving at him from the window of the burned-out townhouse.

When they were ready to leave, Thom, Dupree, Kurt, Fitlanká, and Freda were sitting in the airboat, eager to be on their way. Becka was still trying to coax Alexander Henley into joining them. He refused to leave his townhouse. It was his home and he had no wish to become a wanderer. Becka had a decision to make. Would she stay or would she go? Escape the dreary city or remain to nurse and nurture the old man if he needed it? Henley made the decision for her:

"Go away, girl," he said. "You bother me. I want to be alone and you will just complicate my life if you stay. Be gone!"

Reluctantly, Becka climbed onto the airboat. They waved goodbye to Henley, and Freda lifted the airboat up above the fractured skyline and pointed its nose toward Kansas.

# 32

## 1254 AD, Earth Time…Somewhere in Space

Two ktanyos after the exodus from Klivpokla, the scientist, Zopthmnquiosk, suggested splitting the fleet into five groups, each with three mother ships. These separate fleets headed in five different directions, toward likely solar systems where planets might exist. We know that the mothership called Uoigykwosp landed on Earth many centuries later, its population plagued by the inability to procreate. But what of the others?

Pgikovjela was a large, egg-shaped space ship that traveled with two others in what might have seemed an arbitrary direction. There were no known life-sustaining planets in their path. Their's was a dismal gamble. Half way across the galaxy, or so it seemed, a scientist on the Pgikovjela named Grtrifhoopalr, despaired of ever finding such a planet. The quadrant of space they found themselves in was particularly empty of solar systems. A group of important males and females, four from each of the three motherships, formed a Circle to discuss the problem. Grtrifhoopalr testified and offered a possible solution: change direction.

While that might have seemed obvious, it was a plan fraught with more uncertainty and danger. It meant recrossing all that emptiness with little hope of finding the resources they needed to sustain life: mainly water and the minerals from which they could derive dark matter. These things were typically gotten by capturing comets and asteroids—few and far between in their sector of space. Added to this was the terrifying fact that their supply of dark matter was dwindling—they could end up stranded in the void! Grtrifhoopalr pointed out that there was a black hole not far from them. Why not use the event horizon of the hole like a spring board, flying at it and generating a huge burst of antigravity at just the right moment to bounce away at near light speed?

A black hole—the aliens didn't call it that, but they understood its principles—was a region of space-time formed around matter which was compressed so much that the gravitational waves it emitted allowed nothing to escape from it, not even visible light. The event horizon—the aliens didn't call it that—was a sort of boundary surrounding the black hole. This could pull particles (and objects) into the black hole by bending space-time into something like a funnel. By hitting the edge of the event horizon and exerting an opposite force, they just might deflect and accelerate to the speed of light.

The proposal was accepted and the fleet veered off toward the black hole. The Pgikovjela was to try the experiment first. Grtrifhoopalr had calculated a tangent which would bounce the ship toward a distant solar system where they thought there might be planets orbiting a sun...planets capable of sustaining life. The motherships lined up several thousand miles from the black hole. The Pgikovjela was readied. The command was given and the mothership's pilots steered her toward the black hole's event horizon.

Just at the precise moment that Pgikovjela encountered the event horizon, at the edge where the gravity pull could still be escaped, the gravity waves of the mothership were reversed. So great was the push between the two opposing forces, the ship was indeed flung deep into space at a velocity that neared that of light speed. There arose a rousing cheer from the staff in the control capsule. The other two ships, encouraged by the Pgikovjela's success, ventured toward the black hole with due haste.

Unfortunately, the navigators on the other two ships had miscalculated by a fraction of a degree. Both ships were captured by the event horizon and sucked into the black hole to become additional matter to fuel the fearsome anomaly. Pgikovjela never knew of their fate, so far away was she on her journey into the unknown.

Life went on in the mothership as usual. The Klivpoklaian culture wasn't one to evolve or change very much. Generations were born; generations died. They hadn't been visited with disease and sterility the way that other ship, the Uoigykwosp, had. Not yet. They were well on their way toward a promising solar system. There was every reason to be positive.

Cghenmudwe worked in a lab as an assistant to the head scientist. She was a Grey female, tall for her race, nearly seven feet (by Earth measurement). Tall and as slender as a pflematap vine and wispy too; when she walked she swished. This wasn't an affectation. She just swished through a room in a hurry—she was always in a hurry. This was due to an abundance of natural energy born of body and of mind. It was also the reason she had been given the job over many other applicants.

Cghenmudwe loved to look out one the lab's few windows, out across the wide plaza ten stories below. There was a small park with trees and a pond where water fowl circled and small children played. There were not many moments during her day when she could indulge herself in this activity—only when things slowed down and the others took their breaks or ran errands in other parts of the facility. Today she had such an opportunity and she gazed out the window feeling, for a change, tranquil and no longer hurried.

Behind her on a table covered with glass containers, test tubes and bubbling beakers was a set of petri dishes she had been monitoring. Each contained a culture medium and a strain of one of the various bacteria that had been found recently in food stores kept deep in the mothership's bowels. It was a routine check on the quality of meat and vegetables that had been put aside in case of shortages of fresh food. It wasn't expected that the bacteria would prove to be anything other than harmless. When she turned from the window and picked up her pad to begin writing notes she glanced down at the dishes—and dropped the pad.

Something didn't look right. For one thing, the cultures had grown at an unexpected rate. For another, there was a pattern of concentric violet and crimson rings in one of the dishes. This seemed to portend an unknown and possibly dangerous strain. She would need to notify her boss immediately. She hurried out of the lab to do so.

When she returned with the scientist in tow (the man was not happy at being taken so abruptly away from a game of wkebvoles[12] which he had been playing with some of the off-duty staff) she led him to the table where she had left the petri dishes. The one in question, however, was no longer on the table. It had somehow rolled off onto the floor, landing right next to the pad she had dropped, and was open…and empty.

Thirty ktanyos later a generation had passed and a new one tackled the task of conquering the wide-spread disease that had erupted so gradually from that spilled petri dish. The disease attacked the young and the old, killing the weakest and disabling the rest. There was another, greatly alarming aspect of the epidemic: fewer children were being born.

Finally it had run its course; immune systems rallied against the disease. But a devastating toll had been taken; most of the survivors were sterile. Now they were, like the Uoigykwosp before them, another doomed civilization hurtling through space toward a dubious future.

Work began on a solution. There were still a few who could procreate, who had been resistant to the disease. Only one in ten of the babies was normal. The rest also proved to be sterile. The only solution now was cloning. This was an imperfect process with a limited success rate. Experiments to improve the process began.

Of the four races of Klivpoklaians aboard the Pgikovjela, none were compatible with the others so cross-breeding was impossible. Cloning therefore necessitated finding a source of genetic material to combine with that of the sterile members of each race. This would provide the missing elements attacked by the bacterial infections. The solution was thought to be splicing these genes into a DNA string (a very tricky procedure) and fertilizing with it the ovum from females who were still viable. The search for the genes expanded to include virtually every living thing on the mothership.

Ahtejiqs, fwilhogs, zlthmogs, and even plablikz were tested. There were just not enough similarities to the Klivpoklaian generic codes to allow the splicing. Then came a breakthrough. Someone tried testing a phamleblikz, the ancestor of the plablikz. Its spider shape was repulsive and the notion that such a primordial creature, a predator, no less, should be the savoir of the Klivpoklaian races, was anathema to the population. Yet the scientists persisted. And it seemed as though the problem had been solved.

Cloning now produced a new generation, with each of the four races represented in adequate numbers. These clones interbred and Klivpoklaian civilization moved forward, optimistic once again toward the promising future of colonizing a planet—a planet which long-range sensors had recently detected. The third planet from the sun of a not so distant solar system.

## 1974 AD, Earth Time…Mount Pleasant, Iowa

About 200 miles into their journey, the airboat was hovering above Mount Pleasant, a small town in southeastern Iowa. The town appeared to have been unaffected by the war. Buildings stood intact, people walked along sidewalks or rode in horse-drawn carriages up and down the streets. There were gardens in backyards and flags flying from poles in schoolyards and at the City Hall and in the Central Park. American flags. A good sign.

"We should stop here for supplies," said Freda. We still have a long way to go."

"You worked mind control on us, didn't you? To get us to agree to return to your mothership." Thom still did not trust the Klivpoklaian/Human hybrid and said so.

"I might have nudged you a little. But that sort of thing is difficult with so many subjects to control. I think your fears overrode your reluctance more than my powers of suggestion could have. Anyway, you'll be safe in the Uoigykwosp."

Dupree peered over the edge of the airboat. "Looks pretty peaceful down there. Why don't you let us off here and go on your own way?"

"Your so-called modern technology was disabled by the war. No more internal combustion engines, no electrical grid. This little town has reverted to a life style more suited to a previous century. An agricultural microcosm in the middle of a burned-out nowhere. Interesting."

"You didn't answer the question."

Nor did she as Freda flew over the rooftops of the seemingly idyllic hamlet looking for a place to land. She picked out a field on the edge of town and set the airboat down there. Just as the airboat came to rest a dozen or so of the town's people rushed at them, yelling and brandishing pitchforks, clubs, axes, or carrying stones which they began to pitch at the airboat.

"Peaceful, huh?" Freda raised the airboat up above the hostile crowd so suddenly that the others fell to the floor. "I think you've got your answer."

The Pgikovjela, the mothership that had changed course so long ago, now approached the edge of the solar system. The sun rushed through space chased by a spiral of planets, asteroids and space dust. Probes were sent out to explore the third planet from that sun, the one that looked like it might support life. An astonishing thing then happened: life readings were present—and among these were life signatures that could only be interpreted as Klivpoklaian! Was it possible? Were there beings like themselves on other planets in the galaxy?

The Pgikovjela hung back, orbiting the sun next to a large planet with a swirling red dot. Saucers were sent to explore the third planet. To search for life. To search for Klivpoklaian life. They discovered a concentration of Klivpoklaian life forms in the center of a continental land mass. They discovered the Uoigykwosp, the mothership that had landed in Kansas two decades ago. This was cause for rejoicing. Except for a question: why had the inhabitants of the mothership not spread out across the planet? Why were they still huddled together in the big egg-shaped environment? Why had they not cleared the planet of those other indigenous life forms that roamed like wild beasts? The saucer commanders chose not to communicate with the Uoigykwosp. Not yet.

The Uoigykwosp's observers had seen the two saucers. A check of their data base failed to show any missing saucers; all were accounted for, including those lost in the initial battles with the humans. They knew that at least one saucer had been captured, but the humans had not been able to run it since its control orb had been missing. Had the humans reverse engineered the saucer, built two of their own?

By the time defensive saucers were scrambled, the mysterious others had left the Earth's atmosphere. The observers watched them disappear behind Jupiter. This propounded the mystery. Did the humans have a base hidden behind the giant planet? How had this gone unnoticed for so long? There was only one way to find out. Two saucers were sent to approach Jupiter from beyond its outer orbit. They were not heard from in the next two weeks.

Then the message came: "Salutations, brothers and sisters. We are the Pgikovjela. Request landing on your planet in your vicinity."

Of course the request was granted. The prospect of encountering new members of their own four races, of their former planet, was exhilarating. No one, however, thought to inquire as to the fate of the two saucer crews. The idea that there may have been some changes over the centuries to the psychological or physical makeup of these others also had not occurred to them.

## 1974 AD Earth time...St. Joseph, Missouri

Freda hovered the airboat over the river town of St. Joseph. She was not about to land until she could determine the relative friendliness or hostility of the population. Destruction was evident in the collapsed structures of larger buildings, but many small houses remained undamaged and there were people walking through the streets. Some pointed up at the airboat. No one ran or took cover. Perhaps alien ships were a common enough sight that danger was not anticipated.

Experimentally, she lowered them to within a dozen feet of the ground, at an open area which appeared to be a public park. A handful of the locals wandered slowly, somewhat aimlessly. All of them had a faraway look to their eyes; they apparently were ignoring the airboat, or perhaps they failed to register its image in their consciousness. At least there was no hostile activity on the part of the locals. Freda decided to land.

They sat, silently waiting for the approach of the townspeople or its authorities, if there were any, but no one came closer to them. Kurt came forward in the airboat and sat next to Freda. The two had had little interaction during the time Freda had been at the commune. Now Kurt ventured to speak what had been on his mind for some time.

"You and I have something in common," he told her.

"I have also thought as much," she answered.

"The others don't know, I think. Nor do they know about me. It is probably for the good."

"Are they so prejudiced?"

"There are many tensions. Russians and aliens are the natural enemies of humans these days."

"That is absurd. Once we are back to the mother ship I will see that you are treated with respect. " Freda looked deeply into Kurt's eyes. "Are you skilled yet at thought transfer?" This last she thought to him rather than speaking it aloud.

"I can hear thoughts," he answered, speaking. "But I don't have any experience in sending thoughts. No one to think at."

"Of course. I will help you with that. Concentrate on my face and lean forward toward me. Now think some lovely thoughts to me."

Two of the airboat's occupants were observing the interchange between the hybrid man and woman (they saw only a human boy and an alien girl). These two witnesses were nonplussed at the apparent mutual attractions Freda and Kurt exhibited for each other. Thom was himself attracted to Freda and resented Kurt's romantic inclinations—this he supposed was indicated by the closeness of the two as they whispered together. Becka was furious with Kurt for his attention to Freda and the fact that he had all but ignored herself during the flight from Chicago. Jealousy easily festered where unrequited adoration was concerned.

Fitlanká had meanwhile leaped from the airboat and approached one of the wandering people. He followed along side of the fellow trying to get his attention. After few minutes, he returned. His report to his companions was as follows:

"I tried to engage the man in conversation. At first it appeared that he was oblivious to my existence, as if I were invisible. I suspected that he and the others were under the influence of some drug. Then I noticed something ominous. There were numbers printed on his sleeve. The others had the same clothing, a dismal brown, and all appeared to have the same kind of numbers.

"Off in the distance I saw what looked like a fence. A very tall fence with barbed wire across the top of it. I think we've landed in the middle of a prison camp! The man, and the others...they don't look like Russians to me. Which means... "

"Which means we'd better get the hell out of here," said Dupree.

[12] Wkebvoles is a card game played with a deck of 64 cards divided into 8 suits of 8 cards each. It is a game for four players. For purposes of clarity we will dispense with the Klivpoklaian names and use their human English equivalents. The suits are distinguished by their colors: infrared, red, orange, yellow, blue, indigo, violet, and ultraviolet. Each card in the suit has a pictogram representing an idea of importance, symbolized in an image. These are, in no particular order, mountain, valley, river, lake, night sky, morning sky, fire, and sun. When combined in pairs with one of the cards placed on top of the other, a meaning is created that is either positive or negative. For example, with the pair "fire and lake," it can be seen that fire on top of lake represents a dynamic image of motion and energy (positive), whereas lake on top of fire will obviously quench the fire, resulting in stagnation and destruction (negative).

The cards are shuffled, not so much to randomize them as to align them with cosmic forces which will order the possibilities in a manner beneficial to one or more of the players…a consequence thought to spring from the Kpxk (what we would call karma) of each player. Eight cards are dealt to each of the four players and the remaining deck is put aside. Beginning with the dealer and rotating in a counter-clockwise direction, each player lays down one pair of the same suit. If he or she has no pairs they lay down a single card. Once a suit is played it is "owned" by that player and can not be used by another. Thus four of the eight suits will be played in the first round. It is a good strategy to select the best pairing and place the cards so that the top card creates a positive image.

On the second round, players may either lay down another pair of the same suit they began with, or play a single card of the appropriate suit on top of another player's pair. In playing on top of another's pair, the object is to create a negative image. If no play can be made the player may draw from the deck until he or she gets a card of one of the suits showing on the table. This must then be played whether or not it creates a positive or a negative image.

The game goes on until all the cards have been played. Players' hands will now contain all the cards of the four suits which have not been in play before. The dealer then begins by placing a pair on the table, thereby owning that suit. The play continues until no more plays are possible. The winner is the player with the most positive image pairs showing. The reader may notice the slight similarity to the Chinese Book of Changes, or I Ching. There is no reason to believe this is anything but a coincidence.

# 33

## The Beginning of the End

The (secret) meeting of the Uoigykwosp Circle is in session. The twelve officials, three from each racial group, are assembled to discuss the advent of the landing of the Pgikovjela and its ramifications for their own security and that of the planet. Atklofghewi, a Grey male who heads up what serves as the alien's Intelligence Service (known as JST, or Jwensry Suughbwt Tjaiolp— untranslatable but meaning something like Overtly Suspicious and Nosey Investigators), is speaking to the group. He has assembled some documents to support his comments and these will be projected for the Circle by a holographic device called a ghkewbdr.

Atklofghewi rubs his hands against the gel material of his clothing; his hands are sweating—he is unaccustomed to speaking before such an esteemed body as the Circle. What he is about to relate will seem incredible and most likely will be in doubt: hence the visuals he has prepared as proof of his theory. Already hanging in the air in front of the Circle members is the slightly translucent image of the Pgikovjela, the second mothership to have landed in the middle of Kansas.

"Thank you, your Honors, for the opportunity you have given me to discuss some grave concerns I have about our recent visitors. As you know, the Pgikovjela was given permission to land some 40 gvoplts from our own site. Since the landing, they have spread out across nearly half that distance in an ever widening circle, establishing outposts and clearing the area of any random humans who previously lived in their path."

"We know all this, Atklofghewi," says Mat/3, current leader of the Circle. "Please get to the point."

"The JST became interested in the Pgikovjelaians because of several incidents," continues Atklofghewi. "At the first meeting of their ambassadors and ours they questioned our isolation and noninterference during the human war." (Mat/3 stiffens and displays an irritated expression.) "This could be attributed to mere curiosity but then their chief ambassador, Knmueqroaak, suggested a coalition to remove humans from this continent. This raised a red flag for us since it seems an unusually aggressive notion for a Klivpoklaian."

Mat/3 leans forward, anger flaring in her eyes. "You should not have been privy to the negotiations between the ambassadors, Atklofghewi. That was a closed session. You will reveal your sources for this information and be cited for improper behavior!"

"I am sorry, your Honor, but I cannot reveal my sources. It would endanger an ongoing investigation and put my agents at risk. But please allow me to continue. Surely the rest of the Circle will want to hear what I have discovered."

"Yes," says Aim/1. "Let him continue. I myself was suspicious of the ambassador's request."

Atklofghewi changes the projected hologram to one displaying the full length figure of a Pgikovjelaian male. "Thank you, your Honor. This is a scan we made of an aide to Ambassador Knmueqroaak as he waited outside the conference room during that closed meeting. If you look closely you will notice he is covered with a light fur."

"So he's hairy," Rat/2 blurts out. "I see no reason to incriminate him for being a little odd."

"That's the point. He isn't odd. We have documented others in the Pgikovjela itself who exhibit much heavier hairiness…with considerably darker fur covering, it appears, their entire bodies."

"It is not remarkable that over many hundreds of ktanyos, some interbreeding would produce a variation of body style," suggests Mat/3. "Again you have broken protocol by scanning these people without their permission. You are in serious jeopardy of losing your position."

"There was another incident I need to report. This was kept secret for purposes of security. On a day one llopikm after the meeting, a group of Pgikovjelaians were on a sight-seeing tour of the Uoigykwosp. Someone on level ten had left their pet plablikz running loose. The animal started growing and backing away from the

Pgikovjelaians, as if it were frightened. One of the group took offense at the animal's attitude and aimed a vicious kick at it. The plablikz seized the man's leg in its jaws and bit through his clothing, causing a deep gash in his leg."

"Why wasn't this incident reported? It could have had political consequences," asks Aim/3.

Atklofghewi now changes the projected image to one showing two rendered double spirals clustered with colorful spheres. The members of the Circle turn their attention to this projection, some squinting to better resolve the image.

"The man in question was taken to a dispensary to have his wound treated. We were able to obtain samples of his blood from the discarded wipes. Here you see on the left an example of DNA from a normal Ratiessrvedflynach, one of our own. On the right is the DNA taken from the Pgikovjelaian who was bitten. You can see clearly where the difference is."

Atklofghewi brings a second image up next to that of the DNA molecules. This shows a single helix, very similar in configuration and coloring to that of the Pgikovjelaian one.

"This is DNA from a phamleblikz. Notice that these fourteen strands on the Pgikovjelaian image match their equivalents on the phamleblikz one."

Mat/3 rises suddenly from her seating cube, nearly tipping it over. She is furious. "This is absurd," she says. "It is obvious what you have done. Everyone knows the phamleblikz is the ancient ancestor of the plablikz. The animal's saliva mixed with the man's blood and contaminated it. Your interpretation is not only wrong, it is treasonous!"

Atklofghewi now brings a third image up next to the others. "This is plablikz DNA. It differs from phamleblikz at several significant points. The fourteen strands of similarity which with we are concerned do not exist in plablikz DNA. So your theory is false. Our conclusion is that the Pgikovjelaians have evolved along these lines over many hundreds of ktanyos. How this occurred is unknown. The result, however, has been to produce an aggressive population. There is further evidence.

"We sent undercover agents into the Pgikovjelaia. They have surveyed the population and noted that Aimnegarwfuchees, Matofnblotjuupzs, and Syktijthraxteraq exist in appallingly small numbers. We believe the mutated Ratiessrvedflynachs have crowded the other races out over the years…perhaps purposely, we don't know for sure. At any rate, it is troubling."

"*You* are troubling," says Mat/3, her voice trembling. "Your theory is full of holes and your intentions suspect. I bring a motion to this Circle to censure you and separate you from your position as head of the JST." Then in focused thought transfer to the other Circle members: "Any discussion? Shall we vote?"

It is unanimous. Atklofghewi is no longer the head of the JST.

Two days earlier the airboat arrived at the Uoigykwosp. During Freda's debriefing she revealed that Kurt was an Klivpoklaian/Human hybrid and requested that he be placed under her care and supervision. The other humans were taken to the facility for housing of human subjects where they would be treated well and would eventually contribute to the research into cloning. Becka and Thom despaired of ever seeing Kurt and Freda again. "Shoulda stayed in Chicago," Thom was heard to say as the group was led away.

"My friends…I should be with them," said Kurt.

"No. Come with me. I want you to meet my parents," answered Freda.

"What will happen to them?"

"Nothing bad. Humans lead a good life here. They aren't experimental subjects anymore. They do contribute, however."

"What do you mean…contribute?"

"They will have the choice to intermarry. They won't be forced to. But they will be introduced gradually to our culture and our people. Most will become coupled with one of us. It is a natural thing."

"That might not sound so natural to some."

"You and I are the results of natural coupling. Do you think we were mistakes?"

"No, of course not. It's just a little hard to get use to. And my mother's 'coupling' was anything but natural."

"I understand. But when you meet Knuuplhcanika you will lose your prejudice."

"Knuuplhcanika? Who is Knuuplhcanika?"

"That is the name of their coupling. No longer do they use their old names, Rkohtealnaq and Christianresnik. They are a single unit now."

First she took him to a balcony where he could look out over the edge of the level into the vast empty cavity of the giant egg-like ship; he saw the many levels: agricultural, urban, grazing areas and more. He saw spherical things with people in them flying here and there across the space. He saw the tubes that carried people between levels; these clinging against the walls of the levels, gleaming in the illumination that passed for sunlight, reflecting the greenish glow. He saw strange animals and flying things. He heard the bustling of people going about the routines of their day.

They rode a moving sidewalk into the heart of the urban level. Freda explained the workings of the lifting tube and soon Kurt was rising to the upper stories of a cube-shaped building. He exited the tube at the third floor as Freda had directed, and waited for her to join him. When she appeared she spoke to him verbally rather than by thought transfer:

"You will now meet my parents. They live just up this hallway. They will communicate by thought transfer, although both can also speak human English. It will be polite of you to try to get by using the thoughts, thinking at them as I have shown you how to do. However, I will explain to them who and what you are and where you come from and I am sure they will welcome the opportunity to practice verbalizing."

"I'll give them a good old Midwestern howdy-doo. In my mind, of course."

Freda scowled at Kurt, unappreciative of his little joke. "Come along now," she said.


The human habitat occupied the eastern sector of level nine. Over one thousand human beings lived and worked in an environment which had been tailored to Earthly tastes: gardens, parks, long paths through vegetation that at least vaguely resembled Earth-type forests, and a lake upon which one could navigate a paddle boat. Greys lived there as well. They mingled with the humans.

It was known that Grey/Human couplings were successful in producing offspring, while couplings with the other species rarely had a child which survived its first ktanyo. This was the reality for the aliens—it was accepted, but it spawned irreconcilable schisms between the three other races and the Greys. Now, with the arrival of the second mothership, some believed that things might change for Nordics, Reptilians and Greens. These optimists would be disappointed.

Fitlanká, Becka, Thom and Dupree were on their way in a surface vehicle, a large, oblong bubble with transparent walls. They were certain they were headed for incarceration in some gloomy cell, and torture by experimentation. Fitlanká could not shake the common belief that aliens ate humans—raw, like sushi. He would be flailed alive and rolled into little bite size morsels. Dupree seemed to be the only one of the four that had not succumbed to fear. He tried to calm the others with these words:

"As soon as we see an opportunity, we will escape. I have a plan."

"Mirko...Mirko? Why does that name sound familiar?" said Christian Resnik (half of the coupled entity known as Knuuplhcanika).

"My mother and father were abducted by the aliens back when they were still on the dark side of the moon," answer Kurt. "Maybe you heard of them."

"That explains it. I was up there too, you know. Yes...I think I remember your father. My memory is a bit hazy these days. Getting senile, I guess."

"I guess it's a small world when it gets around to abductions. Father and Mother didn't talk much about that time. It was worse for my mother. She..."

"Knuuplhcanika, I wanted you to meet Kurtmirko because I have decided to become coupled with him. I want you to ask the Circle for permission," said Freda.

If it were possible for jaws to actually "drop," Kurt's would have reached the floor. This was a surprise—not entirely unwelcome, but all the same, nothing he had anticipated or would have wished for.

"But Freda," he stammered, "isn't it a little soon for..."

"Ha! Back in the old days," said Resnik, "they would have called that a 'mixed marriage.' How do you feel, boy, about marrying an alien?"

"Knuuplhcanika, you need to know that Kurtmirko is a hybrid...just as I am. That is why I think it would be a perfect coupling. And the Circle would be interested in our offspring." Freda was determined to convince her parents, and Kurt, of her wisdom in the matter. She looked to her mother for guidance.

Rkohtealnaq smiled at her daughter. "You have my blessing," she told her.

Kurt could only stutter: "But…but…but…" and then was silent.

Twenty years before this, Senator Joseph McCathy, in his maniacal rage, had insisted that the military had been infiltrated by communists. He was partially correct. There were, in fact, a few well-placed Russian spies in strategic positions. It was because of this that when the war intensified, the enemy was able to breach the supposedly impenetrable and atom bomb proof underground bunkers hidden here and there around the country. Even Area 51 fell to the invading armies.

Yet a group of scientists, many with expertise in nuclear science, had escaped and hidden in a place so obvious that it was overlooked by the roving marauders: the Carlsbad Caverns in New Mexico. They had traversed through the exotic chambers called "rooms" by their discoverer: through the Bat Cave, past the Bell Chord Room with its single skinny dangling stalactite, across the Hall of the Giants where columns and draperies of multicolored stone shimmered in the light of the torches they carried, and into Chocolate High with its crazy labyrinth of tunnels delicately arrayed above a river of mud. At the Hall of the White Giant they paused. A huge white stalagmite rose from the floor. It seemed to symbolize something to them about endurance, survival, the vastness of time itself, and the accumulation of knowledge which they shared. As the stalagmite had grown from the slow action of carbolic acid-saturated water, so too could the group achieve something equally monumental and marvelous. If they only persevered.

The elevators used to descend the 750 feet to the entrance of the cavern ceased to operate some months later; the electric grid was down, never to rise again to full power. They had had time, however, to bring into the caves much equipment, including a portable generator, many gallons of petroleum, some pumping equipment and tubing, and a generous supply of uranium rich ore. Within a year they had assembled a crude breeder reactor. Now they would spend their time refining the ore and separating the U-235 from it. The yield of weapons grade U-235 was very small, but the reactor produced plutonium, which in turn produced more plutonium, and so the cycle of building a bomb began.

Some argued for explosive power. This was problematic given the meager resources of the group and the small yields of plutonium they were getting. Others proposed constructing a Neutron bomb—a device of minimal explosive power, but one which would spew deadly radiation in a large circumference around ground zero. Still others suggested jacketing the device with cobalt, thus creating a sort of "doomsday bomb" whose half-life radiation would continue to kill for many, many years. This was deemed impractical, given that reestablishing civilization was paramount once the aliens had been destroyed. And yet...

Now, twenty years after taking refuge in the cave, they were ready. Their only problem was transportation: how to get the bomb to Kansas. They had no airplane, nor were any of them capable pilots. There was still a small supply of gasoline; the generator was not needed as the reactor had produced steam to run an electrical turbine. All they needed was a truck or some other conveyance, and a way to lift the heavy bomb up out of the caverns.

Fitlanká sat off to one side of the group of detainees in the human habitat. He pulled a small leather pouch from underneath his shirt where it had hung on a leather thong. This he opened to spill the contents out into the palm of one hand: a small stone carved like a turtle (a charm related to his clan, the Turtle Clan, the keepers of information and the custodians of the land), and a short belt made from purple and white Quahog clamshells (a Wampum Belt, used by his people—not as money, but to document significant events). The pictures woven into the designs on the belt spoke to those who could read them. The newest addition to this one showed the arrival of the alien spacecraft. Strands of cord had been tied off at the edge of this picture, and dangled from his hand. What might be added, he wondered? What would the next chapter of Oneida history be like?

# Aftermath

The more frightening parts of this story are the ones that are true. The senseless detonations of nuclear weapons, the stockpiling, the so-called cold war, Nationism, bureaucratic stupidity, prejudice and hatred. As I write these worlds, in August of 2017, there is a deranged man in the White House with his (tiny) finger on the nuclear trigger. Narcissism, bigotry, incompetence, bullying and lying are the hallmarks of this man's presidency. Neo-Nazis and the KKK are holding rallies and attacking and killing counter-demonstrators. Where, oh where are those benevolent aliens when we need them?

True: the windshield pitting episodes of 1954. There was at least one theory that fallout from the Bikini tests was the cause of it. True? Ufology maintains that President Eisenhower met with aliens three times. Maybe. In my story Ike dies from his first heart attack. He did not. But he was hospitalized in September of 1955 (not 1954 as in my story) and ran the White House from his hospital bed with Vice President Nixon meekly running errands for him. Mamie did move into an adjoining room and decorate it all in pink including a pink toilet seat.

The Majestic Twelve very probably did exist in the capacity of advice and control of space alien related activities, real or imagined. The men mentioned in the story were real, except for Dr. Albert Forstinger, who is my fictional character. One member of the group, James Forrestal, committed suicide under very mysterious circumstances in 1949.

The Air Force may have contributed to the saucer sighting phenomenon in a cover up of the crash of a spy balloon in Roswell by leaking that it was a flying saucer. Saucer hysteria was real, whether the sightings and abductions were real or hoaxes. The abductions didn't begin to be reported until around 1957 and didn't obtain wide-spread notice until 1961. My aliens started abducting people and cattle right away in 1954, or so my story would have you believe. Greys, Reptilians and Nordics were the most common types of aliens reported to have been seen in the 1950s. Early sightings also involved aliens of a small stature, the so-called "Little Green Men." In keeping with the historical record, I used these types as my aliens, rather than blobby, tentacled horrors or shape-shifting bug-eyed monsters.

Project Blue Book, the Air Force's effort to debunk UFO sightings, listed as many as 720 "unexplained" sightings by the time it closed down in 1969, about 6 percent of the total reports. Some sources maintain the number may be closer to 1500. Over the period in which Blue Book was active, 1952 to 1969, there was an average of 700 sightings per year. The National UFO Reporting Center recently issued a report that UFO sightings peaked in 2014 for a total of 8,619 for that year. If 6 percent of those are unexplainable, that means there may have been over 517 flying saucers seen in that year.

The alien's use of Dark Matter to manipulate gravity for piloting their space crafts makes more sense to me than their using some propulsion system based on rocket fuel or nuclear reactions. The traditional shape of the flying saucer (which dates to June 24, 1947, when Kenneth Arnold reported seeing disc-shaped objects which moved like "saucers skipping across the water") is particularly unsuited for flying in air. The United States Air Force tried unsuccessfully to build one. But if antigravity was the force which propelled the object, its shape would be irrelevant.

The flying boat and the alien's propensity for sword fighting were nods to the Edgar Rice Burroughs novels in his Martian series. I had to overcome a desire to give the aliens a double set of arms.

The Tsar Bomba was a three-stage hydrogen bomb with a yield of about 57 megatons. It was detonated on October 30, 1961, in the Novaya Zemlya archipelago. For purposes of narrative efficiency, I moved the date earlier and ground zero to Wichita, Kansas. The bomb had a potential yield of 100 megatons but delivery of such a weapon by missile would have been impractical if not impossible. Its real function was to prove to the US that Russia was superior in its weaponry.

According to *The Guardian*, stock piles of nuclear weapons totaled an estimated 15,400 worldwide in 2016. That's down about 32 percent since 2010. But these numbers are staggering. Russian and the United States have an equal split of around 14,000—locked and loaded. Considering that a typical nuclear warhead dropped on a large city would kill millions of people, an all out nuclear war would be devastating.

Is there a relationship between nuclear proliferation and the observation by real people of flying saucers? It seems so.

Last question: do *I* believe? Like the character of Agent Fox Mulder in "The X Files," I *want* to believe. Carl Sagan once pointed out that we are "lost in a galaxy tucked away in some forgotten corner of a universe in which there are far more galaxies than people." In all those billions and billions of galaxies there is most certainly the chance that intelligent life exists. He also said that "absence of evidence is not evidence of absence." While it is comforting to some to adopt the irrefragable view that whatever is true must be observable and validated, categorized and circumstantiated by scientific method—there are simply more things in Heaven and Earth, as Hamlet says, than we have yet to dream of in our philosophy.

That is why we dream.

# Appendix A

## Chronicles of World War III

It had started with a bang and it didn't look as if it would end whimpering. World leaders were no longer under mind control by the aliens; they were free to be as vindictive as possible—humanly possible. Fortunately, nuclear arsenals had been destroyed and fissionable materials had been neutralized. Unfortunately, scientists on both sides of the ocean were put to work to develop new weapons of mass destruction. It would take longer then they thought.

Russia and China became uncomfortable allies in the war against the United States and Europe. South Korea and South Vietnam were overrun by Communist forces; China captured Formosa, Japan, and Nepal, and marched into India; Russia easily took territories in Germany and Northern Italy; the combined Arab nations of Iran, Iraq, Saudi Arabia and Turkey forced the Israelis out of the Middle East in one of the bloodiest purges of the war. In Africa there were uprisings in Uganda, Zimbabwe, Libya, Ghana, South Africa, Ethiopia and Nigeria; colonials were brutally executed, then the various factions in each nation began to systematically eliminate each other.

France and England mobilized against Russian aggression in Europe; Spain remained neutral at first, but the fascist elements of its government soon manipulated the military into invading France from the west, effectively placing the French between Scylla and Charybdis. France fell—where Nazis leaders had once stood beaming arrogance beneath the shade of the Arc de Triomphe, Soviet soldiers now goose-stepped in unison down the Champs-Élysées. Soon most of Europe had been swallowed by the hungry Russian bear; only England stood alone against the Red surge.

England called for help; America declined to answer with troops saying only, "Keep a stiff upper lip." This time the blitz over London left little standing. The government surrendered. American had her own problems.

Three Russian subs pelted the Los Angeles Naval Base with short range missiles and entered San Francisco Bay intending to sink more

US ships. Depth charges from the USS Milton destroyed all three. Up and down the West Coast, the Navy of the People's Liberation Army, using Soviet supplied destroyers and battleships, turned their guns on the innocent civilians living in coastal cities. On the East Coast, a Russian aircraft carrier supplied Mig fighter jets in sufficient numbers to protect the bombers that devastated Washington DC. America had been caught with her pants down. But she rallied.

No one was winning, expect, perhaps, those moguls of the military industrial complex whose munitions and aircraft fed the global onslaught and swelled their Swiss bank accounts. They sold to all sides, of course. They gloried in war and bought newspapers and television stations to spread hateful propaganda.

President Dwayne Peterson had bowed to the hawks in congress and thereby kept his presidency intact in spite of having been complicit in the bombing of Wichita. The KGB chairman, Ivan Serov, quietly disappeared along with most of his staff. His mistress, Yulia Borisov was distraught. In China, resources for the war were dwindling rapidly. Russia was fighting on so many fronts she couldn't supply the Chinese to the degree she had in the past. The Chinese people suffered from shortages caused by an overtaxed war industry which devoured resources.

In the United States, the coup occurred three years into the war. Someone leaked a memo that implicated President Peterson in the Russian plot to bomb the alien mothership which had gone so wrong. His best of intensions amounted to little; the cover-up was cited as evidence of obstruction of justice. The call came for impeachment. A special prosecutor was appointed, and summarily fired by the president. A second prosecutor was chosen and a congressional declaration assured his independence from the executive branch. There were demonstrations demanding the president's resignation. Peterson declared martial law. He sent special agents to arrest certain members of congress for disloyalty. Chaos reigned. The generals conferred.

The military coup had been well organized and probably preplanned. Peterson was removed and imprisoned pending a military tribunal. Congressional members were told to go home until the conclusion of the war. The Joint Chiefs of Staff of the Armed Forces now ruled America. What had previously been a defense against invasion turned into an outward thrust of aggression against what was called the Red and Yellow Perils that threatened the American Way. Work on the bomb was accelerated. The generals praised former President Eisenhower (deceased) for his foresight in not ending the draft after the Korean War; they were in need of cannon fodder.

The rush to get the bomb in the United States was hindered by a lack of fissionable material, a resistance toward channeling funds to the development effort, a scarcity of qualified technicians (most had been drafted), and a disorganized government that mismanaged practically everything. In the Soviet Union the problems were similar. At least the US had its nuclear submarine, the USS Nautilus. Cannibalizing its reactor, however, would not have yielded substantial bomb making material. Its usefulness lay in its stealth and long-range cruising abilities.

In the eighth year of the war the first nuclear device had been completed: the United States had won the race. There was only one bomb and its magnitude was only in the five megaton range: barely powerful enough to provide a deterrent threat. The red telephone rang in the Kremlin. "Surrender or a major Russian city will be obliterated," said the caller. "Trakhat' tebya!" came the answer.

A long-range bomber left a hidden airfield somewhere in the continental USA on a gray Sunday morning, headed for Moscow. In midflight it was suddenly surrounded by a fleet of six flying saucers. Supporting fighter jets were helpless against the saucers. The bomber was downed in a field in Western Pennsylvania where its weapon of mass destruction was confiscated by a team of aliens. No one was injured, but now there was little hope for a speedy end to the war. It was the only time the aliens interfered in the world-wide conflict. They hadn't actually taken sides; they had merely acted to prevent the destruction of a world they hoped to inherit—without the advent of a nuclear winter.

The stories of the numerous battles, the ups and downs of the enemy combatants, the hardships that stretched on through the years, would constitute a lengthy narrative beyond the scope of this volume. There was no deciding battle, no clear victor, no sparse spoils to gain—but much brutality and criminal action had occurred against the innocent who had nowhere to run. In the end, the war simply fizzled out like the wick of a spent candle. All sides were lacking the substance and fortitude to continue on into the darkness that had descended upon the world. Now they had to learn how to survive the aftermath. Most of the globe lay in ruins. Populations in western Europe and in the United States formed isolated communities; the enemy still roamed the land—survival depended on close cooperation and stealth. Incidents of armed conflict were sparse, but the danger existed that annihilation could come at any minute. The aliens remained shut tightly in their protective egg-shaped space ship.

# Appendix B

## Alienspeak

| | |
|---|---|
| Ahtejiq | a cow-like animal |
| Aimnegarwfuchee | the race of aliens we call the Nordics |
| Blgiiktmnas tree | its leaves have a healing power |
| Floutb | a  direction, roughly south |
| Fwilhog | a large bird, a source of eggs |
| Gfelpodzex | a cattle prod, can be used as a weapon to stun |
| Ghkewbdr | a holographic device |
| Glrovaktre | term for a laboratory |
| Gvoplt | a unit of measurement, approximately 2.4 kilometers |
| Htyopker | alien name for a flying saucer |
| Klivpokla | the alien's planet, fourth from their sun |
| Ktanyo | a unit of time, similar to an earth year |
| Kza-Tza | an endearing term for grandfather |
| Llopikm | a unit of time like an earth month |
| Matofnblotjuupz | the race of aliens we call the Reptilians |
| Mkehfutwess | a mushroom-like plant grown in dark tunnels |
| Nhuddetkiosos | a rare disease |
| Pflematap | a type of fruit growing on a thick vine |
| Pfsedariotmne | a house for orphans |
| Pgikovjela | a mothership |
| Phamleblikz | ancestor of the Plablikz, wolf-like in behavior |
| Plablikz | a spider-like animal kept as a pet |
| Pzotyklo | a pinkish orange fruit |
| Qwerkl | a unit of time similar to an earth hour |
| Ratiessrvedflynach | the race of aliens we call the Greys |
| Rikthijmb | a dance-like martial art using swords |
| Sjilgezhm | the Grey's name for our earth |
| Syktijthraxteraq | the race of aliens we call the Little Green Men |
| Tpiroleaw | an item of playground equipment |

Byron Grush

| | |
|---|---|
| Twodhlog | the alien's sun, about to go supernova  (Betelgeuse) |
| Uoigykwosp | a mother ship |
| Wkebvoles | a card game |
| Xmkitosp | the Grey's name for our moon |
| Zlthmogs | airborne creatures similar to Earth birds but reptilian |

# About the Author

Byron Grush was born and raised in Naperville, Illinois, just southwest of Chicago. He is a third generation native of that town. Grush studied art and design at the University of Illinois and filmmaking at the School of the Art Institute of Chicago. At the Art Institute he was a student of Gregory Markopoulos, one of the originators of the New America Cinema movement in the 1960s.

Grush then taught at The School of the Art Institute of Chicago, creating a course in film animation in the mid-seventies. He later became an Associate Professor at the College of Art at Northern Illinois University in Dekalb, Illinois, where he taught in the Electronic Media area. He is the author of a book on hand-drawn animation techniques entitled *The Shoestring Animator*. Becoming interested in genealogy, he wrote a trilogy of historical novels based upon what he had learned about his early ancestors.

He and his wife moved to New Mexico in the late 1990s, and opened an art gallery featuring Outsider and Visionary Art in Santa Fe. They returned to the Midwest to retire in the small town of Delavan, Wisconsin, a place that reminds them of their roots. Grush writes, paints and studies Tai Chi.

# Other fiction by Byron Grush

*All The Way By Water*
In which Isaac Grosh brings his wife and eight children to Illinois, traveling by flatboat on the Ohio and Mississippi Rivers.

*Once Upon a Gold Rush*
In which John and James Grosh journey by wagon train to California during the gold rush of '49.

*Road of Stars*
In which White Cloud searches for his father (James Grosh) and helps to build the Transcontinental Railroad.

*Dance Beneath A Diamond Sky*
This historical novel of the Sixties follows a group of young people as they search for identity, love, honor and redemption during the decade or so between the assassination of President John F. Kennedy and the resignation of Richard Nixon.

*Violet at The Breakers: a novella*
Violet might only have been twelve, but she was worldly. When her mother brought her and her sisters to Palm Beach, she hadn't expected to discover the body of a murdered man, or to be pursued by his killer. Nor had she expected a certain lady would be careless with a curling iron...

*The New Unwritten Law: a novella*
"The murder victim is slumped over his desk, a bullet hole in his forehead, a pool of blood spreading slowly on the green felt blotter on which he lies. The only door to the room is locked and bolted from the inside..."

*The Scrapple Eater: a novella*
A young man named Jefferson, seems to be obsessed with graveyards, and with eating scrapple. He has some troubling dreams. He thinks he may have a ghost.

*Romeo's Revenge and Other Wisconsin Stories*
An anthology of twelve short stories about the towns and people of Wisconsin.